Small Town Odds

Small Town Odds

A NOVEL

JASON HEADLEY

CHRONICLE BOOKS
SAN FRANCISCO

Library of Congress Cataloging-in-Publication Data:

Headley, Jason, 1973–
   Small town odds : a novel / Jason Headley.
      p. cm.
   ISBN: 0-8118-4536-2
   1. Young men—Fiction. 2. Fathers and daughters—Fiction.
3. City and town life—Fiction. 4. Underemployment—Fiction.
5. Single fathers—Fiction. 6. West Virginia—Fiction.
7. First loves—Fiction. I. Title.

   PS3608.E23S63 2004
   813'.6—dc22
                           2004012035

Manufactured in the United States of America

Comin' Down in the Rain
Words and Music by Buddy Mondlock. © 1993 EMI APRIL MUSIC INC. and
SPARKLING GAP MUSIC. All Rights Controlled and Administered by EMI APRIL
MUSIC. All Rights Reserved. International Copyright Secured. Used by Permission.

Designed by Steve Jones / www.plantainstudio.com

Distributed in Canada by Raincoast Books
9050 Shaughnessy Street
Vancouver, British Columbia V6P 6E5

10 9 8 7 6 5 4 3 2 1

Chronicle Books LLC
85 Second Street
San Francisco, California 94105
www.chroniclebooks.com

To the loving memory of Hannah.
And the enduring spirits of Bart and Jake.

Burnin' himself out on a limb like a leaf in the fall
He blazed for a while, now he's feelin' all dried up and small
The color's all gone, disappeared near as quick as it came
He says he can't stay up, but he'll only come down in the rain

—Buddy Mondlock
"Comin' Down in the Rain"

SUNDAY

When he was lying still, he could feel every ounce of blood running through his head. Most of it seemed to pound through the swollen bruise above his eye. He thought he could actually hear the blood fall loose from its capillaries and into his skin with every whoosh of his pulse. The bed was as bare bones as they come. Just some cloth, covering a bit of filler, that was never intended to support a man's weight. But it was good enough for County. If you didn't like the accommodations, you were more than welcome to not come back. Eric had been reminded of that on a number of occasions.

He couldn't remember how he'd gotten there, or what he'd been doing just prior that had piqued the interest of the local law enforcement community. But hazy as he was on the details, he was clear about one thing. It was Gina's fault.

A thud echoed down the corridor, followed by the familiar footsteps of Deputy Daniel Moran. Eric stayed still to avoid the pain of lifting his head, but looked at Deputy Moran out of the corner of his eye.

"I'm innocent, Danny," he said.

"No," the deputy answered, "you're not."

"Well, shit," Eric sighed. He looked back at the ceiling and furrowed his brow. "Then what'd I do?"

"I already went through it once, Mercer," he muttered over the clang of the opening cell door. "I'm not reliving it for your benefit."

Eric slowly swung his feet to the ground and hefted his head upright. The pain was offset by a quick flash of light-headedness. "Well if I'm not innocent, why are you opening the cell?"

"Deke posted bail." He hooked his keys back onto his belt and walked into the cell. "I don't know why that half-wit gives two squirts about springin' you all the time, but I'm glad he does. Spares me the trouble of having to clean up after you when the booze or that shiner finally turns your insides out."

He stood, held still for a moment to steady himself against the air, then walked toward the deputy, through the barred door. "I'm not gonna puke," he said.

Deputy Moran smirked. "You always puke."

"We'll see there, Danny," Eric said as he slugged down the hall. "I'm not as predictable as you think."

Eric swung open the door to the lobby and was greeted by a one-man debacle. Deke Williams stood at the front desk, pressing his fingers into an ink blotter, making fingerprints on a scrap piece of paper and a mess of everything else he'd touched.

"Now Deke," Eric sighed, "you know Danny ain't gonna like this."

"What?" Deke said. "I never been fingerprinted before. Just thought I'd try it out. That's what it's here for." He held up the piece of paper, displaying two even rows of five smudged fingerprints along with a batch of other prints around the edges where he'd steadied the paper. "Pretty good, huh?"

The door to the cell block swung open and Deputy Moran looked at Deke and the fingerprinting workshop that used to be his desk.

"Aw dammit, Deke! What in the hell's the matter with you?" he said. He hustled over to his desk, looking for something he could use to clean up Deke's mess. "I swear to Christ, you two are purebred derelicts."

Deke began wiping the ink from his fingers with the paper he'd been using for his prints. "Oh relax, Danny. I was just foolin' around. Besides, Eric didn't have nothin' to do with it. He's no derelict."

"Is that right?" The deputy grinned and shook his head. "Then what the hell was he doing back there in that cell? Again."

Eric pulled his coat on and walked over to the desk. "C'mon Deke, let's get out of here. We'll see you later, huh Dan?"

"I'm sure," he answered as Eric pulled open the door. The bell above the door frame let out a clang as the autumn air blew into the room. Eric reached over with his foot to catch a few leaves that blew in with the wind, then pulled the door closed behind him without looking back.

Deke was over beside his truck, wiping his ink-stained hands on his worn-out jeans. "How's come Danny's so wound up all the time? Ain't like he's saving the goddamn world in there."

"I don't know, Deke. Maybe he's just sick of seeing us every other weekend."

Deke made a face like he'd just smelled a dead animal. "Why would he be sick of us? We're nice guys."

"Yeah, we are. But when your job's the law, we're just work."

Eric climbed into the truck and slammed the door shut. Deke's truck was the kind where you had to slam things to be sure they were closed. The doors, the glove compartment, the tailgate. Deke had once lost a whole case of beer when the passenger door popped open in a tight turn, sending the best part of his paycheck spilling out onto the road.

Eric was sitting in that seat now, looking in the little mirror on the visor, checking out the monstrosity that was once his right eyebrow. Deke was driving along the river on Route 2, a road that had been in need of some new pavement slightly longer than Deke's truck had been in need of a new suspension. So the constant jostling around didn't give Eric much of a chance to get a good look at his wound. He finally stopped trying and flipped the visor up with the back of his hand.

"Who the hell punches someone in the forehead?" he asked.

Deke just glanced over at him, then back at the road, trying to concentrate on his driving. These roads could get curvy before you knew it, and his truck didn't handle like it used to. When he glanced back over and realized Eric was still looking at him, he shrugged his shoulders.

"Well hell, I don't know," he finally answered. "I reckon he was probably aiming for your eye."

Eric flipped the mirror back down to take another look. "Well, he sure as shit missed, didn't he."

Deke glanced over again. "Pretty close though. I mean, an eye ain't very big. If that's what he was aiming for, he damn near got it."

In the mirror Eric could see the spot above his eyebrow was pretty red, almost brown in the middle, and half-swollen. He imagined it was going to be a long time going away. He'd never been punched in the forehead before. Plenty of other places, but never the forehead. Once he'd gotten kicked in the shin with full force. It swelled up and turned about every color imaginable before it finally settled on black and started creeping into his foot. Since a forehead and a shin felt about the same, Eric imagined he might just get a black eye out of this yet.

For a twenty-four-year-old man, Eric felt awfully worn down. Especially when it came time to get help with his memory. On the larger scale of things, he didn't know why he got into fights and thrown into jail. The best he could do was find out why he'd gotten thrown into jail on any one particular occasion. In this case, Deke knew. But he wouldn't bring it up until Eric did.

He'd just drive the truck, look out at the river, and think about fishing. It was a simple bliss Eric had been studying in Deke since they were kids.

"So what happened, Deke?" he finally asked.

"What, you mean last night?" said Deke, still looking at the road.

Eric stared at him for a second. "Yeah," he answered with a shake of his head.

"Well, you know this time wasn't so bad. I mean, this guy was definitely lookin' for trouble."

"Who?"

"Just some hoopie from out Stern Grove. You was playin' pool there and he come up and said somethin' bout how he heard you like to fight."

Eric moaned.

"Yeah, but here's the thing. You didn't even do nothin'. You just told him that wasn't you and kept on shootin'."

Eric could hardly believe the story as it was being told. "Doesn't sound like me."

"Yeah, he didn't think so either. So he just kept at you, saying how you didn't look like much of a fighter at all and how he'd come all this way just to find out what you was made of. But you just kept on like he wasn't even there. Then finally I guess he'd worn his welcome, because he was just standin' there, runnin' his big ol' hoopie mouth like he had been for the past five minutes, when you took the cue ball up in your hand and punched him square in the face."

Eric flexed his fingers into a fist and released them. There was a cut on one of his knuckles and a tenderness in the bones.

"Well that musta fuckin' hurt," he said as he rubbed his fingers with his other hand.

Deke chuckled. "It musta, cause he went down like a turd in a toilet. That's when his buddies came in, swingin' their paws around like they was defending the hoopie universe. After that, it was just your standard Saturday night clusterfuck."

Eric let out a deep breath and allowed the disappointment in himself take hold. "So if there was this big pack of trouble, why was I the only one in jail?"

"Cause you were the only one who didn't run away," said Deke. "So that made you the only one staggering around with your tackle out, pissin' upside the building, telling Deputy Danny what a fuckin' pussy he is."

Eric put his hands to his face and rubbed his eyes with his palms. His hands smelled like stale beer, and nausea crept up on him slow. He wanted to lean on Deke's door in the hopes that it might pop open and spill him out over the ridge, down to the railroad tracks below. His muffled voice crept out from behind his hands.

"Fuckin' Gina."

Deke looked over at him, confused. "Naw, she wasn't there."

Eric sighed, "But I was."

Deke tried to keep his eye on Eric, looking for a clue, but he had to keep turning back to the road to be sure they didn't veer into the hillside.

"What do I owe you for bail then?"

"Aw, I don't know," shrugged Deke. "I still owed you some for helping me roof ol' Taggert's a while back. Buy me breakfast and we'll call it even."

Eric nodded his head and thought it over for a minute. The sun was reflecting off the river with an eagerness reserved for morning-time. The light flooded into his eyes and filled his swollen head, which made his stomach turn on itself.

"Can we do that tomorrow?" he asked Deke. "If Abby puts some of that mess in front of me right now, I could upchuck. And she'd probably take a thing like that personal."

"Yeah, tomorrow's good," he answered. As they came over the crest of the little hill that brought them into their town, they could see green and white flags hanging from all the telephone poles that ran along the highway. Homecoming was Friday, and the whole town was crazy with the idea that they might just beat Cedarsville this year. The Pinely Wildcats had a lot of potential, people would say. That 2-4 record didn't really reflect the quality of the team, they'd argue with whoever would listen. The team's coming together just in time for Cedarsville, they'd declare among their friends and neighbors. It was an annual state of collective delusion that had been validated just once in the past twenty years. Which would be enough to keep it going for at least twenty more.

"You want me to just take you home then?" asked Deke as they got about a mile into town.

"No," sighed Eric as he leaned his head against the back window of the truck. "I need to go by my folks'."

The town of Pinely was barely two miles long from end to end, cradled in the valley between the mountainside and the Ohio River. There was one traffic light, at Main Street. But since there was no real traffic to speak of on Main, it was widely believed that the light existed solely for the purpose of giving directions to out-of-towners. As in, "If you reach the red light, you've gone too far."

When the town first sprung up, it was because of industry. They were drilling oil down the river in Cedarsville, mining coal further north toward Weirton, and right there in Pinely they were making glass. The river was a good, cheap route to transport materials. And once the railroad came in, there seemed to be no end to the possibilities there in the Ohio Valley. It was as though their little corner of West Virginia might just lift itself out of the poverty that had plagued the state since it first staked out on its own during the Civil War. But eventually the economic boom sounded more like a thud. West Virginia coal was deemed too dirty to burn. Cedarsville's oil fields were judged too small. Pinely glass became a mere collector's curiosity. So Pinely itself was left without a purpose. Now the jobs were all at the chemical plants just north of the Mason-Dixon, while there in Pinely, folks worked at the schools, for the city, in the stores, for the church, or in the bars. The ratio of the churches to the bars was one of particular contention to Eric's dad. "When I first came to this town, there used to be ten bars and three churches," he would say. "Now there are only three bars, and I've lost count of how many goddamn churches we have."

One of the remaining bars was the American Legion. As they drove past it, Deke glanced over at Eric, who looked like he was asleep.

"You workin' the Legion tonight?" he asked in a voice loud enough to wake him up.

Eric opened one eye, looked at Deke, and shook his head, no.

The truck made the left onto Shales Avenue and pulled up into the driveway of Eric's boyhood home. Eric opened his eyes when he felt the truck come to a stop. He put his hand to his face, as though the rest might have miraculously healed his wound. Finding that wasn't the case, he looked over to Deke.

"How do I look?" he asked, opening the door.

"Like shit," Deke answered.

"Great," he grunted as he eased himself down out of the truck. He stood there for a second with the door open as he thought it over a little more. "Fuckin' great," he finally exhaled.

He slammed the door shut and walked to his parents' front porch. The truck squeaked out of the driveway, into the street, and with a quick honk of the horn, was off. Eric pulled open the storm door to the house, causing the main door to slam from half-ajar to completely closed. The effort required to open a door that had just shut, seemingly for no other purpose than to spite him, felt like more than he could muster. But he took a deep breath and managed to work his clammy hand on the doorknob. The air in the house felt warmed over and pre-breathed, a disappointing contrast to the brisk air outside.

His mom and dad were sitting at the kitchen table having breakfast. His dad looked over the top of his glasses and watched his son amble forward. Sitting between them at the head of the table was a little girl wearing a crown made of yellow construction paper. She looked up from her waffles and gave Eric a look of equal parts fear and surprise.

"Hey Mom. Hey Dad," he said, stopping in the doorway to the kitchen. He glanced at the girl then bowed his head in mock esteem. "I'm sorry, I didn't realize you were entertaining royalty this morning."

The little girl smiled as her hand absently touched the crown atop her cinder hair. "Daddy, what happened to your head?"

Eric walked over to her, took the crown in his hand, and kissed her on the forehead. He rested the small crown on top of his own head as he walked over to the empty chair at the other end of the table. "See, you've been hanging out with Grandpa for too long," he said nodding in his dad's direction. "He's been asking me that for years now."

"Still valid," his dad mumbled before shoving a bit of sausage into his mouth.

Eric smiled out of resignation and looked back at his daughter. "I just had a little accident, baby. Did you have a good time last night with Grandma and Grandpa?"

"Uh huh," she answered while cutting off a piece of her waffle. "We made cookies and we made a crown out of the colored paper. And Grandma and I played your old records and danced on the bed."

His mom smiled at the girl, then looked at the wound above Eric's eye. "What about you, did you have a good time last night?" she asked.

"Not as I heard it described," he said with a weak smile.

"Well, would you like some breakfast?"

"I could try to put back a waffle if you have any left."

His mom got up and went to the freezer. "Just one?" she asked as she pulled the frozen waffles out of the box.

"That should do," he answered, watching her drop it into the toaster. He looked over at his little girl, whose mouth was full with her breakfast. She squinted a smile at him with her big brown eyes. "Pretty good?" he asked her.

"Mmm-hmm," she answered. "Very good."

"Yeah?" he laughed. "Well, no one toasts a waffle quite like Grandma."

The little girl kept her eyes on her plate as she worked the fork to cut off another piece. "I know," she said with sincerity.

Eric watched her intently as he settled back into his chair. He'd been doing this for the past five years, watching this little girl as she walked, talked, learned, and took on a life of her own. Like no other mistake he'd ever made. He watched until she finally managed, using a combination of the fork and her fingers, to get a piece of waffle free from the rest and into her mouth. Pulling the crown down off his head, he turned to look at his father. "How are you this morning, Dad?"

His dad nodded his head indifferently and took a sip of coffee. "Better than you, I imagine." His weathered eyes shifted in their crow's-feet settings, from his coffee to his boy. "Where'd you sleep last night?"

"Dan fixed me up a bed at County."

The old man put his fork down and looked at his son. "Jesus Christ, Eric—" he started before his wife shot him a look and nodded toward the girl.

"It's fine, Dad," Eric said flatly. "Deke said I didn't even really do anything this time."

"Oh Deke said so, huh?" he laughed. "Well I was just hanging out here last night not doing anything either. How come they didn't come bursting in and drag me off to County?"

Eric's head was beginning to throb. It wasn't even 9:00 A.M. and he'd been sprung from jail straight into an argument with his dad. His mom walked over and put a gentle hand on his shoulder as she set a plate with one dry waffle in front of him. "Leave him be, Dave," she whispered to her husband. "Do you want anything to drink, Eric?"

"Some milk?" he said, pouring syrup on top of his breakfast and cutting into it with his fork. He crammed a huge bite of waffle into his mouth, then looked back over at his father. "It's fine, Dad," he mumbled through the food. "It really is."

He listened to himself chew for a while, trying to pretend he wasn't upset with his dad for nagging, or upset with himself for giving him a reason to. The waffle scratched its way down his throat, half-chewed, and he packed another chunk into his mouth. He stared at his plate, gauging how much more waffle stood between him and any more unpleasantness in his parents' house.

"Gina called last night," his mom said from the kitchen.

Eric tried to swallow, but found he'd either severely misjudged the size of the last bite, or his mouth had gone dry.

"Did you hear me?" his mom asked from just ten feet away.

"Yes," Eric managed to reply through the choking hazard in his mouth. He swallowed hard and took a deep breath. "What did she want?"

His mom shrugged. "Just checking in."

Eric looked across the table at his daughter, hoping for more information. She just smiled. But there was something in her eyes that made it seem like she knew more. A trait she got from her mother.

His mom put the milk on the table in front of Eric, then put her hands on her hips as though she were about to announce she'd found the cure for cancer. "Well, I'm going to go get ready for church! Would anyone like to come with me?"

Eric winked at his daughter. "You're a big girl now, Grandma. You should be able to get ready for church all by yourself."

She smacked him on the shoulder with her dishtowel and leaned down to him. "You could use some time in church, young man."

"Maybe," he answered, "but I'm still gonna pass. My little girl and I have plans. Ain't that right, Tess?"

"What're we gonna do, Daddy?"

Eric stuffed the last of his waffle into his mouth and stood to go to the other side of the table. "I don't know," he said as he put the paper crown back on her head. "But we'd better get started." He lifted her up out of her chair into his arms and then down on her own feet. "So go get your jacket."

She ran around the table, then scurried off to a bedroom around the corner.

"Thanks for watching her last night," Eric said to his mother as he gave her a hug. "Deke was starting to feel neglected."

"You know it's our pleasure to have her around, Eric." She crossed her arms across her body and brought her thumbnail to her teeth. "To have both of you around."

He turned to his dad and gave him a slight wave. "I'm on at the Legion tomorrow night. You think you'll come by?"

"Probably so," he answered.

"Probably so," Eric mocked. "Aren't you coy?"

"What?"

"Free hotdogs, that's what," Eric smiled. "If you aren't there I'll know to fill out a missing persons report."

Tess came around the corner wearing a patchwork jacket with gloves buttoned to the sleeves. "I'm ready, Daddy."

"Well that makes two of us." He held his hand out for her to hold and they made their way to the front door. Eric glanced back at his parents—his mom waving too enthusiastically, his dad sitting, arms crossed, shaking his head—and walked out into the brisk morning air.

This had been Eric's neighborhood for nearly his entire life, from the day he was born until he turned twenty-one. Even though he couldn't really afford it at the time, he moved out when Tess was two. That was when she started to understand the world around her a little more, and he didn't want his daughter asking questions about why she lived with Mommy while he lived with Grandma and Grandpa. Plus it made it difficult for him to feel like much of a parent with his own parents around all the time.

As they walked past Jean Walton's place on the corner, Tess started one of her "remember when" stories. For someone with so few years from which to draw, Tess managed to drum up an astonishing number of stories. On the walk from his parents' house to his place, he could almost guarantee to be asked if he remembered when the two of them had picked apples from the Waltons' tree, or the time they'd built an igloo with the kids who used to live in the red house by the highway, or when they'd found that dead robin under the tree and buried it out in the pines under a popsicle stick cross. Always the same stories, but always told like they were brand new. His dad suffered from a similar affliction. His stories could be told as many as three times in the same day. Eric always figured he was above such blatant repetition. But now, seeing it have its way with both his father and his daughter, he'd come to realize that he wasn't so much above it as he was between it.

When they got to where they could see Eric's house, Tess started running, trying to pull her dad behind her. "C'mon, Daddy!" she shouted, her little legs pounding the sidewalk but taking her nowhere.

The idea of running, even half a block, was more than Eric's hangover could handle. So he held her hand and kept her moving at his pace. "The house isn't going anywhere, Tess."

She just laughed and ignored him. "C'mon, Daddy! Run, run, run, run, run!" When Tess got an idea in her head, it was like gravity. You couldn't ignore it, and you couldn't explain it away. But like a pioneer of aviation, Eric had learned that he could bend the rules a little.

"Okay then, let's race!" he said as he let go of her hand. Her stumpy walk became a full-fledged, stumpy run as her body fought against itself with every step. Eric watched her arms and legs refuse to synch up, but still manage to make good time.

He knelt down on the ground and shoved the palms of his hands into the wet grass. "Daggonnit!" he yelled.

Tess looked back over her shoulder and laughed. "Daddy, you fell!" she shouted as she romped up onto the porch.

Eric picked himself up off the ground and wiped his hands on his pants. "Yeah, I did," he hollered at her. "Lucky for you, cause I was just catching up." He made his way to the porch stairs and ambled up to meet his daughter.

"How'd you fall?" Tess asked, looking at the grass stains on Eric's hands.

Eric took one of his hands back from his daughter to dig his keys out of his pocket. "I'm not sure. I was just hitting my stride, when all the sudden I was down in the grass."

Tess shook her head as she watched him open the front door to the house. "Prolly them ol' boots, huh? They prolly ain't no good to run in."

"They probably *aren't*," he corrected as he ushered her out of the cold and into the living room.

Eric's place was a good-sized house. Certainly more than he needed. But it was nice to have the extra space for Tess. Two bedrooms, a kitchen, a living room, and a big back yard. All for a price that left him enough on which to eat. And drink.

The brown shag carpet was in need of a cleaning. It smelled like pets. The folks who had lived there before Eric had cats, and Eric had a dog for a couple of years before it finally got fed up with Eric's absentminded feeding schedule and ran away.

Eric undid the laces on his boots and sat them beside the door. Tess was sitting on the floor taking off her own shoes, giggling. She reached over and grabbed him by the toe, which had worked its way through his sock.

"This little piggy's going to market," she said, shaking his toe back and forth.

"Honey, I wouldn't touch that if I were you. Your daddy's in desperate need of a cleaning."

She just laughed at him and said, "Yeah, you're dirty from head to toe!"

Eric winced at his daughter's attempt at humor. Sometimes having her around was like hanging out with a member of Hee-Haw. "Good one," he said. "Now let go of my toe and wash your hands. You don't know where that thing's been."

Tess got up and made her way to the kitchen sink. As she climbed up on her footstool and turned on the water, Eric went over to the stereo in the living room. He didn't realize the settings were the same as he'd left them from the night before, so when he turned on the power, the music blasted out at an ear-shattering volume. He heard a crash in the kitchen as he quickly turned the volume knob all the way down.

"You okay in there, Tess?"

He heard her stacking dishes back in the sink. "Yeah. The plates . . . ," her little voice called. Then, to herself, he heard her mumble, "That was loud."

His head hadn't cared for that surprise one bit, so he took a deep breath as he scanned his music for something appropriate. He set the volume at a loud but tolerable level and made his way to the kitchen door. Peeking around the corner he saw Tess on the footstool, washing her hands and shaking her behind to the music.

"Honey, will you be alright if I go take a quick shower?" he called out to her.

"Yep."

He watched her for a minute, but she didn't turn around.

"What are you going to do?" he asked.

"Just dance a little maybe."

She seemed to be true to her word. As soon as she finished washing her hands, she boogied her way toward the paper towels, then over to the garbage. Feeling fairly secure that a five-year-old girl couldn't possibly dance her way into trouble all by herself, he headed off to the bathroom.

The water stung against his eye. That was expected. But the hot water also pointed out other scrapes and wounds. Bar fights weren't like fights in the movies where guys stood there and traded blows. Eric would get into the guy hard and fast, wrap him up, get him on the ground, then punch, kick, bite, and do whatever he had to. That sort of full-body, no-holds-barred action left lots of room for random injuries. And a hot shower would find them fast.

Eric noticed he had quite a few scrapes on his back. Lying on his back had never proven itself to be a winning position, so he figured he must have been at a severe disadvantage at one point during the brawl. He also noticed a pretty good cut on his ankle that looked like it came from a blade or something sharp. This one confused him, since his ankles had been protected inside his boots. He was thinking about the cut when he felt a breeze pull in through the open window and heard the music get louder and more clear. He stuck his head around the shower curtain and saw a little boy standing there with the bathroom door wide open.

"Hi Ewic," he said.

Buddy Piles lived across the street. On top of having a speech impediment that made him sound a little like Elmer Fudd, he also had a social impediment that made him completely unable to feel discomfort in any situation. If Eric didn't know Buddy so well, he'd have been amazed that the kid could casually stand there in a neighbor's bathroom and talk to a grown man taking a shower.

"Hey Buddy," Eric answered. "What are you doing in my bathroom?"

"Can Tess come out and play?" was the closest thing Buddy had to an answer.

"Buddy."

"Yeah?"

"Get the hell out of here."

Buddy turned and walked out of the bathroom, leaving the door wide open. Eric took a deep breath, then summoned his daughter.

"Tess!"

She ran around the corner and stood with her eyes darting from her dad's face to the wall and back again.

"That was weird, huh?" he asked her.

"He didn't want to wait," she said, knowing it wasn't a very good excuse. She looked at him, but didn't really say or do anything. Finally she looked up at the ceiling and said, "Can I go outside and play with Buddy?"

Eric wanted her to go outside and play. He wanted the house to himself for a while so he could lie down and maybe take a nap. He also wanted to make sure that Tess understood that letting Buddy come into the bathroom while he was showering wasn't a good idea. But the cold air was easing in through the window, creating a plume of steam, and Eric didn't feel well enough to try to make an ambiguous disciplinary point involving a kid that wasn't even his. So he just waved his hand at Tess and pulled his head back behind the curtain.

"Yeah. Go play with Buddy," he said through the plastic. "But make sure you wear some play clothes. And a jacket. And not the nice jacket you wore on the way over here." He heard little footsteps stamping away. "And Tess?" he shouted.

"Yeah?" she answered.

"Don't go very far."

"Okay."

He heard her footsteps again, then all he heard was the music. Loud and clear. And the wind was still cutting through the window and across his wet body. He peeked his head out from behind the curtain and shouted for her again. "Tess!"

She quickly came to the door of the bathroom and stood there with her arms hanging at her side. He looked at her blankly, then pointed. "Could you shut the door?"

She nodded her head, grabbed the doorknob with her tiny hand and backed out of the bathroom, pulling the door closed behind her. The music was suddenly muffled again and the air from the window slowed down.

He stood there in the shower taking deep breaths of moist air. His head didn't feel much better, but now, Buddy Piles willing, he was going to have time to take a nap. As he rinsed the last of the soap from his face, he felt a sudden shudder in his body. He quickly opened his mouth and took in a huge breath of air. Leaning forward with his hands on the tile in front of him, Eric steadied himself against a world that had just gone topsy-turvy. Sweat rushed to his skin, was quickly washed away by the water, and hurried down the drain. His stomach heaved against itself, expanding his ribs in a way that helped him discover yet another wound. He moved his hand to his side to feel out the bruise. Just then, a convulsion ran through him with enough violence to make him briefly lose his vision. When the blood rushed back from his face and his eyes cleared, he saw the last bits of bile and waffle swirling down the drain.

He would have been more comfortable lying down in his bedroom, but with Tess out there under the influence of Buddy Piles, he wanted to nap in a more central location. Just a few months prior, Buddy had convinced Tess that she could get water to come out of her ears if she squirted the garden hose up her nose. Buddy was the same kid who'd once deafened himself for two days by shooting himself in the ear with a cap gun, so his intelligence was well documented. But what he lacked in brilliance, he made up for in bullshit. So that afternoon Eric had tried to comfort a daughter with water pouring out of her nose, tears coming out of her eyes, and a headache that lasted well into dinnertime.

The couch in the living room suited him fine for this nap. He turned off the stereo and listened to the pseudo-silence. The house had its ambient noise, he could hear Tess and Buddy playing across the street, and he could hear Buddy's mom bark out the occasional "No, Buddy!" like she was training a dog. Which was oddly more comforting than jarring. But for the most part, it was quiet. He could hear his heartbeat in his ears slowing as his body began to let go of consciousness. A twitch. A strange shudder that seemed to settle in his spine. A soft, cottony sense that muffled his connection to the waking world. And he was almost . . .

Asleep.

The phone rang like a blow to the skull. It was beside his head on the end table. Eric shot upright and knocked it off the table with his arm, bringing it to the floor with a crash of cheap plastic.

"Fuck," he said as he reached one hand for the phone and the other for his head. His breathing got a little exaggerated for a second as he tried to get his bearings. Finally he lifted the receiver to his ear and spoke.

"Hello?"

"Eric?"

"Yeah," he grunted before he recognized the voice.

"Are you okay?"

He knew who it was now and tried to come across as alert. "Oh yeah. Yeah, I'm fine. I was just . . . taking a little nap here."

"Are you hungover again?"

"No, Gina. I'm just resting," he answered.

"Well, where's Tess?"

"She's outside playing with Buddy."

"Oh . . . Buddy."

Her honey-tone couldn't mask her judgment.

"You know," Eric deadpanned. "From across the street."

"I *know* Buddy," she said. There was a pause while she thought of the most motherly thing to say. "You're aware he's a menace?"

"I'm the only guy in town who has to lock his doors at night," Eric said. "I'm painfully aware."

"Well, where are they now?" she asked.

Eric was already tiring of the sad attempts at kindness, wrapped in judgment. Or vice versa. "Last I saw them, they were up on the roof. I'm sure she'll be down any minute now. You want to talk to her?"

"That's not funny."

"It's a little funny," he insisted.

There was silence on the other end of the phone.

"You know, I think Buddy's providing a service," he finally said. "Thanks to him, Tess won't have to do a good sixty percent of the stupid things she would have done otherwise. He does them for her. Look at all the things she's learned so far. Don't cram metal into an electrical outlet. Don't hook your sled up to the mail truck. Don't stick your finger up a dog's ass."

"Well," Gina interjected, "obviously you have your hands full. Which is why you're letting the six-year-old delinquent from across the street watch our daughter. So what time do you want me to come by and pick her up?"

"Anytime after dinner, I guess," he answered. "That'll give us plenty of time to play in traffic, run with scissors, and go introduce ourselves to strangers."

Gina's voice got a little more abrupt. "I'm just making a point, Eric. You don't have to be a smart-ass about it."

"Apparently I do."

"Alright," she said. He could tell he'd pushed her too far. "I don't want to get into it with you. So I'm just going to let you get back to your nap, and I'll come by around seven to get Tess. Okay?"

Eric thought he might want to apologize, but he wasn't really sure what he'd be apologizing for. His mind scoured for an angle. Something he could offer as an olive branch, without giving any ground. An innocuous statement that could sugarcoat the whole situation. But he was too tired. It would probably be easier to just say he was sorry and get it over with. He sighed into the phone as he spoke.

"Could you make it eight?"

Gina was silent for a moment. "Okay." The next pause was even longer. "I'll see you at eight o'clock."

"We'll be here," he answered just before she hung up.

Eric put the phone back on the end table and put his head back on the pillow. Fucking Gina. The hangover. The head wound. The couch that smelled like a dog that didn't even live there anymore. All of it was her doing. How was he ever going to explain it to Tess? Someday it would come up, and he'd have to inform her that her one-and-only mother could erase the future, sully the past, and render the present mundane, lifeless, and generally void of meaning. His mind got so worked up, he wasn't sure he'd be able to get to sleep. Luckily, his body was in charge. It forcibly overtook his poor, scattered brain and smothered it into the throes of slumber.

He heard footsteps. He had no idea how long he'd been asleep, but he knew there were now children in his house. The nap was officially over. It was upsetting, but he didn't feel the need to open his eyes just yet. He admired Tess and Buddy's attempts at being quiet, whispering loudly as they made their way into the kitchen. Even factoring in his bias, Tess was doing a much better job, whispering and tiptoeing far more softly than Buddy. Which really wasn't saying much, because Buddy's idea of whispering was talking at full volume in a raspy voice. And tiptoeing was pretty much out of the question in his junior hunting boots.

Eric kept his eyes closed when he spoke.

"Hey guys?"

The whispering and walking immediately stopped, but there was no answer.

"I don't know what's going on in there," Eric continued, "but I'd like to recommend that anyone who's wearing dirty boots inside my house get their ass back outside."

Again, silence. Then the sound of one little set of boots made its way across the kitchen, through the living room, and out the door. A moment passed before the door creaked open again and Buddy's "whisper" carried across the room to the kitchen.

"I'll see you latew, Tess." Then the door closed behind him.

It was quiet again, and Eric stayed there on the couch with his eyes closed. He could hear Tess moving, but knew she was still doing her best to stay silent. Surely she knew he wasn't asleep anymore. She'd just heard him speak. He listened to her footsteps squoosh across the carpet toward him and stop when she was near him, maybe even right beside him. For a moment, it was so peaceful he felt the nap try to creep up on him for a reprise. It was a welcome feeling, but he was too curious about what his daughter was up to. He was just about to take a look when he felt a sudden pain above his eye.

Shooting up on the couch, his eyes wide open, he saw Tess standing beside him, index finger extended, with a look of shock on her face.

"Jesus, Tess! What are you doing?" he asked, exasperated.

"I wanted to see what that thing felt like."

"It fuckin' hurts, that's what it feels like!"

She winced at the sound of her dad swearing at her, but she didn't mind correcting him. "No, I wanted to see what it felt like with my finger."

He looked at her blankly for a second, then thought it over. His hand reached for his eye. "What *does* it feel like?" he asked her.

"It's kinda puffy," she answered.

"Yeah," he confirmed, "it is kinda puffy." He took his hand down and leaned toward her a little. "What color is it?"

She put her hands on either side of his face and squinted her eyes.

"It's like brown. And then a little purple around the outside."

"Hmm," Eric said.

"Yeah," she continued, "and your eyes are all red too."

"It's like a rainbow, huh?"

She smiled and shook her head. "Like a rainbow in those spots in the driveway from your car."

Eric sat up on the couch and looked out the window. "I have oil slick eye?"

Tess giggled, "I guess so."

He reached out and pulled her up into his lap. "Well, you know, the best thing for that is probably some exercise," he told her.

Tess frowned at him.

"What's the matter? Don't you like to exercise?"

"I don't know," she shrugged. "I've never done it."

"You've never exercised?" he asked.

She shook her head and pointed, "Not like Mommy does, in front of the TV."

"Your mother exercises in front of the TV?"

Tess nodded.

"Well, she's screwed up," he told her. "The TV isn't for exercise. In fact, the TV is the archenemy of exercise. And I'm not sure she should be going around mixing up the two. It just ain't natural."

"It just *isn't* natural," she corrected.

Eric looked at her, caught a little off guard. "You're absolutely right. It isn't natural. That's why we're going to go outside and exercise in the fresh air."

She jumped down from his lap as he stood and looked around the room.

"Let me just get my coat and boots and I'll meet you out in the yard," he told her.

Tess nodded and turned to walk through the kitchen to the back door. As he was leaning over, putting on his boots, he saw her reach for her hood, then stop. She turned her head to see if Eric was looking. Seeing that he was, she made a disappointed face, pulled the hood over her head, and opened the door. Eric laced up his boots, grabbed his jacket out of the closet, and headed for the garage.

In the far corner of the garage, past a box filled with football trophies and high school yearbooks, he found a rake. Right next to another rake. Eric couldn't recall why he had two of something that he only used once a year, but he was fairly certain it involved his mother's hell-bent obsession with yard sales. Just as he was appraising the merits of each rake, he got an idea. He took the extra rake to his makeshift workbench, pulled out a hacksaw, and cut the handle in half. Holding it up to his leg he checked the height, then, satisfied with his work, headed out to the backyard.

Tess was sitting on the concrete step of the porch, waiting for him. He handed her the sawed-off rake and walked toward the tree.

"What are we gonna do, daddy?" she asked, dragging the rake behind her as she walked.

"Exercise," he answered.

He started by the outer edge of the yard and raked the leaves back toward the center. Tess watched him for a while, then started trying to use her half-rake. She had no cadence to her work. She simply dragged the rake across a particular patch of grass until there were no more leaves on it. Whether it took three swipes or thirty, she kept at it until it was done. Then she stepped over to another area. She never stopped looking down, even when she spoke to Eric.

"How come all these leaves came down off the tree, Daddy?"

"Happens every year," he answered.

"Is the tree dying?"

"No. The tree's fine. Only the leaves are dying."

"But they're part of the tree."

Eric didn't want to get into this explanation right now. It was far too technical and scientific. If he tried to simplify it, it was just going to come out as "sometimes a part of something has to die so the rest of it can live." And while that was true to his personal experience, it seemed a bit melodramatic for a Sunday afternoon with a five-year-old. So he decided to skirt around the whole issue.

"Well, they're not a part of the tree anymore, are they?"

This was the way it was going to be, he was afraid. These weren't the sorts of big questions he thought he'd be discussing at this point in his life. He'd imagined a lecture hall led by a scholarly mentor and filled with his intellectual peers. Not once did he picture himself leading a backyard classroom with one small, overly inquisitive pupil. Eric didn't know whether to admire her curiosity, or fear her relentlessness. She was a one-woman inquisition. It would have been intolerable if Eric didn't know that time was on his side. Because, eventually, her onslaught of questions was always undone by the same, inevitable statement.

"I'm hungry."

Eric cleaned up from dinner while Tess took a bath. She'd only just learned that you're not supposed to swim right after you eat or you'll get stomach cramps and drown. So it took quite a bit of parental ingenuity on Eric's part to convince her she'd be okay to take a bath with a belly full of dinner. Her argument was so impassioned and long-winded that Eric settled on a compromise. He found an old whistle in a drawer and told her to wear it around her neck. At the first sign of stomach cramps, she was to blow the whistle and he'd come running in to save her.

He could hear her sloshing around in the tub, giving the whistle tiny toots every now and then to be sure it still worked. He was wiping down the range with a dishrag when he hollered back to the bathroom.

"You bout done in there, Tess?"

He heard the whistle scream back at him.

"Was that an 'Oh my God, I'm suffering tremendous stomach cramps and about to drown' whistle, or a 'Yes, Daddy, I'm almost done' whistle?" he hollered back.

He heard her pull the plug up from bathtub drain as she called back, "The second one."

"Good," he answered. "If you hurry and get done back there, we might have some time to read before your mom shows up."

A few minutes later, Tess came running out from the back hallway, fully dressed with the wet towel flapping behind her like a cape. Her bare feet thumped across the floor as she "flew" through the living room. Her laughter propelled her as she ran around the couch, past the front door, then suddenly screamed in genuine terror. Her body folded to the ground. Eric was surprised to hear himself cry out a little as he rushed over and took her in his arms.

"What's wrong, baby?" he asked.

"My foot, Daddy! My foot!" she wailed.

Eric looked down at her feet and saw blood trickling out from one. He took it in his hand by the ankle and noticed a piece of glass jutting out from it. Tess was pitching a fit, the likes of which he wasn't going to be able to calm. So he decided to roll with it.

"I want you to scream really loud for me, baby."

She obliged with more furor than he'd anticipated. But he kept at it.

"Come on now, I know you can do better. Doesn't it hurt more than that?"

Again she let loose with a scream of a pitch and intensity exclusively reserved for little girls in pain.

"Okay, honey, I think one more scream ought to do it. I'll count to three and you scream all the pain away. Ready? One. Two. Three!"

On three, he grabbed the glass and pulled it out of her foot as Tess screamed with all her might. He reached for the bath towel and wrapped her foot in it to suppress the bleeding, then looked down at her tear-stained face.

"Better?" he asked.

Tess just looked up at the ceiling, breathing heavily. "Yeah."

Eric took a hard look at the glass shard in his hand and thought it over. As his eyes glanced around the room, they stopped on his boots sitting by the door. He pulled up his pant leg and looked at the cut on his ankle, the one he'd discovered in the shower. Wiping away the blood on the glass, he held it up to the light to see it was brown. Beer-bottle brown. He looked back at his little girl and kissed the bloody towel around her foot.

"I'm sorry, Tess."

By the time the knock came at the door, the entire trauma was nearly forgotten. Eric had cleaned the wound, relieved to discover it wasn't as extensive as all the bleeding had implied, and bandaged it up. They were lying on the floor, reading a story, oblivious to the world around them. The knock brought them back as Eric shouted toward the door, "Come in."

Eric was always startled when he saw Gina walk into a room. She was tall, shapely. Her long brown hair cascading over her shoulders. Her clothes hugging in all the right places. She was a walking, talking feminine ideal. To anyone but Eric.

"What happened to you two?" she asked.

Eric looked up at her. "What do you mean?"

"What do I mean?" she blurted. "Your head. Her foot. It looks like you beat the crap out of each other!"

He looked at Tess's foot as he reached for his own eye. "Oh," he said. "Y'know, tough love."

Gina walked over to Tess and picked her up. "What happened to your foot, honey?"

"I stepped on some glass," she answered matter-of-factly.

Eric stood up and put his hand on her bandaged foot. "Apparently it fell out of my boot earlier and she kinda stepped on it." He thought about it for a second, then added, "After she'd taken her bath," as though that might win him points.

Gina just shook her head as she looked at Eric. "What about you? What happened to your head?"

"I'm not sure," he answered.

She shook her head and looked at him like she might like to help. If she only knew how. Which was one thing she and Eric had in common.

"Big game on Friday, huh?" Gina said as she helped Tess with her jacket.

"That's what people are convincing themselves," he answered.

"You don't think we have a chance?"

"We never have a chance against Cedarsville."

"Well," said Gina, "they're gonna have the bonfire rally on Thursday and I thought I'd take Tess along. You think you're gonna go?"

"Yeah, I'll probably see you there," he answered.

"Oh, okay," she said with some hesitance. "Or, I was thinking maybe we could all go together. The three of us." She stopped for a second, then continued. "Like a family."

Eric leaned over and picked up Tess. "Okay then, honey, you've gotta go with Mommy now. But I'll see you later, okay?"

"Tomorrow?" she asked.

"No, I have to work tomorrow," Eric answered. "So sometime after tomorrow."

She gave him a big hug and he handed her over to Gina. Then he looked Gina in the eye and said, "I'm probably going to go with Deke. So I'll just see you guys there."

Lying in his bed, reading, Eric tried to focus on his book, but kept thinking back to what Gina had said. "Like a family." What in the hell did she mean by that? Did she think a synchronized appearance at a high school pep rally was going to turn them into the goddamned Brady Bunch? That's when the puzzle started in his head again. It always started with the same question: What would I have done different?

By the time the puzzle kicked up he didn't even realize he'd stopped reading his book. In fact, he didn't realize he'd set the book down and closed his eyes. Which made it easier for him not to realize he wasn't even working on the puzzle anymore. Because at some point that he didn't even realize, he had fallen asleep.

TWELVE

The weeds were too high. If there was a path to be found on this side of the railroad tracks, it was certainly playing hard to get. Deke had already decimated a swath of weeds with a stick he'd picked up, swinging it like a machete to clear some room for them. Daryl Dinkins decided to use the space to sit down and have himself a bit of rest.

"What are you doing, Huey?" Eric asked.

Kids in Pinely always seemed to end up with nicknames. Some were obvious, like Deacon Williams being called "Deke." But others came from a more imaginative place. No one was really sure when it happened, but at some point, poor Daryl Dinkins's slightly pudgy build and slightly stunted intellect earned him the name "Huey." His Christian name was all but forgotten by everyone except a few stubborn parents and school teachers who didn't feel right about calling him by a nickname they thought was mean-spirited. They didn't understand that any derogatory inspiration for the name had long been forgotten by everyone, including Huey.

Huey was sitting in the dirt, burning ants with a magnifying glass he'd dug out of his backpack.

"I need a rest," Huey said, without looking up.

Deke stopped swinging his stick and looked back at Huey. "A rest?!" he shouted. "We just got here."

"That running wore me out," said Huey.

The summertime life of twelve-year-old boys was made up of long patches of boredom, peppered with brief moments of overwhelming excitement. One of those moments had just passed when they'd cut through the land of the old man in the blue trailer.

They'd crossed paths with the old man in the blue trailer a few times, because if they wanted to play in the woods behind the railroad tracks, they had to cut through his land. Unfortunately, he didn't sanction this arrangement and took it upon himself to let them know it in a most unsettling way. This last time, he passed right by any friendly warnings or gentle reprimands and cut straight into full-blaze, swear-laden threats. Eric, Deke, and Huey were called, among other things, *piss-ants*, *fuckers*, *shit birds*, and one of them, although it was hard to tell who the old man was pointing at, was apparently *a little sonofabitch who oughtta know better*. He went so far as to threaten to sic his dog on them, even though Eric was pretty certain he didn't even have a dog. The whole experience had been so jarring, Eric could hardly blame Huey for needing a bit of a rest.

"Oh man!" Huey shouted, bursting out in a fit of corpulent laughter. "Did you see that one?" His finger reached down to where the light from the magnifying glass had been focused and brought up a bit of black crust. He stayed seated, but held his finger above his head toward Eric. "That used to be an ant!"

Eric leaned in to look. "Yeah, that's pretty cool," he said, to be polite.

Deke stood there, leaning on his stick, shaking his head at Huey. "Are all you rested up now, Huey, or do you need to kill some more stuff first?"

Huey looked up at Deke like he wished he would just go away. But he stood up, dusted off his shorts, and stuffed his magnifying glass back into his backpack. Deke shook his head, then returned to swinging his stick through the weeds. Eric followed behind and focused on looking for a trail.

Huey, on the other hand, was never going to find a trail. He had the attention span of a goldfish, and could rarely even be bothered to keep his eye on a trail once they were on it. Apparently there were just too many other things to look at, most of which were completely made up. He was always claiming to have seen a monkey in a tree, or something shiny—like maybe a piece of a UFO—off in the distance, just farther than anyone wanted to walk. Eric didn't really know much about drugs, but he did wonder what Huey's dad might have been up to when he was younger. This trek had barely begun when Huey already claimed to see something up underneath the tracks. A claim that, out of habit, was met with unmerciful skepticism.

"You're a retard, Huey," said Deke, without even bothering to stop swinging his stick.

"No, I'm serious, man. There's something up there!" He dug around in his backpack while Eric stood behind him, staring up at the tracks. He hated wasting time on Huey's every hallucination, but he hated the idea of missing out on a possible adventure even more. Huey brought out his magnifying glass and held it up to his eye.

"Shoot! I thought this thing was supposed to make things bigger," he said, moving it back and forth at different distances from his face.

"It's not a telescope there, short bus," said Eric. But he didn't give Huey too much of a hard time, because he thought he saw something too. "Hey Deke," he hollered, "I think Encyclopedia Brown here might actually have something this time."

Deke stopped beating down weeds and turned around. "Aw man, don't do that," he said. "You're only gonna encourage him. Next thing you know he'll be seeing dinosaurs again."

"I didn't say it was a dinosaur," snapped Huey. "I said it *could* have been a dinosaur." He paused to put his magnifying glass away, and mumbled, "Either that or a dragon."

"Naw, for real, Deke," said Eric. "I think I see something up there. It looks like there's some metal sticking out from underneath the railroad ties."

Deke walked over to where they were standing and looked up the hill at the tracks. It was about fifty yards away, and up the hill about twenty feet, but it definitely looked like something. Not much really, but something.

They cut through a thick patch of weeds, abandoning all hopes of avoiding poison ivy, and made their way to the spot directly below the something. From there, they could see it was a hole hollowed out beneath the tracks, with a slab of sheet metal lodged directly underneath the ties. The ground on the hillside was soft and covered in weeds, so it took some time to get to the top. Especially for Huey, who must have been the only kid in West Virginia who didn't own a pair of boots. His old worn-out sneakers sent him sliding so often that he probably climbed the distance of the hillside three times during the one trip. But when they got to the top, it was worth it.

What they saw before them was a fort like no other. Some resourceful kid had taken this area underneath the railroad tracks and turned it into a full-fledged home away from home. There were busted-up pieces of wood paneling along the sides, a couple of good-sized rocks to serve as chairs, and the sheet metal above to provide shelter from the rain. There was enough room for all three of them inside, and they immediately felt at peace in the cool, musty air.

"This is awesome!" said Huey. "I told you guys. I told you I saw something!"

"Okay settle down, Huey," answered Deke. "You're like one for a million and seven now. I wouldn't get too cocky about it."

"Yeah but it's a really good one," answered Huey.

Eric agreed, it was a really good one. This fort was better than any makeshift fort he'd ever managed to put together. He normally got himself all worked up during the planning of a fort, but got bored pretty quickly when it came time to put it together. Whoever built this one thought it through. The location alone was genius. No one could ever find it unless they were dumb enough to be trudging around in the mud and high weeds on the other side of the tracks. Even then, they'd be so preoccupied with watching their footing, they'd probably never notice it. If there was no such thing as a Huey Dinkins in the world, it would have been flawless.

But there was a Huey, and he'd already started moving things around in exploration of the fort. He was peeking behind the wood paneling to see what was back there, and picking up the rock-seats to have a good look underneath them.

"What are you doing, Huey?" asked Eric.

"Just lookin' around," he answered.

"For what?"

"I don't know."

"Well," Eric said, sitting down, "let us know when you find it."

Deke was sitting near the entrance of the fort, with his knees pulled up into his chest. "Man, this place is something else. I'll bet it took forever to build." A wistful, faraway look came over him as he began to feel all cozy and right at home. Eric was feeling the same thing. It was like pulling the covers over his head at night during a thunderstorm. Except instead of being surrounded by the warm air of his body and breath, he was enveloped in a cool cover of summer shade.

"Oh man!" Huey cried out in a half-whisper. "Oh man, I found it!"

Eric looked over lazily in Huey's direction. "Found what?" he sighed.

"Oh man, you guys gotta check this out!"

Eric and Deke shook their heads at one another before going over to where Huey was in mid-conniption. He was down on his knees, hovering over a hole he'd discovered beneath one of the rocks. Inside that hole was a freezer bag filled with magazines. Nudie magazines.

"Holy crap, Huey! You're on fire today," said Deke with a punch in his shoulder.

Finding the occasional nudie mag in the woods wasn't unheard of. Eric could never figure out who would go through the trouble to buy, borrow, or steal a nudie mag, then just leave it out in the woods. The pages were always wrinkled and stale from the rain, and smelled like the coldest corner of a stone basement. A smell that was magnified by holding the pages too close when carefully trying to turn them. More often than not, they'd tear, leaving the girl on the page without her head, or tits, or worse. But even old, decaying, and slightly disfigured nudity was better than no nudity at all.

The magazines Huey had found were of a whole different quality. Whoever put these here had learned from the mistakes of woods-porn past. They'd been preserved in freezer bags, sealed in a stone-covered hole, and protected by the shelter of the coolest fort ever made—a distinction only heightened by their presence. Huey opened the bag with an air of reverence and pulled out the top magazine.

"Remember the order," Eric told him. "Let's be sure to put them back in the exact same order."

"Okay," said Huey in a dreamy voice. "I got the first one. It's a *Playboy,* with a . . . girl on the cover . . ." His voice trailed off as he went back to studying the magazine he now held solemnly with both hands.

Deke looked through the bag as he spoke up. "They're all *Playboy*s there, numbnuts. And, wait a minute. Yep, hard to believe, but they all got girls on the cover."

Huey didn't bother to look up, and barely bothered to speak out loud. "I got the first one," eased from his lips as quiet as his breath.

"Alright, Huey's got the first one," Eric said to Deke. "Let's you and I remember that. He'll be lucky if he can remember his name in a few minutes."

Deke laughed and looked over at Huey. Suddenly his brow furrowed and he squinted his eyes. "Are you gonna open it, Huey?" he said. "The naked girls are on the inside, y'know?"

Huey just nodded. "I know. I'm lookin' for the bunny."

"No duh, you paste-eater. She's on the inside."

"No, I mean the bunny logo. They hide it on the cover of every issue. I like to try and find it."

"Jesus Christ, Huey, it's not *Highlights*," snapped Deke, "it's *Playboy*! You want a pen so you can do the crossword in the back?"

Eric had never heard about the bunny logo being hidden on the cover before. He looked at his magazine to see if he could find it, but realized it might actually take the level of focus that Huey was committing and quickly gave up. The last thing he wanted was to catch heat from Deke on this one. The introduction of sex into their lives, as theoretical and intangible as it was at that stage, had left Eric on shaky ground. He didn't know anything about all this stuff. He knew the mechanics of it. That was easy enough to look up in the back of the library when no one else was around. But he had a feeling there was something else going on that no one was writing about in library books. And no one was talking about it, either. Apparently you were just supposed to know everything about it already, because if you ever asked a question, or didn't know what another kid was talking about, you'd be instantly ridiculed.

Eric didn't like not knowing things. Like why, when he looked at the pictures in *Playboy*, with the girls all posed and poised just so, he got that feeling. But when he looked at other magazines, where the girls had their legs all splayed out so they could get close-ups of parts that sort of looked like cold cuts, it made him feel kind of sick. He figured it must not make everyone sick, otherwise they wouldn't take pictures of it and put it in magazines. But not looking at it wasn't an option either, because when you found nudie magazines with your friends, you had to look at them.

As he flipped through, the magazine naturally opened to the centerfold. He normally liked to start at the first set of pictures and work his way to the back, but when he peeked at the centerfold, he couldn't believe his eyes. It was Gina Stevens.

It took him a second to realize it wasn't actually Gina Stevens. But this beautiful, naked girl on the pages of *Playboy* looked so much like her that Eric let out an audible groan of some kind. Deke gave him a funny look, but was distracted before he could say anything.

"It's in the lace!" said Huey, fervidly poking at his cover. "I found the bunny. It's hidden in the lace."

"Way to go, Huey," said Deke, looking back down in disdain. "Now see if you can't find the tits. I'll give you a hint. They're on the girls."

Eric didn't care to see Huey's hidden bunny. Not because he was worried about what Deke might say. He was far too enchanted by the nudity of his would-be Gina Stevens.

Besides being a sophomore at Pinely High School, Gina Stevens was the unknowing object of Eric's massive and mythical crush. She was so bigger-than-life to Eric, and to a lot of other young men in Pinely, that she was always referred to by her full name, to the point where it practically became one. Ginastevens. Deke and Eric used to play a game where they'd find out which girls in town they thought were prettiest using a simple, head-to-head, single-elimination tournament. It was how the Super Bowl was determined, so they figured it was the most fair and accurate way to measure just about anything.

"Tricia Thatcher or Penny Sterns?"

"Penny Sterns."

"Penny Sterns or Alice Whitfield?"

"Penny Sterns."

"Penny Sterns or Christy Anderson?"

"Christy Anderson."

"Christy Anderson or Leslie White?"

"Leslie White."

They knew how to build the game to make it more interesting. There was no point in bringing in the A-players too early. The lesser-of-two-evils contests were a good warm-up to the real key match-ups. But when Eric was on the receiving end, the outcome was always the same.

"Lori Gates or Becky Hayes?"

"Lori Gates."

"Lori Gates or Ginastevens?"

"Ginastevens."

"Ginastevens or Shannon Lopez?"

"Ginastevens."

"Ginastevens or Heather Hynes?"

"Ginastevens."

It got to the point where Deke would only play the game if he was allowed to leave Gina Stevens out of the pool. "Otherwise," he said, "it's about as fun as watching Pinely play Cedarsville. A game ain't no fun if you already know who's gonna win."

This girl on the pages of *Playboy* filled Eric with a mixture of excitement and guilt. She had the same dark hair, falling down over her shoulders. The same blue eyes, gazing out from behind their long lashes. The same smooth curves rendering her body in a soft but defined form. Except this girl was actually showing the so much more that Gina Stevens only hinted at. Which made Eric feel a little like a Peeping Tom.

When the sun broke over the crest from behind them and poured into their newfound fort, the cool shade vanished, replaced by a cruel summer heat that eventually got to the three of them. And while Huey had remembered his canteen, he hadn't remembered to fill it up before he left the house.

"I thought we could just fill it up down at the river," he explained.

"The fish don't even drink the water in the river," said Eric.

"For cryinoutloud, Huey. If we could drink the water out of the river, we wouldn't need the stupid canteen in the first place," Deke added.

Huey looked at Deke, then looked down at his canteen. "It's not stupid," he said.

"Oh God," said Deke, rolling his eyes at Eric. "I didn't mean to hurt your canteen's feelings, Huey. I didn't realize it was so sensitive."

"It's okay," said Huey.

"Great. So let's just put everything back the way we found it," said Deke. "Huey's magazine was on top. Then it was yours, right, Eric?"

Eric surveyed the situation for a moment. The freezer bag, the hiding hole, the rock to cover it all up. He tried taking one last look at his pseudo-Ginastevens, but quickly realized it wasn't going to be enough.

"I think I'm just gonna hang on to this one," he said with as much authority as he could muster.

"What are you talking about, Eric?" asked Deke. "Just put it back in the bag."

"No, I think I'm gonna keep it."

"You can't keep it, man," said Huey. "That'd be like stealin'."

"No it wouldn't," he said. "They're already stolen, right?"

"We don't know that," said Deke.

"Well if you could buy your own *Playboy*s, you probably wouldn't take them out to your fort in the woods and bury them under a rock," he declared. "I mean, if you could buy your own *Playboy*s, you probably wouldn't even have a fort in the woods to begin with. So whoever put these here already stole them from somebody else. And you can't steal something if it's already stolen, can you?"

Deke and Huey were stumped by that one. "I don't know," Deke said with a shrug.

"You can't kill something if it's already dead," said Huey, "I know that."

"Well then," trumped Eric, as though Huey's last point hadn't been completely ridiculous.

"Well what are you gonna do with it? You gonna take it home?" asked Deke. "Your mom'll probably find it when she's cleaning up, and then what?"

Huey thought Deke had a pretty good point and came in to back him up. "Yeah, Eric," he said, "if you just leave it here, you can come back and look at it anytime you want. You live closer than any of us."

Eric had already thought of that. But he'd thought of a few other things as well. Like what if the kid who put these here was taking them from his dad's stash? And what if that kid decided to switch these magazines out with a few other ones some day, just to keep things fresh? Or what if another group of kids found the fort and stole the magazines for themselves? There were just too many loose ends for Eric to be comfortable. He wasn't going to risk losing naked Ginastevens, even if he had no idea what he was going to do with her.

"Mom won't find her," he said.

Deke's face scrunched up in confusion. "Find who?"

Eric realized his mistake and quickly tried to cover. "Look, I'm not asking you if I can take it," he said as he picked up his bag. "I'm just taking it."

Deke and Huey looked at one another bewildered. "Alright," Deke finally said to Eric, then added under his breath, "weirdo."

Hiking out of the woods wasn't as carefree as the hike in. Everybody knew that Eric's backpack now contained stolen goods, but nobody wanted to talk about it. Instead, they talked about what they hoped their moms would be cooking for dinner, what was going to be on TV that night, and which superheroes would win in head-to-head combat with one another. They even ragged on Huey a little bit when he mispronounced "chrysanthemums" so badly they had to have him actually describe it in order to know what he was talking about. But the whole time they were wondering to themselves if they were now criminals or sinners or both.

When they got to the end of the alley, where they would all split up to head home, they stopped and looked at one another. Eric figured it was his job to speak first, so he did.

"You wanna try to get some people together for flashlight tag after dinner?" Eric looked back down the alleyway for a second, then turned back and added, "After it gets dark."

Huey was growing visibly uncomfortable with the whole situation, and answered a little too enthusiastically. "Yeah, that could be fun!"

"Yeah," said Deke, "that'd be . . ." His voice trailed off as he switched trains of thought. "Well you should just call us later if everything's still—if you still want to play."

They made uneasy small talk for a few more minutes, then finally split up to head home. Deke was the only one who even acknowledged the issue in the slightest way, and he saved that for his parting words. "Good luck."

Eric tried to put it all into perspective during the walk home. It was just a magazine. His mom had magazines all over the house, so what could be the big deal about bringing another one home? He figured he should probably just throw it up onto the coffee table with the rest of them. His dad would sure enjoy that. But with every step he took, it changed from being just a magazine to being the filthy, dirty, smutty pornography that it was. By the time he stepped into his living room, he felt so riddled with guilt, he might as well have had a severed human head in his bag.

He wasn't in the door two seconds before his mom was all over him.

"Oh Eric, you've got to come look at this," she said, putting her arm around his shoulder and her hand on his backpack. She led him around the corner and into the kitchen where their neighbor Barbara was standing, holding a little puppy. Either his mom was behaving as though she'd never seen a puppy in her life, or everything was overly exaggerated in Eric's criminal mind.

"Isn't it just adorable?" his mom asked in a dolphin-pitched voice.

The puppy was licking Barbara in the face while she tried to talk. "Do you want to hold him?"

Eric didn't know what he wanted to do. He just wanted to do whatever would draw the least attention to himself. He was smiling. He knew that's probably what he'd normally do when he saw a puppy. Which meant he probably liked puppies. So the answer must be yes. Yes, he would like to hold the puppy!

The puppy didn't seem to care who was holding him, or who he licked. He immediately started licking Eric's face and chewing on his ear. Eric started laughing and even managed to ask Barbara the puppy's name. But he didn't catch the answer, because the useless cur squirmed over his shoulder and started chewing on the top of his backpack. His mom, now ridiculous with glee, didn't miss a beat.

"Aw, he likes your backpack, Eric. You must having something good in there," she said. The next thing Eric knew, she had her hands on the backpack, pulling it off of him. "Here, let me take that before he chews it all up."

And just like that, Eric's world was on its ear. He was holding a puppy. His mom was holding his bag. And his bag was holding naked Ginastevens. He stood there, getting molested by this animal and staring into the manic faces of the two women in front of him. But nothing could pull his awareness away from the backpack his mom was carelessly dangling in her hand.

When the phone started to ring, no one moved to answer it. His mom was in a complete puppy-daze, and Eric wasn't about to lose visual contact with the bag by leaving the room. Finally, his mom snapped out of it.

"Oh, I guess I'd better get the phone," she said, moving toward the other room.

Eric wanted to throw the puppy, dive for the bag, and run for his life. Instead he mustered as much nonchalance as he could and casually grasped the handle of the backpack as she passed by.

"Here, Mom," he said, "let me take that for you."

He expected some resistance, but she just said, "Oh thanks, Eric," and left the room. Thinking she'd be helpful, Barbara extended her hand to take the backpack from Eric, but he wasn't having any of it. He handed over the puppy, and took the bag up close to his body with both arms. A sense of relief washed over him. Then he realized it wasn't relief, it was unbridled elation. He smiled at Barbara and she smiled back, both enjoying the warmth, beauty, and magic of the bundles of joy they guarded so closely in their arms.

MONDAY

"What's in the bag, Eric?"

Deke was sitting at the counter of Abby's Diner, sipping a cup of coffee. He'd taken his hat off, revealing a head of hair that obviously hadn't seen a comb all morning. In fact, based on the state of his hair, and the puffiness of his eyes, Eric figured Deke hadn't been out of bed more than fifteen minutes.

"Just some library books I've gotta return," Eric answered, sitting on the stool next to him at the counter.

"How come you don't just have your mom return 'em for you?" Deke asked.

"I'm gonna walk right by the library on my way to work, so what's the difference?"

"I don't know. Just seems like if your mom's a librarian, it'd be easier to have her do it. Cause she ain't gonna just walk by the library. She's gonna go all the way inside it."

Eric shrugged his shoulders at Deke in disbelief. "Jesus, Deke, does it bother you that much to have books so close to you?"

"No! Hell, I don't care," Deke snapped back. "I'm just trying to make your life easier, that's all."

"Well you're doin' a piss-poor job of it," answered Eric.

Abby Drysdale came out of the kitchen, waving her dishtowel above her head of gray hair. "Alright, you two," she said, "just cut it out. It's too early in the morning to have you fellas makin' everyone else uneasy with all your yappin'."

It didn't seem to bother Abby that her point was undermined by the poor attendance at the diner that morning. Other than Deke, Eric, Abby, and Chet, the short-order cook, the diner was empty, save the ever-present Dwayne Griffith, who'd lost all but the faintest remembrance of his hearing in a mining accident twenty years earlier.

"He started it, Abby," said Eric.

"I doubt that," she said. "Do you know what you want?"

"I want to live to tell about it, so I'm gonna stick to the usual," Deke answered.

She turned to Eric. "How about you, wise-ass?"

"Y'know, Abby, this whole breakfast-cooking thing is your specialty, so I'm just gonna let you work your magic. Surprise me." he said. "As much as you can for under two fifty."

Abby poured Eric a cup of coffee, then disappeared behind the swinging doors to the kitchen. Deke didn't even let him finish stirring in the milk before he started in.

"So do you want in on the pool?" he asked.

Deke's dad ran the most dim-witted betting pool ever concocted. It ran for one week out of the year, the week of the Pinely-Cedarsville game. What had started about thirty years ago as a bit of a get-rich-quick scheme had blossomed into a full-fledged pain in the ass for Deke's dad. In the very beginning, he gave even odds on the game, but limited participation exclusively to citizens of Pinely. Those were fiercely loyal times, and fools from all over town lined up to put their hard-earned money on their beloved Wildcats. Year after year, Deke's dad reaped the rewards of exploiting the loyalty of Pinely. But at some point, people began to realize that, by betting on Cedarsville, they could find a way to win, even when Pinely lost. There were still enough other loyal fools to cover the costs, but this change of events turned it from pure profit for Deke's dad to pure management. It only took two years of that before he realized he had to make some changes. He started giving odds on the game. The question was no longer would Pinely win, but how badly would they lose? This turned the whole thing into one big mess for Deke's dad. He caught grief beforehand about the size of spread. He caught grief afterwards from people who claimed they didn't understand the spread when they'd bet on Cedarsville. And every time he tried to stop running the pool altogether, he caught grief about giving people the chance to win their money back from last year.

"I never bet in the pool," Eric said to Deke. "What makes you think I'd want to do it now?"

"Well, Dad and I were talking, and . . . y'know the point spread is creeping pretty far out there again, so people don't really wanna bet too much this year."

"Yeah," Eric said. "I'm one of 'em."

"Right," said Deke, sipping from his coffee cup. "That's understandable." He stared off into the distance, drinking his coffee, then spoke more into his cup than he did to Eric. "But maybe you could help us out a little, without having to actually bet."

Eric turned and looked at Deke. "What the hell are you talkin' about?" he asked.

Deke pretended as if he hadn't said anything when he saw Abby come through the swinging doors. She put a plate down in front of Deke and said, "Bacon, eggs, and toast for you," then turned to Eric. "And for you, the chef's surprise." She put the plate in front of Eric and waited in anticipation.

Eric looked at the plate, glanced at Deke out of the corner of his eye, then looked back at the plate. "What is it, Abby?" he asked.

She pointed at the concoction, emphasizing each word with her finger as she spoke. "Sausage-cornbread pancakes."

Eric nodded his head in disbelief as he stared at the plate. "Well, I'll be damned," he finally managed to say. He looked over at Deke, who was looking right back at him. "Sausage-cornbread pancakes, Deke."

Deke just nodded and dug into his bacon and eggs. Abby was headed back toward the kitchen when Eric called out to her.

"Hey Abby, am I supposed to put syrup on these?"

She stopped and looked as though she was working a tough math problem in her head. Finally she shrugged. "I'm not sure," she said, before disappearing behind the swinging doors.

He picked up his fork and started prodding at the pancakes a little bit. Deke leaned over the counter to be sure Abby was gone, then turned back to Eric.

"So anyway, you could help us with the pool just by letting us use your name," he said.

Eric had a piece of the pancake on his fork and was holding it up to his nose, inspecting it in every way possible before he put it in his mouth. He wasn't all that interested in what Deke was saying, especially since it didn't make any sense.

"I don't know about this," he said, more to the pancake than to Deke.

"There's really nothing to it," Deke said. "Seven years ago, when we beat those sonsabitches, you were the only one who called it. You were parading around town telling everyone we were going to win, but of course no one believed you. Hell, I didn't even believe you. Losing to Cedarsville was just something that happened every year. Kinda like Christmas. But you predicted that win. You were like . . . ," Deke lost his momentum as he searched for a word that just wasn't there, "whoever that guy is who predicts the future."

"Kreskin?"

"No."

"Nostradamus?" Eric said, before gently placing the bite of pancake into his mouth.

"Yeah," said Deke, excited to be back on track, "Nostradamus. So that got Dad to thinkin'. He's all set to close the spread a little bit anyway, which'll bring a few more people into the pool. But, if he were to close the spread on account of another Eric Mercer victory prediction . . ." Deke nodded his head and smiled at Eric. "You see what I'm gettin' at?"

Eric looked at Deke and nodded his head. "Yes, I do."

"And?"

"And I'm not gonna help you."

Deke sat still for a minute, then turned to completely face Eric. "Alright," he said. "I didn't want to have to bring this up, but Dad wanted me to remind you that seven years ago, you cost him a fuckload of money by beatin' the spread."

Eric laughed, "We didn't beat the spread, dipshit, we beat the team."

"Which was well above what was covered by the spread," he clarified.

Eric could hardly believe the line of logic he was hearing. "Look, Deke, I can appreciate the predicament your dad's got himself in, running a ragtag racket in a podunk town. But I'm not going to apologize for something that happened when I was seventeen years old. And I'm sure as hell not going to let him go around telling people I think Pinely's gonna win. Cause they're not. They're gonna get the ever-living shit kicked out of them, just like they do every year."

"Except that one year," Deke added.

"Yeah," Eric sighed, "well, a lot of strange shit happened that year."

Deke spent the remainder of their time trying to persuade Eric to "get in on the action," as he so sincerely put it. The only effect this had on Eric was to make him devour his breakfast quicker than was probably healthy. He'd wanted to get Abby to bring him a fried egg to go with his pancakes, but he knew that would take a few minutes, and he knew those would be a few more minutes of listening to Deke yap about how his hare-brained scheme was "easy money." So Eric just kept his head down, and kept shoveling back pancakes. When he hit the bottom of the plate, cramming back the last bite, he turned to Deke and smiled.

"I gotta go to work, Deke."

"Aw man, c'mon," Deke whimpered, "you gotta look at it like—"

His words broke off suddenly as Abby came back out to the counter. The piece of white toast in his hand absently sopped up the last of his egg as he stared deep into his coffee cup.

"What's the matter with him?" Abby asked.

Eric stood up and dug around in his pockets for some money. "Oh, he's just upset because I won't let him sully my good name in this town."

Deke looked up at him with a flash of concern that, despite his best intentions, came across as comical. His eyes grew wide as he raised his eyebrows and spoke out of the side of his mouth. "Eric, shut up," he half-whispered.

Eric just smiled at him as he threw seven dollars on the counter. "I can't let him do that, can I Abby?"

"Sully your good name?" she asked. "Hell no." She picked up the empty plates, tucked the money into her apron, and looked up at Eric. "That'll leave you with nothin' to do."

Deke grabbed his hat from the stool next to him and stuffed it on top of his head. "I don't put up with enough shit all day, do I? I gotta start shoveling through it first thing with you two."

Deke was a technician at the Pinely Sanitation Plant. He didn't let anyone else crack wise with the obvious jokes, but he reserved the right to use them whenever he wanted. After all, he was the one who climbed up inside the collective colon of Pinely every day and filled his lungs with its stench. If he could find a scrap of humor in it then, by God, he was certainly entitled to it.

He bummed a pack of matches from Abby and lit up a cigarette as he and Eric made their way to the door. Outside in the cold morning air, they watched the people making their way to the bank, carpooling up the highway toward the chemical plants, and opening the stores on Main Street. It seemed a little too cold for October, but then it always seemed a little too cold when you realized there'd be no more Indian summer to save you from the coming freeze.

Deke blew out a cloud of smoke that mingled with the frost from his breath. "So you pickling anyone today?" he asked Eric.

Eric leaned out past the awning of the diner to catch some of the rising sun peeking over the hillside. "Not today," he answered. "The population of the greater Pinely metropolitan area is alive and well."

"Fuckin' health and happiness," Deke grunted. "Kinda bad for business, huh?"

"Well I'll be pickling 'em tonight at the Legion."

Deke took a final draw from his cigarette and stomped it out with his boot. "Drinkin' and dyin'. Hell, you got a lock on the two steadiest streams of business in town."

Eric closed his eyes as the sun washed over his face. "Well, I haven't seen much of a slowdown in people using the toilet, Deke."

"Yeah," he answered, staring at the ground. The two of them stayed that way for a pause that would have seemed uncomfortable to just about anyone else. Finally Deke wiped his nose on his sleeve and said, "Shit," before turning and walking down the street toward his truck.

Eric headed in the opposite direction and turned up toward the north end of town. With his bag slung over his shoulder and his hands in his coat pockets, he set into a casual pace up the vacant sidewalk. Despite the fact that everything in Pinely was practically right next to everything else, no one walked anywhere. Eric found it kind of silly that people would drive four blocks to the grocery store just to pick up a gallon of milk. But other people found it kind of silly that Eric would walk the length of the town every morning, and do it again every evening, when he had a perfectly good car sitting in his driveway. They used to offer him a ride, thinking maybe times were hard and he was just trying to save on gas. But after a while they began to realize he just liked walking. As with most things about Eric, they didn't really understand it, but they just let him be.

Passing by Pinely High School, Eric took in the annual gross display of school spirit. Swathed in homemade signs of green and white, the place looked like Propaganda Headquarters: Pride Division. The signs encouraged the mighty Wildcats to inflict every variety of unpleasantry on the dastardly Cedarsville Tigers, even going so far as to "Kill the Tigers"—an idea that struck Eric as a bit sadistic for small town life.

Just a block away from the high school was Tremble's Funeral Home. As he walked up to it, Eric ran his hand across the wooden fence out front and a frown crept upon his face. He opened the gate and walked up on the porch and in through the front door.

"Morning, Mr. Tremble," he called out. There was a slight hint of formaldehyde in the air as he hung his coat on the rack in the parlor. Normally the flowers would cover up the scent, but it had been a few weeks since there'd been a service.

"Good morning, Eric," a voice called out from another room. Eric turned to the window and looked more at it than out of it, holding his hand above the sill. He heard footsteps behind him and turned around to greet Mr. Tremble.

"Oh goodness," the old man said, "what happened to your eye?"

Eric had forgotten about his battle scar. Abby was used to seeing Eric banged up, and rarely bothered to say anything about it anymore. Working with Eric every day for the past five years, Mr. Tremble had seen even more of his scrapes and bruises than Abby had, but for whatever reason, he couldn't seem to get used to it the way she did.

"Aw, I just got a little knocked around, that's all," Eric answered. His hand was still extended toward the window as he spoke. "We've got a little draft poking in around the windows. I suppose I'll go ahead and caulk those and weather-strip the doors since it's pretty nice out today. Maybe even get to the fence out there by this afternoon. It's feeling a little unkempt, but a good coat of paint oughtta keep the winter weather off it."

Mr. Tremble just nodded and smiled. He had a perfectly pleasant face. Exactly the kind of face you'd want to have in front of you when dealing with the unpleasantness of burying a loved one. Mr. Tremble handled each family with an impeccable balance of compassion and composure. He made them feel he knew the magnitude of their loss, while serving as an unwavering source of strength. Eric had watched the man console a grieving mother with heartfelt tenderness, then turn around and dictate the logistics of the funeral procession with distant poise. He made his living off the dead. He was constantly in their company. And it infused him with an overwhelming, if heavily compartmentalized, respect for life.

Eric started working for him before Tess was born. He and Gina were leaving the Cedarsville hospital after Gina's first ultrasound when they saw Mr. Tremble loading a body into his hearse with the help of a less-than-enthusiastic orderly. Eric helped them get the body into the hearse, then asked Mr. Tremble if he was going to need any help when he got back to Pinely. He was desperate for a reason not to have to ride with Gina and share in prenatal chitchat, so when Mr. Tremble told him he could use a hand, Eric offered to ride along with him as well. Eric sat in the passenger seat, idly staring out the window. When he turned and asked if he could switch on the radio, Mr. Tremble was impressed at how unruffled Eric was about riding in the hearse.

"Aren't you nervous about being in a car with a dead body?" he asked.

Eric turned away from the window to face Mr. Tremble. "Why, are you?"

"No, not at all. It's just that most people aren't as comfortable with it as you seem to be."

"Well," Eric answered, "as long as he's one-hundred-percent dead, I'm okay with it."

Mr. Tremble looked at Eric, a little confused. "What do you mean?" he asked.

"Y'know, as long as there's no chance of any Edgar Allan Poe—type of nonsense going down." He smiled at the old undertaker. "You've never encountered any of that stuff have you?"

"What," Mr. Tremble asked, "the undead?"

"Yeah."

"Nope," he laughed.

"Right," Eric said, turning back to the window, "then I've got nothing to be nervous about."

Few people ever tried to make Mr. Tremble laugh. They seemed to think that an undertaker must be a dour and somber man. But Eric made regular conversation with him as though he wasn't forty years his elder, and as though there wasn't a dead body in the back of the car. As they loaded the body into the back room, Mr. Tremble asked Eric if he'd be interested in working for him. Keeping the place up and offering a hand with the services. Eric didn't say anything at first. He concentrated on hefting the body onto the embalming table, realizing for the first time the origin of the term "dead weight." When it was safely up on the table, Eric took a serious look around the room. He felt comfortable there, and for one melodramatic moment he felt it was an all-too-appropriate place for him. When he shook free of his moment of self-pity he realized that, above all else, he could use the work.

"I'll be honest with you," he told Mr. Tremble. "I really don't know much about being a handyman. But I learn pretty quick."

"You were in the top of your class, weren't you?"

Eric looked down at his shoes. "Third."

Mr. Tremble extended his hand to Eric and smiled. "Then I imagine you'll learn plenty quick enough."

There was a set of Time-Life books on home repair at the library. It was part of an attempt to make the library a more vital part of the community. Classic literature wasn't exactly bringing them in by the droves, so Doris, the head librarian, acquired some volumes of a more vocational nature. Six years later, Eric was the first person to check them out. But he more than made up for the idle time they'd spent on the shelf. In the first year he worked for Mr. Tremble, he constantly had the Time-Life Home Repair and Improvement Series in his possession. By the time he'd gone through four seasons of handy work and repair, he'd practically memorized the entire series, from *Heating & Cooling* to *Windows & Doors*. A little bit of faith on the part of Mr. Tremble had earned him the most thorough and well-read handyman he'd ever had.

The fence probably could have been painted in August, but August was summer's last gasp, and summer in Pinely rarely went down without a fight. During those hellish, humid days, Eric tried to do as little as he could get away with. It was sandbagging, for sure.

But he always made up for it later, normally when the weather settled down in September. But September had been a high-volume month for the funeral home. On top of the regular autumnal check-outs by the elderly, there had been some accidents. Toby Earle flipped his Cutlass in a rainstorm coming back from Doddridge County. Shane Rubin got himself beat to death with a pool cue at the Buckskin during an argument that, to the best of the witnesses' recollections, had started over something to do with Conway Twitty. And Erica Potter got caught in the undertow of Shale's Creek while she was out skinny-dipping with some young man from Hickory who wasn't her husband. All of this had kept Eric pretty busy during September. So the fence was still in need of a coat of paint that October.

He sat on his milk crate in the afternoon sun, brushing the pale coat onto the fence, when he heard the school bell ring down the block. The serenity of his task was soon disrupted by an erratic stream of kids walking by on their way home. He was just as happy to ignore them, but some insisted on being neighborly. About every fourth passerby would acknowledge him with a "Hey Eric," and he would just nod, smile, and return to his painting.

It was the sound of footsteps stopping right behind him that really drew his attention. He turned around and saw three boys standing there. He was no good at figuring out how old kids were. His best guess was that these three were older than Tess, but still young enough to watch cartoons. They seemed a little startled when Eric turned around and looked at them. It quickly turned into confusion when he didn't say anything. Finally the one in the middle, wearing a Pinely Wildcats t-shirt, spoke up.

"You're Eric Mercer, aren't you?" he asked.

"Yeah," Eric answered, "who are you?"

"Donnie."

"Hey Donnie," Eric said. The awkward pause didn't seem to bother the kids nearly as much as it did Eric, so he decided to try to get to the bottom of things quickly, and directly. "What are you guys doing?"

Donnie took this to be a breezy, conversational question and seemed flattered that Eric cared about his plans. "Oh, we're just going over watch the football team practice," he said. "What are you doing?"

Eric shrugged and held up his paintbrush. "Paintin' a fence."

Donnie looked down one length of the fence, then back up the other. "How can you even tell where you've been?" he finally said.

"What do you mean?"

"It all looks the same."

"Well see, I started down there and I moved in an orderly fashion to here. That's how I know where I've been."

Donnie considered this for a moment, then shook his head. "Oh," he said.

"Oh?" Eric asked. None of this made any sense to him. "What grade are you in?"

"Fourth," Donnie answered.

"I'm not trying to be mean or anything, but you really should have been able to figure that one out."

The kid to Donnie's right had apparently caught up with Eric in growing tired of Donnie's pointless blather. He took a small step forward and pointed at Eric. "My dad says you scored three touchdowns against Cedarsville once."

The three of them looked at Eric as though they expected him to do something extraordinary. But he just nodded his head and said, "Yeah, I did."

Donnie seemed to think he could get back in on the conversation now that it was on the right track. "And you beat 'em," he said with unclear inflection.

"Was that a question?" Eric asked.

"No, you beat 'em," Donnie said, but quickly added, "Right?"

"Yeah, we beat 'em," he said.

"What was that like?" asked the kid who'd cut to the chase.

"I don't know," Eric shrugged. "It was . . . better than losing, I guess."

The kids looked at Eric, a little disappointed. Apparently they'd expected something more dynamic than "it was better than losing" to describe what was possibly the biggest win in Pinely Wildcat history.

"How come you're not playing for the Steelers or something?" asked the kid who hadn't said anything yet. "If you can score three touchdowns against Cedarsville, you should be playing for the Steelers."

"Well if I was playing for the Steelers, who'd paint this fence?" Eric asked.

The kid looked confused. "Anyone can paint a fence," he said.

"Well, apparently Donnie here can't," answered Eric. "He'd just paint the same section of the fence over and over again. Which is a waste of time. And paint."

The kids weren't sure what to do next. They'd expected some type of football hero. Instead they got a guy who could talk in circles and paint a fence really well. Donnie took one last stab at it.

"Do you think Pinely can win on Friday?" he asked.

Eric pointed at the three of them with his paintbrush. "Why don't you guys go on over there and watch them practice for a little while. You know, scout it out. Cause I really don't know. Then, come back here and tell me what you think." He turned around, dipped the brush into the can, and started painting again. "I'll be right here painting," he told them. He stopped and turned around to Donnie. "Actually, I probably won't be right here. I'll be further down that way."

The kids walked toward the high school while Eric returned to painting. He heard them mumbling to one another as they sulked off. It wasn't his intention to ruin their impression of what a football hero was like. He was just sick of being defined by something that had happened seven years ago by the people who were old enough to remember it themselves. He didn't want to have to live up to the hand-me-down expectations of a bunch of kids simply because their parents couldn't think of anything else to talk about.

The light bled out of the sky as it approached the end of the working day. Eric painted his way to the gate by the last rays, then took his brush and paint can inside. He went to the sink in the back room and washed up, cleaning out the brush and leaving it to dry for tomorrow. There wasn't much else to do, so Eric made his way to the office to say goodnight to Mr. Tremble. He found the old man sitting quietly in his chair, staring at the calendar on the wall.

"Hey Mr. Tremble," Eric said with a soft knock on the door frame.

Mr. Tremble looked over at Eric as though he'd just been woken. "Hey Eric," he said with a slight smile.

"Unless you have anything for me, I think I'm all done here today."

"No, no," he answered with a wave of his hand, "go on. It's been another quiet day."

Mr. Tremble made his living from other people dying. It was something he didn't really like to think about. He knew he was providing a service people wanted, and when he stayed busy he believed that. But when there were too many slow days in a row, days in which he wasn't preparing, planning, or performing that service, he was left with nothing to do but think. Once, over a shared flask of bourbon, he'd confided in Eric that when things got too slow, he sometimes found himself wishing that someone would just hurry up and die. Not so he could make money from the service, but so he could stop thinking about the fact that all he was really doing was waiting for someone to die.

Eric dug a piece of lint out of his pocket and went across the office to the garbage can by Mr. Tremble's desk. He threw it away and gently touched the old man on the shoulder as he walked back to the door. "You never know what tomorrow has in store," he said.

"No," answered Mr. Tremble, "you never do."

The American Legion smelled like so many things. All at once. It smelled like cigarettes, whether anyone was actually smoking or not. Someone usually was, but the smell in the Legion was one of cigarettes that had been smoked years before. Maybe by the same person who was smoking at that very moment. Maybe by that person's father. It also smelled like a damp basement, the kind that's just cinder blocks and a concrete floor. The Legion was carpeted, with walls that were done up in wood paneling, but it still managed to smell like a stone basement. Which was actually sort of crisp when mingled with the essence of cigarettes past. Then of course there was the scent of alcohol. It was more of a presence really, since you could never really hone in on the specific smell of beer or whiskey or anything else. You couldn't place any of them individually, but they were all there.

Bartending there didn't take much. The drinks folks wanted always had the complete list of ingredients in the name: Jack & Coke, Vodka Tonic, 7 & 7. All Eric had to do was mix them in a glass with some ice, or twist off a beer cap and slide the bottle down the bar. These deft skills earned him a little extra cash, paid under the table, three to five nights a week.

Eric buzzed himself through the door with his pass card and made his way behind the bar. There were only two people there, but it was bound to pick up by the time Monday Night Football started. Eric hung his bag on a peg on the wall, then hung his coat over it. Mack Shilling was sitting at the bar directly in front of Eric and pointed with a meaty finger as he spoke.

"What you got that bag for, Eric?"

"Oh, I just had to drop off some books at the library on my way over here."

Mack took a drag from his cigarette, speaking the smoke from his lungs. "Hows come you read books so much?" he asked, shaking his oversized head. "You're never gonna read 'em all."

Eric picked up a dishtowel and started wiping down the bar. "How come you fish so much, Mack? You're never gonna catch 'em all."

Mack rolled his eyes as if Eric didn't understand a thing. "Yeah, but fishin's fun," he said.

Eric wasn't about to get into this with Mack. The Legion was the Roman Colosseum of drunken, redneck arguments. He'd seen guys argue themselves blue in the face over things as trivial as the score of a football game they'd played thirty years ago. There was no room for logic, or proof, or anything else that might settle a dispute in real life. In the end, it all came down to how many other people in the room you could get to believe your side. There was little doubt how fishing versus reading would turn out, so Eric quickly shifted gears.

"Who's playing tonight?" he asked as he walked over to the hotdog steamer.

Kirby McDougal perked up and spouted out, "Whaddya mean, who's playing? It's only the Packers and the Bears, the oldest fuckin' rivalry in the history of professional football!"

"Jesus relax, Kirby," Eric shot back. "It's not like I asked when Independence Day is or something. I'm just trying to make some small talk here."

He started loading hotdogs and buns into the steamer. Eric brought in the steamer to make Monday nights at the Legion more eventful. He got the idea a couple of years ago at the county fair. The guy who ran the hotdog stand started telling Eric that he was turning his back on standard hotdogs and moving up to corndogs. He had a theory that people wanted food that was fun when they were at a fair. Apparently meat on a stick seemed more fun to this guy than meat on a regular old bun. Eric didn't have an opinion one way or the other, but he did make a deal with the guy to buy his hotdog steamer at a vastly reduced price. Thus Free Hotdog Mondays began.

His other Monday Night Football theme didn't pan out as well. He bought a set of Yard-O-Beer glasses and brought in a keg of Miller on game night. People seemed to enjoy the novelty of drinking beer out of what was essentially just a really tall glass. They didn't even seem to notice that the glasses were actually only half a yard. But he had to put an end to it when Shank Lewis drank nine of them in rapid succession, then, as he finished the tenth, stood up, shouted "First down!" and passed out, busting the glass and cracking his head on the floor. The trustees at the Legion decided they'd better do away with the Yards-O-Beer before other folks tried to top ol' Shank's drive for glory.

Kirby squinted at Eric as his wiry old legs walked him back to the bar, more out of instinct than free will. "What happened to your eye?" he asked.

"Deke says I got punched."

"I could see that happenin'," Kirby chuckled.

"By who?" wondered Mack.

"Not sure," answered Eric.

"You're not sure?!" shouted Kirby. He turned to look at Mack, then back to Eric in disbelief, causing his wobbly skin to resettle itself once he was finished. "How in the hell can you not be sure who punched you in the goddamned face?"

"Cause I was drunk, Kirby," Eric said. "You know what it's like to be drunk, right?"

Mack laughed a hacking, smoker's laugh. "I been piss-drunk since before you were born, son. But I'd sure as hell remember it if someone punched me in the face."

Eric filled a glass with water and shook his head. "Look, what's it gonna take to get you two to quit chappin' my ass for a little while? If you'll just be patient, some other folks'll show up. They'll get a few drinks in 'em and they'll be all ready to play 'bitch and bicker' with you guys."

True to his word, people slowly started to file in over the next couple of hours, and by nine o'clock there were a good two dozen people there, enjoying their hotdogs and watching the game. Mack and Kirby were at the far side of the bar by this point, giving Stan Winkler the once-over about the dangers of voting Republican. About halfway through the first quarter, Eric's dad strolled in and took a seat at the bar.

"Who's winning?" he asked, pulling a dollar from his pocket and absently adjusting his thinning hair.

Eric reached into the cooler under the bar, twisted the cap off a Miller Lite, and put it in front of his dad. "I think the Pack's got 'em by seven right now. Intercepted one in the flats and took it all the way in."

His dad made some sort of sound that acknowledged what Eric said without really commenting on it one way or the other. The two of them stared silently at the TV screen for a while, Eric's dad nursing his beer. When the game broke for a commercial, his dad looked back over at Eric and thrust his stubbled chin in his direction.

"That eye's not lookin' so good."

"Yeah, it's not feeling so good either, to be honest," Eric answered.

"How'd you hold up with Tess yesterday?"

"Pretty fair. I got a little nap in while she was outside playing with Buddy."

His dad shook his head and laughed a little. "How's Buddy these days?"

"Retarded."

"Yeah." He took another drink from his beer and listened to an argument breaking out in the corner about NASCAR. Eric had drifted down to the other end of the bar to get some empty bottles. When he got back, his dad picked right back up. "So what'd you and Tess do?"

Eric smiled proudly. "We raked the yard."

"Puttin' the poor little girl to work, are you?"

"You know, you can borrow her anytime you want."

"Naw, they're more trouble than they're worth at that age. Maybe in a couple years though."

"What's mine is yours, Dave."

"That's true," he said. "A quarter of her is actually me anyway, right?"

"Yeah, but as soon as I can get the money together we're having that part removed."

His dad swilled back the last of his beer and set the empty on the bar. "If this is the kind of respect you're gonna give me, I'm leaving."

"Going home?" Eric asked, more than a little surprised.

"C'mon, son," his dad admonished. "Going down there by the hotdog machine."

"Oh yeah," Eric said. "That makes a little more sense."

He gave his dad another beer and watched him make his way to the hotdogs. Everyone loved free food, but his dad seemed to love it more than anyone should. Last year, he caught a flu bug that had him lying in bed for three days. But on Super Bowl Sunday he rose from his bed like Lazarus, still packing a major-league fever and loaded to the gills with antibiotics, just to go to the Legion for the free chili and deep-fried oysters. Eric called it a case of psychosomatic wellness.

As the game went to halftime, Eric made his way to the cooler to pull out more beer. Someone buzzed outside, and since he was right there anyway, Eric skipped the club-house security measures and opened the door. Eric half-smiled at the man standing on the other side and nodded at him to come in.

"Hey there, Mr. Dupree," he said as he carried a case of beer around to the back of the bar.

"Hey Eric," the man answered. "Do you need a hand with that?"

"No, I'm okay. What can I get for you?"

Mr. Dupree took the seat at the bar where Eric's dad had been earlier. "I'll just have one of those beers, if that's alright," he said.

Eric twisted the cap off one of the beers from the case and handed it over the bar. "Here you are. Feel free to grab a hotdog over there if you want."

"Naw, I'm okay. I already had dinner."

"So's everyone else. You don't see it slowing them down, do ya?"

Mr. Dupree just smiled and took a sip from his beer. He was a blue-collar man, with simple tastes and lean desires. To him, there wasn't much purpose in eating a barroom hotdog after already enjoying a home-cooked meal. This sort of behavior made him a little suspect to others. He was about the same age as Eric's dad, but they didn't grow up together. Mr. Dupree had only lived in Pinely for the last eight years. One of the few people who had ever moved to Pinely instead of away from it.

"Boy, that's a good bruise on your eye there," he said to Eric. "What happened?"

"He got punched," piped in Kirby on his way to the bathroom. "And don't ask him by who, cause he don't know! You ever hear of such a thing, George?" he said, slapping Mr. Dupree on the shoulder with the back of his hand. "It's not like he got punched in the back of the head. Huh-uh. Punched right in the face. No idea who did it."

Kirby giggled and walked off toward the bathroom, undoing his pants partway before he even got to the door. Eric looked over at Mr. Dupree and shrugged.

"I got punched."

Mr. Dupree nodded and took a drink of his beer. "Yeah?" he said. "By who?"

Eric smiled. "So, how you been, Mr. Dupree?"

"Pretty good, Eric."

"And Mrs. Dupree?"

"She's fine. Just fine."

"That's good."

Eric just stood there smiling at Mr. Dupree and nodding his head.

"Jill's fine too, Eric."

Eric's smile became slightly more wistful. "Yeah. Oh I'm sure she is. She's . . ." He sifted through the next thing to say as a million things rushed through him at once. "Law school, right?"

"This is her last semester," he answered. "You know, she was in town for a little while over the summer."

"Yeah, I heard—" he paused, realizing he'd given away too much, then went on anyway. "I heard that."

"You should have come by to say hello."

Eric sighed ever so slightly into his glass as he took a drink of water. It wasn't really a question, so Eric decided he didn't have to answer it. Instead he tried to change the subject, without changing it completely.

"So did you two go camping when she was in?"

Mr. Dupree was generous enough to go with the change. "Yeah, we went up to Dolly Sods."

"She loved those trips," Eric said with a smile. "She used to go on and on about the fun you guys had. She'd talk about things that happened, but the way she'd tell it, I never knew if she was six or sixteen." He wiped the bar with his dishrag for no real reason. "I'm going to have to do something like that with Tess. Something that's just the two of us."

"How is Tess?"

"Aw, she's—amazing. A handful. But really something else, y'know?"

"Yeah, I do."

"Oh yeah, you would!" Eric answered, realizing they both had daughters.

"Jill asks about her."

"About Tess?"

"Yeah."

Eric suddenly felt like he was walking across a frozen lake. He wanted to see if it would support his weight. To see if he could stand in the center and see it all from a whole new angle. But he was afraid the ice would crack and plunge him into a place colder than he could ever imagine. "What does she ask?" he said, taking a small step forward.

"Just how she's doing. How you are with her."

"What do you say?" he asked, listening for the squeak and moan of the ice.

"I tell her what I know. She's a beautiful little girl. You guys seem happy. She's smart as a whip."

"How do you know that?"

"I saw her reading a story to the rest of the kids at Billy Wallace's birthday party last month."

"Oh yeah?" Eric said proudly. "She likes to read alright."

"I'll bet Jill would really like to meet her."

The ice let out a loud crunch that made Eric take a step backward. Maybe it wasn't as solid as he thought. Maybe it just needed some more time to freeze over all the way—if at all.

"Well, I don't know about that, Mr. Dupree. I mean—" he struggled to find some words to evade the whole thing. A way to not really say anything. He realized he was doubly uncomfortable because Tess was out there on the ice with him. "I just thought it'd be easier on Jill if I was out of her life. Completely."

Mr. Dupree gave him a sad look. "I think you're wrong about that."

"Wouldn't be the first time," Eric answered.

"Look Eric, her life is better because of you. She never would have gone to college. She'd never be in law school right now."

"I wasn't her guidance counselor, Mr. Dupree. I was her boyfriend."

"Well, you were good at both."

Eric reached over and took the empty beer bottle from Mr. Dupree's hand. "I think that may be a little bit of revisionist history there."

The door buzzed open, allowing Deke to bluster in and head directly to the bar. He let out an exhale that seemed to carry the weight of the world. "Fuck," he said. "I need a beer."

Eric handed him a beer and got another one for Mr. Dupree while he was at it. He was about to say something, but Deke had no intention of letting anyone speak until he'd gotten a few things off his chest.

"You wouldn't believe the day—" he switched his attack in mid-thought and came back with, "Guess where I've been up until now. Just now. Work, that's where." He paused for a quick drink of beer, then picked right back up. "Fuckin' hell, man. Imagine your shittiest day of work. Now imagine your job involves actual shit. Then multiply that shitty, shit day by—I don't know," he looked to Eric.

"Pi?"

"Is that a lot?"

"A little more than three."

"No," Deke said, slightly offended. "Way more than that. Like . . . a billion. That's the day I've had. Some slackjaw down at the plant—and we don't know who, because obviously everyone in the place has an alibi—but somebody fucked up one of the valves—forgot the old 'righty tighty, lefty loosy' routine they teach you before you're even allowed to use the goddamned rubber cement in nursery school. So we come back from a little lunch break up on the roof—because nobody likes to eat their lunch in the stink there—I know some of the guys say they've worked there so long they don't even smell it anymore, but that's bullshit cause they're all up on the roof when it comes time to eat. So we come back from the roof and it's just Shit Town, U.S.A. down there. I mean we've got shovels and wheelbarrows and buckets and whatever else we can find to haul ridiculous amounts of shit. If the folks from OSHA or the EPA had been there, we'da had double the amount, cause they'da shit themselves something fierce. It was just that bad. And this is what I've been dealing with from after lunch till just now. I mean, what time is it anyway?" Eric was about to answer when Deke looked up at the TV. "Holy hell, it's the second half?! Who's winning?"

"I'm not sure," Eric answered.

"You're not sure?" Deke said. He looked at Eric, a little confused. "What the hell you been doin'?"

"Talking with Mr. Dupree here."

Deke turned around and saw Mr. Dupree for the first time since he came in the bar.

Mr. Dupree just raised his bottle to him and said, "Hi Deacon."

Deke smiled and clinked his bottle with the upraised one. "Hey Mr. Dupree, I didn't see you there. Gosh, I haven't seen you in a while."

"Yeah, it has been a while, hasn't it? Jill said she ran into you this summer."

Eric looked at Deke suddenly. He knew Deke was aware of this look, because he watched him focus even more intently on Mr. Dupree.

"Yeah, I did," Deke answered. He sauntered around this thought for a nanosecond, then thought better of it and turned quickly to Eric. "Are there any more hotdogs left?"

"They'd be in the steamer if there are," he answered.

"Right," said Deke, lingering at the bar. He looked at Mr. Dupree, then made a face and nodded his head like old men do when they've run out of things to say. A sort of nonverbal acknowledgment that their end of the conversation has dried up. "Well I'm gonna go see," he said. "About the hotdogs."

Mr. Dupree watched him walk off, disappearing into the throng gathered around the hotdog steamer, then turned to Eric. "So you don't even talk about her?"

Eric was a little ashamed, but didn't know what else to say. "No."

"Do you think that's the best way to deal with it?"

"Look, I'm emotionally stilted. Always have been. Ask my mother."

Mr. Dupree looked at him, clearly with no intention of saying anything.

"It's not easy, Mr. Dupree," he said. "In fact, it's worse than not easy. It's really, really hard. If you don't believe me, try it out sometime. Some day when there's nothing on TV or you're on a long drive, think about being me for about fifteen minutes. See how many different ways you can make yourself feel bad about something, like a thought. Even if it's just a little one that jumps in your head for a second and you never really meant to think it at all."

The two of them stopped talking for a minute or two. The Packers came out of a time-out and lined up, three yards from the goal line. When the ball was snapped, there was a massive pileup of bodies, including the running back who was brought down for no gain. This was apparently a crucial play, because the people in the bar were cheering and cursing and calling the coach a dumb sonofabitch.

"Well," said Mr. Dupree. He searched Eric's face for something before realizing he had no idea what he was even looking for. "I don't know," he finally said.

"Yeah, there's a lot of that going around," Eric answered.

"I'll tell you this much," he returned, suddenly alive with something certain to share. "This much I know for sure. You're a good kid. And I think it's just bad luck that probably the only person you ever hurt in your life was my little girl."

Eric wanted to cuddle up with this sentiment, but it was all too squooshy and real for him to handle. "One time I convinced Deke to set fire to his hands after dipping them in rubbing alcohol."

"What?"

"That hurt him," he offered. "Pretty bad too. Lotsa crazy blisters and stuff. If his dad hadn't been laid off at the time, he probably would have gone to the hospital."

Mr. Dupree sort of laughed and took in a mouthful of beer. "Alright Eric, I don't want to make you talk about anything if you don't want to."

"I'll tell you what, if I ever feel like sorting through any of it, you'll be the one I come to."

"Fair enough." He stood up and put on his coat. "Jill's gonna be in for Thanksgiving. You should come up for a visit."

"Maybe I will."

"Really?"

"Probably not."

He smiled a sad smile. "Well then, you should come up for a visit some other time, when she's not around. I only get to see you when you're working."

"Well that's cause I work a lot. If not here, then down at the funeral home."

"Maybe I should come visit you there sometime, just for a change of pace."

"Come down tomorrow. You can watch me paint a fence."

"Maybe I will," he said, opening the front door.

"Really?"

"Probably not."

A wisp of cold air shot in as Mr. Dupree left. Autumn and nighttime did their best impersonation of the coming winter, making Eric feel warm in comparison, glad to be inside with the drunks and the drifters.

Deke lolled up to the bar eating a hotdog, his third. "Where's Mr. Dupree?" he asked.

"He just went home."

"Home? Hell, the game's about to go into overtime!"

Eric took a sip of water and shrugged at Deke, who rolled his eyes and shrugged right back. The two of them watched the Packers squeak one out in overtime, a fifty-two-yard field goal that bounced off the uprights before going through. That was all it took. One crazy bounce of a misshapen ball and the game was over. There was some exchanging of money that Eric wasn't supposed to see, another round of drinks for the hangers-on, then suddenly Eric was all alone.

It was late, not quite closing time, but close enough for Eric to start cleaning up. Bundling up the trash, throwing out the uneaten hotdogs, filling up the cooler. It was all mundane and routine, but he had something else to keep him occupied. Something new going on inside his head, which was like a brand-new toy. It was just a tiny little thing, but it was something he could chew on, turn over, examine from every side, and test in different scenarios.

Jill asked about Tess.

He smiled from the inside, gave one last scan of the bar, and shut off the lights.

SIXTEEN

"I can't see very well."

"Do you need to see?" she breathed in his ear.

It was a good question. He wasn't sure if he needed to see or not. There was certainly enough keeping him occupied with the lights off. Maybe total visual stimulation would be too much. They were naked. Both of them. There was so much bare skin in the bed. Everywhere he reached he found warm, soft, fully exposed skin. He couldn't get over how it felt, his bare chest on hers, the warmth of the spot behind her knee, even the way she looked. He could see a little from the summer moon filtering through the curtains. It cast her in a blush of deep blue that made her seem almost make-believe. Her shoulders were bare, not even the strap of a bra, and her face looked different. It was no longer defined by the space that clothes didn't hide. It was all equal. Face drifting into neck flowing into shoulders. All covered by her soft, soft, beautiful, unbelievably soft skin.

She took his ear in her mouth and bit it slightly, pushing her hot breath against his neck. His skin nearly jumped free from his body, forcing a short pant from his lungs. He scratched her thigh, more out of reflex than anything else, causing her to release his earlobe from her teeth and rest her tongue on the back of it so all he could hear was her breathing.

This was the way it had been for the past hour or so. Constant action, reaction. Call and return. It all felt incredible and, despite the fact that he'd never done anything like it before, remarkably natural. He'd always imagined his first time would be sort of nerve-wracking. Maybe some girl in the back of a car, a lot of groping and confusion, looking forward to the end as much as anything. Because doing it wasn't the important thing. Having done it was.

But this was something else entirely. It wasn't sex, that would come later. And if sex was better than this, he was going to be awfully impressed. This thing with Jill had happened so slowly, he never had time to feel uneasy. Kissing turned into touching. Someone's shirt came off, he couldn't even remember whose first. Everything seemed like the only logical next step. The whole night had been like this, from before the beginning. He knew her parents were away for the night. The two of them hadn't talked about anything, but they both seemed to know. Eric went so far as to replace the condom in his wallet. If something was going to happen, he thought it would be best to use a condom that hadn't been subjected to the heat and pressure of being crammed against his ass day in and day out for the past year and a half.

The condom was far from his mind at that particular moment, though. He was simply enjoying the feeling of her mouth. As her bottom lip slipped between his, he took it in his teeth and ran his tongue across it. When he let go, he leaned back to look in her eyes. The darkness made her pupils seem gigantic, wide open portals inviting him to come in. Come closer. She bit her bottom lip herself, as if to double-check the feeling, before her mouth broke into an enormous smile. She was all smile and pupils, bathed in a nearly nonexistent light.

"Hey," she whispered.

"Hey," he breathed back.

———•———

The year hadn't seemed very promising from the start. There was nothing very exciting about being a sophomore. He was still going to be playing JV football that year. He might get in on a few plays in the varsity games, but probably only on special teams or during blowouts. He certainly wouldn't get to carry the ball. Coach Gleason thought Eric was too soft, too afraid to get hit. He found him to be a little too easygoing, and went so far as to tell him he needed to "develop an appreciation for violence." Nothing had happened over the summer to make Eric feel like he'd done that. He had gotten some thrills from the more vicious parts of *The Picture of Dorian Gray*, which he'd read during a rainy spell in July. But he had a pretty good sense that reading a book on a rainy day, written by a man who'd been incarcerated on account of his sexual preference, wasn't exactly what Coach Gleason was looking for.

There was driving. He'd turned sixteen in December, which had been something to look forward to. But the truth was, he'd sort of been driving for the past year or so. His friend Lisa would let him drive her car on the back streets every now and then, especially when she'd been drinking. So the thrill of driving was actually just the thrill of driving legally.

As far as Eric could figure, the best thing about being a sophomore would probably be *not* being a freshman. Which seemed like a sad way to define it. It reminded Eric of people who, when they saw a cripple or an amputee, immediately started going on about how lucky they felt simply to have their health. Eric just wasn't comfortable measuring his condition by direct comparison to those less fortunate than him. Like freshmen.

It was four weeks into the lackluster year when the new girl walked into Biology. Eric felt a little bad for the girl, not because she looked kind of white-trashy, but because her parents obviously didn't plan their move enough in advance to be sure she'd start the school year on time. Now she was coming in already behind in every class. He would have felt even worse for her if she seemed to care at all herself. When the teacher called on her, she simply said, "I don't know." She wasn't apologetic about it. Nothing in her voice said, "I wish I did know, and by God I'm going to work hard until I do." They were just three words stating a simple fact. I. Don't. Know.

Bio Lab was one of the few things Eric had been looking forward to that year. Bio Lab meant dissecting things and learning the intimate details of their working parts. Previous classes had gotten to choose their own lab partners, but this year Mr. Douglas had decided to do things differently. He was going to assign lab partners himself, and it became obvious after about the third pairing what he was doing. The smart kids, the ones who actually cared, were getting matched up with the, to put it generously, less enthusiastic kids. Eric was pissed. It wasn't his job to teach biology to some derelict who had no interest in learning. It was Mr. Douglas's job.

"Eric, why don't you work with Jill here," Mr. Douglas said.

Eric didn't know anyone named Jill. There were only thirty people in the class, and not one Jill. Then he realized. It was the new girl. Eric gave her a wave and starting walking toward the counters in the back of the room. It could be worse, he thought to himself. He could have been stuck with someone completely unmanageable. Someone like Tyrone Bungard, who'd probably just butcher the entire frog because he thought it was funny. At least the new girl, little miss "I don't know," seemed fairly apathetic. Maybe she'd just stay out of his way and let him take care of things.

He watched her come toward him from his seat in the lab and noticed she wasn't quite as average as he'd initially thought. She was oblivious to the classroom of eyes watching her, and the way she moved tipped Eric off to something. Her "I don't know" was just a polite way of saying, "I don't care." Nearly everyone, including Eric, wore shorts during the first few weeks of school. But this girl was wearing jeans that were faded, acid-washed maybe, and ripped at the knees. When she sat down on the stool next to Eric, the skin of her knee touched his bare leg. She looked him in the eye with something less than a smile, and said, "Hi, I'm Jill."

Her eyes were sort of green, with a little bit of hazel going on as well. Eric didn't know why he noticed this. He couldn't tell you the color of anyone's eyes. Ex-girlfriends, family, buddies, even his own mother. But now he knew this girl Jill had greenish eyes—and a very smooth, warm knee.

"Hey, I'm Eric," he told her.

"Hi Eric. Well, I'm not very good at this stuff, so I hope I don't screw it up for you," she said.

And there was something else different about this girl. She smelled odd. It wasn't like the other girls in his class. They always smelled a certain way. Actually most of them smelled the same, like they all wore some perfume called "Teenage Girl." This girl smelled different, like—

"What are you wearing?"

"What?" she asked.

"Like perfume or . . . what is that?"

She looked at him like he was brain damaged. "Soap?"

Soap! That was it. She wasn't wearing perfume at all.

"Oh yeah," he said as casually as he could. "Well, you smell great."

"What?"

He couldn't tell if she was amused or offended or what. She was probably just baffled. If she was, she'd just be catching up with him. He didn't know how to get out of this one. Telling someone who smelled like soap that they smelled great was just weird. But it was true. So he just decided to stick with the truth.

"Yeah, a lot of girls around here wear a lot of perfume, see. So I've never really smelled a girl who smelled like you."

That didn't sound right either. It was a good try, but the spiraling eddy of weirdness was picking up speed.

"I was under the impression they were teaming up smart kids with average kids on this project," she said. "If I'm supposed to be the smart kid, we're in a lot of trouble."

"No, no, I'm the smart kid," Eric said, before realizing how cocky and demeaning it sounded. "I mean—"

"Believe me, I'm fine with that," she said.

Eric was trying to piece together something to say that would seem normal, gain him some ground in this horribly lopsided, five-minute-old relationship. He just about had something. Some comment about being the new kid in town that he was still fine-tuning when Mr. Douglas put a dissecting tray in front of them. The tray was made of banged-up aluminum and filled with a solid, black, tar-like substance. On top of the black stuff was a frog, splayed out on its back and pinned down by its arms and legs. The soapy-fresh smell of his lab partner was immediately replaced by the strong scent of formaldehyde. It made Eric's eyes water, and he thought it was ironic that the stuff they used to preserve dead things smelled worse than the dead things themselves. He looked over at Jill, who was looking at the frog and shaking her head.

"I'm not touching that thing," she said.

As she gripped him in her hand he felt a rush go through his body. *He* was the only person who'd ever touched him there. This was entirely different. A short wave rolled through his hips and he was afraid the whole thing was going to be over before it started. He quickly pulled away, trading the warmth of her hand for the cool night air.

"What's the matter?" she asked.

He leaned in and kissed her. "Nothing."

"Didn't that feel good?"

"A little too good," he said. His arms were getting tired from propping himself up, and they began to shake. He rolled over onto his side, letting his right hand move to her hip. "This is all new to me, remember?"

She smiled. "I know."

He wanted to be spectacular. He didn't care that it was his first time, he wanted to be a natural. Even though she'd only been with one other guy before, he wanted her to tell him that he was the best she'd ever had. Better yet, he didn't want her to say anything. He wanted her to be speechless, so overwhelmed by orgasmic rapture that she couldn't even find the strength to form a sentence. Maybe even stay that way for so long that he'd momentarily be afraid he might have to call an ambulance. But just before he did, she'd come back from her pleasure coma, look at him with glassy, blissful eyes, and whisper, "That was amazing."

He had a suspicion it wasn't going to work out that way, though. Already he was having problems, and he only had himself to blame. An older cousin of his, whom he only knew from a few disastrous fishing trips with his grandpa, had given him a crash course on sex-ed at a very young age. The guy was stunned when he realized Eric had no idea how babies were made. It really didn't occur to him that it might be because Eric was still a kid. He told him all about it with the kind of enthusiasm and graphic detail that can only be conjured by a long afternoon of whiskey drinking. Included in this bleary-eyed lesson was an explanation of a habit known as "whackin' off." Eric didn't understand the name at all, since there didn't seem to be any actual whacking involved. But that's the way the whole lesson had gone from the beginning. It was supposed to be an explanation of the birds and the bees, but that'd been the last Eric had heard of any animals, except for one mention of a beaver that he couldn't quite figure out.

Whether he fully understood it or not, Eric was anxious to experience this whackin' off. He tried it a few weeks later in the bathtub, and it was everything his drunken cousin had described. Over the years, Eric came to rely on this sleight of hand to ease the pressure of puberty. But it was never about prolonged pleasure. It was all about the release. Now, when such a release would bring to an end all of the fun to be had, he wished he'd used those times more as training than as recreation.

They had fallen into another bout of furious kissing. It reached the point where Eric felt his body was simply inadequate. Not just his body, but hers too. The way they tore into one another felt like they were looking for something more. Like they could maybe rip through their flesh and somehow dissolve into something else entirely. She leaned into him, reaching behind his head to pull him closer. Kissing him with a carnal force, she took his hand and moved it from her hip to between her legs. His fingers fumbled around before finding the exact sensation he'd been hoping for. This warmth. This wetness. He wanted it to surround the best parts of both of them in seclusion.

Eric never figured he'd date a girl like Jill Dupree. She didn't seem to have much interest in what she was doing at that moment, let alone what she was going to do after high school. But she was fun to hang out with. It was as though she liked Eric for reasons other than whether he played sports, or what he wore. Reasons that were so far outside the high school paradigm, Eric had never even considered them before. She thought it was cute the way he'd get genuinely interested in what was being taught in school. She even seemed to be amused, maybe even a little interested herself, when he would read more about a subject outside of class and tell her all about it. For the first time, Eric felt like he could be himself. Not the pretend-self he was around the football team, or the half-self he was in his Advanced Placement classes. Just himself.

But no one was more excited by their burgeoning relationship than Mr. Dupree. He was thrilled when his daughter went from indignant toward school to merely indifferent. But nothing could have prepared him for the changes that came once she went all starry-eyed for her study-buddy. When Eric and Jill lost track of time while preparing for a lab practicum, Jill asked her dad if Eric could stay for dinner. That was the meal that forever established Eric Mercer as a savior in the heart of George Dupree.

"Daddy, what would we do if I wanted to go to college?"

Mr. Dupree was stunned. No one in their family had ever gone to college. He was the first to ever finish high school, and sometimes he wondered if his girls would even make it that far. Beth, his oldest, just squeaked by last year before settling down with a spot welder over in Dunbar. Now here was Jill, who could deliver him joy in the form of a B in any subject, asking about college.

"What do you mean, what would we do?" he asked.

"Well, Eric says his dad has some money put away for him. So when he graduates, he's gonna go to college."

Eric looked up, a little embarrassed. "It's not that much, Jill. Not enough to pay for four years of college."

Jill practically ignored him. "He's been saving up since he was a baby."

"Well honey, if you wanted to go to college, we'd find a way to pay for it," Mr. Dupree answered. "But you have to get into college first, y'know."

"What's that supposed to mean?" she asked.

"I think he means your grades," Eric said, stuffing some food in his mouth.

"Yeah, but we're gonna work on that, right?" Jill said.

Eric looked up at Mr. Dupree. "That's the plan anyway, sir. I don't know why she's been getting all these Cs and Ds. I mean, she's got that attitude thing, but she's really pretty smart. We're gonna tear right through this lab practicum tomorrow. Then what? History, English lit, Pre-calc. Next thing you know, you're up in Cambridge visiting her at Harvard."

"Is that right?" asked Mr. Dupree, uncertain if this conversation was really happening. "You want to go to Harvard, Jill?"

She laughed a little bit. "I don't know, maybe. Where do you want to go, Eric?"

"Harvard's good, I guess. Or maybe Yale. But then I wonder if I might not want to head out West. Y'know, Berkeley, Stanford, something like that."

Mr. Dupree looked at his daughter, who was looking at this boy who was piling food into his mouth while spouting off top-tier colleges like they were vocational schools. "And what do you want to study, Eric?"

Eric looked up from his plate and shrugged his shoulders. "I don't know," he smiled. "I'm only sixteen."

The groping and pulling was falling into a natural rhythm. It made Eric believe if he'd never even heard of sex before, he would have eventually figured it out for himself. That's the way it worked in the beginning. Just two healthy humans, being controlled by hormones sent to propagate their species.

"Maybe um——"

He wasn't sure if she'd said something, or if she'd just stopped talking. He waited for a second for her to finish, but she didn't. "What?" he whispered.

"Maybe . . . Do you have a condom?"

"Yeah."

"Yeah. Maybe you should get that."

"Okay," he whispered. He climbed off her and leaned over the side of the bed, leaving his hips and legs on top of the mattress. His pants were on the floor, within arm's reach. As he pulled them over closer to him, he dug out his wallet. On the inside pocket, the one whose purpose he could never figure out, was the condom. It was brand-new and, although he felt a little bad about turning his back on the trusty condom he'd carried with him for so long, he knew he was smart to err on the side of protection over nostalgia.

He pulled himself back onto the bed and started kissing her again. But the focus had shifted now. This wasn't the indefinable sensual exploration of before. This was foreplay. The condom in his hand meant they were going to have sex. Soon. Suddenly Eric felt the pressure to perform. Because once that package in his hand was opened, the gig was on.

He was lying directly on top of her and noticed for the first time he was sweating. It was the sweat on her chest and stomach that made him notice. The two of them were covered in it, their skin, their hair. He could taste it on her lips when they kissed. She moved her hips into him and he could feel the bone of her pelvis against his.

"Put it on."

Oh Jesus, he thought. Here it goes. This is for real. His stomach did some sort of turn and he felt all rushed out, like he was about to kick the game-winning field goal in the Super Bowl. He leaned back from her and ripped open the condom package. He was glad that once, when he was alone in his bedroom, he'd tried one on just to see what it was like. Right there in the dark, with Jill naked and sweaty underneath him, would have been too high-pressure a situation to be the first time he ever saw or touched a condom in his life. He dropped the wrapper off the side of the bed and started putting on the condom. Looking at Jill, he was practically beside himself. This was going to be his first time. Not with some skank in the back of a Nova out by the power lines, but right here, in the bed of an exceptionally hot, incredibly cool girl. He was the roll of a condom away from making love.

He'd never been in love before. He'd been infatuated more times than he was proud to admit. When they read Romeo and Juliet in freshman English, "unrequited" became his favorite word. The fact that there was no other word for it in his Merriam-Webster's Collegiate Thesaurus only reinforced its distinct and unequaled meaning in his mind. He became convinced he'd been the victim of unrequited love on more than one occasion, and was more than a little embarrassed when Huey, of all people, pointed out that it didn't seem likely that he could be star-crossed with that many lovers in a row.

"I mean, look at Romeo and Juliet," Huey reasoned. "There's no way they'd have killed themselves if they figured someone else might come along. That'd just be stupid. Cause then they'd never meet that someone else, y'know?" He shook his head, waiting for a response, then figured he might not have been clear enough. "Cause they'd be dead. Y'know?"

Eric was annoyed that Huey was teaching him a lesson. "I thought you didn't even read it, Huey."

"I watched the movie," he explained with a knowing wink. "They get naked in it too."

As difficult as it was for Eric to admit, Huey had a point. All of Eric's ideas about love and dating were based on things he'd read in books or seen in the movies. When he decided he liked a girl, typically from afar, he would cook up elaborate fantasies of how he might get into her life. Maybe they'd be in a public setting when some guy, maybe her unappreciative boyfriend, would start pushing her around. Then Eric could spring to the rescue and kick the ever-living shit out of the guy, achieving instant hero/savior/lover status. That way, they could cut straight to the falling in love part, without ever having to bother with getting to know one another on account of their own merits.

With this as his doctrine on courtship and affection, it was no wonder he didn't realize he was falling in love with Jill. She never had the opportunity to become someone he wanted from afar, because she was around all the time. Eric wasn't even sure if they were dating for the longest time. They spent a lot of time together. That was something that boyfriends and girlfriends did. But he also spent a lot of time around Deke and Huey, and he was one-hundred-percent certain he wasn't dating either of those two. He'd had girlfriends in the past, but they were nothing like his thing with Jill. Time with his girlfriends had been a little bit of making out, with a lot of shallow conversation and awkward moments in between. With Jill there was nothing forced or awkward. There was also no making out whatsoever. So, by his experience, there was no way she was his girlfriend. There was only one thing clouding the waters. He thought she was hot.

Jill was one of those girls who'd been dealt a woman's body right off the bat. Girls like that were few and far between. But even more rare was a girl who wasn't completely self-conscious about it. She was sixteen trapped inside of twenty, and making the best of it. She told Eric she appreciated that he didn't look at her the way most guys did.

"I'm not just a set of tits attached to an ass, y'know?"

Eric just shook his head, dumbfounded that she'd just said "tits" in front of him.

"See, the first time we met, you looked me straight in the eyes," she said. "It'd been so long since that had happened I almost forgot I had eyes. You know what I mean?"

"Did you just say 'tits'?"

"Yeah."

"Jesus."

"What?"

"I don't know, I guess I've just never heard a girl say 'tits' before."

"How does that make you feel?"

"Kinda funny."

"Funny how?"

"I don't know, I'm just—I guess I'm just thinking funny things."

"Things about my tits?"

"Jesus Christ, Jill!" He felt the blood rush to his face, and other places. "What are you doing?" he laughed. She laughed too, leaned back on the hillside and closed her eyes to the sun. Glad to have avoided an awkward moment, Eric laid down beside her and closed his eyes. His mind swirled with thoughts before eventually giving way to the heat of the sun.

He didn't know how long he'd been asleep, but when he woke up, he was lying on his side, face-to-face with Jill. She was still asleep, and he watched the grass move when she breathed. He felt a little strange, watching her sleep like that, but he couldn't seem to look away. Slowly, with each breath she took, he began to recognize something. Ambiguous at first, it gained form and presence until he gradually realized he was looking at his girlfriend. He knew that wasn't how it usually worked, that there was normally some spoken or physical confirmation of something like that. But in this case he knew it was different. Just like everything else with Jill had been.

She opened her eyes and looked at him, not at all startled to be inches away from his face. "What are you doing?" she asked.

"Nothing."

The grass waved between them with her semi-verbal answer, "Hmm."

It seemed like a mile or more, but he leaned across the inches between them and, blocking out the light of the sun and all the scrutiny of his overactive mind, kissed her for the first time.

She was propped up on her elbows, trying to get a better look at what Eric's hands were up to. "What's going on?" she asked.

He mouthed some half-answer, starting to say "nothing" but just ending up with, "Nuh——." He didn't want to tell her what was going on. Because what was going on was that he was somehow screwing this up. He'd started putting the condom on, rolling it down after pinching the air out of the receptacle tip, just like they show on the box. But it had stopped rolling after about an inch. Maybe less. She was lying there, ready, and he was dealing with a stubborn condom. He'd only realized, just before she asked what was going on, that he'd put it on backwards. Now he was trying to force it on by unrolling it from the inside, which wasn't very easy, and sort of hurt.

"Seriously, what's going on?" she asked again. This time she sat up onto her hands, bringing her knees up into his armpits. Eric was sweating more than ever now. But it wasn't the lustful sweat of before. This was the hot, stinging sweat of embarrassment, wrapped in tension, covered in overwhelming discomfort. At this point, it took all he had not to simply pull the damn thing off and run screaming from the house, never to speak to Jill again.

"It won't umm——" He really didn't know how to say that he was too stupid to work a rubber. "I'm having some problems here."

"What kind of problems?" she asked playfully, putting her hands around his waist to pull herself closer.

"Well . . . I think I put it on wrong," he said.

"Wrong?"

"Yeah."

She looked down to see what he was talking about. "I think you're right."

"Fuck," he said with a weary sigh.

"It's okay," she said, kissing him on the neck and breathing into his ear. "We'll just fix it."

She brought her hands around from his hips and started taking the condom off of him. It took some doing, but the touch of her warm hands turned it from drudgery into delight. When she got it off, she leaned down to take a closer look, close enough for Eric to feel her breath on him. His frustration was already drifting away, being replaced by a lust that started inside his sternum and ran straight down his stomach to his groin. He had to close his eyes for a moment to the sight of her naked back bent over him. This splendor of smooth skin guided his eye from her shoulder blades to the spot where the swells of her spine disappeared behind her hips. The sight of all this sensual, symmetrical beauty was too much to handle. He felt her start to put the condom back on, giving him a slight squeeze as she rolled it down. The stroke of her hand brought a flash of sensation. A shimmer ran up his back as a familiar twitch turned into a rolling inside his hips. He opened his eyes and felt immediate panic. He couldn't believe this was happening.

"Uh oh," he heard her say as the rolling turned into a pumping that left him spent and covered again in an unwelcome sweat. This time one of shame.

"No," he said.

"It's okay," she said, her hands still on him. She looked up at him and smiled. It wasn't a laughing-at-him type of smile or a feeling-sorry-for-him type of smile, it was just a smile. As if she was still having a good time.

He wasn't smiling at all. He had no idea what he looked like, but he knew it must have been ridiculous, because he was doing something he hadn't done in a long time. He was honestly trying not to cry.

"It's okay," she said again, leaning in to kiss him. He looked at her with disappointed eyes that were so sorry, she actually started laughing.

"This is funny?" he said desperately.

"I'm sorry," she said, kissing him again and wiping the sweat from his forehead. "You just look so sad."

"I am sad."

"Why?"

"Because I just came," he said with frustration.

"Didn't it feel good?" she asked. "I thought that felt good for guys."

"Yeah it felt good, but it wasn't——" He looked up at the ceiling and let out a giant sigh. "It wasn't supposed to happen like this."

She scooted herself closer to him and put her nose to his chin. "How was it supposed to happen?"

"I don't know," he answered, still looking skyward. "There should have been . . . some actual sex would have been nice."

"This is nice."

"What?"

"Being naked with you."

He looked down at her and saw something in her eyes. She wasn't disappointed at all. She looked happy. Suddenly he was overwhelmed again by the sheer amount of exposed skin in the bed. She was beautiful. And she was right.

"Yeah," he answered, "this is pretty nice."

"And we can always try it again later."

A dark cloud moved over him. "But that was the only condom I had with me. And your parents will be back tomorrow afternoon. Then you're leaving to go camping with your dad the next day."

"Then what?" she asked.

"What do you mean 'then what'?"

"Then I'm coming home. Then you'll be here. Then we'll have the rest of the summer to try again." She leaned in and took his earlobe in her teeth. "And again," she whispered. "And again."

He felt a rise run through him and desperately wished he had another condom with him. But he didn't. All he had was the most amazing girlfriend in the world, and an overwhelming urge to pee.

"Lie down here with me," she said. "I want to fall asleep with you."

If that was what she wanted, he could oblige. The trip to the bathroom could wait. He laid his head on the pillow beside her and looked at her. Her eyes were already closed, and the pillowcase moved a little with each breath she took. He felt her knee move up between his legs until their bodies were as close as they could be, her face against his neck, his shoulder as her pillow. He could smell her skin with every breath he took. Soap, with a little sweat. His eyes closed slowly under their own weight as he whispered into her hair.

"I think I love you."

He could feel the breath of her semi-verbal answer on his neck. "Hmm."

TUESDAY

The morning wind blew across his back and made him smile. He'd only been painting for about an hour, but his ass was already tired from sitting on the milk crate. He stopped for a minute, long enough to stretch his back and glance down the length of the fence. He was almost done. Another hour's work at best. It looked way better, no matter what that little Donnie kid said. Plus it had been kind of therapeutic. He'd read a book once on Eastern religion that mentioned something about "the Zen of digging a ditch." After spending yesterday afternoon and the bulk of this morning mindlessly painting this fence, he felt he had a better idea of what that might be all about. Save the occasional tightening in his back and the discomfort of painting the very bottom of the fence posts, he'd found the repetition of painting very relaxing. For the most part, his mind wasn't thinking of anything. It was just up-down, up-down, paint on fence. Maybe the chirp of a bird or the rustling of leaves. Then again, up-down, up-down, paint on fence.

For a while, during the trickier parts around the gate where it was more difficult to lose himself in repetition, Eric's mind did drift off toward something else. Off toward Mr. Dupree and their conversation at the Legion. Actually, it only used Mr.

Dupree as a springboard to get to something far more interesting. Somewhere out there, someone was asking about Tess. Not just someone—Jill Dupree. He hadn't allowed himself to think about Jill in a long time. Which is not to say he hadn't thought of her at all. Just not on purpose. But on this particular day, he opened the gates and let her in.

He limited the memories. No "what if" games and no "remember when" scenes. Just little things. The smallness of her hands. The sound of her voice on the phone when she was tired. The way her hair smelled right after a shower. These things were nice to think about on their own, but soon enough his mind started lurching for more. Nothing good was going to come of that, he knew it for a fact. So he went right back to shutting it all off. No more Jill, no more Mr. Dupree. Just up-down, up-down, paint on fence.

His peace of mind was violated when an ambulance from the Pinely Volunteer EMT squad went tearing up Route 2 with its sirens wailing. He watched it blast down the highway and make a right onto Jackson Street. To the layman, an ambulance meant trouble. But to Eric and Mr. Tremble, an ambulance might mean business. It wasn't a morbid interest, just a professional interpretation. The way a baseball player sees spring showers as bad weather, but a farmer sees them as good growing. Eric hoped it wasn't business for them because he really wanted to finish the fence. A new client meant he'd be busy for the next few days, but it would drive him crazy to have people coming to the funeral home for services with the fence half-painted. The thought of this brought him out of his Zen-like cadence and instead had him painting against some clock that hadn't even been set. He tried to convince himself that it was all in his head, that the ambulance was probably just for someone who'd fallen off their roof while cleaning leaves out of the gutters. But he couldn't seem to shake the tick-tock, tick-tock of the clock in his head. When the bell finally sounded, he knew he'd been right.

It was the phone inside the funeral home. It could have been Mrs. Tremble calling to check in on her husband, or someone from the Rotary Club looking for a donation. But Eric knew that when the siren of the ambulance is still ringing in your ears, the ring of their phone usually meant one thing. He heard the door to the funeral home open and looked up to see Mr. Tremble standing in the doorway, holding his hat and coat.

"Eric."

Eric nodded his head and stood to go. He looked at the remainder of the fence and figured he might have time to finish it while Mr. Tremble was preparing the body. Picking up the crate and the paint, he went inside to get cleaned up. When he got to the hearse, Mr. Tremble was already in the driver's seat, warming it up. Eric hopped into the passenger seat and stared out the windshield as the car backed out of the driveway, turned toward Route 2, and slowly pulled away from the home.

"It's kinda knocking a little bit there. You hear it?"

Mr. Tremble kept his eyes on the road, but tilted his head a little to listen harder. "What do you suppose it is?"

"What's the mileage?"

"Just over eighty thousand."

"Yeah, it's probably just the valves. I'm gonna change the oil next week when I get it ready for winter. Maybe that'll do it."

"Right," Mr. Tremble answered.

This was the way they talked when it came time to work. Eric didn't even know where they were going, and that was fine with him. He just wanted to get the whole thing taken care of without investing too much of himself in the process. If he thought about the dead, their families and the overwhelming sense of loss that filled the place where he worked, he would have been crippled by it all. So he was more than happy to fill his thoughts with meaningless tasks like winterizing the car.

As they turned up Jackson Street, they saw the ambulance coming back down the road. With its lights and siren off, it looked defeated. The driver waved to Eric and Mr. Tremble as he made his way down to the highway and back to the city building. Mr. Tremble guided the hearse halfway up the street, then made a left onto the gravel road that was Eden Drive. Eric hadn't been up this way in quite some time. The Duprees lived in here, and Eric thought it was funny that he might run into Mr. Dupree two days in a row. He figured if he saw him he might tell him that he was just making good on his promise to come visit. It wasn't until Mr. Tremble pulled the car right up to the house where Mrs. Dupree was standing in the doorway crying that Eric realized what was happening.

Something welled up inside him unexpectedly that forced him to clear his throat a couple of times. Mr. Tremble shut off the car and turned to Eric. "Are you going to be okay?" he asked.

Eric took a deep breath and looked at him with wide open eyes. For some reason they had become a little watery, but Eric didn't want Mr. Tremble to think he was crying. "Yeah, I'm fine," he answered. "You?"

Mr. Tremble looked at him with his compassionate, emotionless face. He held his gaze for a second, then, apparently seeing something he approved of, nodded toward the house. "Alright then. Let's not keep her waiting."

Eric stepped out of the car and walked behind Mr. Tremble. They went to the rear of the car, pulled out the rolling cot, and carried it up the steps and into the house. Eric greeted Mrs. Dupree with a hug and listened to her muffled crying bury itself in his shoulder.

"He was just raking the leaves, Eric," she said. "Just a little raking in the morning before we headed over the hill to visit with Beth." Mrs. Dupree pulled away from him and started regaining her composure. "I brought him out some coffee and we sat down on the porch for a rest. He told me that the two of you had talked last night. He was—" She stopped for a second to hold back more tears. "Well, he seemed so happy. I went back inside and he stayed there on the porch for a little while longer, sitting in the sun. I heard him stand up after a bit. I was right there in the kitchen. And he said, 'Dorothy, I'm cold.' Then I heard him fall. He was—" Her eyes swelled with tears and she hid her face in her hands. "He was gone before I got there."

Mr. Tremble stepped forward, placing his hand on her shoulder. "Where is he now, Dorothy?" he asked.

She pointed down the hall, holding her other hand over her mouth. "They put him in the den."

Mr. Tremble looked at Eric, who led the way. It had been over six years since he'd been inside this house, but he still remembered every nook. As they walked down the hallway, Eric wanted to stop and look at things. There were pictures on the wall, some of which must have been pictures of Jill. He wanted to see what she looked like these days. He wanted to duck into her room and lie on her bed again. Maybe see if he could find an old feeling or two she'd left behind. But he didn't stop. He rolled his end of the cot right past her room, past the pictures, and into the den. Mr. Dupree's body was on the couch, covered with an old afghan. Mr. Tremble walked over, removed the afghan, and motioned for Eric to go to the other side. He took Mr. Dupree by the feet and lifted him onto the rolling cot. Mr. Tremble covered him with a clean sheet, and they began to wheel him down the hallway. They never spoke when they were in the house of the recently deceased. The task was always the same, so there didn't seem to be anything to say to one another. And they never wanted to seem to be having casual conversation over the still-cooling body of a person's loved one.

As they passed by the photos again, Eric stole a glance at one of them. He was met by his own, younger face looking back at him. It was a picture of him and Jill that her dad had taken right before the senior prom. Just as the picture was taken, Eric had swooped Jill forward in his arms, causing her to break into a wide-eyed, open-mouthed smile. Mr. Dupree had said it was his favorite picture of the two of them.

"Oh God," Mrs. Dupree gasped as they wheeled her husband's body toward the door. It was common for people to come to the realization of what had happened at various stages of the process, so Mr. Tremble was always careful to make sure they were comfortable with what he and Eric were doing.

"Is it okay if we take him now, Dorothy?" he asked. "Do you want us to wait outside for a while, or come back later?" He looked at her with his compassionate eyes, the ones that let her know that any answer was okay.

She started to walk toward the body, then stopped and crumpled under the weight of her own sorrow. "No," she answered, "go ahead. Take him. He's already gone, right?"

"That's right," said Mr. Tremble. "He is."

They brought up the collapsible legs of the cot when they reached the porch, and carried it down the steps and over to the car. When they'd secured the body inside the back of the hearse, Mr. Tremble walked back up onto the porch and put his arm around Mrs. Dupree.

"You come down whenever you're ready, okay Dorothy? Eric and I will start taking care of things, then you can come and we'll figure out all the details."

She was listening to Mr. Tremble, but looking right at Eric. It was making him extremely uncomfortable, but the last thing he wanted to do was look away. If she needed to stare into his face to somehow feel more in control during all this, the least he could do was not look away. All the same, he was relieved when he heard a car pulling up behind him. It would have seemed more odd to keep looking at Mrs. Dupree than to look behind him, so he tore away from her stare and watched the car come toward the house. Through the windshield he could make out the face of Beth Dupree. Actually, her last name wasn't Dupree anymore. It hadn't been Dupree for as long as Eric had known her. But he could never seem to remember the last name of the guy she'd married, so, to Eric, she was always Beth Dupree. Her face was ashen as she stepped out of the car, but her expression was blank. It was as though she were simply stopping by for an afternoon visit at her parents'.

"Hey Eric," she said, closing the car door with her hip.

"Hi Beth."

She tried to act normal, but she didn't quite seem to know what to do with her hands. She held them at her side, made a motion toward her pockets, then finally crossed her arms up close to her body. "What happened to your eye?" she asked.

"Got in a fight."

"Still doin' that, huh?"

"Seem to be."

She looked up at the big tree looming over top of them. The sunlight was broken up by the leaves, falling on her face in a sparse, uneven pattern. He watched her follow a leaf as it fell from the tree and landed on top of the hearse behind Eric.

"Is my dad in there?" she asked.

Eric didn't like this question. Her dad wasn't in the car. His body was. But Eric knew what she'd meant by the question, and knew this wasn't the time to get philosophical.

"Yeah," he answered. She seemed to be staring a little too intently at the tinted window of the hearse. "Do you want to see him?"

She looked at the window, silently, without a single expression on her face. It seemed like forever, but probably wasn't more than a few seconds before she spoke. "No, it's okay," she said. "I'll see him later."

She turned toward the house and passed Mr. Tremble coming down the porch steps. Eric climbed into the car on the passenger side and watched as Beth let her mother fold into her arms before walking her into the house. It was eerily silent for a few seconds. Eric felt strange about being alone in the car with the body of George Dupree, and suddenly remembered what Mr. Dupree, always a man of his word, had said the night before. About maybe coming to visit him at the funeral home.

They moved the body into the embalming room and hoisted it up onto the table. Eric untied Mr. Dupree's shoes as Mr. Tremble started laying out the tools and supplies for embalming. Left to their own devices, dead bodies could look awfully lifeless. But over the next four to five hours, Mr. Tremble would bleed the body by pumping pink embalming fluid through the femoral artery, on one side of his crotch, and letting the blood run out the femoral vein on the other side. Then he would sew the mouth shut, put him into the suit the family chose, and have Blanche come over from the beauty parlor to take care of his hair and maybe a little makeup. Most of the time, Eric would stick around and help. That usually meant assisting in getting the body in and out of its clothes, and any additional lifting and moving. One time Eric had to massage the hands of a particularly arthritic client to help work the embalming fluid through his extremities. But that was the most delicate work that had ever been required of him.

Eric didn't want to have anything to do with the normal routine today. He felt nearly nauseous as he pulled Mr. Dupree's shoes off his feet, and he couldn't imagine stripping him down and watching Mr. Tremble cut him. The room was already filling with the smell of formaldehyde. This never bothered Eric before, but today it made him think of frogs. He could almost see Mr. Dupree pinned to the table by his arms and legs. He put the shoes over in the corner and leaned against the wall.

Mr. Tremble turned around from his workstation and glanced at the body. "Could you go ahead and get the rest of his clothes for me, Eric?"

Eric knew full well he couldn't do that. There was no way he was going to strip George Dupree naked. Among other things, that would mean he'd disrobed half the Dupree family and seen them as God made them.

"I'll tell you what, Mr. Tremble," he said as convincingly as he could. "I really think I should get back to painting that fence. Folks'll be coming by tomorrow and I don't want the place lookin' like an unmade bed, y'know?"

Mr. Tremble looked at Eric, then glanced up at the clock on the wall. "Alright then. But before you do, why don't you go over to Tug's and get us some lunch?"

"Sure," Eric said, relieved. "What do you want?"

"Whatever looks good and doesn't have onions."

"Okay. One 'whatever looks good, hold the onions,' coming right up."

Walking out the front door of the funeral home, Eric felt better, but couldn't escape some feeling. The air was fresher outside, but something about it seemed the same as in that little room. He walked past Mrs. Redmond's house and noticed the weeds where her flowers had been that summer. As his feet kicked through a pile of leaves on the sidewalk, he remembered how

Tess had been worried that the trees were dying. He'd told her everything was fine. That's what daddies do. But today, he remembered something. Everything dies. In fact, everything was dying right then—flowers, trees. Even daddies.

Tug Winthrop had opened the health food store on Post Street a few years back. Tug was, by the definition of the Pinely community, a hippie. It wasn't just the health food store that made them think so, it was a lot of things. First off was his beard. In West Virginia, beards were for big, burly, huntin' and fishin' type of guys. In fact, some men grew beards exclusively for hunting season. But Tug wore a beard all year long. Actually, he didn't just wear it, he grew it all year long. Plus he was skinny, and had never been hunting. On top of all this was the fact that he dressed funny, he opened a store selling food that most people had never heard of, and he called himself "Tug"—which everyone was convinced wasn't his real name, and if it was he must have been named by a couple of hippie parents, and if he was, well it's common knowledge that the acorn doesn't fall far from the tree. Eric had even heard people say they thought he looked kind of stoned, even though the people who said such things had, in all likelihood, never seen a stoned person in their lives.

It didn't take long for Tug's health food store to become more of a regular old deli and supermarket. He quickly learned that people weren't too interested in vegetarian hotdogs and tofu, but they did seem to like that they could get a sandwich made fresh, right there on the spot. So Tug had refined his menu to include an array of fairly standard sandwiches to which he assigned clever names like The Cattle Call, The Makin' Bacon, and The Sweet Cheeses. Of course, no one ever ordered their sandwich by these names. They'd just ask for roast beef on white. But Tug always tried to encourage the use of the sandwich names by repeating their order back to them as, "One Cattle Call, coming up."

When Eric came into the store, Tug was sitting behind the counter, his hands diligently braiding something.

"Whadya makin', Tug?"

Tug smiled and held up a hoop, the center of which was filled with the beginnings of a spider web. "It's a Chippewa dream-catcher," he said.

Eric nodded his head. "That's what I would have guessed."

"Really?"

"Never."

"Ah," Tug said, rising to his feet. He leaned his lanky frame across the counter to share his handiwork with Eric. "See here," he said, "the web is a perfect circle but there's a hole in the center. If you believe in the Great Spirit, the web will catch your good dreams and ideas, and the bad ones will go through the hole."

"Does it work?"

Tug nodded his head and stared at the strange, ornate loop in his hand. "I don't know," he said. "This is my first one. You want me to make you one?"

"I think you're a few years too late with mine."

"I don't know if I could make another one anyway," admitted Tug. "All this detail work makes my fingers hurt. I'm dying."

"We all are."

"What do you mean?"

Eric recognized his own melodrama. "I don't know," he answered. He took a breath and focused on the menu for a moment. "I need some lunch here. Any recommendations?"

"I made a lasagna today."

"Any good?'

"Yeah."

"Anything weird in it?"

"Like what?"

"I don't know, eggplant or anything like that?"

"No, it's just regular old boring lasagna."

"Meat?"

"Yeah."

"Alright, gimmee two of those to go." Tug started walking behind the deli counter when Eric remembered. "It doesn't have onions in it, does it?"

"No. Why? Are onions weird now too?"

"To some."

Tug rolled his eyes as he turned around to prepare the lasagna. "Oh by the way," he said, his back to Eric, "I hear you like the Wildcats on Friday."

The word shot out of Eric faster than reflex. "No!"

"Yeah," Tug corrected, "someone was in here saying you thought the mighty Wildcats were gonna beat Cedarsville."

"Who?"

"I don't remember offhand."

"Was it Deke?"

"No."

"Was it his dad?"

"No. It might have been Edith Parsons."

"Well where'd she hear that?'

Tug was looking up at the ceiling trying to remember. "Yeah, it was definitely Edith because she said she heard it from Jake Wetzel when she was at the hardware store."

"When?"

"Yesterday. You really think they're gonna win?"

"Fuck no, I don't think they're gonna win! They're gonna get crushed!"

"Yeah, that's what I think too. They're just too small." Tug paused for a moment, lingering on the thought. "I've never seen high school kids so tiny." He looked at Eric with an abundance of sincerity. "Which makes me wonder about those chemical plants, you know what I'm saying? Do you have any idea what those sonsabitches are pumping into the air and the water in the name of profit and progress? I mean, it may only be trace elements, but it all adds up."

Tug shook his head as he put the lasagnas in a paper bag. Eric nodded and hoped he was winding down instead of getting started. Tug's rants on the environment, the state of society, the inequity of government subsidies, and the injustice of American foreign policy were known to be as detailed as they were impassioned. Eric wondered if Tug had any idea that his points were routinely lost on his audience. Simply because, nine times out of ten, the people to whom he preached were focused on the simple injustice of him holding their lunch hostage while he spoke.

Eric was lucky this time. Tug stopped talking, stapled the receipt to the top of the bag, and handed the lunches across the counter. "How come you said Pinely's gonna win then?" he asked.

"I didn't, Tug. It's just a stupid rumor."

"Oh, I see," said Tug. "That's an odd thing to start a rumor about."

"This can be an odd town." Eric handed him the money for the food and hurried toward the door before Tug's brain shook loose another grievance with the state. "Good luck with your dream thing there, Tug," he said. "And do me a favor. Tell people you heard it directly from me that I never said Pinely was gonna win."

"Even if they don't ask?"

Eric thought about it for a second, then nodded his head. "Couldn't hurt."

By the time Beth's car pulled up to the funeral home, Eric had already finished his lunch and the fence. He'd hoped they'd come earlier while he was still painting. That way he'd have a good excuse for not being inside during the business end of things. There were just so many details to sort out, caskets, services, headstones. Most people found it to be terribly capitalistic. Including Eric. So he normally avoided having anything to do with it.

At the same time, he wanted to be there for Mrs. Dupree. He knew Mr. Dupree handled the money for the family. He was a nuts-and-bolts man, while she was all heart-and-soul. Now she was about to walk into a nuts-and-bolts situation during the most heart-and-soul moment of her life. Eric knew he could help her. But a part of him wished he had something else to do instead. Unfortunately, he'd painted the last post of the fence just before they drove up, so he had no choice but to go inside and be of whatever help he could.

He threw the paint can and brush into the milk crate and carried it under his arm as he met the Duprees on the front porch. Mrs. Dupree took his hand, almost out of instinct, and kept walking toward the door. Eric gave her hand a squeeze and leaned down to whisper in her ear.

"You alright?"

She looked up at him with glassy eyes, worn out from crying, and shook her head no. He gave her a gentle smile. "Yeah," he concurred, "me neither."

The inside of the funeral home seemed overly warm compared to the brisk autumn air outside. Eric made a mental note to check the furnace before he left for the evening. A lot of people were going to be around for the next few days, so it was only going to get hotter. Mourners were a lot like the flowers that filled the showing room; they were out of their element and just looking for a reason to wilt. Eric walked Mrs. Dupree and Beth back to the sitting room where Mr. Tremble normally conducted this type of business and had them take a seat. He went around the corner and knocked gently on the door to the embalming room.

"Mr. Tremble?" he called out as he opened the door.

"Yes?"

He poked his head around, but tried not to look at Mr. Dupree's body. "The Duprees are here."

"Oh goodness," Mr. Tremble said. "What time is it?"

"About three-thirty."

"Wow," he said, in apparent disbelief. "Okay, I'll be right out. Do you want to go ahead and get them started looking at the caskets?"

Eric thought about it for a minute and couldn't come up with a delicate way to express his feelings. "No," he finally said, matter-of-factly.

"No?" Mr. Tremble said, although he didn't sound too surprised. "Okay then. I'll be right out."

Eric closed the door behind him and walked back to the sitting room. The two ladies were sitting there, silently staring out the window. Eric had seen blank expressions like theirs on the faces of hundreds of families. It was as though the drove of emotions that overcame people during these times couldn't agree on a look to represent them all, so they simply settled on blank. Like the empty canvas of an artist overwhelmed with options. Eric walked over and sat on a chair next to them. Mrs. Dupree seemed to notice he was there, but kept staring out the window. It seemed like forever before she finally opened her mouth to speak.

"Last night he had one of those . . ." She moved her gaze from the window pane to Eric's face. "He was an odd sleeper, always talking or getting up and moving around the room. One time, when we were younger, he snuck into my room, the way you used to with Jill." Eric tried to hide his surprise, but the smile on Mrs. Dupree's face gave him away. "We thought it might be a little hypocritical of us to point fingers. And we figured you probably weren't getting into any real trouble with us just in the other room. Were you?"

"No, ma'am," he answered quickly, suddenly feeling seventeen again.

"Well, neither did we back then. We just liked being close to one another, you know. To lie there and just pretend we were older, with our own place and our own—" She paused, looking for the idea that was evading her. "Oh I don't know. It was just nice. But one night, we accidentally fell asleep. Which wouldn't have been a problem if it wasn't for George's sleep behavior. Apparently he had some kind of dream that he was being chased, because before I knew it, he was up from the bed and out the door, running down the hallway." She began to laugh as she replayed the memory in her mind. "Needless to say, having a half-delirious boy running through the house at such an ungodly hour didn't go over so well with my dad. And poor George was so confused, he could hardly even string together a defense for himself. I think he half-believed Daddy was the person he was trying to get away from in the first place!"

She sat still for a while, with a smile on her face, letting her eyes drift back to the window. "Anyway, last night he had one of those nights. Not the running around and all, but a lot of jabbering. When he starts like that I always think he's talking to me. But he doesn't even know I'm there at all. He's going on about something, who knows what. All I know is that it's keeping me awake. So I gave him a nudge and said, 'George, be still!'"

She took a deep breath and tried to fight back another round of tears. "That's what I said to him, 'George . . . be still.'"

The sitting room door opened and Mr. Tremble walked in. He was in his most sincere demeanor, walking up to Mrs. Dupree and placing his hand gently on her shoulder. "Dorothy, I want to make one thing perfectly clear," he said in his soft voice. "If you have any questions, any concerns, or if you just want to stop talking about this altogether, you just let me know. Because all I'm here to do is make this easier for you. To make sure we have the service you want. The service George deserves."

Eric had seen this approach so many times. The soft sell. He always admired Mr. Tremble's ability to be compassionate and profitable at the same time. But this time it was different. Even though it was obvious that Mrs. Dupree and Beth were appreciative of Mr. Tremble's offer, Eric wanted him to dial it back a notch. To leave that last sentence off. To not talk about what people deserved, or use the phrase "beautiful service." He wanted him to just be straight with them. Tell them it doesn't really matter what kind of box you put a dead person in, it's going to be covered with dirt and never seen again. And it doesn't really matter how many flowers you have at the service, because people will send so many that it will already be too much. He wanted him to leave the business end of the business behind, just this once.

But Mr. Tremble was just doing his job. He was about to take them into the other room to show them the caskets when Eric noticed something on Mr. Tremble's pants. At first he thought he was mistaken. It was hard to make out from the distance between them. But when he realized for certain what it was, he knew there would be no mistaking it if Mrs. Dupree or Beth saw it.

"Mr. Tremble," Eric said as he stood from his chair, "I think . . ." He realized he had no idea how to handle this gracefully, so he just plowed right through. "Could I talk to you for a second?"

Mr. Tremble turned and looked at Eric, a little confused. "Right now?"

"Yeah," he answered. "If you don't mind, Mrs. Dupree. It'll only take a second."

Mrs. Dupree shook her head, indicating it was fine with her, and Mr. Tremble followed Eric into the next room. When the door had closed behind them, Mr. Tremble spoke.

"What's going on, Eric?"

"Your pants," Eric said, pointing to Mr. Tremble's khakis. "There's blood on them."

Mr. Tremble looked down and saw the trail of blood that had obviously run off his apron. "Oh dear God! Do you think they saw it?"

"I don't think so." He paused for a moment to think. "I hope not."

"Well, I'm going to have to run upstairs and change. Do you think you could just go ahead and show them the caskets? I know you don't want to—"

"I really don't," Eric answered quickly.

"But I hate to keep them waiting."

Eric thought it over for a minute. There was really nothing to do. Mr. Tremble couldn't go back out there without changing his pants. There was no reason to make Mrs. Dupree wait. And in the end, it was his job. So he sent Mr. Tremble off to change, and walked back into the sitting room to face up to the awkward situation.

"Sorry about that, Mrs. Dupree. Beth. Mr. Tremble just needed to take care of one quick thing. He won't be long. So . . ." Eric could barely bring himself to say it. "Umm, if you want—I can show you the, uh, the caskets."

Mrs. Dupree walked over to Eric and touched his face. "It's okay, Eric." He looked at her and realized it couldn't be any less okay. But for her sake, he had to pretend it was. "Let's look at them," she said.

The room where the caskets were held was, in Eric's opinion, ridiculous. It was like an automobile showroom, with the caskets sitting around under just-so lighting that made them all look like a sweet ride. The perfect way to take that long cruise into the great unknown. They even had absurd names like the "Fairfield" and the "Imperial." Eric had always hated that. He thought they should just have numbers. And not even "The #1" and "The #2." They should be weird numbers that wouldn't delineate any value, like the "7107C" or the "26R14." That way everyone could feel okay about their choice, and never have to say, "I'll go with the Ave Maria, please."

Standing there in the room with Beth and Mrs. Dupree, Eric suddenly felt a little overwhelmed by what he was about to have to do. He turned to the tired face of Mrs. Dupree and decided something else entirely was in order.

"Look, Mrs. Dupree, what I'm supposed to do here is talk to you about these caskets, and their features, and tell you why certain ones are better than others. But I really don't feel like doing that." He looked over his shoulder to be sure Mr. Tremble wasn't sneaking up behind him or anything. "The truth is, I don't believe any of these caskets are better than the next. In my opinion, the best casket is the cheapest one. That's going to do the job without costing you too much money. He has a catalog of other caskets you can pick from. All you have to do is say, 'Gosh, I don't know. Is there anything less expensive?' That's my advice for you on all of this. What makes for a nice service isn't the casket or the flowers or any of that. It's the friends and the family who come together to pay their respects. And believe me, Mr. Dupree was a well-respected man. He's going to have a beautiful service."

Eric paused, catching himself using the phrase "beautiful service."

"Mr. Tremble's a kind man. He won't push you toward anything you don't want. But he's also running a business. So he probably won't be the first to mention the least-expensive options. Just ask him. He won't mind. More than anything else, he wants you to be happy with what happens here. Okay?"

Mrs. Dupree's eyes welled up with tears. "Thank you, Eric. You always were—" The words were stifled by her own emotions. Beth came over and put her arm around her mother, then looked to Eric.

"She's right," she said with a soft smile. "You always were."

When Mr. Tremble came in, wearing pants that looked remarkably similar to the ones he'd been wearing when he left, he wasn't at all caught off guard by the scene. In his business, people cried. They didn't need a specific reason. They had the biggest reason anyone could ever imagine. He walked up to Eric and nodded. "How are we doing?"

"We're getting by," Eric answered. "They were just asking if we had anything less expensive to offer."

Mr. Tremble didn't miss a beat. "Of course we do," he said in a gentle, understanding voice. "Hold on one second and I'll go get the catalog."

As Mr. Tremble left the room, Mrs. Dupree slowly regained her composure and looked up at Eric. He imagined if she cried much more, her eyes might wash right out of their sockets. They looked so tired. So overwhelmed by what had to be the worst day of her life. But still, when she looked up at Eric, she managed a smile. A small sliver of peace. And, despite the fact that he'd clearly bitten the hand that feeds him, in that one moment Eric felt, for the first time in a long time, that he might have done more good than harm.

Dusk was short-lived in their little valley. Eric had vague memories of summers at his aunt and uncle's farmhouse in Pennsylvania. The days seemed to last forever there. The sun would pop up on the horizon of the farm and languidly traipse across the sky, bathing everything in warm, golden light. There were no mountains or hills to speak of, so come the end of the day the sun had to set well into the distant horizon, leaving a wash of color in the sky for hours afterward. But there in Pinely it was a different story. The sun only had to travel from the crest of one hillside, across the valley, to the crest of the other. So the days seemed brief enough, even before they began shortening, cutting ballast on their long journey toward the winter solstice. Eric always loved the dusk. To him, that period of not-quite-daytime and not-quite-evening was full of possibility, the way the dawn was to others. The only way to extend the dusk in Pinely was to walk up the west face of the east hillside, going up as the last rays of the sun went down. This was one of the things Eric enjoyed about walking to Gina's house after work.

Gina lived on Seventh Avenue, just off Burrows Street on the east side of town. She had a nice little one-story place with a basement Eric had redone as a rec room for Tess. Gina's house was actually in much better shape than Eric's. Most people considered this in their assessment of who was the better parent. What they didn't consider was that Eric did all the work at Gina's place, fixing up the rec room, reshingling the roof, helping with the plumbing, installing the washer/dryer. He did it because it was his daughter's home. Gina let him because she didn't have anyone else to do it.

Eric lumbered up the walkway that led to the front door and stopped on the porch. Through the front bay window he could see Gina sitting on the couch, watching TV. There was something about her face, bathed in the blue light of the television, viewed through the last wisps of dusk reflecting off the windowpane, that set him in a mood. The wind carried the smell of someone's wood-burning stove, and for a moment, Eric wished he was coming home to this well-kept house, to the pretty face in the blue light. He watched her for a few seconds before knocking gently on the door and walking in.

"Hey Gina."

She started to smile, then stopped. "What's wrong?" she asked.

"What are you talking about?"

"I don't know, you just seem a little . . ."

"I just got here. How could I seem anything?"

She reached for the remote control and turned off the TV. "I don't know," she answered, "you just do."

Eric grunted softly and took off his jacket.

"Do you want anything to drink?"

"You got any beer?"

"I think so," she said, starting to get up.

"Sit down. I can get it."

He threw his jacket over the back of the chair by the door and made his way to the kitchen. The refrigerator was the exact antithesis of his. It was loaded with good, healthy things to eat: fruits, vegetables, juices. Not a trace of spreadable cheeses, Kool-Aid, Jell-O, hotdogs, or anything else that Eric—and Tess—relied on for sustenance at his place.

"So Tess had a good one today," Gina called out from the other room.

The milk wasn't even close to going out of date.

"Oh yeah," he called back absently, "what was that?"

If there was beer in this fridge it would have been exclusively for a "One Of These Things Is Not Like The Other" segment on *Sesame Street*.

"She told me that exercising in front of the TV isn't natural," Gina answered.

Finally he saw the beer, behind half a cantaloupe that he only picked up because he was curious where in the hell Gina found cantaloupe at this time of year.

"Man, I don't know where she comes up with this stuff," he said to Gina.

He twisted off the cap and threw it in the garbage under the sink.

"She told me you said it," Gina answered.

Eric made his way back to the living room and sat down, leaning back on his jacket. "Oh," he said, before taking a drink of his beer.

Gina stared at him for a second, waiting for more. "Oh?" she finally asked.

Eric looked up and, seeing the expression on her face, realized he hadn't provided a sufficient answer. "Well," he said, "I don't know where I come up with this stuff either."

His eyes strolled around the room, taking it all in. The soft light from a cinnamon candle in the corner. The delicate pile of cushions and pillows on the sofa. The framed watercolor in the dining room. These gentle signs of a woman's touch somehow made his heart feel heavy. His eyes settled on a picture of himself, Gina, and Tess on the table next to him. "When was this?" he asked.

"Last Labor Day. At the parade," she answered, watching him closely.

"Funny," he said. "I don't even remember that." He took the picture in his hands and held it in his lap. "Looks like we were having fun."

"We were. Tess kept making this goofy face and covering her ears when the fire trucks went by."

He sat there, silently staring at the picture. Gina watched his eyes squint half-shut, then open again, the way they did when he was working out a problem. He stayed that way for quite a while before he looked away from the picture and up at Gina.

"George Dupree died today."

"Oh no," she said quickly.

"Heart attack while raking the leaves this morning."

"That's so . . . How old was he?"

Eric shook his head. "I don't know. Sixty? Maybe? Beth's only twenty-six, so . . . fuck. Fifty-something? Could that be right?"

"Could be. What's your dad?"

"Fifty—yeah, just turned fifty-four. Holy shit." Eric looked out the front door for a minute, shaking his head. "Holy shit," he said again.

Gina watched him for a moment before she spoke.

"So you'll probably see Jill," she said. "Won't you?"

"What?" he asked, turning back to look at her.

"Well it's her dad's funeral. And you work at the funeral home. So—"

Eric thought about it for a minute. He'd been so overwhelmed with the events of the day, he hadn't even stopped to consider the possible events of tomorrow. Jill would definitely be coming back. She might be on a plane at that very minute. It was going to be difficult—no, impossible—not to see her during the funeral services. It had been six years since they'd spoken, mainly because Eric had been waiting for the right circumstance in which to see her again. Her father's funeral was not the circumstance he'd been hoping for.

He looked at Gina with a bit of panic in his eyes. "This is a bad day."

Gina tried to reassure him. "It's probably time you saw her again anyway."

"Are you fucking serious?"

"Eric!"

"What?"

"Tess is in the other room."

"And?"

"And you're swearing like a pirate."

Eric looked at her and shook his head. "You mean like a sailor?"

"Maybe," she said. "Aren't pirates sailors?"

"I guess," he said, thinking it over for a second. "Hell, are they?"

"I think so. I mean, boats, oceans. What else do you need to be a sailor?"

"I'm not sure." He took a long drink from his beer and let out a loud sigh.

No one spoke for a while. Eric was lost in his own deeply swirling thoughts of funerals, pirates, and high school sweethearts. He didn't seem to have good answers for anything. All he had were problems—and questions.

"Don't you think you should see her?"

He looked over at Gina to be sure it was she who had spoken and not his internal dialogue.

"Jill?"

"Yeah."

He stood up out of the chair and walked over toward the window.

"Of course I should see her. I should have seen her a long—" He stopped in the middle of his thought and turned to Gina. "Have you seen her?"

"I've seen her around once or twice. Summers, holidays, stuff like that. It's a small town you know."

"Oh I know," he said with a short laugh.

"So how is it you haven't seen her?"

Eric leaned against the wall and looked at Gina. There was an uncertain softness that came out in his voice.

"Because I'm not ready."

The thunder of tiny footsteps came roaring down the hall as Tess burst into the living room. "Hey Mommy, when's—" She stopped asking her question when she saw the answer himself standing against the wall. "Daddy!" she shouted as she ran over to him.

"Hey Tess," he said, leaning down to pick her up into his arms.

She took his face in her hands and squinted at him.

"Your eye still looks bad," she said.

"Oh yeah," he said, grabbing her foot and dangling her upside down. "Well how's your foot?"

"Fine," she managed to say between outrageous giggles that forced the blood to her face even faster than the gravity. Eric held her that way as she wriggled and squirmed to get free. He looked over to Gina who nodded in agreement.

"It wasn't that bad really. It's hardly even bled since," she said.

Tess was starting to lose her breath from the laughter and the dangling, so Eric lowered her to the ground. She rolled over and laid on her back, unable to stop carrying on.

"Well if your foot's okay," said Eric, "then why don't you go put it in a shoe so we can go down to Grandma's and mooch some dinner."

"Okay," she said, stumbling to her feet and hustling back down the hallway.

Gina stood up and walked over to Eric.

"Are you going to be okay?" she asked.

Eric looked at her face and nodded his head slowly. "I really don't know," he said.

"Are you sure you want her tonight?" Gina asked quietly. "I mean, are you sure you don't want to be alone? With so much on your mind?"

"Believe me, that's exactly why I don't want to be alone," he answered.

Gina took a step toward him that was both hesitant and deliberate. "You could . . . I mean, we could all stay here."

Eric walked to the chair he'd been sitting on, took the last drink from his beer, and reached for his jacket. Gina clumsily sat back down on the arm of the couch, waiting for him to say something. He put on his jacket and looked down to fasten the zipper. As he pulled it up, his eyes met hers.

"What?" she asked.

"*What?*" he asked in disbelief. "Look Gina, I'm a little unclear in my thoughts right now. Please don't try to take advantage of me."

Gina's face went blank, before quickly flushing red in a mixture of embarrassment and anger. "That's a real prick thing to say," she snapped.

"Who's the pirate now?" he said in mock-reprimand.

Tess bounded around the corner with her shoes on and her laces flapping around her ankles. "Who's a pirate?" she asked.

"We're not sure, baby," Eric said, picking her up and sitting her on the chair. He got on his knee and started tying her shoes. "Maybe me."

"Then you need a patch for your eye," she said.

"And a wooden leg?" he asked.

"And a parrot," she laughed.

Eric stood up and turned to Gina, who had already gotten Tess's coat. "Okay, I'll take her to school in the morning and you'll pick her up, right?"

"Right."

"Arrrrr," said Eric in a deep throaty voice.

"What?"

"I think that's pirate for 'yes.'"

"Arrrrr," said Tess as she put on her coat.

"See," he said, pointing to his little girl.

"Do you ever worry you might be a bad influence on her?" Gina asked.

"Naw," Eric said. "Plenty of people do that for me. Isn't that right, Tess?"

"Arrrrr," she shot back in a little pirate voice.

Eric and Gina looked at each other and let a little laughter spill out of them. His hand dropped to his daughter, who quickly took hold of it. "Come on, Blue Beard. Let's go get some vittles."

"Arrrrr," she said again as they reached the door.

"Okay, that's gonna get old," Eric said. "Let's try and get it all out of our system before we get to Grandma's."

The cold surrounded them as they walked away, hand in hand, filling the night air with the earnest cries of two would-be pirates.

Dinner was always better at Eric's parents' house. When he first moved out, Eric desperately wanted to assert his independence in every arena of his life, including the kitchen. It was a valiant effort, but his culinary ambitions were no match for his rudimentary skills. Eventually, when faced with the mounting evidence of canned goods, frozen foods, and boxes with the word "Helper" in the title, Eric was forced to acknowledge that his cooking skills had been dealt a crushing defeat.

Eric sat at one end of the of his parents' dining room table, the same seat he'd had since he was a kid, and idly picked at his plate. Tess was yammering on about something at the other end of the table, but he couldn't tell what. His mom was doing a good job of keeping her entertained, while his dad just seemed annoyed by something. Eric had been watching him for a while. He seemed to be growing more and more perturbed by the minute until he finally put down his fork and looked at Eric.

"What are you staring at?" he asked.

Eric was caught off guard. "What?"

"You've been staring a hole through me for the past fifteen minutes."

Eric quickly looked down at his plate. "Oh. You just seemed to be annoyed at something."

"Yeah. I was annoyed at you staring at me."

He didn't know quite what to say. He probably had been staring. He wanted to tell his dad a bunch of things that were suddenly on his mind. He wanted to tell him that he loved him. That he really admired the way he'd made something of himself. That he was proud to be his son and wished he could be half as good of a father to Tess.

"Sorry," was all he ended up saying.

"Daddy got in trouble," Tess called out in a singsong voice.

"I did not get in trouble," Eric said defensively. "If I was in trouble he would have hit me. Right, Dad?"

"Funny," his dad answered before looking back down to eat. Eric sat and watched him, wondering if his dad ever thought about the meaning of it all. The way he was eating his pork chops didn't make him seem like a terribly introspective man. In fact, Eric had never really known his dad to talk about much beyond the practical, day-to-day things in life. There just never seemed to be a good time to start into heavy, reflective conversation. He watched his dad slather butter on a biscuit, which only made him realize exactly how little time he actually had. His dad was trading their precious time together for the salty taste of buttery biscuits. How many of those had he eaten in his lifetime? How many biscuits had already begun to steal away the days and hours between them? Time was ticking. But none of that time seemed to welcome a proclamation of love from a son to his dad. Unless that time was right now. He began to work the idea around in his head. "I love you, Dad." That was all he had to say. The words would float across the table and carry them both into a new realm of self-awareness. As the idea became more tangible in his mind, he could almost sense that his dad felt its presence. That he knew something grand and profound was about to change the fundamental nature of their relationship for good. His eyes lifted from his plate, but Eric didn't say anything. Instead, he allowed the moment to become full with the idea. When their eyes had locked long enough for the truth between them to be felt, it was his father who spoke first.

"What in the *hell* are you staring at?"

"What?" Eric said, startled.

"Seriously, Eric. Stop it," his dad pleaded.

"Eric, are you alright, honey?" his mom piped in.

"Yeah, Daddy, are you alright, honey?" added Tess.

Eric looked down the table at his mom and his little girl. "Yeah, I'm fine, ladies. I'm just a little—" He thought it over and decided to just forget about it. "It's kind of been a weird day, that's all."

"Well, you're turning it into a weird evening," his dad said. "So just stop staring and eat your damn dinner."

"Yeah, eat your damn dinner," Tess giggled.

Eric shot a look to his dad. "Now, you would think you'd know better than that."

His dad looked flustered and glanced down at his plate. "Sorry. You just had me all screwed up with your gawking."

"Tess, don't talk like Grandpa, okay?" Eric said.

"Okay," she said, not entirely certain what her dad meant.

"Okay," Eric said to himself as everyone returned to eating. He kept his eyes on his own plate and tried not to think anymore. He tried not to think about George Dupree. About death. About fathers and daughters. Or about who tomorrow might bring.

He was still trying not to think about these things after dinner as he laid on the couch, working the crossword puzzle in the *TV Guide*. His dad was playing a game with Tess in the other room, and he could hear his mom finishing up the dishes in the kitchen. He was stumped. Stumped on the goddamned *TV Guide* crossword puzzle, of all things. Normally he could carry on a conversation and still finish the thing in ten minutes. But his brain had its own agenda at that moment. One that didn't involve figuring out a seven-letter word for WKRP's newsman. He was so engrossed in not solving the puzzle, he didn't even notice his mom come into the room and sit by his feet on the arm of the couch.

"I heard about George Dupree."

Eric looked up at her, but held the *TV Guide* in front of him. "Yeah, we had to go pick him up this morning. How did you hear?"

"Gertie stopped by the library. Said she'd heard it from Alice Newberry when they were at the pool."

"At the pool? It's October."

"Oh, they were doing something for the city planning . . . I don't know. That's just what she said. When was the last time you'd talked to him?"

"Mr. Dupree?"

"Yeah."

"Last night."

"What?"

"He came in the Legion last night to watch the game. He sat there at the bar and we talked."

His mom sat quietly for a moment. He stared at the page of the *TV Guide* but it didn't even register as a puzzle anymore. It was just something to stare at, which was really all he needed.

"How many dead people you suppose I've seen, Mom?"

"I have no idea, honey."

"Five years I've been working with Mr. Tremble. I don't know the exact number, but it has to be closer to a hundred than not. And I've felt things. I've gotten a little queasy more than once. People don't always die pretty, you know. I mean, when people have a closed casket service, I'm the one who closes the casket. But I've also felt other things—more emotional things. It's impossible not to watch a family in pain and not feel anything. But this thing here. Seeing Mr. Dupree. It's like the first time all over again."

Her eyes got soft as she looked at her little boy. "The first time?" she asked.

"The first time I saw a dead person. You know. Realized that people don't go on forever. That things aren't as solid as you like to think."

"When was that?"

"When Jim died."

"Jim?" she asked, a little surprised. "You remember that?"

He nodded his head and tried to fight back a wave of sentiment.

"You were only six. I wouldn't think you'd remember that."

He looked up at his mom and could tell she was trying not to cry. "He died, Mom," he said. "How could I forget?"

SIX

Things were all mixed up and Eric didn't understand any of it. They made him get dressed up. They made him come to this place where everyone seemed to be in a bad mood. And they'd told him things that didn't seem to make any sense. They'd said Jim had gone away. But he was lying right in front of them, all dressed up too. Eric had never seen Jim dressed up before. He pretty much wore the same stain-colored t-shirts all the time. So to see him lying there, wearing a tie, with his hair all combed, was a little strange. But it didn't seem to be worth all this hulla-baloo. His mom had told him that Jim's insides, his soul, had left his body, so Jim wouldn't be able to talk to them anymore. Eric couldn't figure out why his insides would want to do that. It would seem that Jim would get awfully lonely without anyone to talk to. Eric even thought he might get awfully lonely without being able to talk to Jim.

Jim was his grandpa. Eric didn't know any other kid who called his grandpa by his first name. But if Eric called Jim "grand-pa," he'd act like he didn't hear him. Said it made him feel old to have a kid use that kind of language around him. Even though he wouldn't answer to the title, he still did all the things grandpas seemed to do. He let Eric sit on his lap when they watched TV together. He never let Eric pick what they watched, but that was okay most of the time. They'd usually watch *Davy Crockett* or stock car races or something like that. Something that men would watch together, even though they both knew Eric wasn't a man. For one thing, men didn't sit in each other's laps. If that wasn't enough, there was the fact that Eric was only six.

Eric didn't know when he'd first met Jim. He supposed he'd just always been around. He could remember a few beginnings of things in his life. He remembered when the Murphys moved in across the street. He remembered when they got the new station wagon. And he remembered when those men came and put in a driveway where part of their front yard used to be. Everything else just seemed to already be there when he would think back. Including Jim. Jim never had a beginning to Eric. So he couldn't really figure how Jim could have an end.

This place where Jim was lying looked awfully soft and comfy. He thought it might have been the fanciest bed Jim had ever laid down on. Jim's bed—Jim and Eric's grandma's bed, the one they shared—just had regular old sheets on it. But these sheets were way fancier. They were shiny. Eric wanted to reach out and touch them just to see what they felt like, but he was afraid. He didn't know what he was supposed to be doing, so he just stood there beside his mom with his hands at his side. There were flowers everywhere, which made everything smell. Jim always smelled the same, like cigarettes and aftershave. Sometimes they would sit in the kitchen at the table, while Eric ate toasted coconut cookies and Jim smoked a cigarette, and Jim would teach Eric magic tricks. He showed him how to make a quarter appear behind someone's ear, and how to find the card someone had pulled from the deck. These were life-altering skills to have in the first grade, so Eric was always trying to learn more.

More than anything else, Jim liked to do stuff outside. He was all the time hammering something, or drilling something, or working on his truck. Eric would just hang around with him while he worked, asking questions about what he was doing and bringing him the tools he needed from the shed. Sometimes Jim had him run so many errands, Eric wondered what he'd have done without him.

The last project they'd worked on together had been a pretty good one. Jim was cleaning out the gutters around his house. All kinds of gross stuff came out of them. Actually the stuff itself wasn't that gross, it was just leaves and dirt and things like that. But something happened to it all when it spent too much time in the gutter. It turned into a thick, mucky mess. Jim would climb up the ladder, pull the gunk out of the gutter, and fling it down on the ground toward Eric. Then Eric would come over, scoop it up with his hands, and put it in the garbage can. They were a pretty good team, the two of them. Actually, it was the three of them if you counted Eric's grandma.

She would always come out to check up on them, see if they needed anything, let them know when lunch was ready, and always to tell them to "be careful." She wanted them to be careful no matter what they were doing. One time she'd told them to be careful while they were washing the truck. Eric didn't understand that one. What were they were supposed to be careful about? Careful not to scratch the truck? Careful not to get soap in their eyes? In the end, he figured she was just so used to telling them to be careful, she didn't even check to see if they were doing anything dangerous before she said it.

She came around the corner while they were cleaning out the gutters and watched for a minute or two. She saw three loads of gutter gunk get thrown down by Jim, picked up by Eric, and tossed into the garbage can before she piped in.

"Eric, you should be using a dustpan or something to pick up that stuff."

Eric stopped what he was doing and looked at her. "How come, Mammaw?"

"Cause it's filthy, that's how come."

Eric looked down at his dirty hands and realized he had no argument. "But it's more fun this way."

Jim's voice called down from on top of the ladder. "Leave the boy be, Irma. That stuff ain't gonna hurt him none."

"Yeah, Mammaw," Eric added, "it ain't gonna hurt me. It's just old leaves and stuff."

He looked at his grandma, who was looking up at Jim, who had already returned to digging stuff out of the gutters. She watched him throw another fistful of gunk down until she finally caught his eye.

"What?" he asked.

"I'll tell you what," she said, "the both of you are gonna wind up with ringworm or something, fishing your hands around in that crud."

"Oh would you stop it," Jim sighed. "You're gonna make the boy afraid of dirt. Then what? He's gonna be indoors all the time playing pinochle and solitaire, turning into a big ninny."

"Fine," she finally said before turning to go back in the house. "Just be careful."

Eric looked up at Jim who winked and made a shooter with his hand. Eric hadn't quite gotten the hang of winking yet, but he formed his fingers into the shape of a gun and gave Jim a shooter right back.

Eric looked down at Jim's hands, resting by his side in the box and realized something was different about them now. This place was funny like that. If he didn't pay close attention, he'd miss things. Like the music. He didn't even hear music playing at first. It was so soft and quiet, it was like it didn't even come in through his ears, it just sort of crept up around him like the air. But once he really heard it, he realized he'd been listening to it the whole time. That's the way it was with Jim's hands. There was something going on with them. Something different. He looked at them for a long time before he realized. They were clean.

Jim's hands were always dirty, even right after he washed them. He had dirt that had dug itself so far down into his nails and into the cracks of his leathery skin, no soap in the world could get it out. Even when they'd been working on something particularly dirty or greasy and had to use the Boraxo, Jim's hands would never come clean. But now they were. They were so clean, they didn't even look like Jim's hands anymore. If it hadn't been for the anchor tattoo at the base of his thumb, Eric might have figured this fella in the suit, with the combed hair and the clean hands, to be an imposter. That would have been nice if it was true. But Eric had already watched Jim get real sick, so he figured, based on the state of everything else around, that someone at this place just had some awfully good soap.

Eric wasn't helping when Jim fell. He was at school that day. When he got home his mom told him that Jim had been finishing cleaning up the gutters when he lost his balance and fell. It was a pretty good fall from up there on the ladder, Eric knew that much. And there wasn't anything around to break your fall either. Just the sidewalk. So he wasn't too surprised when his mom told him Jim had broken his hip.

Earlier that summer, Kenny Kiminiki had broken his arm doing a Pete Rose into second base during a T-ball game. You weren't even allowed to slide in T-ball in the first place. It was against the rules. But the idea of sliding head first into a base was just too tempting for a showboater like Kiminiki. Unfortunately, Kenny wasn't the most coordinated kid in the Pinely Pony

League, and his attempt to grab the spotlight earned him a fractured radius and six weeks in a plaster cast. It was hot, he wasn't allowed to swim in it, and by the end of it all, that cast was as ripe as a baby's diaper. But when it came off, Kenny's arm was as good as new.

Eric couldn't quite picture how they might put a hip in a cast, but he guessed they'd figure something out. That's what doctors were for, to figure out ways to make people better. If Kenny Kiminiki could recover from a broken arm in half a summer, Eric figured Jim would be back from a broken hip by the month's end. When they went to visit him in the hospital, Eric realized he might have figured wrong.

Jim always looked like he was up to something. Eric's grandma said he was ornery, which was about as good a way to describe it as any. Eric could walk in on Jim taking a nap in his armchair, and he'd still have a look on his face that made him seem like he was up to no good. Once Eric was so certain Jim was faking his way through a nap, covering for something he'd done, Eric sat and watched him for a full twenty minutes. He couldn't quite figure out where his smile was coming from. His mouth was half-open, his eyes were completely closed, but there was something about his face that seemed to be smiling. When a couple of dogs got into it right outside the window, Jim sprung forward and noticed Eric sitting on the footstool, watching him.

"What are you doing, boy?" he asked.

Eric gave him the look of a coconspirator. "You weren't really sleeping, were you, Jim?"

"Well hell yeah, I was sleeping," he answered in a gravelly, post-nap voice. "What did you think I was doing?"

"You looked like you was just purtendin' to sleep."

"How so?" Jim asked, genuinely curious.

"You still looked ornery."

"Well," Jim answered with a chuckle, "ornery doesn't just go away cause you're sleeping."

That's what made Eric guess this broken hip thing might be more than he'd originally figured. Because when he saw Jim lying in the hospital bed, he noticed all the ornery had gone away. Jim looked sad. He was lying there on the thin bed, in his thin robe, just staring at them as they walked into the room. Eric's mom and dad went to his bedside immediately, but Eric stayed back, slowly working his way to the foot of the bed. Jim spoke to Eric's folks, answering their questions, but every word seemed so heavy and lifeless that Eric couldn't help but wonder if Jim had been zombified like in those old black-and-white movies. He half expected him to reach over and suck his mom's brains out.

When the doctor came in, looking at a clipboard, he explained to everyone around that Jim had taken a hell of a spill and was lucky he hadn't broken anything else. It seemed like a stupid thing to say, because at that moment, Jim couldn't have looked any less lucky if he was trying. Eric thought about telling the doctor as much, but changed his mind when he saw something happen to Jim's face.

Jim always seemed to be smiling, without ever actually doing it. When he did break into a full-on smile, it was bigger than life. A big, toothy grin that took over his entire face, forcing his eyes to all but disappear behind tiny slits, and causing deep wrinkles to show up out of nowhere. But when the doctor told Jim he was lucky, he smiled. It wasn't the smile that always seemed to come out of him from the inside, and it wasn't the face-claiming, tooth-baring smile he knew. His lips stayed together and pulled thin as they turned up at the corners forming something that could pass as a smile, if you didn't know Jim. But there was no smile in his eyes. None at all. In fact, his eyes looked even more sad lingering above this weak smile.

Jim's face didn't look sad anymore there in the fancy box. It didn't look ornery either. It just looked like a face. Nothing else. Eric heard one of his cousins say it looked like Jim was just sleeping. His cousin had never seen Jim sleep before.

Jim stayed in the hospital for a long while after the broken hip. The doctors told him he wouldn't be able to get around as well for a while. Maybe even forever. But if he stuck to his physical therapy and kept a positive attitude, he'd be able to recover to an acceptable degree. The idea of Jim not being able to go outside, move around on his own, hit things with a hammer, this didn't sound like Jim at all. Apparently it didn't sound like Jim to Jim either, because when he got home he really wasn't himself anymore. Eric still went to visit, trying to get him to teach him magic tricks and stuff, but Jim didn't seem all that interested. He had dinner brought to him in his chair, and even then he rarely ate it. He would just watch the TV all day. Some days he wouldn't even do that. He'd just look outside through the window. Eric's grandma used to tell Eric things would get better soon. She'd tell him that Jim would be up and moving around again in no time. "He's still weak from the fall," she'd say to anyone who asked. But as Eric moved from being six to being six and a half, he started to wonder how long someone could be crippled by one little accident that happened so long ago.

Jim didn't recover to an acceptable degree, as the doctors had said he would. In fact, his recovery was so less-than-acceptable, he had to go back to the hospital. Eric heard it described as "complications" due to the broken hip. But he overheard another doctor tell his grandma that Jim's attitude alone, his unwillingness to eat, to do his exercises, and to believe he could get better, was amounting to a slow suicide.

"If he doesn't want to walk out of this hospital," the doctor told her, "he can just keep doing what he's doing."

That must have been what Jim wanted, because that's exactly what he did. He rarely touched his food, eating only the pudding if they served it for dessert. He hardly ever moved, except to change the channel, or turn the TV off when the after-school cartoons came on. He didn't seem to believe in anything anymore. He would just offer up his weak smile when someone commented that he was looking better that day.

Through it all, Eric's grandma sat at his bedside and waited for him to get better. Anytime Eric came to visit at the hospital, she would be there beside Jim, resting his hand in hers, gently stroking the top of it with her other hand. Sometimes, there was so little to do, so little to talk about, Eric would just sit and watch her hold his hand for hours on end. It seemed to comfort Jim in some way. But at the same time, it seemed to help him give up. It was like every stroke of her hand was wiping away a little more, until eventually there'd be nothing left of him at all.

This was the first time Eric had seen his grandma away from Jim in months. She was on the other side of the funeral home, wearing a dark dress that didn't seem to fit quite right. It wasn't a dress Eric had ever seen before, so he figured it was maybe just for things like this. It seemed like she must have been smaller the last time someone died. She was standing by Jim, still checking up on him even at this point, when she saw Eric looking over at her. She nodded her head and gave him a lifeless smile, just like Jim's.

She'd picked that up from him near the end. The two of them would offer their double-barreled flimsy smile to everyone who walked into the room. Good news. Bad news. It was all met with the same indifference. Seeing how there always seemed to be more bad news than good, it was probably better to stake out some middle ground. When the doctors told Jim he'd developed pneumonia due to lack of nutrition and exercise, there could have been a lot of emotion. But there wasn't. There were just weak smiles and nods of the head that said, "We know." No matter what the news, they acted like they already knew it. Later Eric realized they didn't really know about the pneumonia, or the circulation problems, or the blood clot. Those were just the means. When Jim and his grandma smiled and nodded their heads, it was in acknowledgment of an end.

The day Eric thought he'd started helping Jim get better was one of the happiest days of his life. His grandma had fallen asleep, right by Jim's side as always, while Jim looked toward the window, even though the shades were drawn. Eric was sitting in a chair on the other side of the room, pulling things out of his pocket to see what he'd accumulated that day. He had a rubber band, a silver rock he'd found down by the railroad tracks, a tiny plastic gun from a GI Joe toy, half a baseball card, a dandelion that had stained most of the card yellow, and a quarter. He'd forgotten all about the quarter. His mom had given it to him in case the Good Humor truck came by that day. He wondered if he might be able to get something from the vending machine down the hall and climbed down off the chair to go see. As he reached the door to the room, he got an idea, and turned back toward the bed. Being careful not to touch any of the tubes running into Jim's arm or nose, Eric crept up close to his head and looked hard behind his ear.

"Gosh, Jim," he said as Jim turned his head to look at him, "I can understand you not eating that food or doing those dumb exercises, but you really should wash behind your ears."

He reached his hand behind Jim's ear, brushing against the stubble on his cheek, then pulled it back out again, producing the quarter for Jim's amazement. He knew Jim wouldn't really be amazed, since he was the one who'd showed him the trick in the first place, but he figured it was worth a shot. Jim looked at the quarter for a minute, looked over at Eric, then smiled. It started in the wrinkles around his eyes and slowly worked its way down to his mouth as it spread open to reveal his half-crooked teeth. Eric didn't know what to do. He just smiled back at his long-lost friend and said, "Hey Jim."

All the dark clothes, soft music, and sad faces made it seem impossible that Jim had smiled at him, really smiled, less than a week ago. Now he was lying in a box. Eric didn't know how long they were supposed to stand there, or what they were even supposed to be doing. His dad seemed the same as he always did, except more so. His mom seemed the exact opposite. He stuffed his hands in his pockets and waited for a sign that they'd be able to leave soon. He didn't know what to do with Jim now. But then, he hadn't known what to do with Jim ever since the fall. His hand found a coin in his pocket and he fished it out to take a look at it. It was a quarter. He thought it over for a minute, then decided to go ahead and try. No one had seen Jim smile at him in the hospital, so he thought maybe, if he could get Jim to smile now, everyone might really appreciate it.

As he reached out toward Jim's ear, the back of his hand brushed against Jim's smooth cheek. It was cold. So cold, Eric was startled and a little scared. He pulled his hand back quickly, dropping the quarter, and watched it fall on Jim's chest and slide into the breast pocket of his jacket. He looked up at his mom, who had watched the whole thing.

"Mom?" he said.

She looked down at Jim and started to cry. His dad put his arm around her and awkwardly tried to comfort her. Eric watched his parents for a second as a strange realization came over him. He rubbed the back of his hand and looked at Jim's face. There was a small streak where he had touched him. A streak where his face had a little less color. It had been so cold. He could hear his mother crying as he looked off at the candles behind Jim. A sudden sadness overtook him and he watched the candlelight grow blurry. He blinked it clear, but it only lasted a second before the candles slowly blurred out again.

WEDNESDAY

If he'd realized it was going to be so cold, he probably would have driven his car. Tess plodded along beside him, holding his hand and breathing frost into the air. Tess was not a morning person. She picked that up from her dad. As usual, the two of them had gotten a late start, stuffing breakfast cereal into their mouths as they absently stumbled around the house trying to get ready. For an unfocused, half-asleep team, they were remarkably efficient. With barely a word spoken between them, they managed to get dressed, have breakfast, and make it out the door by a somewhat reasonable time. Now they were walking together hand in hand, on their way to Tess's school, where she would arrive no more than ten to fifteen minutes late. This wasn't satisfactory for them, it was exceptional. So there was no reason to feel rushed.

Tess lifted her hand, the one holding Eric's, to her face. When she moved it back to his side, the cold seemed intensified on his hand. He looked down and saw a freshly applied, glistening line of snot running up the back of his hand.

"Hey."

"What?" Tess asked.

"Use your other hand for that."

There was no visible response from her until a half a block

later when another drop began falling from her nose, which she tended to with her other hand.

The grass on people's lawns was gray with frost, and some of the cars driving by had tiny holes of visibility on their windshields, melted away by blasting defrosters on the inside. The sidewalk was covered with fallen leaves that Tess absently kicked through. She normally rode the bus when she was coming from Gina's house, but when she was with Eric, he liked to walk her there. It wasn't really on his way, and nine times out of ten he made her late, but he liked to do it just the same.

When they got to the school Eric could see Miss Vicky, Tess's kindergarten teacher, through the classroom window. Vicky Robinson had been married for about twenty years, but had been known as "Miss" Vicky since before the days when she was Eric's kindergarten teacher. She happened to look up and see Eric and Tess coming toward the door, so he waved and tried his best to look sheepish. Miss Vicky rolled her eyes and turned back to her classroom to squelch a small uprising that had broken out in the corner. With the school door in range, Tess let go of her dad's hand and walked a little faster, perhaps just realizing she might be late for something.

"Bye, Daddy," she said, without turning around.

"Hey," he called out, a little perturbed that she didn't want to give him a hug or some other more ceremonious good-bye. She stopped and turned to face him, her brown eyes framed by the hood of her coat, and her nose pink from the cold.

"What?" she asked, in a cloud of breath that floated up and dissipated into the air just above her head.

"Tell Miss Vicky I said I'm sorry you're late."

"Okay," she said. Then, her fear of tardiness confirmed by her own father, she turned and ran toward the door. He watched the classroom for a minute until he saw his little girl come in through the door. Miss Vicky went over and helped her out of her coat, but not before Tess got one more good wipe of her nose across its sleeve.

There was a lot of work to do at the funeral home that morning. It had been decided that the funeral would be on Thursday. Usually they'd have the viewing over two days, for a couple of hours in the afternoon and a couple of hours in the evening, then have the funeral on the afternoon of the third day. This gave people with different schedules, shifts to work, and family responsibilities ample time to come by and pay their respects. In a small town like Pinely, a funeral was a community event. Unfortunately, there was another community event on the horizon that was bound to take precedence. The Pinely-Cedarsville game. If they had the viewing through Thursday night, no one would be there anyway. They'd all be over at the bonfire rally, which would leave the Duprees with an empty funeral home echoing with the sounds of cheering fans and pep band music. An emotional juxtaposition no one wanted to be a part of. A funeral on Friday afternoon would have been even worse. People would have been running around hanging signs, setting up the field, getting ready for the game. There was even a pretty good chance that someone might end up wearing a Pinely Wildcats button or ball cap to the funeral. So while everyone was in agreement that yes, it was terrible that George Dupree had to die so close to game time, and yes, he certainly deserved more respect than to have his final rites of passage scheduled around a high school sporting event, these were the conditions by which they were all forced to work. So the viewing would be limited to one day, and the funeral would take place tomorrow afternoon.

That meant Eric had to get the funeral home ready by two o'clock that afternoon for the first shift of viewing. He and Mr.

Tremble would, in all likelihood, have to work through lunch. So Eric decided to swing into the five-and-dime on his way to pick up some snacks for the two of them. As he was paying for the cheese crackers and RC Cola, he saw a solitary figure trudging down the sidewalk on the opposite side of street, hands in pockets, a cloud of breath puffing out from his head. Eric grabbed his snacks and change and went to the door.

"Deke!"

The figure stopped and turned to look behind him.

"Over here, numbnuts," Eric shouted. Deke turned and looked across the street, but Eric was already halfway to him by the time he'd figured it out.

"What are you doing down here?" Deke asked.

"I just dropped Tess off at school. What are you doing telling people I think Pinely's gonna win on Friday?"

"Aw man," Deke said, pulling his hands out of his pockets to begin really making his point. "I've got such a good explanation for that."

"I can't imagine how. Last thing I remember, you said, 'Hey, can my dad tell people you think Pinely's gonna win?' And I said, 'No.' So I don't really see any reason why Tug Winthrop would be asking me if I actually think Pinely's gonna win."

"What'd you tell him?"

"I told him no, you dumb fucker!"

Deke looked instantly disheartened. "Oh," he said after a pause. "Well you're probably wondering why he thinks you think that, huh?"

Eric felt a flash of anger that prevented him from speaking right away. "Yeah, I was curious."

"Well, you remember on Monday when I showed up late at the Legion cause of that emergency at the plant? See, that ate up my whole damn day. I mean, you've never seen such a mess. Shit by the gallon in there. So I didn't get a chance to call Dad, to let him know what you'd said. And when it got to be so late in the day, and he still hadn't heard from me, he just assumed no news was good news and went ahead with the plan."

"He doesn't hear from you, so he just assumes I said yes?"

"Uh-huh."

"Why would he do that?"

"He's just a silver-lining kind of guy, I guess."

Eric was fascinated by the Williams family logic, and would have loved to spend the next few hours picking it to pieces. But he was already running late and just wanted to get this all behind him.

"Listen, Deke, I gotta go. But you need to tell your dad to stop telling people that. Because I'm not going to go along with it."

"But Eric, this is gonna make us look real bad."

"You're probably right."

Deke looked down at the ground and scraped his boot on the pavement, trying to remove something Eric couldn't even see. Eventually he stopped and stood completely still. "Fuck," he finally said, under his breath.

"I gotta get to the funeral home, Deke."

"Okay," he muttered.

Eric started walking away when he heard Deke call out to him. "Mr. Dupree, huh?"

Eric stopped, but didn't turn around. "Yeah," he said.

"That's messed up."

"Yeah."

"The showing today?"

"And tonight."

"Alright then, I'll probably see you tonight."

Eric rocked back on his heels then forward on his toes to see how cold they were getting. It felt like he'd probably need a new pair of boots before the winter came if he wanted to get through it with any degree of comfort. "Alright then," he called out to Deke and set off walking toward the funeral home.

As he passed by Blanche Rivers's place, he saw her just coming out of her beauty shop.

"Whaddya say then, Blanche?" he called out from the sidewalk.

"Oh, I'm just heading up to the home," she answered as she made her way down the concrete steps. Blanche was probably older than Eric's mother, but he wasn't really sure. She was the type of lady who wore so much makeup and had her hair frosted so far beyond recognition, there was no telling how old she actually was. By doing herself up like a middle-aged trailer tart all her life, she'd obscured all sense of age. Which may have been her plan right from the start. Eric could picture himself telling her, in all sincerity, that she hadn't aged in years even well into her eighties. If she wasn't in her eighties already. "You think we can walk there together without starting up any rumors?" she asked in her best flirtatious voice.

"Any rumors like that start up, I'm not going to deny 'em. Something like that'd be good for my reputation."

"Can't imagine what would be bad for it," she answered.

"Don't push me, young lady. I can get mean."

"What'd you have, whiskey for breakfast?"

"Cheerios."

"I think I'm safe then," she said as she stood on the sidewalk holding out the tackle box she used as her makeup kit. "Why don't you quit threatening me and try being a gentleman for a change?"

Eric reached out and took the tackle box from her, then extended his other arm like an escort. "Are you into that gentleman shit?"

"Don't know," she said, taking his arm. "No one's ever tried it before."

"Well, if it gets you all hot and bothered, you just let me know and we'll duck behind some bushes along the way."

"That's just like you to tease an old woman like that."

"I ain't teasin', Blanche. Women hit their sexual peak later in life, don't they?"

Blanche chuckled to herself. "Not this late, baby. My sexual peak was wasted on a no-good mechanic whose favorite thing about sex was the nap afterward."

Despite her inability to make herself look even remotely natural, Blanche had a true gift for livening up the dead. All the pink embalming fluid and special lighting in the world wasn't going to matter in the end without the proper touch of makeup to a corpse. While everyone understood they were looking at a dead person when they came to a funeral, no one wanted the person to actually look dead. Blanche had been making sure of that for years now. It wasn't what she'd imagined herself doing when she started her beauty parlor, but it was steady, dependable income. And since Blanche had the most popular parlor in Pinely, most of Mr. Tremble's clients had been Blanche's clients just prior. Which gave her a pretty good sense of how they liked to look.

Blanche and Eric's walk to the funeral home was filled with joviality, banter, and sexual innuendo every step of the way. A passerby might think they were on their way to catch a movie, if there was a movie house in Pinely, or off for a day of shopping, if there were any real stores. But when they came to the gate of Tremble's Funeral Home, their demeanor changed both suddenly and subtly. It was an unspoken agreement, but one that held like the letter of the law. A body in the home was deserving of its own respect. Mr. Tremble believed this implicitly. He said that while, scientifically speaking, a person's life may end with a clear abruptness and certainty, there was still a particular measure of ceremony involved in truly laying that life to rest. "Just because a person dies," Mr. Tremble would say, "doesn't mean they don't live on." He believed his work was an important first step in taking that person's life out of his or her hands and giving it to those who now needed it most.

As they walked inside, Eric noticed the air inside the funeral home was already too warm. He'd forgotten to turn the furnace down the night before. Mr. Tremble was a slight man who enjoyed the comfort of a warm room, especially during fall weather, so he would never be the one to notice. Which meant it was up to Eric to be sure the guests would be comfortable. He walked to the thermostat and dialed it down to what would be well below comfortable in any normal situation. But he had to make up for lost time.

"Good morning, Blanche," said the smiling face of Mr. Tremble as he made his way around the corner.

"Mornin', Wilson," said Blanche.

Eric always found it amusing that Blanche called Mr. Tremble by his first name. She was the only one who did, as far as he knew. Eric had been working for Mr. Tremble for years now and still couldn't bring himself to do it. But Blanche didn't think twice about it. In fact, Eric imagined if Blanche saw Mr. Tremble in a place that didn't require a certain level of deference the way the funeral home did, she might even go so far as to call him "Willie."

"I'm glad you could make it in on such short notice," Mr. Tremble said. "It just doesn't seem right to have to schedule around such a thing as a football game, does it?"

"No, it ain't right," said Blanche, "but it's smart."

Mr. Tremble just shook his head and sighed. "I guess so. There's just so much compromise in life, you'd think you'd at least be spared it in death." Mr. Tremble stood for a minute handling his handkerchief before looking over to Eric. "Feels like there's a bit of a chill in here, Eric."

"I just turned the thermostat down. To get ready for the flowers and people."

"Oh right," he nodded. "Well then, Blanche, we should get to it. There's a lot of work to be done yet and the family will be showing up in a few hours."

As Blanche and Mr. Tremble disappeared into the back room to get to work, Eric felt a sudden chill himself. He wanted to think it was just the thermostat adjustment taking effect. But he knew it had a lot more to do with Mr. Tremble's mention of the impending arrival of the Duprees.

The day of a first showing was a busy one for Eric. He had to set up the chairs and ready the guest book. There was lighting to deal with, patio furniture to clean, ashtrays to set out on the porch, and bathrooms to tidy and stock. If there was one thing that truly surprised Eric when he first started working for Mr. Tremble it was the matter of the bathrooms. Inevitably, there would be a guest—a family member, a close friend, or someone who'd let an old grievance go unreconciled just one day too long—who would be so overcome with grief, they would barricade themselves in the bathroom. The only thing more amazing to Eric than the time these people would spend in supposed private exile during an all-too-public ceremony, was the amount of toilet tissue they managed to go through. The first funeral had caught him completely off guard. The bathroom was cleared of tissue so quickly, he assumed some grief-stricken soul had the added misfortune of suffering the ravages of a gastrointestinal disorder. But by the second or third service he began to realize that the bathroom at a regional dysentery clinic wouldn't have the kind of toilet tissue demand he was experiencing.

He was loading up the Charmin under the sink when he heard his name being called from the front door. As he poked his head around the corner, he saw Ernie Gilmore standing there with his Herman's Florist hat and his clipboard in his hand. Ernie started to chuckle when he got a look at Eric.

"Holy hell," laughed Ernie.

"What?"

"Your eye."

Eric touched his brow and felt at the tender spot he'd tried to forget. "Oh yeah," he said. "Apparently I got punched."

"Yeah, no shit. I saw you," said Ernie, before lifting a brown bottle to his lips and taking a drink.

"You were there?" Eric asked.

Ernie shook his head and snickered some more. "To be honest, I'm surprised anyone got close enough to actually punch you. You were swinging your arms like a damn windmill."

Ernie took another drink from his bottle. The label was peeled completely off the glass, but there was little doubt as to what it was.

"Are you drinking a beer, Ernie?"

"It's no big deal," Ernie shrugged. "As long as all the deliveries are right, no one cares." He took another drink and belched, then suddenly poked Eric in the chest with the hand holding the bottle. "I was about to get laid."

Eric looked around to be sure Ernie wasn't suddenly talking to someone else.

"On Saturday," Ernie said. "I was well on my way to gettin' some serious pussy before you cue-balled that dipshit between the eyes."

Eric shook his head and tried to shake out any series of words that would seem appropriate. "Well I'm sorry about that, Ernie. If I'd only known I would have—"

"Don't get smart with me, Mercer!" Ernie gave him a malicious, but amused, stare that put Eric off balance. "If you're gonna be a fuck-up—like the rest of us—that's alright. But if you're gonna be a bigger fuck-up than *all* of us one night, then turn around and act all better than us the next day—" His smile grew a little more friendly before he spoke again. "Well, someone might just come along and take you down a notch."

Eric was afraid to say anything. His brain had been so well wired to dispatch smart-ass remarks, it was nearly instinctual. He never imagined it could some day bring him to within one slipup of a midmorning bludgeoning at the hands of a half-drunk florist's assistant. So, he just stood there and waited it out. Ernie finally gave him a demented smile and slapped him on the shoulder.

"I'll pull the truck around to the side and let's say we unload these flowers."

"Good idea," Eric said as he quickly closed the front door behind him.

It was a popular rumor around Pinely that Ernie Gilmore had once beaten his first cousin to within an inch of his life. He'd been found one morning on Ernie's lawn, a thin layer of dew melting the dried blood on his face, his right shinbone jutting through his corduroy pant leg, and his left eyeball tenuously uncertain as to whether it wanted to reside in or outside of its socket. Ernie was inside sleeping. He told the police he had no idea how his cousin got there. And once he came out of intensive care and could maintain consciousness for longer than ten minutes at a time, his cousin told the police the same exact thing. So with no clues, no witnesses, and no charges pressed, Ernie was left to go on with his regular life. Although he could be a fairly charming guy when he wanted to be, most people, understandably, tried to steer clear of Ernie Gilmore from that point forward.

Eric wasn't so lucky. Every death in Pinely meant an encounter with Ernie. And while he wasn't necessarily afraid of him, he did have the lingering sense that Ernie was working with live ammo. So Eric's approach was always one of respectful caution, while maintaining as much silence between them as he could manage. They were all but done bringing in the flowers, just two bouquets and a wreath away, when Ernie shattered the silence.

"Is it true you think Pinely's gonna win on Friday?"

"No," Eric said emphatically, a little surprised to find himself taking such a bold tone with Ernie. "That's not true at all."

"You sure? Cause I heard you said that."

Eric laughed a little. "Well I didn't."

"I heard you did though."

Eric looked at Ernie and slowly thought out every word in advance. "Ernie, look," he said like a man trying to talk his way out of a fight, "don't you think I'd know if I said something like that?"

Ernie stared at him. "Probably," he finally said.

"Alright—" Eric started, but Ernie wasn't done.

"But you didn't even remember I was at the bar on Saturday."

Eric tried to sort it out on his own, but figured it would be quicker to ask. "What?"

"You don't remember I was at the bar. So how do you know you didn't say Pinely's gonna win, then just forget you said it?"

"I just know."

"Yeah? *How* do you know?"

Eric was stumped. If this were a court of law, he'd be in a tough spot. Somehow Ernie had painted him as an unreliable source regarding his own activities, his own company, and now, his own opinions. It would take a series of witnesses to bring any clarity to the situation. Witnesses that would have to include Deke, who would probably tell the truth, and Deke's dad, who would probably lie. So by the end of it all, the waters would be more cloudy than they'd been in the first place.

"Look, Ernie," Eric said with a hint of pleading in his voice, "I've got a lot of work to do."

Ernie held Eric inside his standard menacing ambience before finally handing over his clipboard and tilting his head back to drink the last of his beer.

"Yeah," Ernie said after he'd finished the beer. "Me too."

Eric signed for the delivery and cautiously handed the clipboard back. "So that's it?" he asked.

Ernie threw the empty bottle into the bed of his truck, shrugged, and opened the truck door. "You want somethin' more?"

"No," Eric said quickly and with confidence.

"Well alright then," Ernie smirked before slamming the truck door closed behind him. His left arm hung out the window and down the side of the door, and Eric could see Ernie looking at him through the side mirror. "You watch yourself now, Mercer," Ernie said before starting up the truck.

Eric nodded and mumbled, "Okay," before Ernie landed two solid whacks on the truck door with his open palm and dropped it into gear.

Eric watched Ernie pull away from the funeral home. He needed to go inside and take care of some work, but more than that, he needed to let his legs stop quivering. He didn't know why Ernie got such pleasure out of terrorizing him like that. But if it brought Ernie half as much pleasure as it brought Eric discomfort, he could see how it would be hard to pass up.

The back room was stuffy from the lights and the busy, warm bodies of Blanche and Mr. Tremble working on Mr. Dupree.

"Oh hey, Eric," Blanche said when she noticed him standing in the doorway. "How does he look?"

Blanche always asked Eric's opinion on these matters. Mr. Tremble was far too polite to ever nitpick over the job Blanche did. But Eric wasn't. He thought it was a complete travesty when someone was forced to go out for their final hurrah wearing too much eye shadow, or with overly rosy cheeks. So he'd give it to her straight, assuming power of attorney for those who could no longer speak for themselves.

"Pretty good, Blanche," he answered. "Something seems a little funny. But it could just be the suit."

"That'll do it sometimes. I don't know why they don't just bury folks in the clothes they normally wear."

"I don't know," Eric shrugged. "Might be along the same lines as why people get all dressed up for church. Wanting to be presentable for the Lord, I suppose."

Blanche smiled. "I guess it is a special occasion."

Eric nodded, "A once in a lifetime event."

Mr. Tremble stood back away from Mr. Dupree's body and studied it for a few seconds before moving a bit and studying it for a few seconds more. This was his final check-off. After he'd stood in six or seven different places to check his work, he took out his handkerchief, wiped his brow, and said, "Well, I suppose we've done all we can for him now."

This was Mr. Tremble's customary line, as well as Eric's cue to help get the body into the casket. He was a bit uneasy settling Mr. Dupree into the last bed in which he'd ever lie. But it was his job. Once they got him in the box and Blanche had touched up his hair one last time, they left George Dupree to his own devices before his big day started.

Out in front of the funeral home, Blanche smoked a cigarette while Eric kept her company.

"Do you ever get nervous about that, Blanche?"

"What? Smoking?"

"No, you don't get nervous from smoking," Eric corrected her. "You get cancer."

Blanche took a long draw from her cigarette and talked the smoke out of her lungs. "We're all gonna die of something, honey. And I don't care much for surprises."

"Control freak."

"To the bitter end."

Eric watched her take another draw and tried not to let himself believe that Blanche might have some perversely ingenious plan there. "No, I meant don't you ever get nervous about giving someone their final haircut and all that?"

"Why would I be nervous about that?"

"Well what if you give them a bad one?"

"I don't give bad haircuts," she scoffed. "It's bad for business."

"Yeah," Eric said, "but what if you did? I mean, that's the last haircut that person's ever going to have, and you just screwed it up."

"No I didn't," Blanche shot back.

"Hypothetically, Blanche. We're talking about the realm of possibility here."

"No we're not," she said. "*You* are. Why would I want to think about a bad haircut I've never even given?"

"Don't you just wonder what could happen? If you did one thing differently, what that might mean?"

Blanche crushed out her cigarette on the brick of the funeral home. "Are we still talking about me here?" When she looked at Eric, he tried to casually look away at the trees across the street. "Cause if we are, I'd tell you that I don't have the kind of time and energy it takes to imagine what a haircut might look like. You know why? I'm too busy cutting the hair."

Eric had barely begun to ponder Blanche's words when he noticed Beth Dupree's car coming down the highway toward the home. He could make out two silhouettes in the car, which immediately set him on a math project involving Mr. Dupree's time of death, time zone considerations, the length, in hours, of a flight from the West Coast, and the current time on his watch. He came to the conclusion that it was entirely possible that she could have made it. That Jill Dupree could have flown back in time to be in that car at that exact moment. He was surprised at how quickly panic rushed through his entire body. Almost as quickly as it dissipated when he saw that it was Mrs. Dupree, and not Jill, riding in the car with Beth.

He watched as the car stopped in front of the funeral home and Mrs. Dupree, after a few words with Beth, stepped out of the car alone. It may have been something in her walk, or the lines in her face, but he could tell the emotion that had lain so heavily on her the day before had only intensified overnight. She walked toward him and Blanche as Beth pulled the car away from the curb and headed north into traffic.

"She's going to the airport," Mrs. Dupree said when she got close enough to be heard.

"Oh yeah?" Eric said with as much nonchalance as he could muster.

"It was tough to get a flight before this morning," she continued as she took Eric's arm and walked toward the door, "so Jill won't be here until the evening showing." When they reached the door, Mrs. Dupree stopped and looked at Eric. Her eyes shone with the tears she'd probably been fighting back and letting go of all night long. "I'm all alone this afternoon," she said.

Eric put his hand on hers and shook his head. "No," he assured her, "you're not." She squeezed his hand gently and smiled with her eyes, just enough to work loose a tear that had been trying hard not to fall. She wiped it with her hand and took a deep breath.

"I suppose we should check in on George," she said, turning back toward the door. They walked into the lobby, arm in arm, with Blanche one step behind them. Mrs. Dupree would have some time to approve the work that had been done on her husband. Blanche would see to it that everything was as perfect as it could be in such a situation. In about an hour, the public would be there to participate in the strange ritual of seeing a dead body. Then in about six hours, Jill Dupree would get to see that same dead body. And a ghost.

The afternoon went smoothly. The only real problem was with Eric. Normally collected and properly aloof while working a showing, he was having some difficulty keeping his casual cool. He felt like he was personally responsible for Mrs. Dupree, so he was doting on her during every free moment he got. Twice he went up to the coffin and made adjustments to the flower arrangements that were so minor, Mr. Tremble had to ask him what he was doing. But more than anything else, Eric was convinced it was far too warm in the home.

He would have asked Mr. Tremble what he thought, but he'd never known him to be too warm in all the years he'd worked there. He asked Mrs. Dupree, but she said she was fine and assured him she probably wouldn't need anything else for a while if he wanted to do some of his other work. Mack and Kirby both showed up, which was the first time Eric had seen them anywhere other than the Legion in years, but they both said the temperature was fine to them. Even the thermostat was on their side, claiming to be a cool but comfortable sixty-eight degrees. But

Eric didn't care what any of them said, including the scientifically calibrated thermostat. He was hot. During the last half-hour of the showing, Eric sat on the porch and tried to cool off. But even the fall breeze didn't seem to be helping. If it weren't for the matter of his age and gender he'd think he was menopausal.

When Mr. Tremble walked out onto the porch at the end of the showing, Eric was sitting with his jacket wide open, a thin film of sweat resting on his forehead.

"Aren't you cold?" Mr. Tremble asked.

Eric looked up at him incredulously. "No," he said.

"Well I hope you're not getting a fever. Go home and rest. Maybe take a nap," Mr. Tremble advised. "I'm going to give Mrs. Dupree a ride home since her girls aren't around, okay?"

"Okay," Eric answered.

"We'll see you back here tonight."

Mr. Tremble walked around the corner of the porch and disappeared out of sight. Eric heard both car doors close and the engine of Mr. Tremble's Lincoln take to life. Eric could feel his ears turning blood red as another wave of warmth rifled through him. He didn't know what was wrong, but something inside him told him how to fix it. He stood and ran over to Mr. Tremble's car trying to get his attention before he pulled out onto Route 2. The two quick raps he landed on the driver's side window made Mr. Tremble jump and slam on the brakes. As the car jerked to a stop, Mr. Tremble looked at Eric with equal parts relief and exasperation. The power window wheezed its way down and Eric channeled the spirit of Deke and tried his hardest to look absentminded.

"What is it, Eric?" Mr. Tremble asked.

"Sorry, Mr. Tremble, but I just remembered something," he said. "Did I tell you—I don't think I told you—that I couldn't get off at the Legion tonight?"

Mr. Tremble looked at him for a second before he spoke. "That's odd."

"What is?"

"I thought that Martin fellow was always ready to cover for you."

"Normally, yeah," Eric said, ignoring how the lies burned on the way out. "But tonight he just—he had something going on. Family . . . issue, maybe?"

Something passing down the road caught Mr. Tremble's eye. He watched a black Monte Carlo drive past them, its music blaring for all the world to enjoy, before looking back at Eric. "Okay, well, what can you do, right?"

"Right," Eric said solemnly, even though he felt a strange punch of enthusiasm in his stomach.

"Well, you rest up before you go to work there then. Because I'll need you good and healthy tomorrow." He looked over at Mrs. Dupree who was sitting patiently looking out the windshield. "We both will," he added before rolling up the window and easing out onto the road.

Eric stood and watched them drive off, feeling a range of things at once. Shame, relief, a little fatigue. But more than anything else, he realized he felt a little cold. He reached down, zipped up his jacket, and walked toward the south end of town.

He'd heard the phone ring while he was standing at the urinal, but he was already too committed to the task in hand. By the time he came around the corner, Martin was standing behind the bar chatting away on the phone. Eric shot him a look, to which Martin immediately responded with a shrug of his shoulders. When he hung the phone up a few seconds later, Eric was ready with his reprimand.

"Now what'd you do that for?" Eric asked.

"You were back there pissin'," Martin answered, his frustration evident in his voice. "What'd you want me to do, just let it ring?"

"Yes! Just let it ring. I'm supposed to be working here right now. Even more importantly, you're *not* supposed to be working here right now. So if the phone rings and I'm not here for some reason, have someone else answer it and tell them to tell the person on the phone that I'm in the bathroom but that I'll be right back."

Martin looked at Eric for a second, trying to let it all process. "Why aren't you at the funeral home again?"

"I've got a touch of necrophobia."

"What's that?"

"An irrational fear of dead bodies."

Martin dried a glass with his bar towel. "Whaddya take for that?"

Eric took his seat at the bar right next to the phone. "I'm not sure," he said. "Maybe just a little rest or something. Let it run its course."

"Well, good luck," Martin offered as he drifted toward the other end of the bar to get Kirby a beer.

Eric had come here right after dinner and begun his charade of "working," which basically consisted of sitting at the bar and answering the phone on the outside chance that Mr. Tremble, or anyone else, should call to check up on him. Wednesday was generally a slow night at the Legion since a lot of folks had lodge meetings or church to attend. It was pretty much just the diehards tonight, which was fine with Eric. He didn't need the excitement. He was too busy trying to figure out if there was any possible way he could get out of the funeral tomorrow afternoon. He definitely wanted to pay his final respects to Mr. Dupree, but he couldn't think of any way to do it *and* avoid seeing Jill at the same time. Other than a disguise. Which he'd entertained well beyond the point of plausibility about an hour ago.

"How come you aren't at Dupree's showing?" Mack asked as he pulled up a barstool.

"I've got my hands full here," Eric answered.

"Yeah, it looks it," Mack said dryly.

"What are you doing here tonight?"

"Escaping."

"From what?" Eric asked.

"Stupidity, apparently."

"You might have come to the wrong place."

"Wait till you see what you're up against," Mack started. "It's no big secret I've put on some pounds, right?"

At the other end of the bar, Kirby barely got started on a wisecrack before Mack cut him off with a swift, "Shut it." He didn't miss a beat before he continued, "So this afternoon I send Twilah down to the Goodwill to get rid of some stuff that don't fit so good no more. A few pairs of pants. Some shirts I don't really wear. And I tell her, while she's down there, to pick me up a couple pair of old Wranglers. One pair of 38s, one pair of 36s. Just something I can mess up and not worry about." He paused just long enough to make Eric think he'd forgotten his own story, but once he picked it back up, Eric realized it had been for dramatic effect. "Now, she comes back with *seven* pairs of jeans and about five shirts. Seven! Now what in the hell am I ever gonna need seven pairs of jeans for? Plus, now I got five more shirts I ain't never gonna wear. *And* I'm out sixty goddamn dollars!"

"Want a beer, Mack?" Martin offered from the other side of the bar.

"Wouldn't you?"

Eric had heard Mack bitch and grumble about his wife Twilah something nearing a billion times since he'd known him. He even had childhood memories of Mack complaining about her to his dad at Legion picnics and other social functions. Way back then, he thought poor Mack must be completely miserable. Now he was old enough to realize Mack had been lucky enough to find the true love of his life. Though he was still sorting out whether Mack loved Twilah, or just the bitching about her.

The door opened by the front of the bar, and Eric saw Deke walk in, dressed like he'd just been at the funeral home, which was no real surprise. What did come as a surprise was seeing Huey strolling along two steps behind him.

"Good Lord," Eric called out, "someone call Betsy and let her know her husband got loose again."

Huey smiled and tried to sound authoritative. "Betsy knows I'm here."

"See there, Mack," Eric goaded, "I always said if you hang out in here more than two minutes you're gonna hear someone tell a lie." Eric reached for the phone. "So you say Betsy knows you're here, Huey? I'll just give her a call and let her know you made it safe."

"Hold on now," Huey said, making an honest, and genuinely clumsy, reach for the phone. "She doesn't really know I'm here. But she knows I'm at the funeral home."

"Well Huey, despite the sad state many of us are in, this is still a far cry from a funeral home," Eric said.

Huey was desperate to change the subject. "What happened to your eye?" he asked.

"My old lady kicked the hell out of me for going to a bar when I said I was going to pay my respects to the dead."

"You ain't got no old lady," Huey mumbled.

"Hell no he don't," added Deke. "Last time I even seen you with a woman was . . . Hell, I don't even know. Gimmee a hint."

"Marla—" Eric started before Deke cut him off.

"Marla Spencer, that's right. The one you didn't want to date anymore because, if I remember correctly, she, and I quote, 'didn't provide much in the ways of intellectual stimulation,'" Deke laughed. "How did you ever weasel out if that was your only excuse?"

"I just told her the truth," Eric said.

"Oh yeah," Deke chortled, "and how did that go over?"

"Some people don't find honesty all that refreshing."

Deke shook his head and stared at Eric in disbelief. "Tits just aren't good enough for you, are they?" he scoffed. "No. You have to have intellectual stimulation."

"Who's Marla Spencer?" Huey asked at the mention of the word "tits."

"She lives across the river in Jasper," Deke answered. "A place you know nothing about because you haven't left your god-damned house but three times since you got married."

"Speaking of which," Eric said, "how exactly are you going to convince Betsy you were at the funeral home when you go home smelling like the Legion?"

"Whaddaya mean?" Huey asked.

"Have you not noticed the distinct smell of cigarette smoke and stale beer all around you?" Eric countered.

Huey sat there for a second, allowing his nose to work over the air. "Aw shit, Deke!" he whimpered.

"Don't worry about it, Huey," Deke said putting his arm around him. "We'll stop by a strip club on the way home to cover the smell."

Huey took hold of the beer Martin had put in front of him and took a long drink from it. It seemed if he was going to get in trouble, which he obviously was, he'd might as well enjoy it.

"How come you weren't there tonight?" Deke asked Eric.

"Oh," Eric murmured, "there was some confusion about the schedule here between me and Martin."

Deke looked at Eric, but Eric just stared at the phone that was still resting under his hand.

"You should have came," said Huey with a half-beer's worth of smile on his face. "Jill was there."

Eric felt something roar up inside him and tried to keep it to himself. "Yeah," he said, "I should have. It'd be nice to see her again. Sometime."

"So you think you're just going to be able to avoid her the whole time she's here?" Deke asked.

"I'm not avoiding her," Eric sniped back.

"No?" Deke said, before shouting down the bar. "Hey Martin, what's Eric doing here tonight?"

"Answering the phone," Martin called back.

"Well fuck me," said Deke. "I'm going to stop paying my dues here if this is the way they're gonna be used. One guy to get the drinks, another to answer the phone. That seems a little excessive, don't you think, Huey?"

"I don't know," Huey said with a shrug. "A little, I guess."

"I'm going to see her at the funeral tomorrow," Eric answered.

"Are you?"

"Well I have to, don't I? I mean, I work at the fucking funeral home."

"Well, you managed to not be there tonight. So what's to stop you from coming up with some way of avoiding tomorrow, then just laying low till she leaves."

"When is she leaving?" Eric asked, a little too eagerly.

"How the hell should I know?"

Eric was growing frustrated with his so-called friend. "Well, you seem to be a goddamned expert on everything else here tonight."

"It don't take an expert to figure you out sometimes, dickhead."

Huey looked up from his near-empty beer and pouted at his friends. "What are you guys fighting for?"

Eric shook his head and elbowed Deke in the ribs. "Dammit Deke, not in front of the boy."

The situation seemed to diffuse for a second while they all sat quietly and drank their beers. Until Huey opened his mouth again.

"Hey Eric," he said, "someone told me you said Pinely's gonna win on Friday."

"Who told you that?" Eric asked, shooting a look at Deke that could have split his skull.

"Ummm, I can't remember," said Huey. "Musta been someone at work. Or maybe Betsy told me."

"Well, hell yeah, it must have been someone at work or Betsy," chimed Deke. "Those are the only people you ever see, you fuckin' shut-in. Honestly Huey, why don't you just go out and get yourself put under house arrest and get it over with. You'll get a nice ankle bracelet to wear. You can watch all sorts of TV. It'd be Shangri-Fuckin-La, wouldn't it?"

"What do you think about that, Huey?" Eric asked.

Huey sat there looking from Eric to Deke and back again. "I don't want to be under house arrest," he finally said.

"No, not that," Eric said. "What do you think about me predicting Pinely to win on Friday?"

"Oh," Huey said, thankful his brush with incarceration was narrowly averted. "Well, to be honest, it seemed like kind of a stupid thing to say."

"Yeah, I agree," said Eric.

Deke smiled as he crossed the line, "Then why'd you say it?"

The spray of glass and beer seemed to come from all directions. People at the other end of the bar actually slid off their stools and made the first motions of heading for cover before they realized it was just Eric, who'd slammed his half-full bottle to the ground, just seconds before grabbing Deke by the throat.

"Maybe this'll stop me from saying stupid things," he snapped. "What do you think, Deke?"

Deke's face was turning an unusual shade of red, but his eyes, although bulging out a bit more than usual, seemed to remain calm. He managed to push enough air through his windpipe to whisper out a response to Eric's question. "I doubt it."

Huey looked like he was about to shit his pants and cry for his momma. But everyone else in the bar was watching with a casual interest, like they were watching it on TV. That's because, since Huey had all but disappeared since getting married right after high school, the people in the Legion all knew something he didn't. Eric wasn't dangerous right now. Because Eric wasn't drunk.

Sure enough, the storm passed just as quickly as it arrived. Eric looked suddenly and thoroughly embarrassed by the whole scene. He eased the grip on his friend's neck and sat back down on his bar stool.

"Yeah," he said to Deke, "you're probably right."

Deke sat down next to him and they both turned back to the bar as though nothing had happened. Huey, on the other hand, was still standing, looking like he'd just seen a UFO being piloted by Elvis Presley himself.

"What in tarnation was that?" Huey asked.

Eric cocked his head and gave Huey a bewildered look. "Tarnation?" he said.

Deke laughed and spun to look at Huey. "Who are you, Yosemite Sam?"

"What?" Huey said defensively. "People say that."

"Yeah, four-foot cartoon people," laughed Eric.

Huey took a cocktail napkin and started cleaning the beer off of his stool.

"Why are you bothering with that, Huey?" Deke asked. "You're already covered in beer from Dr. Jekyll's little outburst."

Somehow, in all the excitement, this fact had completely eluded Huey. He glanced down, saw spots of beer soaking into his clothes, and looked as though he might cry. "Awww daggone it, Eric. Betsy's gonna kill me for sure now."

"Relax, Huey, it'll cover the smell of the smoke."

"Shit fire," said Deke, throwing back the last of his beer and standing up. "I'd better get this poor son of a bitch home before all this excitement kills him. He's like the boy in the goddamned bubble. All that time in his safe house has left him ill-prepared for the outside world."

"Yeah, that'd probably be for the best," said Eric. "Hey Huey, if Betsy gives you any grief, just tell her Mr. Dupree was part Irish and the whole thing turned into a big drunken wake."

"Was he?" asked Huey.

"What?"

"Part Irish?"

"Maybe," shrugged Eric.

"German on his dad's side, Dutch on his mother's," said someone by the door.

The numbness that struck Eric was so sudden he thought he might have been kicked in the spine. Then he realized it was the opposite of numbness. A wash of feelings all competing for the same limited space in his body. It was as if he suddenly had to make a long speech in front of a million people. When he really only had to say two words. To one person.

"Hi Jill."

She was standing by the door, not ten feet away. Her hair was longer. Eric noticed that right away. He wanted her to smile, but that didn't seem likely. She'd gotten her ears pierced. That was different. Eric was sure he'd spoken out loud. If not, he'd meant to. But now that he was so uncertain about it, he couldn't really say "hi" to her again. If he had said it, she would have said something by now. Unless he'd lost all sense of time. There was something else different about her. Her eyes. No. Her nails had grown out. Very ladylike. It *was* her eyes. They were different. Yet the same as the last time he'd seen her. She'd been crying.

"Hi Eric," she finally said.

Huey turned around to see Jill standing there, which made Eric think either it hadn't really been that long between their salutations, or Huey was enormously slow. It was even odds on the two.

"Holy crap!" Huey said upon realizing the situation.

"What's wrong, Huey?" Jill asked.

"Yeah, what in tarnation's wrong, Huey?" added Deke with a grin.

"Nothin'," Huey said quickly, looking back and forth between Eric and Jill. "But I mean, isn't this a big deal right here?"

Eric wondered if it really could be a big deal once a ham-handed oaf like Huey had acknowledged it. But the fact that he couldn't think of one appropriate thing to say or do made him believe it must still be somewhat big, as deals go.

"Big deal?" Jill said. "I don't know. Eric, does this seem like a big deal to you?"

Eric nodded slowly and looked across the giddy smirk of Deke, the bewildered face of Huey, and the dismal, wood-paneled walls of the Legion. "Considering the budget, yeah."

The smile was brief and really only came from her eyes, but it did happen. Eric saw it. Deke must have too, because he picked up his coat and elbowed Huey near where his ribs probably were underneath his girth. "Let's go, Huey. Don't forget, you've got your own big deal waiting for you when you get home."

"Crap," Huey mumbled.

"The mouth on this guy," Deke cracked as they walked toward the door. "You can have my seat over there if you want, Jill. The only downside is it's right next to him," he said pointing to Eric.

Jill looked at Eric. "I thought you were working?"

"Yeah, I am," Eric sputtered, "you know. I'm just—" He looked at Martin who shrugged as he mixed another drink. "I'm answering the phone."

"It's a union thing," Deke offered before opening the door for Huey. "Hey Jill, I can't make it tomorrow because of work, so . . ." He trailed off as he tried to think of exactly what it was he was trying to say.

"Thanks," Jill said with a nod.

"Okay then," Deke sighed. "Well you kids have a nice time catching up on the past . . . six?"

"Yeah," Jill said.

Deke turned and looked at Eric. "Six years." He shook his head and thought it over. "Well. Pace yourselves."

As the door closed behind them, Eric watched the actual Jill Dupree, not the semblance of her he often fashioned from worn-out memories and late-night longing, walk over with what looked like every intention of sitting down next to him. He stood up and looked down at the broken glass and beer on the floor, instantly thankful for Jill's timing. If she'd shown up a few minutes earlier, she would have seen Eric in red rage with his best friend's throat in his hand. Although not an entirely inaccurate portrayal, it wasn't the first impression he'd want to make after all these years. He halfheartedly scooted the glass under the bar with his foot and looked at Jill.

"Hi," he said.

Her swollen eyes darted from his face to the floor and back again. "Hi," she finally said.

He watched her for a second before he realized it was his turn to talk. "Your hair looks nice," he said.

Her brow wrinkled and he could almost make out a tiny smile on the corners of her mouth.

"What?" he asked.

"I don't know," she said with a shake of her head. "Just seems funny."

"What does?"

"Six years," she said. "And we're gonna talk about my hair."

Eric shrugged. "Gotta start somewhere."

"I guess," she said.

They looked at each other in darting glances.

"So it's longer, right?"

"Probably," she said. Her hand went to her hair and combed through it with her fingers. "I don't remember."

"I do," he heard himself say a little more quickly than he meant to. "It's a little longer."

She nodded and looked at just about everything but Eric. "So where," she started, then reloaded. "How come you weren't there tonight?"

He leaned back on his stool and tried to think of something good. "Do you want to sit down?" he asked before noticing Martin standing right behind him at the bar. "Over there," he added.

She agreed, and they both made their way to a table far away from the jukebox.

"Don't worry, Martin," Eric called back to the bar. "I'll clean up that mess."

"Goddamned right you will," Martin grumbled with as little tact as possible.

The red vinyl chairs they sat on didn't seem on par with the import of the circumstances. This was a big deal. That much had already been confirmed. One that called for more than cheap plastic seats and air heavy with cigarette smoke and the voice of Waylon Jennings. But this room was certainly accustomed to settling old scores. Drinks and favors were paid out swiftly. Money, begrudgingly. But the worst thing you could owe someone who walked through the Legion doors was an apology.

"Mom said Dad was here the night . . . before."

It made him sad just to look at her. "Yeah, he came in for a beer."

She stared just over his shoulder at the jukebox, as though she was trying to make out the titles from where she sat. "Things seem the same here."

"Mostly," Eric answered. "Tess changes."

Her eyes shifted and met his. "She's five?"

"And a half," he added. "She'd want me to make that clear."

The tabletop was cold under his bare arms. For some reason, he remembered a picture he'd once seen in the newspaper of a mine shaft that had collapsed in the southern part of the state. People died. The whole place was turned to rubble. But the folks from the company and the guys from the United Mine Workers said they were going to rebuild the mine. Eric couldn't seem to get his mind around how they could ever do that. It seemed like an enormous task. But then he thought about it. The whole thing was such a complete disaster, at least there'd be no lack of ways to start making it better. The hardest part would probably be forgetting what you were trying to do, and just focusing on the shovel in your hand.

"I'm sorry, Jill."

It came out so quickly and easily, it was hard to understand why he hadn't been able to say it years ago. He almost didn't believe he'd said it just then. But he had. Her eyes gave it away. The tears splashed off the table as quickly as they came to her eyes, and he watched her hand streak them across the formica to try to make them disappear.

"God," she said, covering her eyes. "What's going on?"

"I don't know." He felt like he'd uncorked something he might not be able to control. "I just—I don't know at all."

"It just doesn't seem fair for it to be like this."

All this time, she'd felt the same way. After all that had happened. He couldn't believe it.

"Think of all the things we never got to do," she sobbed. "There was so much."

"But you're still doing it, Jill. That's as important as anything."

"But it wasn't supposed to be like this." She was crying so hard now that Eric wished he was one of those types of men who carried a handkerchief with him all the time. "I'm finishing law school, Eric. Law school! Me. I wasn't even supposed to go to college, and now I'm going to be a lawyer."

Was she actually thanking him right now? He apologizes, and she gives him credit for the wonderful things that are happening to her. He went weak under the awareness that he let this girl get away.

"This was supposed to be our big moment together." Her eyes were red, but this vision she was painting seemed crystal clear. "But instead I'm here, all alone. And I have to listen to one person after another tell me how sorry they are."

"What?" Eric said.

"Oh God," she said with sudden sympathy. "I know you mean it. I'm sure everyone means it. It's just that all evening, everyone's so sorry. But I'm the one—" She tried to hold back the tears, but they'd already started up again. "I'm the one without a dad."

Her dad. Of course she was talking about her dad. Any idiot would know that. But then, he'd always felt like he was a particularly special kind of idiot at times.

He scooted his chair to her side of the table and put his arm around her. Moments before, when he was the lord of his own selfish delusions, he would have been too nervous to do any such thing. But it was obvious that right now Jill wasn't his ex-girlfriend, she was George Dupree's daughter. Her face burrowed into his chest and she cried the way people do when they feel they've lost everything. Eric was used to comforting these kinds of people at the funeral home. It was a first for him at the Legion.

It was a bizarre juxtaposition to what was going on around him. People laughing, the phone ringing, drinks being served. But, in his experience, there was no good time to break down and cry your eyes out. You had to seize the moment when it came.

His instant of reflection was interrupted by the sound of Martin calling for him from the bar.

"Eric."

"What?"

"The phone's ringing."

"Well answer it."

"I thought you were doing that."

He craned his head around to look at Martin, who was standing by the phone looking directly at him. It was obvious he could see Jill crying on Eric's shoulder.

"Not anymore," Eric answered.

Martin picked up the phone, and Jill picked up her head from Eric's shoulder. She wiped her eyes and tried to smile, but her face seemed too tired to make that kind of sudden transition.

"Oh God, I'm a mess," she said.

"Aren't we all," Eric countered as he scooted away from her on instinct.

She took a deep breath that Eric could hear fighting its way through her clogged nasal passages. Her puffy eyes seemed to go blank for a moment, staring at something that clearly wasn't in the room. Then, in an instant, she was back.

"I should go home. Mom and Beth are there and—I should just go."

Eric fought back his best instincts and nodded in agreement. "Okay," he said as he stood with her and walked her to the door.

"I'm just a little mixed up, you know?" she said as she buttoned her coat. "So . . . I don't really know why I came down here tonight."

"Well I'm glad you did."

"Really?"

It was just one of those things you say, but it seemed true, and he told her as much.

"I'll see you tomorrow?" she asked.

"Yeah."

"And we'll talk about what's been keeping us busy for the past six years?"

Eric thought it over. "I've got a visual aid."

He watched her walk out the door and tried to feel good about how relatively non-disastrous the whole encounter had been. Still, he couldn't help but dwell on his "apology." It was supposed to be *something*. A coming clean. But it turned into a cliché of compassion. The most upsetting part was that he'd have to apologize all over again. Except next time, he'd to have to be much more specific.

EIGHTEEN

How many beers had he had now? Not only had he lost count, he'd lost feeling in his teeth. He was sure the two were related. He didn't care, really. It was just one of those things you wanted to know for the next day. "Man, I had at least six beers last night." If you over-exaggerated too much, sure as the sun came up, someone would call you on it. So it was best to try to keep some sort of running tab, at least within a beer or two.

Then again, he wasn't going to see any of these people ever again. What did he care what they thought? He wasn't one of them anymore. He could tell the whole lot of them he'd downed a case and a half, then swam the river to Ohio. Everyone would know he was lying. But they couldn't stop him from going away. They could talk about what a huge liar Eric Mercer was. How one night, the summer after they'd graduated high school, and right before he headed off to Brown University, he claimed to have drunk a case and a half of beer then swam clear over to Ohio. And he wouldn't have to hear one word of it.

"Dude," someone suddenly screamed in his ear, "how many beers have you had?"

He turned and saw a sweaty, shirtless Deke wobbling next to him. "A case and a half," he said without blinking an eye.

Deke devoted as much attention as he could spare without falling over entirely. "Fucking liar!" he shouted with a sick grin on his face. "If you're going to drink a case and a half, you'd better drink more. Cause you've got at least . . ." His voice trailed off as simple arithmetic joined the tasks of maintaining balance and focus. "How many beers is a case and a half?" he finally asked.

Normally, Eric would be able to help his friend with this problem. But while he wasn't certain how many beers he actually had downed, he knew it was enough for math to be completely out of the question.

"More than I've had," he said.

"See!" squealed Deke. "I told you you were a fucking liar!"

Deke danced a short jig to the fiddle of the Charlie Daniels Band playing on someone's car stereo at the other end of the field. "Fire on the mountain, run boy, run!" Deke sang along to the music. "Devil's in the house of the rising sun!"

The air was a dark, wet blanket laying across all of them. In the moments when people were putting a new tape in the stereo, or when a strange hush fell across the crowd the way it sometimes does, the sound of the creek would seep up the bank and mingle with the buzzing cicadas. And every now and again, the blanket of hot air would lift for a moment and a cool breeze would dart across the field. But for the most part, it was just hot and loud.

Chad Alexander was one of those kids who was allowed to throw parties. No one was sure if his parents were really cool, or really stupid. No one bothered to ask. The important thing was that Chad threw parties. Good ones. And this had turned out to be one of the best. His parents' camp was nice, on quite a few acres out over the ridge. There weren't any other camps around, so there was no need to worry about disturbing anyone's peace. This was a luxury that some people had been taking full advantage of all night long by screaming at the tops of their lungs anytime something remotely exciting happened. A reminder that they'd all finally graduated high school? "Yeee-ha!!" A couple of extra logs on the bonfire? "Oh yeeaaahh!" Bocephus once again confirming that he drinks whiskey by the gallon? "Fuckin' A!"

There wasn't much for any of them to do at this point in their lives. They were just in between. No more school. No more football. Nothing to do until some of them went to college and the rest started trying to find jobs. Their graduation was supposed to be a big, life-changing deal. But here they all were, a month later, still hanging out and getting drunk together.

"Hey . . . hey, seriously," Chad yelled into Eric's ear. He wasn't sure where Chad had come from, but there was no doubt he was there now. "Look at the moon. Ain't that somethin'?"

Eric looked up at the bright full moon hanging over them. Sometimes, out in the woods, you could see more stars than you'd ever imagine could fit in one sky. But not tonight. The thick air lying on top of them was almost visible. Especially when you looked at the moon. All around it, for what looked like a mile, there was an eerie ring of fog.

"You know, Mercer. I'm going to miss you," Chad slurred. "I know, I know. We never really hung out or did things together, but all the same, I knew you were a good guy. And I think we had a connection. You know what I mean?"

Eric agreed with Chad and smiled. This was the sort of smoke they'd all been blowing up each other's asses for the past six weeks. As soon as it became undeniably clear that some of them were never going to see each other again, they all became much more tolerable to one another. Apparently even a promissory note of absence can make the heart grow fonder. Eric wasn't sure if it was the fact that Chad had thrown such a good party, or if it was the less than a case and a half of beer he'd drunk, but when he agreed with Chad about their unspoken connection, he almost meant it. And as he stood there with his arm around his sweaty, drunk pseudo-friend, a part of him wondered if he might actually miss Pinely when he left.

"Chad," he said.

"Yeah?"

"I gotta go piss. You know what I mean?"

Chad agreed that he did, and staggered off to enjoy a similar heartfelt moment with another of the party revelers. Eric stumbled over toward a tree and positioned himself to, at the very least, allude to discretion, even though there was no doubt what he was up to. As he undid his pants and listened to the sounds of the party going on behind him, he felt a million miles away. In front of him, the woods offered serenity. All he had to do was turn his head a little to alter the mixture of party volume and wooded silence in his ears. That silence was broken when his urine splashed loudly on the flat leaves of the plants at his feet. It was a temporary breach, but he felt somewhat guilty he'd brought the party to this sanctuary in such a undignified way. But it had started now, and he was powerless to stop it, so he leaned against the tree to settle in for what was feeling like a long spell of relief.

Jill might be doing the same thing right now, he thought, and he smiled at the idea that they might share the connection of simultaneously peeing in the woods. She'd gone on a camping trip with her dad, just like they'd done every summer since she was eight. She looked forward to that trip like nothing else. Ten years now they'd been doing it. Eric couldn't think of any tradition he'd been a part of for that long, other than attending Pinely public schools. And now that was over too.

He'd been invited along on their trip this year. Ever since Eric had turned Mr. Dupree's average student daughter into a future college coed, Mr. Dupree was under the impression Eric could spin straw into gold. Jill seemed to want Eric to come along too, but he just didn't feel right about it. It might have even been fun, although Eric wouldn't know because he'd never actually been camping. Eric's dad's idea of the outdoor experience was having a beer on the patio. But this wasn't the time to find out what camping was like. This trip wasn't for him. It was for Jill and her dad. He wasn't about to bust up a tradition like that. He and Jill would have plenty of time together when they left Pinely.

Eric was still pissing when he heard Deke behind him. "There you are," Deke said as he ambled up beside him and unzipped his pants.

"Do you need to be that close to me?" Eric asked.

"What do you mean?"

"I mean there's goddamned woods everywhere you look out here, and you come over here and whip your pecker out right next to mine."

Deke looked down at what he had in his hands, then rolled his head to look at Eric's.

"Dude!" Eric yelled as he moved quickly to block Deke's prying eyes.

"What?"

"Aw, fuck me!"

"What?!"

"You made me piss on myself."

Deke looked over, saw a dark spot about the size of a fist on the leg of Eric's shorts. He broke into a fit of laughter, punctuated with ample pointing.

"What'd you do that for?"

"You got shit in your ears? You made me do it," Eric snapped.

"I never even touched you," Deke laughed.

"Well you came sashaying over here like you wanted to cross streams or something. It made me jittery."

Deke zipped up his pants and nearly lost his footing as he turned back toward the party. "Come on," he said. "Let's go fill 'em back up again."

"What am I gonna do about my pants?"

Deke looked at the spot on Eric's shorts with the sort of intensity he normally reserved for box scores and card games. As he stared, his head began to bob slowly. The unlikely possibility that Deke was actually coming up with a solution began to work its way into Eric's mind, despite his better instincts. The bobbing continued for a long while before Deke switched his gaze from Eric's pants to his face to deliver his hard-thought conclusion.

"Yeah, I don't know," he said with the utmost conviction.

Eric looked at his friend and decided not to even attempt a guess. "Well at least you tried."

"I did. I really did."

Deke was going to get a job with the city after the summer was over. His cousin had worked for the Pinely Water Works since he got out of high school twenty years ago and now he had a Chevy truck with a plastic bed liner and an aboveground pool in his backyard. Deke didn't dare to dream such dreams out loud, but Eric was well aware that, despite the Bible's clear command against it, Deke coveted this life his cousin had carved out for himself.

Even though it was clear Eric was going to be leaving him behind, Deke didn't seem to really care. Eric wasn't sure if that was because they'd been around each other so much Deke couldn't, in his wildest conceptions, picture a day when they wouldn't be. Or if it was because if Deke had any feelings about it at all, those feelings would remain locked in the vault where southern men keep such things safely hidden. Either way, Eric was grateful for it. Deke might have been uncertain about his feelings toward the whole thing, but Eric wasn't. He knew he was going to miss Deke. And he'd just as soon not have to talk about it.

If it was going to come up at all, it was most likely to happen on a night like this. Eric was drunk. He'd been drunk before he and Deke had their pissing excursion. But somehow another beer had found its way into in his hand. And his hand couldn't seem to stop it from going to his lips, even though his lips couldn't seem to really feel the beer anymore. His inhibitions were MIA and his judgment had lost all sense of duty, which meant that, if he didn't keep a careful eye on things, he might start talking about his feelings. Which he desperately wanted to avoid.

The rumble up the road was rubber tires on gravel. As the headlights jostled toward the camp there was the occasional pop of a stone being squeezed under a tire and launching into the night. Eric could see two sets of headlights, but wasn't sure if that meant one or two vehicles. He closed one eye and looked again. Still two sets of headlights. That meant he wasn't seeing double, which he knew was good. But he had to close one eye to be sure, which he knew was bad.

The vehicle in front was a pickup that belonged to Danny Moran. He was four years older than Eric so they never went to school together, but they still knew each other. Mainly on account of the fact that Danny would find his way to a high school party any time he was in visiting from Wilton State College, which was almost every weekend. Anyone who'd ever talked to Danny was painfully aware that during his senior year the Pinely Wildcats came within one game of going to the state playoffs. And the more you saw Danny, the more you learned about his illustrious football career. It was extraneous information since everyone had watched him play. That was all there was to do on a Friday night in Pinely. But he was generally forgiven his lack of conversational topics because he always brought beer.

This time he'd brought beer and other people. It was alumni weekend in Pinely, which meant a lot more people were in town part-timing at Danny's full-time habit, reliving the glory of their high school days. Undoubtedly, Danny had stumbled across a few of his old buddies and decided to lead them out to Chad's party. Eric didn't have a problem with that really, as long as they brought their own beer. He was about to turn and go find someplace else to stagger around drunk for a while when he noticed something about the person in the front seat of Danny's truck. He'd realized it was a girl right from the start, but it wasn't until she'd gotten out of the truck and into the light of the bonfire that he realized who it was. Ginastevens.

She and Danny had dated for a while when they were in high school together. Eric remembered the one time in his life he wished he were Danny Moran. Danny's senior year was the first time in years anyone had given Pinely a chance to beat Cedarsville. Of course, they still managed to lose. Eric remembered Danny standing outside the locker room, his face gray with disappointment, his hair wet from the shower. He looked inconsolable. That's when Gina pulled up in her car. Eric watched Danny mope over and get in, then he saw the most amazing thing. Gina put her right hand on the back of Danny's head, gently pulled him over toward her, and kissed him. She didn't care that they'd lost. She just kissed him, then drove off through the gate. Eric thought it would have been the perfect ending to a movie—if it were him sitting in Ginastevens's car.

"Holy shit," Deke said from right behind him. Eric was surprised to find himself caught off guard by Deke once again. Alcohol brings out different things in different people. Some become singers. Some become criers. Some become dispensers of timeless truths and ancient wisdom. Deke apparently became a ninja. "What's Gina Stevens doin' here?"

"I don't know. Danny brought her."

Deke looked like he'd just swallowed a urinal cake. "What's Danny doin' here?"

"Maybe he was afraid we'd all forget they almost went to state his senior year."

"Maybe," Deke said, before throwing back his head to empty the rest of his beer. "I'm going for another. You need one?"

It struck Eric as an interesting choice of words. He was sure he didn't *need* one. But he knew he was going to get one just the same. He cast one last glance over toward Danny's truck, but Gina was already gone. It was a small party, so he was sure he'd get a chance to stare at her more later. Plus he was getting drunk enough that staring wouldn't make him the least bit uncomfortable. Even though it might be another story for her.

Deke was forging ahead without him in search of more beer. Folks had their beer stored in coolers all around the campsite, but the more they drank, the more likely they were to forget where they'd put their stash. This led to people drinking the closest beer they could find. Someone had drunk all of Deke and Eric's a while ago, so they were forced to swindle, steal, or sweet-talk their way into someone else's cooler every time they needed another. Deke had a real nose for finding the best spot to get more beer. No matter how drunk he was, he could remember which cooler belonged to which person. So he kept himself and Eric out of the coolers of people who turned into fighters when they drank, and got them into the ones that belonged to the sloppily docile.

Jeremy Withers was standing next to the fire, staring pie-faced at the moon. Deke moved subtly, but deliberately in his direction, with Eric a few stumbly paces behind. Jeremy was, by most measures, a complete simpleton. He'd graduated with them, but it was clear he'd done so without the benefit of actually receiving an education. He was no smarter in his cap and gown than he'd been in his jeans and t-shirt the day he walked into Pinely High six years earlier. He seemed like the perfect candidate to drop out. Yet he didn't. He stuck it through until the very end when the faculty and staff realized the only way they were going to be rid of him was to process him through, into the real world and out of theirs. About the only thing he excelled at was attendance, a skill that had now been rendered useless.

"Hey Jeremy," Deke said with an almost demented smile.

Jeremy turned his face away from the moon toward the two of them. "Deke," was all he said.

Deke wasn't about to let the oddity of Jeremy Withers sway him from his task. "Good party, huh?"

"Yeah," he said and looked back toward the moon. Deke wasn't sure what Jeremy was looking at, so he looked up toward the moon too. Eric didn't want to be left out, so for the next few minutes they all three stood there, not saying a word, staring up at the bright full moon and the misty ring encircling it. "So what are you going to do now, Deke?" Jeremy suddenly asked, without looking away from the sky.

"What do you mean?"

"I mean, since we don't have to go to school anymore."

"Well. I'm gonna get a job," Deke said. "Maybe work for the city."

Jeremy nodded his head thoughtfully, then looked at Eric. "What about you?" he asked.

"I'm going to Brown."

"What's that?"

"A college."

"Huh," Jeremy grunted before turning to look at the moon again. Deke and Eric exchanged a series of confused looks before Deke finally decided to cut to the chase.

"Say, Jeremy, you think we might be able to have a couple of your beers?" he asked.

"Help yourself," Jeremy answered.

Deke thanked him and quickly reached into the cooler. He grabbed two beers, looked at Jeremy who was still looking at the sky like it was his job, then grabbed two more. He and Eric then scurried off toward the cabin to get some distance between them and the fire.

"Why'd you get four?" Eric asked.

"Well I figured we might want them, and I'll be damned if I'm gonna go through that again," Deke said. "What the fuck's wrong with that guy?"

"He's probably just drunk."

"Well so am I, but you don't see me staring at the sky like I'm waiting for the mother ship, do you? Jesus!"

Deke rocked his head back and forth in disbelief as he dug around in his pocket for something. Eric had found the exchange with Jeremy to be a bit odd, but it didn't get to him the way it apparently had Deke. When Deke's hand finally sprung loose from his pocket, it was holding his car keys. He took one of the cans of beer, turned it over, jabbed the key through the bottom of it, and handed it to Eric.

"What are you doing?" Eric asked.

"We're gonna shotgun these so we don't lose 'em," Deke said, piercing the bottom of another can.

"So we don't lose them?"

"Well if we go walking around with two beers each, we might put one down and forget where it was, or someone might come bum a beer off of us. This way, we drink one right now, then drink the other one while we walk around and stuff."

His logic fully explained to his satisfaction, Deke tilted his head back, placed his mouth over the hole he'd punched in the bottom of the can, and popped opened the top of the beer. Eric watched as Deke's Adam's apple jumped three times in rapid succession. "Holy shit," Deke said as he pulled the empty can away from his face and smiled a wobbly smile at his friend. "Your—" he said before a giant belch ripped out of his mouth in place of words. "Your turn."

Eric mimicked Deke's routine and felt a rush of beer rocket down his throat. The last bits spilled over the corners of his mouth and into his ears as he struggled to keep up. When he lurched his head forward, he immediately felt three times drunker than he'd been before, and struggled to stay on his feet.

"How do you feel?" asked Deke.

"Holy shit," Eric said.

"Yep, that's about right. C'mon, let's open these ones and go find something to get into."

Eric steadied himself against the cabin for a second and let out a series of small, but sturdy belches. "Boy Deke, I'm pretty messed up now."

"You're not going to puke are you?"

Eric hadn't even thought of that. He stood still for a moment and tried to get some sense of what might be going on inside him. The problem was, he felt so numb, he would have had just as much luck trying to figure out what was going on inside of Deke. "I don't think so," he finally guessed.

"Okay. Let's go then."

"Where?"

Deke looked around intently, but couldn't come up with anything. "Inside?" he offered.

"I don't think so," said Eric. He was growing more and more certain that he wasn't going to throw up, but if he did, he wanted to be outside.

"How about over there by the creek?" Deke pointed. "There's some people hanging out there."

Eric could just make out some shadows in the distance and decided to take Deke's word for it that they were people. He nodded his head and they both made off for that direction. Eric knew he was stumbling, but he couldn't seem to do anything about it. The dampness of the grass was working its way through his shoes with every step. He looked down to watch his feet kick through the tall weeds, and his mind drifted off, lulled into a trance by the rhythm of his own footsteps. His shoes got darker as the moisture clung to them, and he began to wonder what sort of tiny insect worlds he was stomping through so carelessly. He'd just begun to feel like a terrible monster for all the destruction he'd so obviously perpetrated on the defenseless inhabitants of the grass, when someone grabbed him by the arm and pulled him backward.

"Where the fuck were you going?" asked Danny Moran.

Eric swung his head to look at him, but had to squint his eyes to focus. "We're going over there by the creek to where those people are," he said. He pointed to show Danny what he was talking about, but all he saw in front of him was a six-foot drop-off and a gurgling creek below.

"Is anyone responsible for this sad sight?" Danny asked the crowd standing around him.

Deke came rambling over, knocking into people along the way and trying not to laugh. "There you are, young man," he said. "I have been worried sick about you."

"I almost fell into the creek, Deke," Eric said, then laughed out loud. "Creek Deke," he repeated. "That rhymes."

Deke laughed right along with him while Danny just watched and shook his head. "Well aren't you two a sight? Mr. Touchdown and his little buddy Deke, drunker'n all hell."

"Well, it's a party!" Deke answered, a little too loudly.

"And you two are just a couple of party animals, aren't you?" Danny said condescendingly.

"No wait. No. I'm the animal," said Eric. "Not him. Me. Cause here's the thing. I just killed a whole bunch of things on my way over here."

"What are you talking about," laughed Deke.

"It's not funny, Deke. There are, in the grass, there are things . . . that live there and I killed them because I couldn't pick up my feet. I'm too drunk, and I couldn't pick up my feet. And because of that, they're all dead!"

Eric said the word "dead" with enough volume and conviction to make everyone around them turn and look. Eric didn't seem to notice, but Deke did.

"Nothing. It's fine," he said, like a cop at the scene of a crime. "Nothing's dead. Brain cells, maybe."

Danny apparently decided that giving them a hard time wasn't going to be as fun as he originally thought and drifted off toward a few of the other people. Deke shoved Eric and laughed when he almost fell. The two of them stood there, laughing and drinking their beers until they heard a voice behind them.

"Hey Eric."

They both turned and saw Gina Stevens standing there, smiling. Eric concentrated on not sounding drunk before piecing together the words, "Hi Gina."

"Whoa," Deke said from just over Eric's shoulder.

Gina glanced at Deke, but kept her focus on Eric. "What happened to your shorts?" she asked.

Eric looked down at the dark spot on his shorts from his urination mishap and focused on trying not to tell the truth. "I spilled some beer on them," he said, still staring at the spot.

"Nice," said Deke.

Gina gave Deke an even stranger look this time. "What's wrong with him?" she asked Eric.

"He's drunk," Deke answered for himself.

"He is," Eric agreed.

"How about you? Are you drunk?" she asked.

Eric looked up at her face and noticed something strange about it. He'd only spoken to Ginastevens a few times before, and it was always in passing. She was older than him. She had a job. She hung out in different social circles. So he never felt like he'd had much to say. Certainly nothing she'd be interested in hearing about. But when he looked at her face at that particular moment, it looked as though she was very interested in listening to what he might have to say. As a matter of fact, it looked like she might be interested in more than that.

"Oh, I'm a little drunk," Eric lied.

"Me too," she said.

"Me too," said Deke, just to confirm the point.

Gina looked at Deke like he was an annoying little brother. "What's your name again?" she asked.

"Deacon 'Creek Deke' Williams," he said before busting into a chuckle.

Eric tried not to laugh, but he couldn't help it. He quickly regained his composure and smiled at Gina. "It rhymes," he said.

Gina smiled back, but looked a little confused "Okay," she said. "So I hear you're going to some big university this fall."

"Brown," he said. "It's in Rhode Island."

"That's far, huh?"

"From here, yeah."

They both stood there and looked at each other, with Deke looking at the both of them. Eric wasn't at all sure what was going on, but he didn't think being drunk had anything to do with that. He didn't know if he was supposed to keep looking at her, or do something else. He couldn't think of anything else to do offhand, so he just stuck with the staring. It was Deke who finally snapped them out of their bizarre three-way stare fight.

"Hey Gina, you want a beer?" he asked.

She looked away from Eric and over to Deke. "Sure," she said.

Deke took the leg of his shorts, wiped off the mouth of the beer he'd been drinking, and offered it to her. "I only took a couple of sips."

Gina stared hard at the beer, then shook her head in protest. "No, that's okay," she said. "I don't want to take your only beer."

"It's okay," he smiled. "I can get another one."

"He's got a real knack for it," Eric said.

Gina looked at the two of them, then hesitantly took the beer from Deke's extended hand. "Well," she said with uncertainty, "thanks."

"No problem," said Deke. "I'll catch up with you guys in a little while. I gotta piss like a ten-peckered dragon. And find me another beer."

Deke ambled off into the night, tripping over nothing in particular, then looking back to see what it might have been. He saw Eric watching him and laughed as he pointed to the ground at the spot where the nothing was. With Deke gone, Eric was even less sure what he was supposed to do. He had his beer at least. He was thankful for that.

"So, Ginastevens," he sighed.

She looked at him and waited for more. When he stood there taking another sip from his beer, she realized she might be waiting in vain. "So what?" she finally said.

"So," he said while he tried to think of something. "How's that job? That insurance thing you do?"

Gina took a drink from her beer, then looked over her shoulder as though she was about to litter, or rob a bank, or tell a secret. "You want to go for a walk?" she said when she turned back to Eric.

Eric thought about it for a second. A walk might be nice. Walking is healthy. There was nothing else to do. He knew he couldn't walk as well as he normally could, but he could surely manage to walk for a little while without hurting himself or someone else. "Okay," he said. "Where do you want to walk to?"

"I don't know. Let's just head over there, away from the house."

As they walked away, Eric turned and saw Deke standing by the bonfire again, staring up at the moon with Jeremy Withers, neither of them talking. His feet got tangled up from not watching where he was going and he stumbled into Gina a little bit.

"Sorry," he said quickly.

"It's okay. It's dark over here, huh?"

"The moon's pretty bright though. I mean, I can really see you."

She smiled, and the moonlight made her look like a goddess. Or a ghost. Eric couldn't tell which.

"It's too bad you're going so far away, Eric."

"What do you mean?" he asked. He was already tired of walking, even though they'd just started. It was taking way too much effort, and he wasn't certain, but he thought he might just want to pass out and get it over with.

"I mean to college. Rhode Island is really far."

Eric was confused. "What do you care?" he asked, only because he couldn't think of a nicer way to say it.

She stopped walking and looked at him. "I care. I never really got a chance to know you."

Eric smiled. "You mean, in the biblical sense?" he asked, feeling awfully clever in his drunken state.

"What's that mean?"

"Oh, that's how they used to say it in the old days."

"Say what?"

"When they . . . had sex. That was the way—like if I had sex with you, I would say, 'I have known you.'"

"Really?"

"Yep."

Gina giggled and sat down on the grass. "You're pretty smart, huh?"

Eric was so glad she'd decided to sit down, he quickly laid down and watched the moon swirl above him. "Sometimes," he answered. He watched the moon and wondered if he was too far away from the rest of the party to go ahead and pass out. It would be an awfully nasty morning if he slept out there in the tall grass all night. And there was no way Gina could carry him back to the cabin by herself. But she could go for help, and maybe that was good enough.

As he was considering the logistics of passing out, he could hear the grass rustling. At first he thought he might have developed superhuman hearing, but then he remembered his head was essentially buried in the grass, so it wasn't that abnormal that he'd be able to hear something rustling in it. He didn't have to wonder long about what it was. Gina's face soon blocked out the sky as she looked down at him.

"Eric?" she said, very quietly.

"Yeah," he answered.

Her face came down even closer, then passed completely out of his line of sight. Her breath on his ear quickly disclosed her location. "I'd like to know you," she whispered.

Eric barely had time to consider if she meant the regular way of knowing someone or the biblical way. When he felt her mouth on his it became clear. He didn't know what to do, so he kissed her back. That's what you do in situations like these, he thought to himself. Before he knew it, he was tangled up with her in a way that was certain to lead to some good old-fashioned knowledge of one another.

The back of his mind was becoming just as relevant as the front, or vice versa, and it couldn't help thinking about the *Playboy* magazine he'd had in his closet for the past six years. That was the Ginastevens fantasy. It was curious how this rapidly developing reality might match up. Soon the summer air was on his chest, and hers. Everything moved so quickly, it seemed like he couldn't do anything about it. And everything moved so slowly, it seemed like it wasn't even him. The warmth that suddenly surrounded him pulled things back to regular speed. He was having sex. With Ginastevens. He knew there was something wrong with that, but he couldn't think what. He didn't have to wonder long, because just as soon as it started, it was over. He felt himself let go and his mind suddenly opened. As he remembered, his face went from flush to pale.

"Are you okay?" Gina asked, kissing him on the forehead. "Why'd you stop?"

"Oh Jill," was all he could think to say.

THURSDAY

Jill was crying. Eric could tell she was trying to be stoic about the whole thing, but it was an awful lot to deal with. She probably still had jet lag. Now, at an hour when she'd probably still be in bed back home, she was getting ready to bury her father.

Of course he wanted to talk to her, try to comfort her in some way, but he had a job to do. For the next few hours he wasn't Eric, former lover of the deceased's daughter. He was Eric, dutiful employee of Tremble's Funeral Home. His obligations weren't overwhelming in number, but each thing he did carried a meas-ure of importance. This was it, the big show. Stick the landing, big smiles, a graceful bow, and make your exit. That was how he normally considered a funeral. Today was different. He was try-ing as hard as he could to make it feel like any other service. But it wasn't.

The morning rituals hadn't given him much trouble. Other than a slight hangover he'd managed to earn himself after Jill left the Legion the night before, there was nothing to slow him down. In fact, he found if he worked diligently enough and focused on the work at hand, he could almost forget whom the service was for. Almost. Still, it seemed no matter which task he fixed himself on, there was some reminder. He set up the chairs for the attendees with no problem. It was when he marked off the front seats for the family that he felt something soften behind his sternum. He arranged the flowers at the front of the room, choosing in advance which ones would be taken along to the cemetery. It was the wreath that spelled out "Dad" in orange blossoms that sent a sudden rush to the back of his eyes. On and on like this he worked, keeping his perspective by denying himself any connection. It was hard enough when he was there alone. Now she was there, crying all by herself.

He knew she wouldn't want to be so emotional in front of all the people. Or he used to know she wouldn't want that. He wasn't sure if she didn't mind such things anymore. Just like he wasn't sure if he could comfort her like he used to. But most of all, he wasn't sure if he'd be able to keep it together himself if he got too close to her in any way. It would be a pity if people saw her crying when they showed up. But it would be a disaster if they saw him.

So he left her alone. Her mom was around somewhere. And her sister. That would have to be their job right now. He had several of his own. The registry at the front was in need of a new pen. Someone had left the cap off overnight, allowing the soft tip to dry up completely. Eric always tried to keep a spare at the table, but since he'd skipped out on his obligations the night before, small details like that were missed. He preferred the felt tip for occasions such as this. It flowed. It seemed almost calligraphic when taken in hand. And it didn't press ruts into the next page the way a ballpoint could. He was rifling through the bottom drawer of Mr. Tremble's desk, where he kept a healthy supply of the perfect funeral pens, when he heard Tess's voice behind him.

"Hi Daddy."

"Hey baby," he said as he turned around. "Don't you look nice today."

She was standing there, wearing one of her favorite funeral dresses. She had three. One was a rich, almost regal shade of purple that made her seem like a wise woman trapped in a tiny body. Another was navy blue with oversized buttons on the front and a prominent, but tasteful, bow on the back. The one she wore today was black. She almost never wore that one. He wondered why she chose it today.

Eric's mother, whom Tess had guided to the office upon her delivery to the funeral home, was also wearing black. "You look nice too, Eric. Don't you think so, Tess?"

Tess nodded her head. "Who's the man in the box?" she asked.

"His name is George Dupree," answered Eric.

"George Dupree," Tess repeated to make it stick. She thought it over for a second or two, then said, "Okay."

"Okay. Well Daddy has a lot of work to take care of, so—"

"I know, Daddy. I'll be good."

"Okay then," he said getting down on one knee. "I'll see you out there."

Tess waddled over into his arms, gave him a quick hug, then turned and walked through the office door toward the funeral parlor. Eric stood up as he watched her go, then turned his focus back to the pens.

"You know, your dad doesn't think that's normal at all," said Eric's mom.

"Doesn't think what's normal?" he asked.

"The way Tess likes to come to all the funerals."

Hearing what his father considered abnormal in the field of parenting was fascinating to Eric. This was a man who would drag his ten-year-old boy along to the all-day dirt track races in

Pennsboro with a cooler full of beer and two sodas. And when Eric inevitably drank both of his sodas and was, by some aberration of modern science, thirsty again a few hours later, his dad would simply tell him to have a beer. This was normal, according to his dad. But a little girl enjoying a ceremony where there are lots of flowers, and music, and people dressed in nice clothes was abnormal to him.

"Bob and Rita Crane come to every funeral in town whether they know the people or not," Eric said by way of an argument.

"Your dad doesn't think Bob and Rita Crane are normal either."

"Yeah, well a lot of people don't think *he's* normal, you know."

"Like who? No one's ever said that to me."

"Of course they haven't. You married him. They probably have their doubts about you too."

Eric could tell his mom was getting flustered with him, which he normally enjoyed. But he didn't have the time to revel in it the way he'd like, so he just went back to looking for his pens. He finally found the box in the back, hidden behind a pack of chewing tobacco that Mr. Tremble had obviously tried to stash away from all public, and private, knowledge. Eric thought it was cute that Mr. Tremble might actually think he could hide his habit when he spit into the very bushes Eric trimmed all summer long.

"So how are you today?" Eric's mom asked.

"Pretty good. You know," he answered as he tested out a pen on a scrap of paper from the garbage.

"Deirdre Martin said you weren't here last night."

"What was Deirdre Martin doing here?" he asked. He picked up the pack of tobacco and began marking on it with his new-found pen.

"She wasn't. Lilly Carson was here because she's a secretary out at Carbide where Beth's husband works. Anyway, Lilly saw

Deirdre when she was walking home last night, and Deirdre told me when I bumped into her at the flower shop."

"I swear to Christ, this town should just get surveillance cameras and get it over with."

"Eric," she protested.

"Seriously. It's more intricate than Big Brother, the system around here. It would make George Orwell's head spin."

He knew she was performing one of her patented combinations of eye rolling and head shaking at that moment, but he didn't look. He was too busy admiring his tobacco graffiti. Where the warning label had once cautioned of the likelihood of cancerous growths and certain doom, it now read: "Warning: May cause prosthetic lips."

"Well?" his mom asked.

Eric was genuinely confused by this. "Well what?" he asked right back.

"Well why weren't you here last night?"

"You may not be aware of this, Mom, but I already have a boss here."

"What are you trying to say?"

"I'm trying to say mind your own business. Politely."

She wrinkled her brow and tried not to look hurt. "Well, you failed at that."

"Yeah," he sighed. "Well, add it to the list."

Her eyes went soft. She attempted a smile that came off as a sad smirk, then turned toward the door. "You're not—" she started, then let out a sigh. "That's no way to talk about yourself."

He closed the drawer with his foot and looked her over, amazed at how quickly she could be hurt. "I'm sorry. There's just too much going on right now, Mom," he said. "That's all."

"I know," she said, in a way that almost sounded believable.

His arm settled on her shoulder as he guided her toward the door. "Alright," he said, turning off the lights behind him. "Then let's get out there and have ourselves a funeral."

The parlor was filling up quickly and he was sure quite a few people had missed signing the registry because of the pen. He got the new pens to the table just as another wave of people rolled in. Eric was surprised at the attendance. George Dupree was a nice man, but he never seemed like a pillar of the community. He was just a friendly guy who would help you build a fence or fix your toilet. By the turnout, he must have extended those small courtesies to everyone in town.

"So what's the deal, Eric?"

He hardly recognized Coach Gleason without his whistle and shorts.

"It's a funeral, Coach," he answered. "A series of rites and customs to honor the dead."

Gleason glared at him and fought back an urge to demand he run laps right then and there. "I mean about the game, smart-ass. You've got the whole town all confused."

"Wait a minute, I'm not taking the fall for this town getting confused about things."

Coach Gleason grabbed him by the sleeve and led him over to a corner. "Look, I hear from one guy you think we're going to win tomorrow. Then I turn around and hear from someone else that you specifically said we're going to lose."

"Who told you that?" asked Eric in exasperation.

"Tug What's-his-name—if that even is his name—over at that hippie food store. I just needed some milk," he quickly added to explain what a regular guy like him could possibly be doing in a health food store.

"What exactly did Tug say?" Eric asked.

"He said you were in there the other day and you wanted him to specifically tell people you didn't think Pinely was going to win on Friday."

In retrospect, Eric suddenly thought, he shouldn't have told Tug to tell anyone anything. This was a guy who could barely keep your sandwich order straight ten seconds after you dictated it to him. He should have known he would have screwed up something as nuanced as what Eric did or did not say about Pinely's chances against Cedarsville.

"Look, Coach, I didn't say either of those things, actually. It's all just a big misunderstanding."

"Well let there be no misunderstanding about this," Coach started. Gleason was always good at twisting *your* words around to make *his* point, and suddenly Eric felt like he was standing behind the bleachers on a hot August day in full pads, about to bear the brunt of the twisted logic of a high school football coach. "A lot of people are hearing this stuff, and a lot of people are believing it. Including the kids on the team. So you can either have everyone in town running around thinking you said two things at once, or you can straighten it out yourself."

Eric looked at him for a second, expecting there to be more. "That's it?" he finally asked.

"Yep."

"Okay," Eric said and started walking away.

"Wait a minute," Coach said, "What are you going to do?"

"I'm not going to do anything," Eric answered.

"Are you serious?"

"Look," Eric said with a weary sigh, "Deke got me into this mess. I tried to straighten it out, but foolishly involved Tug, and managed to make it even worse. Now you want me to fix it again.

But see, I'm starting to notice a pattern. This is like trying to wipe off napalm. I'm just spreading it around. So now I'm just going to control the burn."

"Well that's not very responsible," Coach said with disappointment in his eyes.

Eric felt a tug on his jacket and noticed Tess looking up at him. "I've got enough responsibilities today, Coach." He looked down at his little girl and winked. "What is it, honey?"

"Mr. Tremble told me to tell you he's almost ready to get started," she whispered loudly.

"Okay, you go in there and wait for me in our usual spot."

He watched his little girl scamper off, then noticed Coach Gleason was still standing near him. "The service is about to start, if you're staying," he said to Coach.

"Of course I'm staying," Coach huffed. "I'm here for George Dupree. I just figured I'd take care of this when I saw you."

Eric loved that Coach Gleason thought he'd taken care of anything. "What do you know of Mr. Dupree?"

"He was always a big supporter of the boosters. Even after his kids graduated."

The athletic boosters was practically a religion to Coach Gleason, so it made sense he'd come to pay tribute when one of his flock had fallen.

"Okay well, have a seat then."

"Right. But we'll talk about this later."

"I hope not," Eric said and walked out the front door to gather up the folks enjoying one last smoke on the porch.

Once the service started Eric started to notice a change. He normally watched these things with a strange detachment, he and Tess standing in the back looking at the flowers and listening to the music. He'd heard the same Bible verses so many times, they'd lost all meaning. He'd heard and sung the same funeral hymns, they were like pop songs on the radio. But on this day, he couldn't seem to distance himself from what was happening right there in front of him. Instead of preoccupying himself with indifferent thoughts about the details of the service, he found himself actually listening to the preacher as he spoke at the lectern. Eric recognized the opening verse as a Psalm. One he'd heard before, but was somehow hearing for the first time. It said someone was "like a tree planted by streams of water, which yields its fruit in season and whose leaf does not wither." Out the window, the trees were ablaze with the colors of fall. One last gasp of life before the long, hard winter ahead. The preacher could have been using the verse to talk about Jesus or God or the Holy Spirit, but at that moment Eric really hoped he was talking about George Dupree.

All around the room, Eric saw familiar faces playing new roles. A funeral in Pinely was always a community event, with folks putting down their normal, day-to-day preoccupations and taking up occupations of a different kind. Bessie, the organist, was in a quilting circle with Beth's husband's mother. Beth's husband himself was a pallbearer, along with his two brothers and his dad. The other two pallbearers were Kip Sullivan and Gary Morris, both members of George Dupree's Thursday night bowling league. Burt Higgins, who ran the seed and feed shop in town, had volunteered to drive the flowers out to the cemetery in his pickup because George Dupree had taken his son to the hospital one summer when the boy fell out of a tree right in front of his car. The only one who didn't really seem to have a direct connection to the whole thing was the preacher. The Duprees weren't faithful churchgoers, so Reverend Thomas had been brought in simply because if they ever did go to church, for the occasional Christmas Eve or Easter service, it was at the Methodist church over which he presided. But even though he wasn't a faithful attendee of the church, George Dupree was known to talk to God. So at the very least, he and Reverend Thomas had a friend in common.

After the Bible verse and a little talk about the afterlife, the preacher moved on to the topic of what a good man George Dupree had been. Eric didn't know if it was the use of past tense, or the fact that Reverend Thomas probably couldn't have picked Mr. Dupree out of a police lineup when he was alive, but something about these words struck Eric as unusually sad. Was this the best any of them could offer a man like George Dupree? This tiny room. These canned sentiments. These words from the dog-eared pages of a worn-out Bible. He thought he'd done everything he could to have a good service, but suddenly he realized he'd done the bare minimum. The exact same thing he'd done for everyone else. Nothing more. And suddenly, for the first time while working a service at Tremble's Funeral Home, he began to cry.

It was subtle. It was controlled. But there was no doubt that he was crying. He was thankful everyone was facing the other direction so he wouldn't be seen. In fact, if he hadn't had to pull his hand free from hers to wipe away a few of the more assertive tears, even Tess wouldn't have noticed.

When Tess first started asking about what he did for a living, Eric was hesitant to go into much detail. But she kept pressing until he relented and brought her along to a funeral. It seemed strange to have a child at a funeral for a person she didn't even know, but by the end, Eric decided it was a great idea. Tess wasn't at all traumatized by the experience. She did have a lot of questions, but she seemed fully satisfied by the matter-of-fact answers he gave her. Eric thought he might be onto something. A public service of sorts. Don't let the first dead person your child sees be someone they know. Let it be a complete stranger. That way, the kid learns about death long before it's something that's taken away their grandma, or cousin, or dog. After that first funeral, Tess became as regular an attendee as Bob and Rita Crane. She would stand and enjoy the service, sing along to the hymns, and even offer a solemn "I'm sorry for your loss" to the grieving families.

She normally stood still as a statue during the prayer. She knew to do that from going to church with her mother. But as Reverend Thomas launched into the prayer, Eric noticed Tess wasn't bowing her head. She wasn't even standing still. She was turning back and forth at the waist with her arms extended outward. He only noticed because she'd struck him in the hip during one of her turns. He made two quick wipes across his face to be sure there were no tears before grabbing her by the arm. She looked up. He gave her one of his "stop it" looks, but she quickly looked off and took a step away from him. When Reverend Thomas finished up with the customary signal for audience participation, "We ask all of this in the name of the Father, and of the Son, and of the Holy Spirit," Tess topped it off with an exaggerated "Amen" that actually turned a few heads in the back rows.

This was enough to quickly flip Eric's emotional coin from sadness to frustration. He didn't know why she was behaving like this, and he didn't have the time or space to find out why. She wouldn't even look up at him. It was the sound of the organ launching into a wildly upbeat intro that turned his focus back to the service. The last he'd heard, the funeral hymn Mrs. Dupree had chosen was "What a Friend We Have in Jesus." A solemn, steadfast hymn with a proven track record. This was something else entirely. It was energetic, bouncy, and in direct conflict with what he regularly associated with a funeral service. As the voices began singing, Eric could hear Jill's voice above all the others:

> *There are loved ones in the glory,*
> *Whose dear forms you often miss;*
> *When you close your earthly story,*
> *Will you join them in their bliss?*
> *Will the circle be unbroken*
> *By and by, Lord, by and by?*
> *There's a better home awaiting*
> *In the sky, Lord, in the sky.*

This was unprecedented. People were suddenly swaying to and fro to the rhythm of the music. Some started clapping their hands. Even ol' Bessie was bobbing along behind the organ like she was sitting in with Booker T. & the M.G.s. Eric could barely get his brain around it. If he'd known the words, he would have sung along. But he didn't. So he was left with nothing to do but exchange confused looks with Tess, whose once vast knowledge of the ins and outs of funeral services was now being dwarfed before her young eyes. This wasn't a funeral, this was a party. And she looked fully ready to bust open a piñata if called upon to do so.

The music and jubilation carried on for several more verses than Eric ever would have guessed. It got to the point where an organ solo, although never executed, wouldn't have seemed completely out of line. It was refreshing to see a room full of hillbillies forget just how white they actually were. But, as demonstrated by the well-crafted box at the front of the room, all good things must come to an end. Inevitably they ran out of uplifting stanzas to sing and clap along to, and the music wound to a close. It was easy to get lost in the moment of a song, but suddenly people found themselves awkwardly returned from their uplifting holiday, still standing in a small town funeral home, with the messy business of burying George Dupree yet to go. The preacher said a few "hallelujahs" and "amens" to attempt a transition, but it was clumsy at best. After offering another prayer, people began dispersing quietly out onto the porch as the pallbearers went to work.

Mr. Tremble, normally the most soft-spoken and gentle man on the planet, was actually quite firm when instructing the pallbearers. He'd tried being kind and subtle when he first started in this business. He left people to their own common sense when it came to carrying the casket, thinking it didn't require much instruction. It took an alcoholic pallbearer, a busted casket, and an inconsolable widow to convince Mr. Tremble that people's own common sense had no place in the funeral business.

While Mr. Tremble was commanding the pallbearers, Eric and Burt Higgins loaded the flowers out the side door and into his pickup truck. The hearse was parked right beside it, ready to be pulled around front when everything was ready. Once the majority of the flower loading was taken care of, Eric made one last sweep through the parlor, while Tess went out the side door and waited for him. He was just shutting off the overheads that lit the casket when he heard Mr. Tremble order the pallbearers not to touch anything, then walked over to Eric.

"Eric, I need you to do me a favor."

"Sure, what is it?"

"The Duprees are a little tight in their car, so the youngest girl, Jill, needs a ride. I thought maybe you could take her out there in my car while I drive the hearse. Since you know her and everything, I thought it might be better." He paused for a moment, then added, "This is a time for friends and family."

Eric wasn't certain he was either of those things to Jill, but he agreed with Mr. Tremble anyway. As he walked out the side door, he saw Tess sitting on a step with a flower in her hand.

"Where'd you get that flower, Tess?"

"There are so many," she immediately defended. "I just took one."

"That's stealing, honey. You know that, right?"

"Nobody's even going to know."

"*I* know," was Eric's retort. "And *you* know. Are you calling us nobodies?"

Tess just hung her head and sulked. Normally she would have returned the flower immediately, but Eric could tell she was in the mood to dig in her heels, so he just left it alone. "Listen, I need to drive to the cemetery in Mr. Tremble's car, so—"

"But I want to ride in the big car with George Dupree," Tess quickly interrupted.

"I know, honey, if you'd just listen for a second." He could feel himself beginning to get frustrated. "You can still ride in the big car if you want, but Mr. Tremble will be driving. That's all."

Tess threw down her flower and protested, "But I want to ride in the big car with you and George Dupree!"

Eric felt his face rush red as he grabbed Tess under the arm and yanked her to her feet. "I don't know what's wrong with you today, but you're going to go straight home if you keep behaving like this. Do you understand me?" She was wriggling her arm to try to loosen his grip and refused to look at him. With her face pointed down, the only thing he could really make out was her lower lip sticking out in a bold pout.

"It's okay," said Jill from somewhere behind him. "I wouldn't mind riding with you and George Dupree, myself."

Eric turned and saw her standing there, her face still tear-streaked, but smiling. During funerals, people's emotions were as random as summer weather. But it was still a strange combination to see on a face he knew so well.

"No, it's okay, Jill. We'll take Mr. Tremble's car. You don't need to do that."

"I don't mind. Really," she said in a way that seemed convincing. "I wouldn't mind one last ride with Dad." She barely got the last few words out before her eyes spilled over a little more. She quickly wiped them away and regained her composure. "So is this Tess?" she asked.

"Yeah," he said, looking down at his daughter, who was still pouting and rubbing her arm, hoping her dad might think he'd actually hurt her. "Or her evil twin. We're not sure today," he added. "Tess, this is Jill Dupree."

Tess looked up and her eyes got suddenly wide. She looked at Jill and said hello, but cast a few nervous glances at her dad. Jill crouched down in front of her and extended her hand.

"Hi Tess. It's nice to meet you," she said.

Tess put her tiny hand in Jill's and shook it. Eric wasn't sure how she knew to do that, but assumed it had something to do with television.

"Your daddy and I were very close friends when we were in high school. Did you know that?"

Tess shook her head, no, and just stared up at Jill.

"She's adorable, Eric," Jill smiled.

"Yeah, most of the time," Eric answered. "Are you sure you want to ride in the hearse? We don't have to do what Tess wants. We're way bigger than her. We can push her around."

"No, it's okay. I'd honestly like it."

Eric reluctantly agreed and did one last check to be sure they had everything they'd need. Just as they were about to get in the hearse, Tess perked up and darted off. "My flower," she said as she ran over to the step where she'd been sitting. She picked it up, dusted it off, and put it to her nose to check that it still smelled okay. Eric noticed it was one of the orange blossoms that had gotten to him earlier. The ones that spelled out "Dad" on the wreath. As she walked back to Eric to get in the hearse, she tugged on his coat sleeve and motioned for him to come closer. Eric put his face down next to hers and listened as she whispered.

"That girl has the same last name as the man in the box," she said.

Eric nodded. "Small world, huh?"

Tess nodded right back, then climbed across the driver's seat to sit in the middle between her dad and this other Dupree.

Once Mr. Tremble's übercommand had delivered the casket into the back of the hearse without incident, the procession was ready to begin. Tess loved riding in the hearse because they got to ride right behind the policemen. They were the first ones to run a red light if the chance presented itself, and she would laugh when they went through the intersection. It was cute, but it also made Eric wonder if she had a taste for lawlessness that would someday have to be appeased in a more reckless fashion. It was a ridiculous thing to worry about, but he did it just the same. He was a dad.

There would be no red lights to run today. They were only going to the Pinely Cemetery, and the town's one red light was south of where they were heading. As they rolled up the highway, Eric was torn between wanting to make small talk with Jill, or giving her a moment of respectful silence. The small talk idea was quickly taken off the table when he noticed Jill was crying again. He focused on the road and took a few deep breaths to keep his own emotions in check. It looked like it would be respectful silence for the duration of the ride. The idea had barely settled in his mind when the radio suddenly sprung to life. No one would have guessed it by looking at him, but Mr. Tremble truly enjoyed the classic rock station up in Wheeling. He was apparently one of the few people alive who had actually taken a liking to the music his kids listened to when they were growing up. So when Tess turned on the radio, the rockin' sounds of Led Zeppelin quickly, and loudly, filled the air. Jill jumped in surprise while Eric fought some distant primordial urge to kill and eat his young.

"Tess!" he shouted as he turned the radio off with one quick flip. She knew he was looking at her, but didn't turn her head. "I'm sorry about that, Jill," he said.

"That's okay," she answered while catching her breath. "It was just a little . . . I wasn't expecting that."

"No. Nobody was."

He glanced from the road to Tess and back again as many times as he could, just to be sure she wasn't cooking up any more deviant behavior. To the average onlooker, she looked calm enough. But her furrowed brow told Eric there may be more to come.

The cemetery came into view as they drove to the top of the hill at the north end of town. Some of the headstones were decorated with fresh flowers, probably placed there to commemorate a birthday or anniversary or day of death. But most of the plots were just covered with the red, yellow, orange and brown leaves from the trees that surrounded the property. The brick gate at the front had a plaque that announced they were about to enter the Pinely Cemetery. As they signaled off the road, Tess turned to Jill.

"Hey Jill? You know why they have that fence up around the cemetery?" she asked.

"No, why?"

Tess could barely hold back her giggling long enough to spit out the answer. "Because people are just dying to get in."

Cyanide pills, Eric thought to himself. This is the exact reason why he should always carry cyanide pills with him. One for him, one for Tess, and it would all be over. It was partly his own fault for telling her that joke in the first place, so it wouldn't be right to only make her take one. No, it would have to be both of them. But surely a death by sudden poisoning would be better than enduring this kind of intolerable embarrassment.

"Again," Eric said to Jill, "I am extremely sorry."

"Eric, you used to tell me that joke about once a month, remember?" she answered.

She had a point. It was the sort of joke his dad would tell. One he swore he'd never repeat. But sure enough, every now and then when he was leaving or coming to town, he'd find himself sharing this flimsy excuse for humor with his fellow passengers. "Yeah, but that was different."

"No," she said, looking out the window. "It wasn't that funny then either."

The last leg of the ceremony couldn't move fast enough for Eric. He just wanted to get Mr. Dupree in the ground and get Tess back to her mother. Reverend Thomas said a few more words, then led them all in one last prayer for eternal rest and salvation for the soul of George Dupree. The leaves had been cleared away in a perfect rectangular plot, the dead making way for the dead. Eric had Tess's hand locked in his to make certain she didn't break free and do a soft-shoe number on the casket as they lowered it down. The preacher finished his prayer, and Mr. Tremble began to close the casket one last time. That's when Jill asked him to wait for just a second.

She walked up to her father's coffin, reached into her purse, and placed something inside the casket. From where he was standing, Eric couldn't see what it was. After she took a step back and smiled a little, she told Mr. Tremble to go ahead. He nodded and continued with his duties, letting the lid down softly. Then it was over. The body was left to be lowered later, so people simply had to get up and walk away. There was no signal, no fanfare. Nothing but a short walk across the hillside, and a quiet car ride home.

He and Tess didn't say much to each other on the ride back to the funeral home. At first, Eric thought he was giving Tess a good old-fashioned dose of the silent treatment. But sometime during the walk to Gina's, he began to wonder if he hadn't wound up on the receiving end somehow. She was stomping along stubbornly, gazing into the tops of trees, or studying the cracks of the sidewalk. Anything but looking at him. He would have been truly perplexed by her behavior, if it hadn't already pissed him off so much. Being a good parent meant working past destructive emotions and moving toward productive ones. He'd read that somewhere. He'd read a lot of these sorts of things in various parenting books after Tess was born. And he agreed with most of them. But he could never manage to put them into practice. It seemed like such a waste to get rid of a good batch of anger so quickly. It was like spitting out gum before it'd lost all its flavor.

Besides, he thought to himself, whatever Tess was upset about was almost certainly juvenile. She actually *was* a juvenile, so it seemed indisputable. He was angry about something concrete. Her immature behavior. Clearly she'd started it, so there was no reason for him to break the silence. This was his silent treatment, not hers. She only decided to give him the silent treatment after she realized she was getting it. As he built this seemingly foolproof case in his mind, he almost began forgetting why he was doing it. Was it for his own convincing? Was it for Tess? It wasn't until they walked through the front door of Gina's house that he remembered. She came around the corner, drying her hands on a dishtowel, and looking at Eric and Tess as though they were two yetis that had just wandered in from the snowbound hills of the Himalayas.

"I believe this is yours," Eric said, nudging Tess toward her mother.

"What—?" Gina started. "I thought you were going to have her for another hour or so."

"I was, if she hadn't gone and behaved like a complete juvenile during the service."

"Eric, she is a juvenile."

Gina was making the exact argument he'd made in his own head. But somehow, when she said it, it seemed to have the opposite effect. He didn't know why that was, but he didn't have time to figure it out. He was going to have to debate on the fly.

"I realize that," he said in order to establish that he did posses some knowledge, "but part of the whole funeral agreement is that she doesn't act like one."

"Like a five-year-old?"

"I'm five and a half," Tess piped in.

"You see," Eric said as though he'd just found the smoking gun, "this is exactly what I'm talking about."

Gina shook her head at Eric. "Okay, I don't know what you two are doing, but if you want to leave her here with me, that's fine."

"I think that would be for the best right now," Eric answered. He tried to believe he'd won the fight, but knew he'd just been spared by the ref.

"So we'll just see you at the bonfire tonight?" Gina asked.

Eric shrugged. "I really can't recommend getting her around fire," he said, pointing to Tess. "She's liable to burn the whole town to its foundations."

"Eric, what is wrong with you?" Gina snapped.

"Look, I'm not the one who behaved like a spoiled monster during the funeral service today," he said.

"Well I'm not the one who cried like a big baby."

He looked at Tess as she partly hid behind her mother's leg. Her face was defiant and remorseful at the same time. It was obvious she wanted to look away, but Eric knew she wouldn't. Her stubbornness was a particularly potent distillation of his own.

"You cried at the funeral?" Gina asked.

"A little bit," he answered, still looking at Tess.

"Are you okay now?"

He wanted to keep watching his daughter to see what might be going on inside her head, but Gina's inquiry caused him to involuntarily look up at her. "Of course I'm okay now," he said in disdain. "I wasn't wailing over his open grave or anything. I just got a little sad during the service."

"And you cried," Tess said spitefully.

"I know," Eric shot back.

"Like a baby," she added.

There were a hundred possible responses. Only after it came out of his mouth was Eric certain he'd chosen the worst one. "I'm gonna make you cry like a baby."

"Eric!" Gina shouted, looking none too amused.

"Okay," he said as his hands shot up in his own defense, "that wasn't called for. It's just . . . a little complex to explain all of this. To a little girl."

"So you just act like one too?" Gina snipped.

Eric sighed. "Do we really need more name calling here? Is that the solution?"

"No. I imagine the solution might involve actually trying to explain yourself to your daughter."

Eric looked at Tess, who still had the same defiant look on her face. Sooner or later she'd have to learn that sometimes it's better to give ground than to stubbornly hold it. That was a lesson he could teach her.

"That might be one way to do it," he said to Gina.

"So what are you going to do?" she asked.

"Right now?"

"Yeah."

He looked at the wall and tried to imagine what it might feel like to do what Gina was asking. Would he feel like a hero? Would he feel like a milquetoast? It was an unknown picture he couldn't quite color in. Luckily, right next to it was a fully realized image that was well worn around the edges. "I'm going home," he heard himself say.

As he walked out the door and down the stairs, he felt strangely liberated. He knew that sometimes it felt good to work through problems. But for some reason, it always felt good to walk away from them. The brisk air seemed to lift the sweat from his face and carry away a whole heart full of steam he'd been building all day. There may have been good-byes back at Gina's. There may have been plans to meet up later. He wasn't sure. Once he'd made the decision to walk, it was all a formality. His dress shoes sounded dainty on the concrete. It was still the cadence of his walk, just with a different pitch. He listened to the familiar rhythm and tried not to think about anything. A task he found remarkably easy.

When he reached his house and turned on the lights, things were pretty much as he'd left them that morning. Clothes on the chair. Shoes on the floor. Dirty dishes on the TV tray. The only thing different was Buddy Piles sitting on his couch.

"Jesus, Buddy!" Eric shouted in surprise.

Buddy, unfazed, looked up. "What?"

"What are you doing here?"

"I like it heew. It's quiet."

"That's cause nobody's home."

"Pwob'ly."

Eric wished there was someone else in the room to hear this, just to be reassured he wasn't the one out of perspective. "You know a man can shoot a trespasser in his own home. It's perfectly legal."

"What's a twespasser?" Buddy asked.

"You."

Buddy's forehead practically folded over on itself as he thought that over. "You don't have a gun," he finally said.

"How do you know that?"

The shrug was almost imperceptible. "You don't seem like you would."

Eric wondered how a kid like Buddy Piles could know what type of person has a gun and what type doesn't. Buddy's dad had a gun. He'd woken up the whole neighborhood one night when he shot a possum that had somehow gotten into his kitchen. Said he thought it was a wolf. No one seemed to mind the fact that there were no wolves in West Virginia, which almost made Eric want to get a gun so he could fire off a few rounds at a pterodactyl some night. He never did. Still, Buddy didn't know that. All he knew was his dad had a gun. And that Eric and his dad were completely different. So maybe it was deductive reasoning on Buddy's part. Eric didn't have time to think about it long since Buddy was apparently all done with the quiet he'd been seeking just moments ago.

"Where's Tess?" he asked.

"At her mom's."

"How come?"

"Cause that's where she lives."

"How come you're all dwessed up?"

There may have been scientific instruments that could measure the space between Buddy's trains of thought, but Eric was certain they were large, expensive, and owned by the government. "I was at a funeral," he answered.

"What's a funewal?"

"It's like a party," Eric said without even thinking. "Like one last party for a friend."

"Do they have games?"

"Hey Buddy?"

"Yeah?"

"You've gotta go home now."

"Okay." Buddy popped up off the couch and walked toward the door. Eric watched him and wondered what it must be like to be completely unflappable. If Buddy could hang onto that trait, Eric thought, he could somehow end up ruling the whole world. Unfortunately, he wouldn't even think to enjoy it.

"Hey Buddy," he called out as Buddy opened the door.

"Yeah?"

"You didn't climb in through the window or anything, did you?"

"No," he said, shaking his head. "The door was unlocked."

"Duly noted."

Buddy spent a second trying to understand what Eric meant by that. He looked at him blankly, hoping for some type of clue. Once he was sure he wasn't going to get one and that he wasn't going to figure it out on his own, he turned back to the door and walked out into the now unmistakable night.

Standing there in his living room he realized Buddy was right. It was quiet there. He looked around the way a person does when they're about to do something silly, then turned off the lights and sat down on the couch where Buddy had been before. It was still warm. In the darkness, the quiet was amplified. It wasn't perfectly still like the booth he'd sat in as a boy to get his hearing checked. It was stillness colored with subtle sounds. He heard Buddy open his front door across the street. There was a hiss from the heating vent in the baseboards. There was his own pulse whooshing inside his ears. He sat there for a while, listening to his heart push blood around, and tried to picture nothing. But his mind wouldn't have it. Each rush of blood brought a new image. It was like a slideshow of people and places. His dad—*whoosh*—Tess—*whoosh*—a touchdown—*whoosh*—Gina—*whoosh*—Jill—*whoosh*—Mr. Dupree—*whoosh*—a coffin. On and on until he finally stood up and turned the lights back on.

How long had Buddy sat like that, he wondered? How empty must that kid's mind be? He turned on the stereo to provide some type of distraction and listened to a song about someone he didn't know. About problems that weren't his. He took off his tie, and started changing into clothes he wouldn't mind having smell like smoke.

Eric stood next to the bonfire, between the high school and the football field, and watched with dismay as the band brought their instruments to the ready position. The Pinely pep band was one of the least inspiring musical collectives ever assembled. Somehow, in Eric's mind, it didn't seem right to have such a small group of people be able to produce sonic atrocity on such a massive scale. Yet there it was in front of him, cacophony in concentrate. With every tune the band bleated out and stumbled over, the crowd seemed to actually be sapped of the very pep the band was supposed to be providing. It was just barely better than the cheerleaders, who were more plentiful than locusts. By the time Eric graduated, the cheerleading squad had swollen to a size that anyone in their right mind would consider unnecessary. Since then, it had doubled. There were actually more cheerleaders than there were football players, which Coach Gleason would always attempt to comment on when he was in the throes of one of his patented fits of inarticulate rage. At one point, there had even been a boy on the cheerleading squad. A fact that had some of the more traditional members of the Pinely community rereading the pages of Revelation in their well-thumbed Bibles.

The music and the cheers were just a prelude to the main event of the night: inspirational speeches from pimple-faced boys. It was a tradition of the bonfire pep rally, and one that had been viewed differently at every age of Eric's life. When he was little, he used to listen to the words of the football players with awe. If they said they were going to win, he believed them. If they said it was going to be a tough game, he got worried. Once he was in high school, he didn't hear the words anymore. He was too busy constructing words of his own, waiting for his turn to wax wise on the difficulties that stood in the path of the fearless warriors who called themselves the Pinely Wildcats. Now he listened to the words for the sheer fantasy of it. Young kids acting needlessly brave and tough, while old men hung on their every word and draped them in the colors of their own nostalgia. Eric was trying to inoculate himself. Drinking the poison to lessen its effects. For the past six years, he'd been fine. But he was always wary of the day these teenage words would ring with a certain reverence. If that happened, he was prepared to walk away from the rally and never return.

Once the pep band had put its finishing touches on a particularly feeble rendition of the Pinely fight song, Coach Gleason made his way to the front of the bonfire. Eric was breathtaken at how unimpressive a figure he cut against the flames. If Jim Morrison were to stand in front of a crowd with fire as his backdrop, it would feel nearly apocalyptic with intensity. But with Coach Gleason there, his paunch jutting over his belt line, his hair carefully groomed in a style that was almost certainly never in style, the air seemed calm and orderly. The fire, rather than looking like a manifestation of social uproar, seemed like the well-crafted and thoughtful effort of a sports-loving community.

"Tomorrow's game," Coach Gleason began, "is a rivalry." He paused here. His public speeches were lousy with such pauses. Most of the time they could be passed off as being for dramatic effect. But occasionally a Gleason pause would be so long, and so poorly placed, it seemed as though the sum of the English language had collected itself quickly and fled his consciousness for good. "Some folks might look at the town of Pinely and the town of Cedarsville and say the only thing that separates us is a thin, city line. But they'd be wrong. There's actually a chasm."

This line garnered a lot of "That's rights" and nodding of heads from the people in the crowd, which was practically the whole damn town. Eric nodded too. But only in appreciation of Coach Gleason's accurate use of the word "chasm."

"One and nineteen," Coach said with an exaggerated punch. "That's our record against Cedarsville over the past twenty years. One and nineteen! That, my friends, is a chasm."

Eric always tried to use a new word at least three times when he learned it, just to help make it stick. He wondered if Coach Gleason had just learned the word "chasm." If so, he was only one more use away from making it his own. Unfortunately, it seemed he was going to boost his vocabulary at the expense of the pep that so many people had come to rally within themselves. Because his chasm theme was a real downer.

"Seven years!" were the next words Coach overemphasized. "That's the amount of time that's passed since we last beat Cedarsville. Seven . . . years." He looked around the crowd to be sure everyone here could appreciate this statistic. "That, too, is a chasm."

Well that oughtta lock it, Eric thought to himself. "Chasm" was officially the intellectual property of one Coach Wilford Gleason.

"How old are you then?" he heard Coach ask someone on the other side of the fire.

"Five and a half," came the little voice. Eric looked across the fire at the face of his daughter, standing against Gina's legs, staring at the strange man hunkered in front of her.

"This little girl has never known a Pinely victory over Cedarsville," continued Coach Gleason as he walked around the fire to see the rest of the faces. "Hasn't happened. From the day she was born until this very night. And two years before that. The Pinely Wildcats haven't beat the Cedarsville Tigers."

Eric wasn't exactly sure how he felt about Tess being used as a tool in Gleason's reverse pep talk, but he was fairly certain he wasn't okay with it.

"I guess it's not as bad as it used to be. There were kids on that team, the one that won seven years ago, who had never known a Pinely victory over Cedarsville. High school age kids. We were asking them to do something they'd never even *seen* happen before." Again he paused. A nice, drawn-out, Alzheimer's-length pause. "But they did it anyway," he finally announced. He was vamping the drama up so high, Eric half-expected him to begin soliciting donations to help keep the Lord's mission strong.

"There was a playoff berth on the line then. A lot at stake. But no one really believed we could win." He shook his head and stared at the ground for a moment. "Hell, I even had my doubts. But there was someone else who didn't have any doubts at all. 'We're going to win.' That's what he said. He said it to me. He said it to the team. He said it to anyone who would listen."

Eric wasn't comfortable with the direction this whole thing was going. Gleason was talking about him now, and everyone knew it. He could feel the eyes beginning to turn in his direction. Some tried to be coy by just casting the odd glance, while others all but squared up to him. Still, Eric didn't look at them. He focused on Coach with all the concentration he could muster, and half-wished Gleason would just go back to picking on Tess.

"People thought he was crazy. Cocky. Stupid, even. And they'd still think it to this day if it weren't for one thing. He went out there and played as hard as he could. And we beat the Cedarsville Tigers!"

This evoked a round of applause and cheers from the crowd, as though they were watching the final seconds tick off the clock all over again. It even got a little rise out of Eric as he briefly allowed himself to remember that night. He was quickly startled by his own nostalgia.

"Isn't that right, Mercer?" was the question Coach Gleason suddenly posed to him. In front of everyone.

"I'm sorry, was I there?" he answered quickly, never being more thrilled to have a wise-ass answer at the ready. The crowd chuckled and the drama of the moment dissipated a little. Enough to make Eric hope it might go away completely.

Coach Gleason didn't find it amusing. But then, in all the years he'd known him, Eric still hadn't sorted out exactly what Coach Gleason *did* find amusing. He only knew it never had anything to do with what happened to come out of Eric's mouth.

"See, he likes to kid around," Coach Gleason managed to finally say. "Which is why we're all confused." He turned to address the crowd. "How many of you heard that Eric Mercer said we're gonna win tomorrow?"

Hands went up all around. Little kids, old women, high schoolers, legionnaires. Even Deke and his dad had the balls to raise their hands. It was about half the town in all.

"Now," Coach Gleason continued, "how many of you heard he said we're gonna lose?"

This time it was the other half of the town. All with hands raised.

"So I guess we're all wondering the same thing, Eric. Which is it?"

He tried staring at Coach Gleason hard enough to give the old prick a heart attack, but it didn't seem to be working. He just kept looking at Eric with that smug grin, while motioning for him to step out to the center, nearer the bonfire. There was a lot he could do with this time, he thought, this kind of attention. He could turn it around on Coach Gleason. Have him explain why, in his twenty-two years of coaching at Pinely, he'd only managed to orchestrate three victories over Cedarsville. Or he could involve Deke and his dad. Make them rationalize their ludicrous attempt to tamper with the handicap on a high school sporting event. Hanging from the red brick of the school building were the handmade signs, flickering with the light and shadows from the fire. "Leave your heart on the field," said one particularly creative one. It struck Eric as a good motto if you win the game. But not a very good one if you lose.

"You see," he found himself starting, "when I played football . . ." He paused. Coach Gleason might have paused longer a time or two during his speeches, but not many. The bonfire popped behind him as he tried to think of something to say. "When I played football," he said again more quietly, "it wasn't my passion, or my life. It was just something I did. It's a small town. There isn't much to do. So . . . I played football."

He could tell the people in the crowd were searching for some sort of meaning in his words, but were having a hard time with it. Between Coach Gleason's "chasm" routine, and this little uninspiring discourse on passing time in a small town, they were entirely unclear as to how they were supposed to feel.

"I wasn't very good, really. I was . . . okay, I guess. I don't know why I knew we'd win that game back then. Sometimes you just . . . I don't know, you just know things."

He looked across the fire at the scrappy group of kids wearing Pinely football jerseys. There were a couple of big kids, stocky boys who managed to look a little more like football players than the rest. But for the most part they were small. Smaller than he ever remembered being at that age. One of the smallest of the bunch stood there, his jersey tucked into his jeans, looking at Eric with a sad sense of hope. They all were. He knew they were going to lose, no doubt in his mind. If he said otherwise, he'd be lying.

"You're gonna win," he said with conviction.

He could feel their hearts jump just as quickly as his dropped. Those kids had more hope than he had reputation, he thought. There was no reason for him to take it away before the coin toss had even happened. They'd have plenty of time to learn their own lessons about the bitter sting of hope.

The band moaned to life again, taking another shot at the fight song, and the cheerleaders appeared from all sides like ninjas to lead the crowd in a sing-along. Eric wanted to stick around and hear the players make their speeches, but he knew he'd just feel bad for them this time. Plus he didn't want to have to deal with the backslapping grins of Coach Gleason or Deke. As the pep pandemonium built, he slowly made his way in the opposite direction. The only exit was through the gate, which was being blocked by a portion of the cheerleading squad that was about to attempt some type of vaulting acrobatic maneuver that seemed sure to end with an ambulance ride. Rather than try to sneak around and risk being seen at the exact moment some poor girl landed hip first on the ground, Eric ducked behind the concession stand for a moment of planning. And peace.

The music, cheering, and merrymaking may have been out of sight, but Eric could still hear it plain as day. He sat on the cold grass and listened to the band grind to an anticlimactic finish. There was a moment when it seemed like no one knew quite what to do after all the excitement and music was over. It reminded Eric of the funeral that afternoon. But eventually, one of the captains of the football team started talking in an overly dramatic tone about how beating Cedarsville was the first sure step to curing cancer, or some such exaggeration. Eric tried to tune it out by listening to the hiss of car wheels on the road. There weren't that many cars driving through Pinely, so he'd occasionally catch a bit of something about this game being "the biggest moment of our lives." It was only because he was trying to listen to anything but these words of wisdom that he heard the sound of footsteps on the grass. He wasn't sure who'd seen him escape to his hiding place, but there was no doubt the footsteps were heading in his direction. He watched the corner of the old wooden building that served as the concession stand, waiting to see who his hunter might be. It would have been silly to run. Which was the only reason he didn't.

"What are you doing back here?" called a familiar voice in a half-whisper. As she rounded the corner, Eric found himself looking up at Jill Dupree.

"What are *you* doing back here?" asked Eric. "I thought you'd be at home with your family."

"Oh I was," she said as she plopped down next to him, "but I just felt like going for a walk. There's just so much—well, people are sad one minute, then smiling about Dad the next. I tell ya, it's an emotional roller coaster back there." She smiled at Eric and sighed.

"Have you been drinking?" he asked.

"A little. We had some cocktails in Dad's honor. I may have honored him a little more than everyone else." Her crooked smile and limp speech told the rest of the story. She cocked her head back and looked up at the sky. She didn't seem to have much else to say, so Eric gave it a shot.

"So this afternoon," he asked, "at the graveyard?"

"Yeah?"

"What was that thing you did at the end? You put something inside the casket."

Jill smiled, but looked a little embarrassed. "It was—a garden trowel," she confided. "You know, just in case."

He didn't mean to laugh, but he did. "That's a first. I've never seen that before."

"How long have you been working there?" she asked.

"Forever," he sighed. "Maybe a little longer."

Eric could hear someone with a xylophone lightly practicing on the other side of the concession stand. He was glad to hear someone practicing their instrument. It gave him hope that maybe the other band members would see this kid and inquire as to why he was playing so softly and by himself.

Jill drew his attention back to their side of the stand. "So you're a funeral . . . person and a bartender?"

"These days."

"So this is Plan B?"

Eric couldn't spit out his answer fast enough. "There was no Plan B. There was only Plan A."

"Well," she said, "it was a good one."

"Seems to be working out for you."

"No. This is my Plan B too."

Eric sat up and looked at her. "Law school was your Plan B? I got shafted here."

She let her head roll to look him in the eye. "Plan A was to be there with you."

He sat and looked at her beautiful face and tried to think of something to say. "Yeah," he muttered, "well, mistakes were made."

Her face suddenly turned sour. "Don't call her a mistake, Eric. She's a beautiful little girl."

"I wasn't——" he started defensively. "Are you talking about Tess? Jesus, Jill, go easy. That's my daughter. I wasn't calling her anything. I was just saying."

"Oh God, I'm so sorry," Jill said. "I just thought you were . . . The way I heard it was——"

"It's okay," Eric said. Jill seemed more repentant than was necessary, which made Eric feel he may have overreacted. "I just——" He looked at his feet and shook his head. "I don't know."

"It's hard, huh?"

Eric laughed. "It's fucking impossible." He looked at her, then off at the road. "You have no idea."

"You could tell me," she said.

He looked into her green eyes, into this face he'd thought about more times than he'd even let himself realize. And he trusted her.

"I love her," he said, "more than I've ever loved anyone." He was surprised to be fighting back emotions he normally kept in check. "Including you." Her face looked so understanding. Not at all hurt at being demoted in his emotional hierarchy. The sort of face that could handle a dark secret that had never before been spoken. "And," he started, a little uncertain of himself, "I wish she'd never been born."

It seemed suddenly quiet. More quiet than before. Eric felt a pained smile affix to his face and looked away from Jill. He didn't know what else to say. Or if he'd said too much.

He heard her breathe like she was about to speak, but she never got the chance. The drummer counted off the fight song and, suddenly, abysmal music filled every cranny of the air. Eric shook his head in disbelief and turned to tell Jill the clamor wouldn't last long. He leaned in toward her ear and was surprised to find her mouth instead.

He didn't know how it had happened. Her lips were every bit as soft as he remembered them, and the two of them fell into a long-lost, comfortable rhythm. It was all so unanticipated, he found it difficult to concentrate. His mind replayed the few seconds before she started kissing him, to see if he'd missed a signal or a sign. But each time he drifted, he was pulled back by what was happening in front of him. On top of him by that point.

She was so warm, and familiar, and in no way diminished by his own well-worn memories of her. She was perfect. Her hair brushed against his face as she pulled back and looked in his eyes. They were the same as they were years ago. The same as the first day he'd met her. He was trapped in some time that didn't exist. An amalgam of that moment, and years past. There was no more music in his ears. No more thoughts in his mind. Just a beautiful face he'd missed. More than he'd let himself know. She leaned in again and kissed him with such tenderness, he thought she must be made of light and air.

The world around him sounded like it was moving in an odd time. The ground crunching underneath him, crushed by a hundred footsteps. He felt like a prince. Like a poet. Like anything besides what he actually was.

"Daddy?"

On the other side of the fence was Tess. She was holding Gina's hand, walking home from the pep rally, like everyone else.

"Are you okay?" Tess asked.

Eric quickly bucked Jill off him and hustled to his feet. "Yeah, honey," he said in his calmest voice. "I'm fine. I was just—"

He didn't get a chance to try to explain before Gina said, "Come on, Tess," and pulled her down the alley toward their home. Tess glanced back and looked even more surprised than before.

"I know that girl," he heard her say to Gina. "She has the same last name as the man in the box."

Eric looked on the ground and saw Jill there, discarded. She was trying to bring herself to her feet, but was too turned around by the sudden change in circumstances. From kissing her ex-lover to picking leaves out of her hair.

"I'm sorry, Jill," Eric said as he helped her get up. "I was just a little thrown by that."

"Yeah, me too."

"I didn't mean to . . . do that. To cast you aside. It was just . . . I wasn't expecting her. Obviously."

The look she gave him was so strange, he didn't know what to do. Luckily, she seemed to. Her hands cupped his face and pulled it toward hers. She gave him a long kiss that felt like dusk, slowly wrapping his mind in blue. She held him like that for a while, then said she had to go, and walked around the corner of the old wooden building. He stood there, waiting to see her walk past the fence. It was the shortest way home for her, but she must not have been looking for that. Because when he turned around, he saw her walk across the football field and disappear into the darkness.

SEVENTEEN

He didn't hurt as much now. Which must have had to do with the lights. They were just tiny one-inch light bulbs. Regular white light. Four ninety-five for a box of ten at the Western Auto. Next to the other things for sale there, they didn't seem remotely impressive. Given the choice between bicycles, riding lawn mowers, bird feeders, or the little white lights, almost anyone would choose any of the former. But at that moment, from where he stood, those lights were the most significant, precious, and beautiful things on the entire planet. That's because they were attached to a large green board, arranged in a certain way, and lit in an exact configuration. One that read Wildcats: 20, Visitors: 14.

At halftime, Eric could barely move his arms. He had to unhook his shoulder pads and bend at the waist to let them slide over his head. Those corn-fed fuckers from Cedarsville always hit hard, but tonight they seemed especially vicious. They knew Eric said Pinely was going to win, and they seemed determined to physically remove any such notion from his mind, or any other part of his body that might harbor it. By that point they'd done a good job. Pinely was down 14 to 7. Eric was down more than that.

The one Pinely touchdown had been hard fought. Two shots at the end zone had gained three yards, then lost two. It was on third down that Eric finally punched it in. A quick handoff from the quarterback, then a four-yard push that seemed like a mile. He thought he was running face first through a junkyard. Hit in the legs, pushed from behind, torn at the arms, then slammed to the ground. Even after the whistle, they kept hitting him, this time with fists. When the pileup was cleared by the officials and he was back on his feet, he was attacked by his own players. They were smacking his helmet and shoulder pads, jumping on his back, and screaming "Touchdown!" It was the first series of the game.

In the halftime locker room, Coach Gleason had some sort of coaching seizure. If Eric had the strength, he would have rushed to stuff something in Gleason's mouth to keep him from swallowing his tongue. But he was too exhausted. And he'd long held the suspicion that Gleason was beyond all help anyway. He ranted in some half-language about blowing a perfectly good lead, threw some things around for dramatic effect, then stormed into his office and slammed the door behind him. This was the leadership and guidance he provided.

It was only one touchdown, Eric told himself. Hardly even a lead, really. That ball was shaped funny. It could take a strange bounce at any moment. But when the team took the field for the second half, the crowd was strangely subdued. They didn't seem to think any team could possibly come back from a seven-point deficit. At least not a Pinely team. Not against Cedarsville. They had thirteen years of proof to back them up.

Standing on the sidelines before the second-half kickoff, Eric looked up into the stands. Everyone was there. The kids from school were all piled at one end in the "cheering section." Some huddled under blankets to keep out the cold air. Some were making their own warmth together under those blankets. Jill was standing at the top of the bleachers, bundled in his jacket, trying to look optimistic. Near the middle of the stands were the diehards, who looked like they were at a funeral. They wanted this victory more than they wanted their next breath. And Eric had promised it to them. He began to think that was a stupid thing to do. Especially since he didn't even care that much if they won. Certainly not as much as the people in the stands.

He could see Deke's dad looking like he was about to have an aneurysm. Eric's prediction had apparently set Mr. Williams's amateur betting pool out of whack to the point where he wasn't sure if he wanted Pinely to win or lose. He just knew he wished Eric had never said anything. Eric's dad was sitting just a few seats over from Deke's, wearing pretty much the same expression. He didn't have any money on the game, he was just the worrying kind. He checked things twice. He planned well in advance. He tied his shoes in double knots. Eric had never adopted this over-attention to detail. He shot from the hip, said what he felt, and tied his shoes once. Which brought Pinely a touchdown in the third quarter.

Up the middle again, after a long drive from their own twenty. Pinely had taken it piece by piece. Three yards. Then five. Two here. Four there. It had gotten them to within sixteen yards of the end zone. Then up the middle went Eric. Some sonofabitch had him by the foot. He was stuck, standing upright, an easy target for the next Cedarsville player who got there. The sort of tackle that puts people out of games. He tugged a couple of times. There should have been a hit. A bone-crushing strike to be studied on the game film—or the X-rays. But it never came. Instead, he popped free. He'd somehow shaken loose of his tackler. And his shoe. Cleat then sock, cleat then sock, all the way to the end zone, and it was tied 14-14.

This sent a rumble through the Pinely crowd. They weren't sure if it was time to break out the hope they'd stored away so long ago. But they were at least trying to remember where they'd put it.

Deke stood next to him on the bench while he retied his shoe. "That was pretty lucky, huh?"

Eric glanced over at him. Deke wasn't even looking at Eric, he was staring up at the scoreboard. "Which part?" Eric asked.

"When your shoe came off."

"Yeah," Eric agreed, "pretty lucky."

"Were you counting on that much luck when you said we were going to win?"

Deke had been hounding Eric about his prediction all week. He knew full well Eric wasn't the type to have premonitions. And even if he was, this one would have been tainted by the fact they'd both watched the same NFL Films special about Super Bowl III over at Huey's house. Deke immediately made the connection between Joe Namath guaranteeing a New York Jets win over Baltimore, and Eric suddenly predicting a Pinely victory over Cedarsville. Of course, Eric vehemently denied it every time he brought it up. Which only made Deke bring it up more.

"No," Eric said in answer to Deke's question. "I was hoping for a lot more luck than that."

Unfortunately, there wasn't much more luck to be had for a while. And in the middle of the fourth quarter, Eric thought maybe their luck had run out entirely. His mind had wandered again. It happened. For Eric, the game of football could get very mechanical. Very rhythmic. Into the huddle. Listen to the call. Down in a stance. Run the play. Over and over until something good, or something bad, happened. All he really had to do was remember the play. The rest of his brain could think about other things.

So off it went, considering the Friday Night Stage that was Pinely High School football. It struck him as odd. That so much hope, excitement, and passion could revolve around a game being played by teenagers. It was pageantry on a grand scale. Lights, music, colors, commotion, all swirling around an organized display of brutality and violence. The stands filled with parents, pitting their children against those of their rivals for the mere spectacle of it all. And in the middle, boys becoming young men, seeking to warm themselves in the only spotlight their small town could provide.

Eric was in the middle of it all, crouched in a three-point stance, ready to run a play. The problem was, his mind had forgotten to take note of exactly which play was called. Information he would certainly need. He was hoping for one of those moments where time seemed to slow down, so he could at least try to remember what had been said in the huddle. Something about a "one," maybe? He was almost certain it was a running play. If not, then definitely a pass. Unfortunately, time didn't slow down. The ball was hiked and the play was in motion, so he had no choice. He ran. He took off to the right and hoped for the best. Mike, the quarterback, was holding the football out to his left, which made Eric realize he'd probably gone the wrong way. It was a busted play. Mike would just have to keep the ball and do what he could. Or—a less reasonable option—he could spin all the way around and try to force the ball into Eric's arms as he ran past. Eric felt it jam against his hipbone as he crashed into the line. Staggering backward and looking on the ground, he watched as the strange brown ball was covered by a black-and-orange jersey. It was much later than he'd wanted, but time finally did slow down.

He watched the pileup around the ball. Joining in might have helped, if it didn't seem so futile. He knew where the ball was.

Under the Cedarsville player. Number 64. *That* he could remember. Not the play that was called in the huddle. The play that, if properly executed, could have helped them all avoid this unpleasant pileup of human bodies. All because of a loose football that, in all likelihood, had helped Pinely snatch defeat from the jaws of victory. The football that looked an awful lot like the one sitting on the ground, two yards from where Eric was standing.

They'd run the drill hundreds of times in practice. When there's a ball loose, you fall on it. Cover it up, hold it with all your might, and wait for the referee to take it from you. He hadn't seen it come out from the pile of players, but he was pretty certain the football in front of him was the same one he'd fumbled just a few seconds before. He ran toward it, crouched to fall, when he realized something. Almost everyone on the field was in that giant pile. So he reached out his hands, felt the rough leather run against his fingertips, and scooped the ball into his arms.

Along the sidelines he could hear people yelling. Like lions had been unleashed on the crowd. Pure pandemonium. Eric couldn't see another soul around him on the field, but there was a clicking noise he couldn't seem to shake. Right behind him, every step of the way. It sounded like it was gaining ground. Which only made him run harder. But no matter what he did, he could still hear it. Maybe even getting louder. At any moment, he'd be taken down from behind, that's what he thought. But that moment never came. He ran harder and harder until his feet broke free from the yards of green and stood in the painted grass of the end zone.

When he turned to look for an official, there was none to be seen. He was all alone. No other players. No officials. Nothing. If his heart hadn't already been pounding from his sprint down the sideline, it would have started then. Because he was almost certain he'd run the wrong way. The pounding of his heart filled his ears as he looked down field. There were players from both teams looking his way. The people in the stands were on their feet. Finally he spotted an official. He was running down the center of the field, surrounded by most of the Pinely players. He only stood out because he had his hands in the air. Both of them extended above his head, signaling a touchdown.

Eric looked up at the scoreboard and watched as the white lights, those beautiful white lights, changed their pattern. Like a bold, new constellation. Wildcats: 20, Visitors: 14. They were winning. He wanted to celebrate, but there was still too much time left on the clock. It was only one touchdown, he reminded himself. Hardly even a lead, really. That ball was shaped funny. It could take a strange bounce at any moment.

Coach Gleason smacked him on the helmet when he ran to the sidelines. He was happy about the score, but still pissed. "That's not the play I called," he said.

Eric took off his helmet. "What *did* you call?"

"Split red, thirty-one dive."

Eric looked at Gleason for a second, then up at the scoreboard. "We'd have never scored on that one," he finally said.

He could tell Gleason wanted to choke him. More than usual. But it wouldn't look very good to be choking the player who just put them in the lead. So he smiled and told Eric to get out of his way so he could watch the extra point attempt.

The water from the plastic bottle tasted sweeter than it ever had before. The bottles normally made Eric nauseous, because some guys on the team would suck on them like a nipple instead of squeezing the water into their mouths from a safe and hygienic distance. During one particularly exhausting practice back in September, Eric had watched Chuckie Beckmeyer mouth a bottle with such intensity he thought he might actually take the thing to homecoming. "Christ on a crutch, Chuckie!" he finally snapped. "Why don't we all just make out and get it over with?"

From that day on, Chuckie, who missed the point completely, refused to go into the shower room until Eric was done.

"Man, you sure ran fast," said Huey. He was standing there with Deke, both smiling like they'd escaped from prison.

"I thought someone was behind me."

"There wasn't anyone for miles."

"I kept hearing a noise right behind me."

Deke laughed. "You were running from a noise? Hell, you were probably making a shitload of noise just from running so hard."

Eric hadn't thought of that. The clicking sound he'd heard was probably his own shoulder pads rattling from the force of his footsteps. He'd been running away from himself the whole time.

"This is huge, man," Huey said, too seriously to be laughed off. "Thirteen years. Look at those people up there."

They all turned and looked up into the stands. People were happy. Hopeful, even. They had the look of folks waiting for a reunion with their long-lost loved ones. At least most of them did.

"Boy, your dad doesn't look so good, Deke."

Huey, never a master of understatement, had actually been extremely delicate in his description. Deke's dad looked like panic and rapture were using his insides as a battlefield. He was smiling, sweating, and looking a little like he was about to cry. He noticed the boys staring at him and tried to wave.

"Yeah," Deke said, turning back around, "he's been pretty mixed up ever since you popped off about winning."

Eric kept looking at the crowd. He didn't want to gloat, but there was something nice about basking in the golden adulation they poured down over him. The faces were smiling. They were grateful to him. He wasn't entirely sure what he'd done to deserve such gratitude. It was just a game. That's what he'd told himself a thousand times. There wasn't any doubt in his mind. Still, he said it again, just to be sure. It's just a game.

"Look at ol' Danny Moran," Huey said with a chuckle.

Danny was standing down by the Cedarsville end zone, leaning against the chain-link fence. The white vinyl arms of his letterman's jacket were draped over the fence, making his hands bulge red from lack of circulation. He was looking out onto the field, but it didn't seem like he was really watching the game. Cedarsville went for a long pass that was badly overthrown. It skipped off the gravel track and smashed against the fence just a few feet from where Danny was leaning. The metal links crashed loud enough to make Danny jump back from the fence, almost tearing the sleeve of his jacket.

"This is probably the worst day of his life," Huey laughed.

Eric agreed. They'd all heard enough stories from Danny over the years to last them a lifetime. But still, Eric couldn't help but feel a little sorry for him. Pinely football had been the highlight of his life. They'd almost made the playoffs his senior year. A fact he always deemed worth repeating. But it wasn't going to be a very impressive fact if this team actually *went* to the playoffs. Especially if they did it by beating Cedarsville.

The Tigers were held on downs and punted the ball away with two and a half minutes to go. Eric grabbed his helmet and ran onto the field. The crowd was deranged. He wouldn't have been surprised if, when the game was over, half of them dropped into frenzied fits requiring medical attention. Regardless of the outcome.

"Just a few first downs," Mike said in the huddle. "That's all we need. Hold onto the ball. Stay in bounds. No penalties. Got it?" Everyone nodded their heads. "Okay. It's split red, thirty-one dive. Eric?"

"What?"

"Got it?"

"Split red, thirty-one dive," Eric repeated. "The old way, right?"

A few guys laughed as Mike shook his head. "Yeah, the old way. On one. Ready—"

"Break," they roared with a clap of the hands and jogged up to the line of scrimmage. And with that little bit of ceremony, they began trying to pound away at the clock. Two and a half minutes. In football time.

The hits were like hammers forging steel. Each carry of the ball, each blow to the body, was changing him. All while Cedarsville hoped for a fluke. One strange bounce to change everything. But the yards stacked up as the seconds fell away. Until there was no time left.

The moment locked, never to be undone.

He stood on the field and watched the stands empty. Everyone wanted on the field, except for the Cedarsville players. They just wanted off. His own teammates swirled around him, hooting and hollering and throwing their helmets in the air. He could see his mom and dad standing by the gate, waiting for him to make his way to the field house. There wasn't much of an opportunity to concentrate with people hitting him on the shoulder pads and slapping him on the back. "We're going to state!" was the most intelligible cry he heard. The rest was ecstatic gibberish.

Eric wasn't sure what to do. He tried to tell himself it was just a game, but it didn't sound right. People were going Grade-A bat shit all around him. How could it be just a game if it made an entire town that was normally pretty dreary and dejected all smile at the same time? Smile, hell. It was like there was a nitrous leak. People were beside themselves, and he was in the center of it. He breathed in the commotion and felt something inside give. They'd won the game. He'd scored every touchdown. He'd predicted the win in the first place. It all whirled around his brain until, finally, it had to make an escape. Everything seemed warmer and he felt his ears pull back to make room for a smile that barely fit on his face.

"Son of a bitch!" Deke yelled in his ear. "Son—of—a—bitch! Can you believe this shit?"

Eric wasn't sure how to answer that, so he just mumbled and shook his head. There were so many people around him now, he could barely see. Coach Gleason was waving a football above his head, looking like he'd just landed on the moon. Everyone around Eric was wild. Hitting him, shoving him. Displaying their joy through brute force. That's why he was so startled, amid all the jostling, to feel a soft touch on his bare arm. He looked at the slender hand on his arm and followed it all the way to its owner. A smiling Gina Stevens.

"Good game, Eric," she sang out to him.

He nodded a few times and felt his smile extend even more. He was sure there was something he was supposed to say after that. Something fairly common and well rehearsed, but he couldn't think what it was.

The crowd began to move, en masse, toward the field house, carrying Eric along with it. They moved right past Danny Moran, who was still hanging over the fence, trying to look happy. He looked up and gave Eric an anemic smile and wave. It was such a sad display, Eric felt a little piece of joy actually shrivel up inside himself. But then someone kissed him. Full on the lips and with reckless abandon.

"I've never kissed a big-time football hero," Jill said with a smile that almost rivaled Eric's.

"Me neither," he said. "What's it like?"

She instantly slammed back into him for another kiss. When she'd finished, she threw her head back, pretending to think. "It's pretty nice," she finally said.

This is the way life should be, Eric thought to himself. Being celebrated as a hero. Being kissed by a beautiful girl. Pinely was, at that exact moment, the most perfect place in the world.

"Hey Jill, I was thinking," he said. "Maybe I'll just stay here in Pinely and live like a hero."

"You think this is your big moment? The peak of your life?" she laughed.

"Could be," he said.

"Well, that might not be a bad idea then," she shrugged. "But you'll have to do it without me."

"Really?" he said in mock-indignation. He looked around at the chaos he'd helped create. "Okay. But I'm giving this all up for you."

She kissed him again. "I appreciate it."

Just before he made his way into the field house with the rest of the team, he looked up at the lights on the scoreboard. They radiated in their perfect pattern. And even though he knew it wasn't physically possible from such a distance, he swore he could feel the warmth of their simple white light.

FRIDAY

He was alive again, thanks to Jill. The touch of her skin, the look in her eyes, every bit of it had awakened him in ways he'd all but forgotten and left for dead. An old friend—Possibility— had even made a surprise appearance in his head. Eric couldn't remember the last time any consideration of the future had stopped by for a visit. For the past few years, his thoughts had been strictly reserved for complex reworkings of the past. But there he was, well into the night, forgetting about the things that could have been, and carefully handling delicate ideas of what might yet be. He was a little shaky with such thoughts at first, but then it all started coming back to him. There was a time when Possibility was the favorite toy in his toolbox. He could wield it with such deft precision, entire worlds could shift, appear, transform, and practically live on their own.

Eric crafted new landscapes for the first time in years. He would go with Jill to California. Work for a year, establish residency. Get his brain ready for college. College. He and Jill would take the love that was obviously still there between them, and weave it into a grand tapestry of passion. If anything, their love would be even stronger because of their time apart. He would study hard and learn great things. About the histories of civilizations, the religions of man, the ways of science. He'd read so much about all these things already. But he was certain the halls of higher learning would dwarf the piecemeal education he'd fashioned through the Pinely Public Library. He would see the Pacific. Get a sunburn in February. Live the life he'd always known was out there for him.

There was, of course, the matter of Tess. It seemed strange to him that this piece of the puzzle had stumped him for so long. He'd done the right thing. He'd stayed, been a father. But how long was his obligation? The most intense parts were behind them now. The early stages. A child's mind develops most rapidly before the age of three. He'd read that in one of his books. Now she was five. And a half. She knew things he'd never taught her. She was picking things up on her own. He wasn't a day-to-day influence in her life anymore, but one of a thousand influences that were multiplying by the minute. There's a shelf life on the importance of fatherhood. He didn't need his dad. Hadn't for a while. Besides, it wasn't like Eric was going to stop being her father. He'd still be able to handle any crisis with words and thoughts. Plus he'd come home and see her as much as he could. If she wasn't too embarrassed by him. Which seemed to be starting already.

It all made perfect sense. It was the most logical and clear-headed idea to pass through his brain in so long, he could hardly sleep. It would take some time for everyone else to get used to. People grew accustomed to things moving in the same direction, or not moving at all. It was called inertia. Eric remembered that from his science classes in high school. It applied to physics, but Eric had come to believe in social inertia. He was living proof of it. An object at rest tends to stay at rest, until acted upon by an outside force. That was the phrase he remembered. He'd needed an outside force for so long. So it was pure perfection when Jill called and asked to meet him at Abby's for lunch.

"Last night was a huge mistake."

They hadn't even ordered yet. Not even coffee. He could still feel the cold vinyl of the booth through his jeans.

"It was . . . I don't know. I was drunk, and all mixed up. Being here, seeing you. Burying dad. And I just wanted—" She paused and looked down at her hands. If she'd had coffee, she could have handled the mug or even taken a sip while she looked for the right words. But she didn't. That was her own damn fault, Eric thought. "I just wanted to feel a connection with something," she finally said.

"Some. Thing," Eric heard himself say as he looked over his shoulder for Abby.

"What?" Jill asked.

He waved at Abby and pointed at their booth. "So not *me*," he said to Jill. "Not even some*one*. But some*thing*."

"Oh, I didn't mean it like that."

"You said it like that."

"Can I get you guys something?" Abby asked, pulling her notepad from her food-stained apron.

"Something," Eric said with widening eyes. "You mean like, food?"

Abby looked over the rims of her glasses at Eric. "Are you new here?" she asked.

"He's just giving me a hard time," Jill explained.

"Lucky you," Abby sighed.

"But by 'something,' you mean something inanimate, right?" Eric continued.

"Yeah," Abby said, rolling her eyes, "I'm afraid our lobster tank's busted."

"Well what do you think, Jill?" he said, looking at the menu. "Do you see anything here you might be able to feel a connection with?"

"I'll have the club sandwich," she said politely to Abby.

"Club sandwich?" Eric nodded, "I could see that. Lots of layers and flavors. More than one opportunity to connect there. Me? I think I'm just going to keep it simple and go with the chicken-fried steak, thank you."

Abby jotted down their orders, shaking her head the whole time. "There are plenty of empty tables," she said to Jill, "if you get tired of this shit."

"Thank you, I'll consider that."

Once Abby had made her way back to the kitchen, it seemed like the two of them had nothing to say anymore. Jill watched someone out on the street tying green and white balloons to a telephone pole. Eric watched Jill. She seemed taller than she was in high school. It struck Eric as an odd thing to notice about someone who was sitting down.

"You and I," she started, still staring out the window, "we're different people now."

"What do you mean?"

"What do I mean?" she said, as though he'd just asked what color the sky is. "You're a dad, Eric. You're a bartender. You work at a funeral home."

"But I'm still the same person I always was," he pleaded.

"Maybe," she said with a sad smile, "but I'm not."

The smell of bacon and chicken-fried steak on the skillet was drifting from the kitchen, mingling with the cigarette smoke of the diners at the counter. It was the sort of thing Eric wouldn't have noticed normally. But now that he did, he couldn't seem to concentrate on anything else.

"I'm never moving back to Pinely," she continued. "There's nothing here for me."

Was this air even safe to breathe, he found himself wondering? Pork and grease and carbon monoxide, all mixing together like that? He didn't know what mustard gas was made of, but he felt pretty certain these ingredients would do in a pinch. It seemed impossible there could be room for any oxygen in that mixture. They were almost definitely being poisoned, and Jill didn't even seem to notice.

"This is a great place to grow up. A great place to raise kids. Which is why you're never going to leave."

"I can leave," he managed to say. His voice sounded distant, like it was coming from another room. Probably one of the first signs of hypoxemia, he thought. "I've been thinking about it. About trying to pick things up in California."

Suddenly, he was ripped from his dreamlike state by words that rang out like a gunshot. "I have a boyfriend," she said.

It was a concept that was allowed to hang in the festering air, because at that moment, Abby arrived with their lunch orders in hand.

"Club sandwich," she said with a smile, placing the dish in front of Jill. "And chicken-fried steak for you, sunshine."

Eating the food in front of them seemed like the obvious thing to do. There was no need to dredge up any further unpleasantness. Eric picked up his fork and started cutting through his steak. It seemed more unhealthy than usual, given his earlier concerns about the air quality, but it would just seem strange not to eat it now. So he stabbed a chunk of the meat and crammed it into his mouth, happy to have an excuse to not talk for a while.

"His name is Rodney," Jill suddenly said.

Eric looked at her plate and noticed she hadn't even touched her sandwich. "Who?" he asked through his mouthful of food.

"My boyfriend."

Eric could feel his eyes squinting. It took an inhuman amount of force to swallow his bite of steak. "What'd you tell me that for?"

"I don't know, I thought—" Her hands smoothed over the already sleek surface of the table. "I thought you might like to know."

"That your boyfriend's name is Rodney?"

"I don't know," she said in exasperation.

"Well I don't either," he said. "You asked me to lunch for some reason. And so far all we've talked about is that you and I are different now. You have a boyfriend. His name is Rodney. Oh, and of course, we covered the fact that I can serve as a nice pacifier in a pinch."

"I just didn't want you to misunderstand what happened last night. To think there was something . . . going on between us."

"Well I'm sure that'll come as quite a relief to Rodney when you explain all this to him. 'You see Rod . . .' Do you call him 'Rod,' or is that too—explicit?" He could tell Jill was becoming less and less amused by him, but he was already in the throes of a whole different sort of inertia. "'So it's like this, Rod. I was straddled atop the young man with my tongue in his mouth because I missed you so much and I just wanted to feel a connection with something.' Does that sort of shit actually fly in California? Cause I don't think it would here."

He'd loaded her guns for her. The eyes gave it away. He was bare chested, splayed out, and tied down, waiting for her to fire that last comment right back through his heart. At first he thought she was just working out the wording. Fashioning it into a particularly deft variety of "Fuck you, you hypocritical prick!" But as each second passed in peace, he began to realize she had no intention of blasting back. It was worse than if she had.

"Sometimes I wish things were different," she said. "But they're not." Her eyes welled up again, but she held herself together. "Dad always said, 'There's a reason there's no rewind button in life. Nothing would ever get done.'"

Eric wanted to say something, but was afraid it would just come out mean. He seemed to have an abundance of mean inside him at the moment. Even when he thought it might stop her from standing up, putting on her coat, and leaving money on the table, he couldn't think of one thing to say that didn't involve the word "Rodney."

"I have to go, Eric," she said.

He nodded in agreement and watched her walk away. It seemed like forever, the time it took her to get to the door. He wanted to do something. He, at least, wanted her to look back. But she didn't. She kept her eyes forward and walked straight out the door.

Eric looked up at the stadium lights when he felt the first drop of rain. Standing against the fence, Eric watched the Pinely players gorge in a gross display of over-exuberance. Occasionally, one of them would stop and stare at the dim lights on the old, tattered scoreboard as though looking for more proof. Something even more concrete than a giant green board lit up with white lights. Eric wanted to tell them that sometimes the unexpected, no matter how clearly it's presented, can be difficult to comprehend.

"Un-fucking-believable!" Deke was shouting. "My dad's trying to figure out how to kick himself in the nuts right now."

Pinely had won the game. Everyone was still trying to figure out how, but there it was on the scoreboard, plain as day. Wildcats: 6, Visitors: 0. The Cedarsville quarterback was tackled out of bounds on the first series of the game. It was a clean play that would have been uneventful if he hadn't slipped on the gravel track and broken his ankle. That put Cedarsville in a bad spot right from the start since, like most teams on the small school level, they didn't really have a backup quarterback. The closest they had was one of their receivers who, when there was some extra time in practice, would take a few snaps from the center. He didn't really know the plays. He wasn't even all that good at taking the snap. So the Cedarsville offense was reduced to four quarters of fumbled snaps, busted plays, and generally unproductive attempts at moving the ball downfield.

Luckily for Cedarsville, the Pinely offense consisted of a lot of the same, despite their quarterback being in perfect health. Their sterile offense produced little in the form of excitement until, late in the fourth quarter with the clock ticking away to nothing, Coach Gleason reached deep into his bag of trick plays. Everyone had a different opinion of what had actually happened, but the one thing they all seemed to agree on was that the play involved some heavy, and possibly even illegal, misdirection on the part of the Pinely players. It was more like a thespian production than a football play. Gleason was yelling at a player who seemed to be off the field, but was actually standing in bounds. The quarterback acted like the ball had been hiked over his head, when it was really snapped to the running back. Just as he reached the line of scrimmage, the runner turned and tossed the ball to the quarterback, who threw it downfield to the player everyone thought was out of bounds in the first place. There was high drama as the poor kid bobbled the ball for a good ten yards before finally getting a grip on it and carrying it into the end zone. Had there been midgets or an elephant involved, it could have rivaled the greatest productions of Barnum & Bailey. As it was, it was simply the cap to one of the most improbable victories in Pinely Wildcat history.

"I mean seriously," Deke was yelling right in Eric's face, "Dad is just shittin' himself right now," he cackled. "And he blames you."

"Me?!" Eric said in disbelief. "What'd I do?"

"I'm not sure. Something about your prediction."

"Prediction?"

"Predicting Pinely was going to win."

The rain was picking up now, but Eric was determined to settle this then and there. "Now I know this was quite a few days ago," he said with as much patience as he could muster, "but you still might be able to remember that I didn't predict anything. This was all his stupid idea."

"Yeah, but then you went and did that thing last night."

Just the mention of last night made Eric's mind whip around in contradiction. There was love, passion, and plans, all slammed in the door of rejection. But not one idea relating to anything Deke might be talking about. "Did what?" he asked.

"Gave that little pep talk," Deke said as though he'd just uncovered whodunit.

"What are you talking about?"

"You said to those guys, 'You're gonna win.'"

He could feel the water trickling between his shoulder blades. "I thought that's what your dad wanted me to say!"

"To everybody else. Not to the players. He thinks you went and inspired 'em."

"Deke," Eric laughed, "it took a broken ankle and a last-minute circus act for them to win. I'm flattered your dad holds my inspirational abilities in such high regard, but I *really* don't think I had anything to do with this one."

"Fuck no you didn't!" Deke shouted with a maniacal look in his eye. "That's just what he thinks. He also thinks wrestling is real, so I wouldn't worry about it. I'm just telling you he's pissed. So, you know, don't talk to him or anything."

"Do I ever?"

Deke just shrugged and crammed his hands in his pockets. "What say we get on outta the rain?"

"You want to go over there by the field house?"

"Hell no," Deke sputtered. "I wanna go to the Legion."

Eric looked up again at the scoreboard and tried to ignore the feeling that was working its way around inside him. "It's just a game," he heard echo in his mind. This time, the parts that saw it differently were a lot less agreeable. He wiped the wet hair from his eyes and looked over at Deke, who was watching the Pinely players out on the field.

"Look at these lucky little sonsabitches," Deke said.

Eric turned to see what Deke was noticing. Maybe he saw boys, like they used to be, allowing themselves to get caught up in a perfect moment. Or maybe he saw himself, standing on the field seven years ago, with his whole life ahead of him.

"They're probably all gettin' laid tonight," Deke said, with the weight of the world in his voice. "It's depressing."

Eric wasn't sure if he was joking or not, so he chose not to say anything. Poignant silence was always a safe option. He watched Deke stare at the players for a second more before he realized he had no idea what was on Deke's mind. An idea that disturbed him more than a little.

"Come on, Deke," he said. "Let's get out of here."

Deke nodded and started walking toward the gate and out to the highway. Neither of them had an umbrella, but they were both too wet to care. As they passed by the players gathered under the goal post, someone called out.

"Hey Eric!"

It sounded like a girl's voice. But when Eric turned he saw one of the Pinely players waving at him. A kid who was so young, his voice was still settling on a pitch.

"We did it," he shouted through his full-throttle smile. "Just like you said!"

Eric managed to toss the kid a half-assed thumbs up, which seemed to tickle the boy beyond all proportions. He immediately shot one right back, with more enthusiasm than such a lame signal should ever warrant. The higher the boy's spirits rose, the further Eric's heart sank, until there was nothing to do but traipse through the rain with his childhood friend, in search of warm shelter and cold beer.

The scene at the Legion was already ridiculous. Bolstered by their vicarious victory, the crew around the bar was loud and getting louder. A situation that wasn't going to be remedied by the fact they were drunk and getting drunker. Any hope of a quiet entrance was shattered by the raspy voice of Kirby calling out to Eric the second he walked through the door.

"Hey, look who it is!" he shouted. "It's Pinely's own fortune-teller. You're just a regular . . ." He lost momentum, but quickly resigned himself to ask for help. "Aw, what's that big word I'm looking for?"

"Charlatan?" Eric offered as he shouldered his way to the bar.

"Maybe. Is that the one who can see the future? I thought it was 'para'-something."

Suggestions came down faster than the rain outside.

"Paratrooper?"

"Parakeet?"

"Paraplegic?"

"Parasol?"

Kirby looked out over the bar to see who said that. "What the fuck's a parasol?"

"You know, a little umbrella," answered Tony Riggs. "Like women used to carry when they wore hoop skirts and shit like that."

The whole bar burst out laughing at Tony, saying things like "You love men!" and "Your daughters are safe, but hide your sons." Ridicule at the Legion was always served up without bias or mercy. It didn't matter if you were a kid, a cripple, a cop, or the goddamned mayor. Tony was blind. Had been since a hunting accident three years before. People were dying to tease him even then, since he'd gotten himself shot in the face by carrying a turkey over his shoulder while still tooting on his bird call. No one blamed his cousin for shooting him. Not even Tony. Still, there was just enough tragedy involved to keep people from making fun of him. It wasn't until he decided to get a Seeing Eye dog that he became fair game again. Staggered by the cost of the well-trained beasts, Tony opted to save a few bucks and buy a used one whose owner had passed away. The dog had served its prior master dutifully for years. Maybe a few too many years. Tony hadn't had the dog for six weeks before it became obvious something was wrong. A quick veterinary exam revealed that Tony's discount dog had begun to develop cataracts, which officially tilted the scales of Tony's case from tragedy to comedy. The onslaught of "blind leading the blind" jokes that came Tony's way more than made up for the fact that everyone at the Legion had been so well behaved in not making fun of him for being shot while impersonating a turkey.

He took the parasol jokes in stride by giving them all the finger.

"I thought sign language was for the deaf, Tony," someone shouted, ushering in another wave of laughter and guffaws. Eric had to shout in order to get the two beers he wanted. The bar was packed, so Eric and Deke were forced to sit at a table right next to Kirby and Mack.

"Seriously," Kirby started before Eric even had a chance to relax, "anytime you think about playing the lottery, you let me know. I'm going in right behind you."

"Me?" Eric asked before taking a long pull from his bottle.

"Yes, you. You're the one with the spooky knack for predictin' the future."

"Oh yeah," Eric sighed.

Deke chuckled to himself and lit up a cigarette. "What the fuck would you do if you won the lottery anyhow, Kirb?"

"Shit fire, son, I've got a whole plan detailed out and hid under my mattress. Step One: Get the fuck out of town before Doris gets her hands on any of the money. Step Two: Pick me up a nice BMW."

Mack almost fell out of his seat, he turned around so fast. "BMW?!" he bellowed. "What the fuck you want with a piece of shit foreign car like that?"

"It happens to be a high-quality, precision driving machine, dipshit."

"What, a Cadillac ain't good enough for you? A nice Town Car, maybe? Something American made?"

"Fuck you. It's my lottery money," Kirby said with enough conviction to make Deke jump a little in surprise. "When you win the lottery, buy as many Cadillacs as you want. I'm gettin' a BMW."

"Alright, wait a minute," Mack said, leaning well into Kirby's personal space. "If you gotta be all big for your britches and European and all that, get a Mercedes. It's okay to buy a Mercedes now, cause Chrysler bought them."

Eric, who had watched this sad exchange in silence, couldn't let this one slip by. "So they're allowed to buy an entire foreign company, but Kirby can't buy one fuckin' car?"

"Hey, mind your own business, nibshit," barked Mack.

"I thought he was the one who was going to pick the winning numbers," said Deke.

"So?"

"So it's kinda his business."

Mack stared at Deke for a second, smoldering even more than the cigarette hanging from his stumpy fingers. "Then you mind *your* fuckin' business. How bout that?"

Eric cocked his head back and finished the last of his beer. "Arguing about spending money you don't even have. It's a wonder we don't get more tourists in this town." He stood up and nudged Deke in the leg. "You want another?"

The light shone dark through the brown bottle in Deke's hand. "No," he said, "I still got like half a beer here. You might want to pace yourself a little."

"You might want to stop telling me what to do," he said before making his way back to the bar.

The topic of conversation never managed to veer too far from the wonder and spectacle of the evening's victory over Cedarsville. Eric found himself with little to say about it, so he spent most of his time listening. And drinking. No one could seem to say enough about what a spectacular game it had been. But since it was basically four quarters of drudgery followed by one wild play, the discussion constantly revolved around every nuanced speck of minutia the great trick play could provide. There were men at the bar who'd recounted the birth of their first child with less detail and enthusiasm. As Eric listened to them, he would have sworn the play had happened in a suspended time that allowed for the thorough dissection of nanoseconds. But his breaking point didn't come until a few hours later when it deteriorated into a comparison of locales.

"Well I was down by the south end zone, so I saw that kid break wide open from the start."

"See, I was standing right behind the bench, so I thought for sure it'd been a wild snap."

"Yeah, even from under the press box it looked like that."

"Well I was right there behind them, so I saw the snap. But I wasn't expecting the toss back."

"Aw come on!" Eric finally screamed. "This isn't 'Where were you when Kennedy was shot?' You were all in the same fucking place!"

Everyone stopped what they were doing and tried to find the right look to wear on their faces, torn between being angry that he'd interrupted their fun, and being ashamed that he was right. As was the case with sudden outbursts, Eric didn't have much to say once he'd popped his cork. It was just a quick blast that needed to get out before it caused an instant ulcer. Most people, once they'd erupted, felt compelled to continue. To justify their outburst with further rambling while they had the momentum. Not Eric. He was satisfied that he'd gotten everyone to stop talking. There was nothing else to add. Everyone stared at him, and he stared right back. He wasn't oblivious to the attention he'd drawn to himself. He just didn't care. In fact, with that area of discomfort remedied, his mind had already drifted off to another. He stood, and to no one in particular, made an announcement of sorts.

"I gotta piss."

No one said a word. They just watched him bump into the table, knock over the beer bottles he'd so diligently emptied, and stagger down the hall to the restroom. It took a full turn of the record in the jukebox before everyone forgot their moment of awkward embarrassment and returned to their in-depth analysis of the game.

There wasn't much point in having lights in the Legion restroom. From the smell of the place, they didn't seem to help people find the urinal. No one spent any time primping in front of the mirror, so the lights weren't helping there either. It wasn't the sort of bar where folks gave two shits how they looked. They already knew. They looked bad. The lights weren't helping people read at all. There was a notice by the sink reminding the bartender to wash his hands. A condom machine in the corner advertising "Savage Bliss: For maximum stimulation." And a sign over one of the urinals that said "This toilet doesn't flush. It's out of order." But there wasn't any soap at the sink. No one came to the Legion to get laid. And, from the streaked letters of the sign on the urinal, it looked like someone had already pissed directly on it. Eric figured they should rip up the floor, throw out the mirror, quit depressing everyone with the condom machine, and turn out the lights. Just a dark, dirt room where you did your business and got back to drinking.

He stood, listening to himself ring against the porcelain. The smell of the bathroom, which should have made him nauseous, was only making him angry. It seemed ridiculous he could be held hostage in this disgusting place by his own bladder. He looked at the sign on the urinal next to him. He hated that he lived in a place that would deem it necessary to have a sign that followed something as clear as "This toilet doesn't flush" with an additional statement like "It's out of order." Even more than that, he hated that someone could be stupid enough to actually urinate on such a distinctly unambiguous sign. But more than anything else, he hated that he had to breathe air that was ripe with the misguided waste of these same fools who constantly surrounded him. Even when he was all alone.

His body must have sensed he was reaching his breaking point because the endless stream suddenly stopped. He quickly zipped up and made his way to the sink. The water splashed against the stained basin with slightly less force than his own outpouring at the urinal. He filled his hands and splashed his face a few times over, hoping to chase away the fire that had started to build behind his brain. The water dropped from his face in tiny beads as he stood up and looked into the mirror. He looked bad. His eyes, more red than white, stared back at him, goading him on. He knew what they wanted. To stir things up. To touch up the fading bruise that hovered over them. He obviously hadn't drunk himself into submission, so there was only one other option.

But Eric was tired of playing the only option left. He wanted to try a new one. To go home, lie down, and see if he could make it through the night without finding any trouble. It seemed like a bold plan. Perhaps a bit ambitious, given his current state, but he was willing to risk failure for the chance at success. He wiped his face on his shirtsleeve and opened the door. He tried not to notice that the smell outside the bathroom wasn't much better than the smell inside. He even tried to pretend he didn't hear the people at the bar still discussing the greater nuances of the astounding trick play. But there was no ignoring the bellowing voice of Deke's dad making his way across the bar.

"There you are, you sonofabitch!"

Serenity gave way to survival, and Eric suddenly found himself right in the thick of it.

"You cocksucker!" Deke's dad was shouting. "You loud-mouthed stain!"

Deke was right behind his dad, trying to get him under control as he barreled past people's tables, knocking over their drinks along the way. Eric just stood his ground and tried to focus on his original plan of not getting into trouble. A plan that seemed infinitely more difficult the closer Deke's dad got. He wasn't too confident in his self-control, so he took the added measure of putting his hands in his pockets, hoping to reduce the chance of sudden calamity through poorly mannered reflexes.

"Hey Mr. Williams," he said, rocking back on his heels a little. Having his hands in his pockets made this sort of neighborly pose feel completely natural. "How's your night going?"

"I think you know——" Deke's dad started to answer, before tripping over the leg of a chair in front of him. If laughter were a cushion, everyone around him would have provided a soft landing. As it was, he landed clumsily with a loud thud. Some change spilled out of his pockets and a litany of curse words spilled out of his mouth, but he quickly found his way back to his feet, surprised to be standing just six inches away from Eric. "You know damn well how my night's going, you little dickweed!"

"Actually I don't," Eric said.

"Well don't you worry, cause I'm gonna tell ya." His hot breath parted on either side of Eric's face, landing its boozy sting in his eyes. Eric tried to ignore its potency and focus on finding a way out of the situation. He looked at Mr. Williams, who was contorting his face and making a sound like his head had a slow leak. The hissing sound got louder, until it finally sprayed forth in a bold declaration. "Shitty!"

This was not the sort of indignity Eric would normally allow to go unpunished. He'd just been spit on by an old, drunk psychopath. The fire ran to his face, and the faint taste of metal came to his mouth. But he kept his hands, now fists, firmly planted in his pockets.

"Deke?" Eric said sternly.

Deke looked like he didn't know whether to shit or wind his watch. He just danced around in place, trying to see if he could somehow, through his own enthusiasm, get everyone to settle down.

"Hey Dad," he said, "why don't we just sit down and have a couple of drinks?"

"I don't need any more drinks!"

"Well, that's probably true," Deke sighed, "but you don't need to be gettin' all tangled up with Eric either."

"I'll tell you what I need," he shouted, pointing his finger in the air. Eric saw the finger come toward him, but didn't really believe Mr. Williams would use it. It landed with a jolt on Eric's sternum. "I need this filthy shit-stick to pay me back all the money I lost because of his big mouth."

The first poke in the chest came as a shock. The second, third, and each one after was anticipated, dreaded, and added to the increasingly difficult task of letting all this slide. Eric stood, fists in pockets, and allowed himself to be jabbed so many times, he practically had an out-of-body experience. Mr. Williams continued his diatribe, surrounding Eric with his drunken breath and waling his foul, bony finger against his chest with increasing intensity. Finally, on his concluding point, one that was lost on Eric since his words had long since turned into incoherence riding a breathy chariot of stink, Mr. Williams planted his finger and pushed with deliberate force. Just enough to knock Eric off balance. He shifted his footing and let one hand drop from his pocket to keep from toppling over, just as Mr. Williams put the final touch on his tirade.

"Ya fucker!" he yelled, leaning his face in toward Eric for added force.

His loose hand was like a dog set free in the park. It'd been cooped up too long and needed to run. It swung up from his waist, over his head, and came crashing down across the bridge of Mr. Williams's nose with a loud crack. His knees buckled, and the whole bar watched as he crumpled into an uncomfortable looking pile. Eric stood there, still, one hand swinging at his side, the other firmly planted in his pocket. He looked like someone waiting for a bus, or watching a parade. Except for the blood on his pants.

"Holy fuck," Deke shouted. "You just beat up my dad!"

Eric looked down at Mr. Williams, then over at Deke. He wasn't certain what to do. His original plan was shot to hell.

"You think he's alright?"

"Hell, I don't know," Deke said. "I've never seen him take a punch before."

"From the looks of it, he hasn't taken many."

"Guess not."

They both stood over the heap that used to be Deke's dad and looked at each other.

"Maybe you could help me put him in the booth over there," Deke said.

"You don't want to take him home?"

"Well . . . eventually," Deke said. He stood for a moment, looking down at his dad and shaking his head absently. "I thought we might have a couple more beers first."

If Eric had thought about it, it would have seemed strange. But since he didn't, it sounded like a pretty good idea. Everyone was still on their feet, watching as Deke and Eric scooped Mr. Williams off the floor and laid him out on the cushioning of a vinyl booth. Then they all watched Deke reach into his dad's front pocket and fish out something.

"Car keys," Deke said, holding them above his head.

"He drove here?" Eric asked.

"Yep."

"How'd he manage that? He was fuckin' hammered."

Deke shrugged his shoulders. "He said it took some doin'."

The two of them watched Mr. Williams for a little while longer, making sure he was still breathing. When they were satisfied he'd be okay on his own, they turned around and headed to the bar. Martin was standing there, watching them as they came over. "Is he gonna be alright?" he asked.

"I suppose," Deke said.

"How bout a couple of beers, Martin?" Eric asked.

Martin was normally pretty quick with an order, but this time he just stood there, shaking his head. "I don't think I can do that."

"What are you talking about?"

"Well, you're pretty drunk," he said. "And you just beat up Deke's dad."

"I hardly beat him up!" Eric protested. "I only punched him one goddamn time!"

Martin shrugged. "Did the trick."

"So Deke's dad's got a glass jaw and I don't get to drink anymore?"

"It wasn't really his jaw," Deke offered. "You hit him more in the nose."

"Truth is," Martin said, "you should probably just go."

"Go where?"

"I don't . . . ," he started, then shifted. "You know the rules. You fight, you go."

"Aw c'mon, Martin," Eric shouted. "That wasn't a fight!"

"It wasn't much of one, but it counts."

Eric stood and looked at him, feeling the blood surge back to his head. He tried to talk in a collected, even tone. "Look Martin, if you get me a beer—it'll save me the trouble of having to come back there and get it myself."

The two of them stared at each other with an intensity normally reserved for matinee westerns. The rest of the bar was staring too, but they had to divide their focus between the two, while Martin and Eric could concentrate solely on one another. Eric waited for Martin to get him a beer. Martin waited for Eric to leave. Everyone else knew neither of those things was going to happen, so they all waited to see what sort of third option materialized. Hoping for something dynamic.

No one really saw Eric jump, they just saw him land on the other side of the bar. Deke dropped to the ground, clutching his face, a hail of shattered glass descended around him, swept off the bar by Eric's legs. Eric tried to calmly make his way to the cooler, but Martin had already pulled out the baseball bat they kept behind the bar. He swatted Eric in the back of the legs, bringing him to his knees. Just as soon as Eric pressed his hand to the ground to try to get up, he felt the bat land between his shoulder blades. With his face on the floor, breathing in the stale beer collected there, Eric knew better than to try to stand up again.

"That was unnecessary, Martin," he said.

"You have to go."

"I just want a beer."

"I'm calling the cops."

Eric laughed and waved his hands above his head. "Okay, I give up. Are you going to hit me again?"

"Are you going to leave?"

"Yes."

Eric pried himself from the floor and took a step to come out from behind the bar. Martin stepped too, but was surprised to find Eric turned around to face him. Somehow, in one swift motion, Eric pried the bat from his hand and brought it crashing down on the bar, sending glass flying in a storm. He pressed the blunt end of the bat underneath Martin's chin and smiled.

"You call the fuckin' cops," he said before turning around and throwing the bat toward the back wall. "I'll be at home if they need me."

Everyone thought they should do something. But no one tried to stop him as he picked up his coat, strolled across the room, and walked out the door.

At least the rain had slowed down. When he was in the Gas N' Sip it had picked up so much he could hardly see the street outside. A torrent that roared against the awning louder than thunder. After walking half a block toward his house from the Legion, he'd thought better of it and made his way toward the Gas N' Sip. It'd occurred to him that maybe he shouldn't go home. Martin was just enough of a hard-on to send the cops to his house over their little tussle. Besides, he still wanted a beer. He could have easily gone to the Eagles. It was closer. But it was obvious his social graces were just slightly less plentiful than his luck, so he opted for a six-pack and some isolation.

Unfortunately, to get the beer he still had to talk to the kid at the checkout counter. Which is where it all went south. Had the kid just done his job and sold him the beer, there wouldn't have been any trouble. But he didn't. He decided instead to concern himself with Eric's well-being. Saying "I don't think I should sell you that" was the first mistake the kid made. One from which he never fully recovered.

"Why the hell not?" Eric asked.

"It seems like you're plenty drunk already," the kid explained.

"Why do you say that?"

The kid looked like he didn't want to be having the conversation any more than Eric did, but he felt compelled to continue. "For starters, you kicked over that Pepsi display in the back there."

Eric looked where the kid was pointing and saw about a dozen two-liter bottles of Pepsi strewn about the floor in total disarray. He'd heard a crash, but thought it was just the storm outside. All he could offer by way of an apology was a half-hearted shrug.

"Sorry bout that. I'm a little clumsy sometimes." He reached into his back pocket and fished out his wallet. "So how much for the beer?"

"I really don't think I can sell you this," the kid said, growing increasingly nervous.

"Well is there any beer in the store you can sell me?"

"I don't think so."

Eric looked at the kid and tried to smile, but what developed on his face was more of an annoyed dementia. "And why not?"

"Cause you're drunk."

"Yeah," Eric grunted, "I am. It took me the better part of the evening to get drunk. Now you're gonna go and fuck it all up! Now how bout you show a little respect for someone willing to see a job through to the end, and just sell me the beer?"

"What if you go outside there, in the condition you're in, and hurt somebody?"

"Don't worry, I'm not driving."

"You don't need to drive to hurt someone."

"I don't need to go outside to hurt someone."

When the kid reached underneath the counter, a quick flash of panic rushed Eric. He figured it would be just his luck he'd run across the Dudley Do-Right of convenience store cashiers, willing to shoot him over a lame threat and a six-pack of cheap beer. But all the kid came up with was a telephone and a threat of his own.

"I'm going to call the cops," he said, trying not to sound scared.

"The cops?" Eric laughed. "What are you going to tell them? That I'm standing here, with money in my hand, trying to buy beer?"

The kid wasn't sure what he was going to do, but he held the phone like it was a powerful weapon. His only defense.

"Here's how we'll do it," Eric finally said. "I'll put some money down on the counter here. Figuring in the cost of the beer, plus tax, this should be more than enough. It'll even leave you a little something for your trouble." The kid watched as Eric counted out the money and gingerly slid it across the counter, as though it were a hostage situation. "Now," Eric continued, "I'm going to take this and go. And we can both get on with our evenings."

He walked toward the door, pushing aside the rain as he swung it open. The kid was incensed that his authority at the Gas N' Sip had been subverted and shouted out to Eric in an ugly and desperate voice.

"I'm going to call the cops!" he screamed. "I know who you are!"

As the door swung shut behind Eric, he turned and jammed against it with the palm of his hand, just above the sticker that read "Pull." The kid was terrified, looking at Eric's face through the door, glowing sinister in the green light of the vending machine beside him. With swift feet and monstrous force, Eric ran to the other side of the machine and rocked it until it toppled over on its side, crashing down in front of the doorway. Leaning over the wreckage, he gave the door handle a good tug, but it slammed into the toppled machine and didn't budge an inch.

"Do you?" he shouted through the glass at the kid, before picking up his beer and walking off in the pouring rain.

That was when he'd gotten the most wet. The rain had settled down since then. He'd made his way to the lot behind the abandoned Quaker State and sat drinking his beer. When he finished the first one, he threw the bottle against the cinder-block wall of the old deserted building. It shattered with a loud pop and chimed down over the paved lot. The taste of beer was becoming increasingly unpleasant, and his tongue was coated in a bitter residue coming from inside his own mouth. But he was excited by his new diversion and was eager to finish the next beer so he could smash the bottle. It didn't take him long to down the beer, but this time he surprised himself by shouting, "Another beer, Rodney?" as he let it fly.

Rodney. What kind of name was that supposed to be anyway, he wondered? A name for an uptight little bootlicker, he imagined. It suddenly crossed his mind that, even though he hadn't seen his name tag, he wouldn't have been the least bit surprised to discover the kid trapped inside the Gas N' Sip was named Rodney. He seemed like a Rodney if ever he'd laid eyes on one. By the time he finished the third beer, he threw the bottle with so much force he almost fell over, screaming out, "Take that, Rodney!" as the glass vaporized against the wall.

He started laughing. To himself at first, but slowly rising until it reached a deranged cackle. He just didn't know what to do anymore. With a sharp flick of the wrist, he twisted off the cap of his next beer and began pouring it into his mouth from arm's length, spilling it down the sides of his face and into his ears. Something tickled against the back of his throat making him cough. The spray of beer launched into the sky, then fell over him with the rain. His beer was still half-full, but he couldn't wait anymore. He turned around and launched the beer with feral abandon, but was surprised to find he'd staggered to within a few short feet of the wall. The shards of glass ricocheted against him—off his hands, down the back of his shirt, into his face. He dropped to the ground and landed with a wet squish. At first, he couldn't tell if he was bleeding. The rain, sweat, and beer made it hard to tell. But suddenly he was bathed in a bright, white light. It shone over him with unrelenting intensity, and brought to life all the colors around him. The yellow leaves in the gutter beside him. The sparkling green glass of the shattered bottles. And the rich red blood from the cuts on his hands.

"I shoulda known," came a voice on the other side of the light. "People been calling you in all night."

Eric brought his hand over his eyes to try to block the light, but it didn't do any good. It wasn't until the person moved the flashlight out of his eyes that he could begin to make out the figure in front of him.

"Deputy Dan," Eric smiled. "Looks like you got here just in time."

"For what?" Danny Moran asked, shining the light around the lot.

"Well, I only got two beers left. One for each of us."

Danny shook his head and turned the light on himself. It danced off his badge, throwing random patches of light into the darkest corners of the abandoned lot. "I'm on duty, dickhead. Someone said they heard a madman screaming and throwing bottles."

Eric looked up at him and shrugged. "Haven't seen him."

"Yeah, that's the problem," Dan muttered. "Did you do this to yourself?"

"Do what?"

"Well, you're bleeding."

Eric looked at his hands and shook his head. "Rodney did it."

Dan shut off the flashlight and just stood there. Eric was glad to have the light off. His head rocked back against the wall, and he felt something loose inside his mouth. He rolled it around with his tongue, against the inside of his cheek, letting out short grunts of pain the whole time. There was a strange taste in his mouth, like iron. When the object finally reached his lips, he pulled it out with his fingers and held it up to catch what little light was available.

"Glass," he said to Danny.

"Man," Danny chuckled sadly to himself, "I wish I had a camera right now."

"I wish I had magic powers," Eric answered.

"What?"

"That's what I always wish for," he explained, then spit the blood from his mouth.

"Fuck," Danny sighed. "You don't even have regular powers."

He watched Eric spit a few more times, then slowly try to get to his feet. It was a painful sight. Eric winced as he scooted his back up against the wall. He said something to Danny about glass down his shirt, but he didn't switch tactics. When he'd finally righted himself, he looked around the lot, then straight at Danny with a silly grin of accomplishment. "What now?" he asked.

"Let's go to the car."

"Well all right!" Eric shouted in mock glee. "What a fucking day I'm having! Bullshit lunch. Bullshit game. Bullshit from everyone in charge of the world's beer supply. And now, the true topper, a bullshit ride with my ol' weekend buddy. Mister Deputy Daniel Moran himself."

"What's your fuckin' problem, Mercer?" Dan snapped.

"I'm drunk, Dan. What's yours?"

Dan was trying not to get upset, but Eric was certainly making it difficult. "You think you're better than me? Is that it?"

"At what?"

The flashlight popped to life again, and Dan shone it directly in Eric's eyes as he walked toward him. Eric couldn't see a thing and was surprised to find himself practically lifted off his feet and walking around the corner of the building, entirely against his will. With swift efficiency, Dan opened the back door of the cruiser, crammed Eric's head down under the doorway, and shoved him into the back seat. Eric's protests about his abandoned beer were stifled by the door slamming shut behind him. He waited quietly until Dan came around to the driver's side and climbed in behind the wheel.

"You may not have heard that last part," Eric said, "cause you kind of slammed the door right in the middle. But my beers are still over there by the dumpster." Danny didn't say anything. Eric watched him through the cage that separated their compartments of the vehicle as he started up the car and pulled out of the lot. "You don't know what I had to go through to get those beers," Eric continued.

"Yeah, I do," Dan barked. "That poor kid at the convenience store had a twenty-minute asthma attack after you left." He looked in the rearview mirror at the sweaty, bloody, beer-soaked mess Eric had made of himself. "You truly are a fuckup, you know that?"

"Naw," Eric protested, "you just caught me at a bad time."

"Yeah well, what's that thing they say? If it looks like a duck and it acts like a duck, then it's a duck."

Eric sat silently, looking out the window of the car at the town of Pinely scrolling past. The car smelled like leather. And authority. Eric wondered how it always managed to smell like that when half the time it was full of drunks and criminals. It was something he thought about every time he rode in a police car. He'd just started considering the intensity and grade of saddle soap they must use when something dawned on him. "What about the Ugly Duckling?" he said.

"What about it?" Dan asked.

"He turned out to be a swan in the end."

Dan shook his head. "They knew something was wrong with him the whole time. I mean, he was never really a duck."

"Well," Eric grinned, "maybe I'm not really a fuckup."

"Maybe," Dan said as he turned into the market at the end of town. "But I wouldn't bet on it."

The engine went silent. Dan pulled the keys from the ignition, turned to Eric, and told him to wait there. Eric was immediately curious as to where Dan thought he might run off to. There were no door handles in the back of a police car. That was common knowledge, at least to Eric. It only briefly crossed his mind that Dan had probably never been in the back of a police car. Only the front.

He watched Dan stroll across the parking lot to the pay phone on the other side. He couldn't tell what he was saying. Or who he was talking to. He couldn't even read his lips. These were the exact situations where magic powers would come in handy, he thought. It wasn't a very long conversation and before he knew it, Dan was hanging up the phone and walking back toward him. And Eric was trying to pretend he hadn't been studying his every move. Dan settled back into the driver's seat, but made no motion toward starting up the engine. He just leaned back in his seat, the leather crunching under his weight, and looked at Eric in the rearview mirror.

"Some game, huh?" he finally said.

"Tonight?" Eric asked.

"Yeah."

"I guess. I mean," Eric sat and thought about it for a second. "No. Actually it was a shitty game," he said. "Some play though."

"Not quite the ass-kickin' you laid on them, huh?"

"I don't know," Eric sighed. "I guess not."

"What was it like, going to state?" Danny asked, still watching through the mirror.

Eric looked at the eyes reflecting back at him and tried to decipher their strange, sad look. "It wasn't anything, Dan. We lost in the first fuckin' round. It was just a letdown, really."

Dan grunted a little and shifted his gaze out the window. The silence settled over them as they both considered that word, "letdown," on their own terms. "And how's Gina?" Dan finally asked.

"She's fine, I guess. It's a small town, don't you ever see her?"

"Yeah, I see her." His radio squawked to life, the dispatcher barking out something about someone picking him up some pizza if they had the chance. Dan turned it off, then thought better of it and turned it back on, but down to a whisper. "She wants you more than anything, you know?"

"Yeah well," Eric said. It was something he'd picked up from his dad over the years. Something he said when he didn't really have anything to say. "I wish I could want her," was what he finally came up with. "Things would be less confusing. I think."

"What *do* you want?"

"Well that's an oddly insightful question from you there, Danny. I wouldn't have expected it." He looked up and saw those eyes staring back at him with that same strange look. Like they needed an answer. "I don't know," he finally said. "I know what I used to want."

Tiny wrinkles appeared on either side of the eyes in the mirror, but it was hard for Eric to tell if they were smiling or wincing. Dan took a deep breath before he spoke. "Me too."

A car drove into the lot and pulled right up beside the cruiser. Eric had been wondering why Danny wasn't taking him to the jailhouse, a quandary that was solved as soon as he saw the other car. It was a true piece of shit. The sort of thing no one would drive unless they were stricken by crippling poverty or sentimentality. Even in the poor lighting of the parking lot, there were visible bubbles of rust underneath the paint, which was chipped in some spots and fading everywhere else. The antenna was snapped off, which didn't really matter since the radio hadn't worked in years. Eric couldn't see the radio from where he was sitting. He just knew. It was his dad's car.

"Wait here," Danny said again, then stepped out of the cruiser.

Eric watched his dad shake his head as Dan spoke to him, never once letting his eyes drift in the direction of the backseat where Eric sat. After they'd talked for a few minutes, Eric's dad offered his hand to Dan. They shook like they'd just casually negotiated the price on a new washer/dryer, and Danny made his way back to the cruiser. He swung Eric's door open and stood to one side.

"Alright, shithead," Danny said. "You can go now."

Eric looked out the open door and could see his dad sitting behind the wheel of his "car," staring straight ahead. "Come on, Dan," he said. "Just take me to jail."

"I'm doing you a favor, dumb-ass."

"I'm not so sure."

His legs stretched out in front of him and felt surprisingly solid on the ground. The air was particularly cold since the rain had stopped. As he stood up he looked at Dan and tried to smile. "How do I look?" he asked.

"Like a train wreck."

Eric nodded and ran his fingers through his hair in a last-ditch attempt at making some sort of improvement. He walked over to the beater, opened the door, and sat down next to his father. He looked out the window to see if Dan might reconsider on the whole jail idea, but he was already back in the cruiser. Its engine roared to life, and Eric and his dad watched as it did a loop around them, then turned off onto the road. As the taillights faded into the distance, they were left in relative darkness. And total silence. His dad's breathing was the only sound in the car. It reminded him of the way his grandma used to breathe.

"Have you just given up all hope, son?"

The question caught him off guard. Or not so much the question, as the sudden sound of a voice. He'd been concentrating so hard on the breathing.

"Well, it was either that or booze," he managed to answer, "and man has to have a vice."

His dad still didn't look at him. He just stared out the windshield like he was focusing on the road. Like they were driving somewhere. "You beat up your best friend's dad. You terrorized some poor kid at the Gas N' Sip. Then you kept everyone who lives around the old Quaker State awake by hollering at the top of your lungs and smashing things like a half-wit imbecile." He took a shallow breath, like it hurt to do much more. "Does that just about sum up your night?"

"Those are the highlights. Yeah."

"Don't you think you're getting a little too old for this shit, son?"

"Well you're only as old as you feel, right?"

His dad turned his whole body to face him. Eric looked over, but just out of the corner of his eye. As fearless as he was in a bar fight, he couldn't quite handle bearing the full brunt of his father's disappointment. It was gravity times a thousand.

"Let me tell you something, son. You're not the first person in the world who hasn't had things go his way."

Eric was already uncomfortable. "I know that."

"You do?" he said, sounding somewhat surprised. "Well think about this. Think about how long you've been alive. You're going to have to live that many years again just to get where I am right now. Then, you'll probably live at least that many again before you finally check out. You have to live your whole life two more times."

"So?"

"So you might want to start living like your whole life's ahead of you. Not behind."

Eric looked down at his blood-crusted hands and gingerly felt for any glass that might be caught in the mess. It hurt to touch them, but it was a welcome distraction.

"I loved walking around this town being the father of the kid who beat Cedarsville," his dad continued. "But I was even more proud of you when you got accepted to Brown. And when you got all those scholarships, I was really proud. And really relieved." He tried to laugh a little, but it turned into more of an odd cough. "But you know when I was the most proud of you?" He paused long enough to make Eric wonder if it wasn't a rhetorical question at all. "When you decided to stay and be a father to that little girl."

Eric knew he was still looking at him, but he couldn't bring himself to look up from his hands. He was sure there was no more glass in there, but he kept searching. "It kills me to see you so at odds with yourself," his dad said. "With this whole damn town, it seems." His dad reached over and put his heavy hand on Eric's shoulder. "You just made a mistake, son. That's all," he said. "But mistakes aren't remembered by what you did. They're remembered by what you did next."

Eric thought he was going to look up at his dad, but his head rolled right past him and looked out the window instead. The clouds that brought all the rain had moved further down the valley, revealing the kind of night sky that only exists in cold seasons and small towns. Eric searched the stars, looking for something specific.

"You see that star right there?" he asked his dad.

"Which?"

"The bright one there in the middle. It's a little less blue and moves kind of different than the rest."

His dad craned his neck to see what Eric was talking about. He had a bad angle from his side of the car, so he had to lean over Eric to see. "Oh yeah," he said, his eyes squinting a little.

"I used to make all my wishes on that one. You're supposed to wish on the first star you see at night, you know? But—I thought I'd have better odds if I stuck with the one star. I didn't want to spread my dreams across the night sky all willy-nilly."

"That one right there?" his dad asked. "The reddish-looking one?"

"Yeah."

"That's Mars, Eric."

Eric looked at his dad, then looked back out the window at his star. "Really?"

"I'm pretty certain."

He stared at it like he was seeing it for the very first time. "How do you know?"

"Not sure. It's just one of those bits of information you pick up after you've been around as long as I have."

"So I've been wishing on a planet?"

"Apparently."

He gave it one last look, then sat back in his seat and shook his head. "Well, that explains a lot."

He wanted to laugh. He also wanted to cry. And to top it off, all the beer, fighting, and fatigue were catching up with him. His eyes flickered a few times, unsure of how to deal with everything that was going on, inside his body and out. He took a deep breath, exhaling a soft refrain of "Fuckermotherfuckermotherfuck."

The two of them sat in the car in total stillness for a while. Eric occasionally glanced out his window at Mars, then shook his head in disbelief that his carefully planned, intricate network of dreams had been, in all likelihood, negated on an astral technicality. His dad watched him, then finally broke the silence. "You know, Eric," he said, "that person you thought you were gonna be? He never really existed."

Eric nodded his head. "Yeah, well," he sighed. He'd never thought of that. But it was completely true. "I miss him just the same."

His dad started the car and dropped it into gear. It creaked its way out of the lot and onto the road. The heat from the vents blew across Eric's neck, making him feel dopey and thick, but his face felt cool against the glass of the window. The things outside his mind swirled by in graceful sweeps of slow motion and pulled Eric down into the gentle fold of unconsciousness.

NINETEEN

He could barely even see things by the side of the road, they were launching by so fast. Deke was hellbent and hospital bound. There was nothing for Eric to do but hold on and hope that when they got there, they wouldn't be in need of any medical attention themselves.

"Now seriously," Deke said with a strange conviction in his voice, "there are a few things we need to talk about before this baby comes along."

"What's on your mind, Deke?"

"I know this seems a little last-minute, I just always thought there'd be time. Nine months goes pretty fast. But have you thought about names at all?"

Eric was surprised to find himself hanging onto the dashboard with both hands, his knuckles bone white. "You mean for the baby?"

"Well yeah!" he shouted. There was no real reason for the volume, but he was obviously excited by the circumstances and his role in them. "Actually, it's not so much the 'baby' I'm worried about. If it's just one, call it whatever you want. It's twins I'm thinking of."

"Twins?"

Deke looked over at him with a knowing nod. "It happens, you know." He looked back at the road just in time to notice he'd drifted over the yellow line. The truck jerked back into its lane with a quick tug of the wheel. "So if you have twins, don't go all cutesy with the names, you know what I mean?"

"You'd better just go ahead and spell it out for me," said Eric, his eyes now locked on the road.

"You know," Deke explained, "don't name 'em shit like 'Barry and Bobby' or 'Danny and Denny.' Don't even go 'Travis and Jarvis.' It's too close."

"How about 'Huey and Louie'?" Eric asked with a slight smile.

"No!" Deke shouted. "Are you even paying attention to me? This is serious shit I'm talkin' about here. You gotta let these kids have their own identities. That means no silly names, no matching raincoats, none of that shit."

Gina had gotten an ultrasound scan during the fall, so Eric was sure there would be no twins. But he didn't have the heart to break it to Deke, who constantly seemed more excited about this pregnancy than anyone else. Maybe than anyone ever.

"Alright then, Deke," Eric reassured him. "None of those names. What about girls?"

"Girls?"

"It happens, you know," Eric said. "Are there any twin girl names I should avoid?"

"Yeah," Deke said quickly. "'Gina and Tina.' 'Vicky and Nicky.' 'Deborah and Darla.' Any shit like that. But that's not . . . listen man, you better hope it's a boy."

"Why?" Eric laughed.

"I'll tell you why," Deke said with as much force as he could muster and still operate a motor vehicle. "Because if you have a boy, you only gotta worry about one dick. But if you have a girl"—he nodded his head at Eric as though he were about to bestow upon him the wisdom of the ages—"you gotta worry about all of 'em."

He tried to laugh as he told Deke he was being ridiculous. But he wasn't entirely convinced. Deke may have actually been right, which saddened him on a multitude of levels. He listened to the truck's engine groan as Deke pushed it up the highway toward the hospital. It sounded like the pistons could shoot through the hood at any moment. Outside, the hills were busting green and flowers were starting to bloom. April showers bring May flowers. He wondered if his child would learn this little truth in rhyme. His child, who was on the way.

The summer hadn't gone as planned. Neither, for that matter, had the fall or winter. Deke may have been under the impression that nine months went pretty quickly, but Eric wasn't. Time moved differently in Pinely. Especially if you weren't supposed to be there in the first place.

He was pretty stunned to see Gina Stevens standing on his porch that July afternoon. He hadn't heard from her since their little tangle in the woods during alumni weekend. Which was fine with him. He'd been riddled with guilt, but wanted desperately to pretend the whole thing had never happened. No one else seemed to know about it, so he was hoping to get off to college—him at Brown, Jill at Providence College—and leave the whole drunken mess behind.

"What's going on, Gina?" he asked.

"I really need to talk to you about something."

This was no good at all. She wanted to talk about what happened, which would only gum up the gears. But Eric had no choice but to listen. If she didn't talk about it with him, she'd certainly talk about it with someone else.

"Sure," he said in an airy, nonchalant voice. "What's on your mind?"

"I got one of those kits," she said. "Actually, I got two, because I didn't believe it at first. And they both . . ." She trailed off for a second before she regathered herself and looked Eric in the eye. "I'm pregnant."

Eric suddenly looked over his shoulder for some reason. "What?" he asked when he turned back.

"I'm pregnant," she said again.

He could feel his head shaking, just slightly, back and forth, the way his Uncle Pete's used to do when Parkinson's first set in. "No," he said, bluntly. A slight cough that tried to be a laugh escaped his mouth as he said, "That's ridiculous."

"How is it ridiculous?" she asked.

"Come on, Gina, you're being—" He stopped for a moment, but was surprised to find that his head was still shaking. "It was just the one time."

Gina shrugged and looked a little pained. "I guess that's all it took."

He looked at her, hoping she would crack a smile. Praying she would reveal it all to be a big joke she'd cooked up, just for a laugh. But it never came. "So what . . . ," he started before stepping out onto the porch and letting the door close behind him. "What are you going to do?"

She looked down at her feet and sighed. "God, what a mess."

He watched her for a second, but she didn't look up. "Listen, I can—I have some money from graduation. And I can make some calls, find out where—I don't know, probably have to go up to Wheeling, maybe? Pittsburgh? Wherever. I can drive you—and—we can just . . . Just get it taken care of. You know?"

Gina looked up at him and shook her head. "Oh, I can't—" she started. "That's not really an option for me."

Eric couldn't understand how she could so quickly be eliminating options. "Well wait a minute," he said. "Who else have you told?"

"No one."

"Right. See, so no one would know," he said. "You wouldn't have to worry about what people thought or anything like that."

She tried to smile before she spoke. "Eric, that's not really the point."

"The point?" he snapped. "It's a complete fucking accident. There is no point!"

He saw her cheeks go flush, but her voice stayed calm. "I know this isn't easy. Believe me, I know. But I'm keeping it." She put the palms of her hands up toward Eric, like a magician with nothing to hide. "It's my decision."

"What, I don't get a decision?" he asked.

"You kind of made one at the party."

"No, I didn't," he said. "I made a mistake. I was too drunk to make any decisions."

"I know," she said. "So was I. But that doesn't change anything, does it?"

"Well, it could," he said, throwing his hands up in the air. "All we have to do is figure out how you're suddenly in charge of all the sober decision making."

"I just am," she said. He watched her chew on her bottom lip as it went pink to white and back again. "Like it or not, it's my choice to make."

"Well," he said, "enjoy your choice. Because like it or not, I'm leaving for Brown next month."

He'd made his decision then and there. And his case for leaving was strong and manyfold. He needed to make something of himself if he was going to support a child. He'd worked too hard and too long to let his whole life change because of one night. He was too young to be any kind of father figure to anyone. It would be even more confusing growing up with two parents who didn't love each other. By the time he finished college, he'd be better prepared, and the kid would be old enough to realize important things. The list went on and on in his mind. He was certain, if he'd taken the time to write it down, he could have papered the streets of three counties.

But his mind allowed a counterargument. Two points that undid all the rest. The first came courtesy of Jill. When she'd come back from her camping trip with her dad, she was full of life. She and Mr. Dupree rolled up into the driveway, smelling of dirt, smoke, and humans gone sour, smiling like they'd just pulled one over on the world. They looked like refugees, but for the next week all Jill could talk about was how much fun she'd had camping with her dad. How the time she spent with him was worth more to her than almost anything else in the world.

The second point was just a feeling. An imagining of a feeling, really. The one he'd have knowing a child would walk through his hometown, looking for someone to call "daddy."

It smelled like spring in the Duprees' house. No matter what season it was outside, Mrs. Dupree always managed to make it smell like a fresh new start. Jill sat on the couch in her parents' living room, her hair still wet from the shower, looking at a map of Rhode Island. "Look at all the water. The bays and the ocean. Do you think it's too cold to swim?"

Eric felt like he was going to be sick. He was afraid to even open his mouth, because every word he said was deception. Worthless interference for the words he'd come there to say. Words he still hadn't sorted out.

"I can't believe we're actually going to a state that's smaller than West Virginia. Seems ridiculous, doesn't it?"

His tongue felt numb inside his mouth. "Jill, I don't——" He felt his ears go red and his heart pick up speed. "I can't go."

"What?" she laughed. "Is Eric Mercer getting cold feet? Homesick for Pinely already?"

He felt his eyes begin to swell as the room closed in all around him. Jill looked up from her map and stopped smiling. "Oh God, Eric, what's wrong?" she said as she moved closer to him.

Eric leaned into her. His head hung low in her chest as he tried not to cry. He wanted to stay like that, with her arms around him, right there in that sweet-smelling room, forever. "I fucked up," he said. He tried to find more eloquent words, but couldn't. "I fucked it all up."

Her fingers poured through his hair. "You fucked what up?" she asked. "You've got to——" She put her face to the top of his head so he could feel her breath when she spoke. "You're scaring me, Eric."

"The party, you know. I went to Chad Alexander's party with Deke. And, we were so drunk."

"I remember. You told me."

"Yeah. I almost fell in the creek. But Dan——Danny . . . and he brought Gina Stevens. And Deke went to get another beer. So Gina——we were talking, there. And I just wanted to pass out." His breath seemed like it would barely sustain him anymore. "And——she kissed me."

"Gina Stevens kissed you?"

"Yeah."

Jill leaned back so Eric's head couldn't rest on her anymore. He looked up and saw a face that was suspicious, but still understanding. "Did you kiss her back?"

If that were the absolute pinnacle of his transgressions, it would be gut-wrenching to answer "yes." But he had more. "She's pregnant," he said.

Her eyes locked onto him, but she didn't say a word. He waited, hoping she had something to say. Finally it got too uncomfortable. "I was just so drunk," he said. "And I swear to God, we were just talking. Then before I knew what happened—"

"Well, do you know what happened now?!" she said.

"I guess so," he answered. "I don't . . . not really."

"Well, it sounds like you have proof, the two of you. That should help you piece it together."

"Jill, I don't want you to be angry."

"Yeah, well I didn't want you to fuck Gina Stevens. So it doesn't seem to matter what either of us want, really."

"Jill, I—"

"Why did you do this?"

"I don't know," he said. "I hardly remember it."

"Who else knows?"

"That it happened?"

She looked disgusted. "Who else knows anything?"

"I've only told you," he said. "So, you . . . and, well, Gina—"

"Me and Gina," she said. "That's nice." She wiped the palms of her hands on the couch cushion. "How do you even *know* Gina Stevens?"

"I don't," he said. "I've barely ever spoken to her."

Jill kind of laughed to herself. "Well, she's a pretty girl though, isn't she?"

"Jill, don't—"

"Don't what?!" she asked. "Don't you—" She stood up from the couch and barricaded herself inside her crossed arms. "I want you to go now."

Eric went to the door and let it close behind him. Jill looked gray and scattered on the other side of the screen. "Maybe I'll call you later?"

"No."

He tried not to look hurt. "Tomorrow, maybe?"

"I think—" She looked up at him and walked toward the door. He could see her eyes swelling red with tears as she got closer. "Goddamn you, Eric," she said, and closed the door from inside.

The fall brought big changes for everyone. Deke's dream came true. He got a job working for the city at the sewage plant. Dan Moran got on with the county Sheriff's Department and was equipped with a nice dark uniform, a bright shiny badge, and a big black gun. All the tools he needed to become the authoritative prick Eric always knew Danny could be. And Eric took a job working for Mr. Tremble.

One afternoon, as he left the funeral home, Eric was surprised to see Gina walking down the sidewalk. Their interactions exclusively revolved around the pregnancy now. He was always fair. He always did his part. But there was never anything more. It was all he could do not to be openly hostile to Gina, who had gone from lifetime infatuation to life-altering burden.

"Hey Eric," she said as she shuffled up next to him. "Just getting off work?"

"Yeah," he said.

"Me too."

"It's only four o'clock."

"Yeah," she said as she pulled her hair back out of her eyes. "I go in earlier."

There were only five blocks between the funeral home and where Gina would turn off to go home. Eric picked up his pace just slightly and began a reverse tally in his head. Half a block went by before she spoke again.

"So, how are you doing?"

"Fine."

Another quarter block.

"I'm fine too," she said.

"Good."

A full block of silence.

"You know," she said, the annoyance heavy in her voice, "I am a person, Eric."

"Okay."

"Well, would it kill you to act like you like me?"

He was nearly halfway there. "I used to like you, Gina. Look where that got me."

She gave him a cold look. "Have I been unkind to you?"

Eric wasn't sure what she was getting at, but was certain he was going to lose this game. Which immediately pissed him off. "Are you trying to be unkind to me?"

"Jesus, Eric! Is that what you think?"

"I don't think, Gina," he said. "It doesn't do me any good."

This was true. Lately, he hated to think at all, because when he did, terrible thoughts inhabited his brain. He didn't want to think about the possibility of a miscarriage. He certainly didn't want to feel a strange elation inside when he did. He just couldn't help it. Every day that Gina called with a smile in her voice, he felt sick. Then he felt sick again for feeling sick in the first place.

When they finally reached the turnoff for her street, Gina stopped, right in front of Eric. "We're going to be parents, Eric. For the rest of our lives," she said in a pleading voice. "Is this the way it's going to be the whole time? Is this our relationship?"

"We're having a baby," he said, stepping around her. "Not a relationship."

By the winter, Deke was badgering Eric to go out on a date. There was a girl from Jasper who was friends with a guy Deke worked with at the plant. She'd gone out drinking with them after work, and Deke got the idea to play matchmaker.

"She's good-lookin'," Deke swore to him.

"She's good-looking, or she has big tits?" Eric asked, too familiar with Deke's deep-seated admiration for the well-endowed.

"Both," Deke said with a sly smile that almost convinced Eric he might mean it.

"Why do you want me to go on a date so bad anyhow?"

"Cause that's what humans do, you fuckin' cyborg!" Deke bellowed. "You been walkin' around here like a real unpleasant prick since the summer. If I had any other friends, I'd be hangin' out with them. But I don't. So I gotta try and fix you."

"Well," Eric said, "I severely doubt anyone would want to date me, what with a young lady already walking around, heavy with my illegitimate child."

"You'd be surprised," Deke said.

Eric just shook his head. "I've had enough surprises for a while, Deke."

What Eric wanted, more than anything else, was someone he could really talk to. The way he could talk to Jill. But he didn't have that anymore. What he had instead, nearly every day he left the funeral home, was five blocks of unsolicited small talk with Gina.

He hated it. Every step of it, every word they shared, every second he had to spend with her. He was sure of that. And just to be doubly sure, he reminded himself of it before he left the funeral home. Still, it got to be where sometimes, when he wasn't careful, he almost enjoyed Gina's company. Where, if he really let his guard down completely, he almost looked forward to seeing her. It confused him. Because at times like that, the five blocks started to seem shorter. And Gina Stevens started to seem like a real person.

"I thought you drove everywhere," Eric said one afternoon.

"I like to walk."

"Really?" he said. "Because I didn't even realize you had legs for the longest time, you were always inside that red Rabbit of yours."

She smiled at him. "That car made me wildly popular when I was seventeen."

Eric glanced at her out of the corner of his eye, and caught a glimpse of her perfect face. "It might not have been the car."

Gina turned away from Eric for a second. He only caught a quick glimpse, but he thought he saw her blush. They walked in silence for a few steps before Eric spoke up again. "You seem to be taking this much better than me," he said.

She was exceptionally pregnant by then. The kind of pregnant where a person could openly comment on her pregnancy with no fear of being wrong.

"Taking what better than you?" she asked.

"This whole thing. I mean, look at you," he said with a laugh. "Look what I've done to you."

She laughed and put her hands on her distended belly. "Right," she said. "Well, what can you do?"

"You can get angry," Eric said. "Or sad. Or upset that things didn't work out the way you'd planned."

"I didn't really have a plan, so . . ."

Eric looked over at her, waddling along, beautiful, swollen, and content. "How could it be that I had so many plans and you didn't have one?"

"I'm not smart like you," she said.

"Oh yeah," Eric laughed, "I'm a fucking genius. Managed to land myself a lifetime sentence in Pinely, West Virginia."

Gina shook her head. "Why are you so down on Pinely?"

Eric looked over at her and felt a grimace take over his face. "Why are you so goddamned chipper about everything?"

"Does that bother you?"

"Yes!" he snapped. "Jesus Christ, look at yourself. You're too young to be having a baby."

"Well so are you."

"I know! That's the—Have you even been listening to me?!"

"It's hard not to. You're yelling."

"Well!" he shouted. His head rocked back and forth, slowly trying to bring some order to the thoughts inside it. His breathing slowed down, and his voice was reserved when he spoke again. "I find you exhausting sometimes. That's all."

"Me too."

"You exhaust yourself?" he asked.

"No," she said. "*You* exhaust me."

They walked slower these days. Eric assumed it was because she was bigger. But he wasn't entirely sure it wasn't him setting the pace.

"You wanted to do other things," Gina finally said. "Things you can't do here. It's different for me. I guess I always knew I wanted to have kids someday. Just not now. And not necessarily with you."

"What's wrong with me?"

"I have no idea," she shrugged. "I don't know what's right with you, either. I hardly know you at all."

"What do you want to know?" he asked.

Gina walked along for a minute, thinking through her options. "Tell me one of your plans," she said.

"It was just one big plan, really," he said. "All linked together."

"Well, how did it start?"

Eric tried to smile but knew he didn't pull it off. "Get the fuck out of Pinely," he admitted.

Gina looked over at him. "So the whole plan's ruined?"

Eric nodded his head. "Seems that way."

"Well," Gina said. Her hands absently rested on her stomach. "Then you must hate me for sure."

Eric walked along, looking straight ahead, but didn't say anything.

"Eric?"

"Yeah?"

"Wait a minute," Gina said. She stopped walking and turned to face Eric. "You *hate* me?"

He could feel his face trying to settle on an emotion to convey. But he had no idea. His eyes darted from her face to the ground and back again. He shook his head and looked for the truth. "Not all the time," was what came out.

"Oh my God," Gina said. "I'm actually carrying the child of someone who hates me?"

"Wait," Eric pleaded. "What'd I just say?"

"Oh, I'm sorry—someone who hates me, but not all the time."

"Look, Gina," Eric said.

"What?"

He looked at her, but couldn't come up with anything to say.

"Right," Gina said. She looked like some vagabond sadness had found its nest. "Well, if you don't mind, I'm going to turn up here," she said. "Spare you having to hate me for another block."

He walked two blocks, by himself, and tried to think if there were any more ways he could foul up this whole situation. Gina was pretty. Actually, she was beautiful. She was nice. And, most importantly, she'd been nothing but straightforward with him from day one. The only flaw he could find was that, one summer night, she'd had a complete lapse of judgment. Right along with him.

He didn't know what she deserved, exactly. But he was certain it didn't involve being hated. No matter how precariously. He turned and started walking back toward the other end of town. Flowers always helped. At least in the movies they did. He would find out what time Gina started work in the morning and have flowers there waiting for her. When he got to the door of the insurance agency where she worked, he was a little surprised to see her red Rabbit parked in the lot. He walked in the door and smiled at the middle-aged woman behind the front desk.

"Hey there"—he glanced at the nameplate on the woman's desk—"Shelly. Is that Gina's car out there?"

"Yeah."

"Did it break down or something?"

"I don't think so."

Eric looked through the front window at the car, then back at Shelly. "Well, she went home already, right?"

Shelly looked at him like he'd just spoken Swahili. "It's only four-thirty," she said.

"But she comes in early."

"Gina?" Shelly laughed. "Hell, if she came in on time we'd all crap our trousers."

Eric looked around to be sure he was in the right place. That they weren't both talking about different Ginas. "I don't know what you're talking about," he finally said.

"Well, I don't know what you're talking about either. So we've got that in common," said Shelly. "She'll be back any minute now from her walk, if you want to confuse her for a while."

"What do you mean, 'her walk'?"

"She goes on a walk every day about this time. Says it's good for the baby."

Eric felt the puzzle coming together in his mind, but didn't want it to. He put his hand on Shelly's desk and turned to look at the car again. Maybe there was an explanation. He glanced back at Shelly, but she simply pointed in the direction he'd just been looking and said, "Here she comes now."

Gina didn't see him until she was halfway to the door. When she did, her face told Eric that any explanation she had was going to be unsatisfactory. She opened the door and stepped inside, but didn't come any closer.

"What are you doing here?" she asked.

"I was going to have some flowers delivered for you."

Gina looked like she was about to cry. She looked at the ground and dug the toe of her shoe into the carpet.

"But enough about me," Eric said. "What are *you* doing here?"

Gina looked at Eric, then nodded toward the door. "Maybe we could talk outside?"

"Mr. Shipley called about his claim," said Shelly. "Wanted you to call him back before the end of the day."

Eric turned toward Shelly as he opened the door. "She won't be too long," he said. "Promise."

Outside, the cars whipped by on Route 2, picking up speed as they approached city limits. Eric went to lean against Gina's car, but then changed his mind. He stood there, still, waiting for Gina to say something.

"I didn't mean to, Eric."

"Didn't mean to what?" he asked. "Lie? Every day?"

"I just thought if you got to know me—"

"Well, I know you now."

Gina shook her head in frustration. "What's so wrong with wanting this to work out?" she pleaded. "What's so bad about having a nice, pretty girl want to spend time with you?"

"What's so wrong with telling the fucking truth?" he asked.

"Would that have worked?" she asked. "Would you have come out to dinner with me, or gone for a walk, or given me the time of day if I would have just asked?"

Eric looked at her and shook his head. "I don't know," he said.

"No," she said, "you wouldn't. Because I already tried."

"So you cook up this elaborate plan?"

"Yes."

"Well, when did this plan start?" he asked. "I mean, we've already had six months of it. Where did it begin?" He paced back and forth a few steps before stopping right in front of her. "What about this?" he said, pointing to her belly. "Did you plan that, too?"

"No!" she said, her eyes open wide.

"Well, you've certainly proven to be a credible witness, so—"

"No, Eric! You've got to believe me."

"Believe you?! If you weren't the size of a fucking truck I wouldn't even know whether to believe you're pregnant!"

Tears came to her eyes and spilled over all at once. Eric had never watched someone cry and feel absolutely nothing. But he did now.

"I just wanted—"

"I don't care," he said. "I really, really don't care. About anything anymore." He watched her cry for a second more, then turned to leave. "So thanks for that," he said and walked off.

Eric could see the red lights flashing in front of them, just in front of the line of cars that were already stopped, waiting for the train. There was nothing odd or curious about it, except that Deke was speeding up instead of slowing down.

"You gotta stop here, Deke," Eric said, trying to sound calm.

"No," he said in voice that sounded a little too much like someone talking in a TV show or movie, "we're gonna make it."

"Like hell!" Eric shouted. "Stop the fuckin' truck!"

"You're gonna miss it," Deke pleaded.

"I'm gonna miss a lot of things if you get us fuckin' killed!"

Eric tried to think of something poignant to say. Deke was already in the other lane, speeding past the drivers who were in control of the common sense the good Lord gave them, and Eric was certain the next words out of his mouth would be his last. He could see the train coming. It was much bigger than Deke's truck. There was no doubt what would happen if it hit them. And there was little chance they could keep that from happening now. Eric was beyond asking Deke to stop, because it was obvious that hitting the brakes would only slow them down. Of course, that didn't keep Eric from pressing his leg into the floorboard of the truck, searching for some phantom brake that wasn't there. The whistle of the train sounded like it was coming from inside the truck. The scream of the whistle merged with Eric's own scream of pure terror, both of which were suddenly drowned out by a tremendous crashing sound. Eric was surprised not to be in overwhelming pain, and was even more surprised to suddenly hear an even louder crash than the first, like the truck was being separated into all its distinct pieces in the most violent manner imaginable. He was thrown against the dashboard, and his door swung open, sucking styrofoam cups and scraps of paper out onto the pavement and under the truck.

"Close the door!" Deke yelled.

Eric reached out, slammed the door shut, and noticed the train roaring by behind them in the sideview mirror.

"Did we catch air?" Eric asked.

"Hell yeah, we did," Deke laughed. "That was pretty close, huh?"

He said it like they'd almost missed the start of a movie. Eric could feel his entire body going numb, starting at his feet and slowly working its way up, coating him in a hot layer of sweat along the way. He looked at Deke to see if he was having any similar experiences. He was not.

Eric tried to think of a way to explain to Deke what had just happened. To find the words to put it in the proper perspective for him. But every time he started trying to piece it together, he felt like he might throw up. In the end, he decided to let Deke enjoy his sweet oblivion, and let his stomach enjoy its lunch. He put his head back, closed his eyes, and tried not to open them until the truck was safely parked at the hospital.

There was no Gina Stevens listed as a patient at Chance Memorial Hospital. Deke paced the lobby, trying to look collected, but falling far short of it. Eric, on the other hand, wasn't worried. He was indignant. His arms were flailing above his head, demanding that the woman check her records again, in an interrogation that made the Inquisition look like child's play.

"You're not really listening," he said through clenched teeth. "Her friend called and said Gina and her mother were already on the way here. I, on the other hand, was at the south end of town. *Not* already on the way. So you can see how I find it hard to believe that I'm here now, and she's not."

"Well you are," the woman said.

"And so is she," Eric said wearily. "So just do me a favor and see if you can't find her."

Deke stopped his pacing for a moment. "Are you sure this is the right hospital?" he asked.

"Deke," Eric sighed, "you're not helping."

"I'm trying to."

"And yet you're not," Eric said.

"Did you tell her it's with a 'v'?" he asked, undaunted.

"What?"

"Stevens," he said. "With a 'v,' not a 'ph.'"

"Listen," the woman said, clearly growing tired of her new company, "I've been working this desk for the past four hours, and there ain't no one come in to deliver no babies. Not with a 'v,' not with a 'ph.' Nobody. Now——"

When the doors burst open, the woman was just getting warmed up. If anyone had been paying attention to her anymore, they would have seen she was disappointed to have to abandon her speech during the opening remarks when all the good stuff was yet to come. But they'd all turned to see Gina, splayed out on a gurney, being wheeled through the lobby toward someplace more important.

"Oh thank God you're here," Gina's mom said to Eric.

"Yeah, we're here. Where were you?"

"We got stopped by a train," she explained. "This doctor who was out front says she's really far along, so you'd better get in there."

Eric hurried through the swinging doors to catch up, turning around one last time to get a final glimpse of the world before everything changed for good. But there were no bright, shining signs. He just felt a strange wave of melancholy, saw Deke watching him with a sad look of envy, and heard Gina's mom tell the woman at the front desk that her daughter's name was Gina Stevens. "With a 'v.'"

No one even asked him to wash his hands. That was one of the things Eric found strange about the delivery room. They didn't make him wear one of those blue gowns. They didn't even check his I.D. He said he was the father, and they took his word for it. It really didn't seem they were taking as many precautions as they could have. For all they knew, he was some drifter who'd just rolled around in lye and who suffered from a highly contagious variety of chronic eczema. Not the sort of guy you'd want hanging around a place where a baby is about to be born.

After a while, it became obvious to Eric why they believed he was the father. Gina was constantly calling his name and asking him to help her breathe. At first, he wasn't sure what she could possibly mean about helping her breathe. Seemed like the sort of thing a person had to do on their own. Then he remembered about the Lamaze classes. He didn't really remember what they'd learned there, he just remembered they'd gone. But that seemed to be enough for Gina. She squeezed his hand and breathed a certain way, while he absently mimicked what she was doing and glanced around the room at what else was happening.

He was glad to see all the machines there, with their tiny lights flashing and their little computer screens saying all sorts of indecipherable things. It made him feel like professionals were in charge. Which was for the best. Gina was a sweaty, blubbering jumble, breathing like an emphysemic and bellowing some sort of warning to neighboring tribes of impending danger. He, on the other hand, couldn't feel his legs. It was frighteningly similar to the feeling he'd had in the truck with Deke. Only more so. This was a deadness that was threatening to overtake all his senses. So the beeping, whirling machines were his only assurance. A signal that, when he finally lost all sense of space and time, someone intelligent would still be in charge.

He wasn't panicked. It was just the opposite. He didn't care. He found himself thinking about the strangest things. There was a bar attached to the bed Gina was lying on. It came up from the frame, across the width of her body, and back down on the other side. Every now and again, she would reach up and grab it. Pull herself with Herculean force and push until her face turned a shade of red he'd only seen on the face of crying babies. He enjoyed the strange symmetry of that. Then he wondered who'd thought to put that bar there in the first place. And how Gina ever knew to use it. He watched the doctor, perched between

Gina's knees, studying her crotch with unfailing intensity. The doctor was saying things to Gina, encouraging her to have herself a baby, but all the while, focusing on that spot where her legs met in the middle. It struck Eric that he was personally responsible for this whole production, yet he'd never once seen Gina's crotch. It had been dark, he'd been drunk. The whole thing had gone down with very little pageantry or attention to detail. He had half a mind to sneak down there and get a look at it while he had the chance, but Gina seemed pretty adamant about having him right there beside her. So he did his duty, as best he could understand it. Gina didn't look at all good in the lighting of the delivery room. She looked pale and bleak, washed out on all sides. Not exactly radiating the glow of impending mother-hood. The room needed some softer light. Maybe a few candles, a fireplace in the corner. He understood the doctors needed good-quality light to do their thing. But a series of lamps with amber shades could surely suffice. He looked up at the fluores-cent bulbs flickering above them and wondered how no one had thought of this before. Gina seemed to subconsciously agree, because she squeezed his hand with the force of a vise. He winced and suddenly felt even more resolute about the whole thing. He was, at the very least, going to see if he couldn't find a way to work with the lighting they had. To throw a few switches and come up with a better configuration. He was just about to set off on this illuminating task when he happened to glance down at the doctor and notice he was holding something. A baby.

"It's a girl," someone said, and Eric watched as the doctor cleaned it off and reached for the scissors. The umbilical cord was dangling from its stomach, marking a path back to its origin. Eric definitely wanted to see that, but couldn't seem to move. The doctor cut through it, making a sound that was unlike anything

Eric had heard before. It wasn't loud or startling or bracing in any way, just new. There was a deliberate certainty to the way people were moving now. They were cleaning, cutting, swaddling, and generally making quite a fuss over the little thing. When they were certain there was nothing horrifically wrong, they presented the tiny bundle to Gina. Eric could hear her talking to the baby, but was more fascinated by the goings-on around him. He watched a guy come in and pick up bits of umbilical cord and other unclaimed fragments of birth and scoop it all into a small, orange bag. He wondered where they keep things like that. And how they dispose of it. Is there a special landfill, or do they burn it all? And if they burn it, how many bits of airborne afterbirth had he breathed over the years? He was on a perfectly good mental tangent when someone interrupted him to see if he wanted to hold the baby. It wasn't that he didn't want to, he just had other things on his mind at that exact moment. But he knew that wasn't the right answer. So he said okay, and the nurse brought the tiny little wad of blankets toward him.

Everyone else had been handling it with two hands, but that didn't seem necessary to Eric. It was such a tiny little thing. The nurse placed it in his arm, and Eric stood there cradling it like a football. It moved a lot. Squirming around in his arm, probably trying to figure out what had happened. Eric didn't want to drop it, so he was hoping someone would come take it way from him soon. A nurse walked over and Eric extended his arm, ready for her to take the baby. But she just smiled and moved some of the blankets around.

"That's your daddy," she said to the baby. "You see him there? He's your daddy."

Eric looked down and saw the tiniest face in the world looking back at him. It was bright pink, and he was fairly certain her eyes were brown. Just like his. She fidgeted in his arm so much, he didn't even notice the feeling on his other hand at first. It wasn't until she held still for one brief moment that he realized.

Gina was resting his hand in hers, gently stroking the top of it with her other hand. He watched her for a while, wondering why it seemed so comforting. So familiar. It seemed just right for the surroundings. Like exactly the sort of thing someone should do in a hospital. Then he remembered, and his hand looked older. Like his grandpa's. Just like Jim's. He looked back at the face of his daughter, just as she opened her brown eyes. And something inside him broke.

His sobbing became so abandoned, a nurse came to take the baby away. But Eric wouldn't let her. He held his daughter close to his body with both arms and whispered into her young ears. Gina, the nurses, and the doctors all watched and worried, but Eric wouldn't let go. He just kept crying. And whispering promises no one else would ever hear.

SATURDAY

He was talking to himself. That's what woke him up. He was in his old bedroom, in his parents' house. A lot had changed since he'd moved out, but he still recognized it as soon as he woke up. His mother had repainted the place, added a little trim of wallpaper, filled it with knickknacks. She even took out the bed and put in an old corduroy couch she'd found at a garage sale for only fifty-two dollars. It wasn't a bedroom anymore, it was a "sitting room." Eric didn't really understand what that meant, especially since his mom and dad still did most of their sitting in front of the TV in the basement. But it was better than if she hadn't changed it at all after he left. It was hard enough getting on with your life in a small town like Pinely without having a standing shrine to your adolescence preserved for posterity.

His face felt raw on one side, etched with deep ridges from the corduroy fabric of the couch. He tried holding his head in several different positions, but none of them seemed to help with the pain that was throbbing behind his eyes, toward his temples, down his brain stem and into his shoulder blades. A few deep breaths offered some support, and when he felt he had the strength, he gathered his feet underneath him and stood. The sunlight peeking in from the side of the blinds caught him in the eye and almost dropped him back down to the couch, but he managed to withstand its laser-like intensity and stay upright. He stood there, looking at the room, sweating from exertion and wondering how his dad ever managed to get him in there in the first place. He didn't remember walking. And he knew his dad couldn't carry him. The sheer physics of the problem started to make his head hurt again, so he abandoned it altogether and decided to see if he couldn't find something in the kitchen that might make him feel better.

The high-pitched wheezing of the blender was another blow to his stability. He took slow, lumbering steps toward the sound, the noise growing louder as he got closer. But he was full of hope that if he got close enough, whoever was operating the beastly appliance would see him and have pity. If not, there was slightly less hope that he might be able to wrestle control of the blender away from the uncaring soul and put a stop to the clamor himself. Luckily, the first scenario was the one that played out. His mother was standing behind the counter whipping up some fruit concoction that looked frighteningly like vomit. When she saw Eric trudging toward her, she let out a short scream and quickly shut off the blender. As the blades spun to a stop, she shook her head and laughed a little at her own outburst.

"Well, I didn't know you were here," she said.

"Neither did I," answered Eric. He managed to pull himself up to the kitchen counter and have a seat. "Where's Dad?"

"Golfing."

Eric squinted at the idea. "Golfing? Hell, he can't golf."

"No one's told him that."

"Is the course even open in October?"

"No. That's why he goes," she said with a shake of her head. "It's free." She picked up the glass pitcher from the blender and pointed it at Eric. "Do you feel like a smoothie?"

"Yeah," he coughed. "Why, do I look like one?"

"You don't look very good," she said in a way that made Eric certain she was being kind.

"That's good. I don't want to surprise anyone."

"Do you want some food or something?"

He wanted something, but he couldn't even begin to figure out what. The idea of fruit was appealing, especially in easy-to-ingest liquid form, but he was still wary of the puke-like appearance of his mom's blender potion. He decided to roll the dice and held out his hands toward the pitcher. "Can I smell that?" he asked.

His mom started to hand it over, then noticed his scabbed and dirty hands. "Oh Eric," she asked, "what happened?"

Eric looked down and tried to explain it as clearly and articulately as possible. She'd want the details, so he gathered as many as he could muster. "I fell," he said.

Her face flashed disapproval, but she quickly thought better of it. "Well at least you got back up," she said. "That's the important thing, right?

Eric nodded in agreement, then was struck with a strange realization. "Are you speaking metaphorically?" he asked.

"I don't think so."

He watched her for a second or two and realized she was telling the truth. "Just checking."

The smoothie smelled much better than it looked, so he decided to give it a shot. It oozed into the glass and he immediately began having second thoughts, but he went ahead and brought it gingerly to his lips. It was surprisingly refreshing, if a little difficult to drink, and soon he was taking large gulps from the glass, following them with deep, satisfying breaths that hurt less and less every time.

"So," his mom asked, "did you get in a fight last night?"

"Not really," he answered.

"Why'd the police call here then?"

Since he didn't end up in County, he wasn't really sure what he would have been booked for. He thought about what he'd done the night before and compared it to other things he'd had noted on his record. "I guess I was disturbing the peace," he answered.

"So how long do you suppose you're going to keep doing this?"

"Doing what?"

"Disturbing the peace."

He took another drink from his glass and was surprised when a chunk of something dropped into his mouth. His gag reflex kicked up quickly, but he fought it back and eventually discovered it to be a piece of banana. "I think I'm about done," he answered, chewing the banana with his back teeth.

"Do you ever wish you had a brother?"

"What?" Eric asked, once again surprised by his mother's ability to change topics without the slightest warning or even clumsy attempt at a transition.

"You know, growing up," she continued. "Or even now that you're older. Do you ever wish you had a brother?"

He knew from experience that this topic, in all likelihood, meant nothing at all. The question had probably resided in her mind for approximately two nanoseconds before it popped out of her mouth. But Eric couldn't help but wonder if she had some strange idea in her head about the positive effects a sibling relationship might have had on him. Or about trying to get pregnant again, which led to sudden images of his parents having sex, which was no help whatsoever to his already precarious state of health. "Believe me, Mom," he said emphatically. "If I sat down and made a list of wishes, that one wouldn't even make the first page."

"Really? What would you wish for?"

"Magic powers."

"That's a good one," she said with genuine enthusiasm. "What would you do with those?"

"Well," Eric started to answer. He had an exceptionally detailed plan for how he would put such powers to use, one he'd been thinking about and revising since he was thirteen. No one ever asked about it though, so it was purely for his own benefit and amusement. But now that he had his opportunity to show how cleverly he'd planned his application of such fantasy powers, he was distracted by something else. "Is that clock right?" he asked.

His mom turned around and squinted at the digital display on the microwave oven. "Yeah," she said, "that's right. Why?"

Even in his state of depreciated brain capacity, there was something that struck him about the time on the clock. The most obvious was that he'd slept until noon. Since his dad consistently awoke at the crack of dawn, whether he wanted to or not, Eric always held his own ability to sleep in as a source of pride and genetic good fortune. But there was still something nagging at him. He wasn't supposed to pick up Tess until later. He hadn't made any plans with Deke that he could remember. Then it hit him. He wasn't doing anything. Jill was.

He stood up quickly and turned to his mom. "How do I look?"

"Like you lost the rodeo," she said.

"Shit," he sighed, sitting back down.

"What's the matter?"

"Jill's gonna be leaving for the airport in a little while."

"So go take a shower."

It seemed like a valid idea. A shower would certainly be a good first step. But there was still the matter of his dirty, sweaty, blood-stained, beer-soaked clothes. "What about—?"

"You still have some clothes in your closet, I imagine," she answered, without even really being asked.

He was a little afraid to imagine what sort of clothes he might have left behind. Something that was barely in style when he first started daydreaming about magic powers, no doubt. But it was surely better than what he was wearing now. He looked at the clock one more time, craned back the last of his smoothie, and scuttled off toward the bathroom, somehow limping with his entire body and soul.

The shower was as refreshing as anything that causes blood and glass to fall from your body can be. He didn't have the time he needed to really investigate the scope of his wounds, focusing instead on getting rid of any visible grime and noticeable stink for which he might be responsible. Soon enough, he was clean and dry, standing in front of his closet, and staring at his miserable wardrobe options. It wasn't going to be pretty. He found an old pair of Lee jeans that fit fairly well, a white gym sock with a red stripe at the top, a gray sock with two blue stripes, and a t-shirt that said "Visualize Whirled Peas." He was thankful it was sweatshirt weather, so he could at least cover this bold reminder of what he'd considered clever when he was younger. Standing on an old trunk, he rooted around in the top of his closet for something warm and long-sleeved. He found a fairly innocuous thermal shirt that would do and grabbed hold of it. It seemed a little heavier than a thermal should be, and once he brought it down from the closet, he realized something was wrapped up inside it.

A magazine dropped from the shirt and landed on the couch. It was a *Playboy*. The coveted *Playboy* he'd stolen from the woods. He forgot all about being in a hurry and sat down. The pages felt so familiar under his fingertips as he turned them, past the articles he'd never read, past the jokes he'd memorized and told over and over again, right to the pages he'd spent more time studying than any homework assignment he'd ever been given. It was amazing. She looked just like Gina.

He looked at the curves of her tanned body, the lines of her face, the way the skin wrinkled just around her knees, the only place it wrinkled at all. His face felt warm, and he could hear his breath growing more shallow just like when he was a kid, listening for the sound of his mother's footsteps outside his room. Ginastevens. The words hadn't run together in his mind like that for years. It was strange to feel this way toward an imaginary Ginastevens, when the real one was in his life nearly every day. There was something different about looking at the centerfold now, though. It used to simply be a visual exercise, but now there were other senses involved. It was like he knew how soft her skin was, what she smelled like, how she tasted. It seemed so real. He was slow to realize these sensations were his actual memories of Gina.

Footsteps came tapping down the hall, and he quickly stashed the magazine under the cushions of the couch. His mom opened the door and jangled a set of car keys at him. "You can take my car if you feel okay to drive."

He never felt okay to drive his mom's car. It was massive. She was of the old-fashioned opinion that bigger cars are safer, and insisted on owning the most unwieldy behemoth that could still operate on a standard-size road. The last thing he wanted to do was drive a car where he felt he should be barking orders to a crew, but the clock told him he was running short on time.

"Okay," he said. "That might be helpful."

She held her hand there, waiting for him to come get the keys, but he wasn't about to stand up. His lecherous walk down memory lane had left him in a state that was inappropriate to showcase in front of his mother.

"Just leave them on the counter," he said. "I'm going to sit here for a minute or two longer. Catch my breath."

She shook her head in disapproval then went away. When he felt the coast was clear, both inside and outside the room, he pulled the *Playboy* from the couch cushions and carefully returned it to its hiding place in the closet, but not before stealing one more longing look at its middle pages. His sails suddenly full with the wind of coital musings, he closed the closet door and headed for the kitchen to get the keys.

The afternoon sun lit the smiles on everyone's faces as he drove through town. At first, Eric couldn't figure why everyone seemed so pleasant. It was a nice day, with warm sunlight on the skin followed by a cool breeze chaser. Just the sort of contrast that kept the mind alert and alive. But there was more to it than that. Then he passed the football field and saw a couple of kids standing there, their fingers laced through the chain-link fence, staring at the grass on the other side like it possessed some sort of otherworldly power. That's when he remembered. Victory had set euphoria free on the fine people of Pinely. Cedarsville had been defeated. All was right with the world. Everyone else in town probably had a pretty good night, he imagined, with the obvious exception of himself, Deke's dad, the kid at the Gas N' Sip, and anyone who lived within shouting distance of the Quaker State. But percentage wise, that wasn't too bad. It was a small town, but even Eric had his limitations on the amount of havoc he could wreak in one night.

He'd been drunk. That was some form of an excuse, anyway. Unfortunately, he didn't have that to blame for his lunch with Jill. All he'd had to drink by that point was two glasses of apple cider, an RC Cola, some buttermilk, and a hot chocolate. At best he could claim the mixture had resulted in some behavior-altering chemical reaction, but it would have been a lie. The truth was, he'd just been an asshole. It hadn't exactly been a dream reunion for the two of them, but all Eric wanted now was to make sure Jill didn't leave angry. Not again.

He maneuvered his mom's road tank down the gravel drive and saw Mrs. Dupree standing in front of the house crying. Just like she'd been when they'd shown up with the hearse. The breeze was blowing leaves from one neighbor's yard to the next, all culminating in a fiery kaleidoscope of color at Mrs. Dupree's feet. When she saw the car coming toward her, she quickly tried to regain her composure, wiping away her tears and fixing a halfhearted smile on her face. Eric could tell she didn't recognize the car, but she stood firm, friendly, ready to greet another in what was probably an endless parade of well-wishers and stewards of grief. When she finally recognized Eric behind the wheel, no small task, given the face-to-car ratio, her smile took on a more genuine quality and she took a few steps toward the car.

"What brings you out here, Eric?" she asked as soon as he'd opened the car door.

"I'm canvassing the town, getting reactions to the great Pinely victory last night. So, would you describe yourself as enthusiastic, thrilled, excited, or apoplectic?"

She smiled at him even more and shrugged. "What's that last word mean?"

"Pretty much the same as the rest of them," he said.

"I'll go with that one then."

"A lot of people have."

"Are you here to see Jill?" she asked.

"If she'll see me," he said, the humility painfully obvious to both of them.

"Well I'm not sure what you did this time," she said, "but I imagine I can coax her out here. You want me to lie?"

"If you have to."

She went into the house and left Eric by himself. Leaning against the car, he watched the leaves chase each other through the yard, tumbling over one another and pinning themselves against the base of the house. Where Mrs. Dupree's flower garden used to be, there was only a pile of mulch and rotting leaves. Eric stared at it for a while, remembering how much time she used to spend on her hands and knees, tending to her garden with her miniature tools. His thoughts quickly drifted to Mr. Dupree, growing roots of his own, with a garden trowel as his only earthly possession. He heard the door swing open and turned to see Jill walking out on the porch, zipping up a puffy blue coat that was obviously her dad's. He didn't move toward her, but simply raised his hand in a submissive wave.

"What happened to your hand?" she asked.

"I fell."

"I bet."

"I'm glad you haven't left yet," he said.

"Why's that?" she asked. "You hoping for another opportunity to parse my words and poke fun at my boyfriend?"

It struck Eric as odd to hear her use the word 'parse.' It wasn't the sort of thing she knew before she'd left the first time. "No, I came by to . . . That wasn't the way I wanted . . ." He couldn't seem to find a string of words that sounded right together, so he just cut right to the heart of it. "I'm sorry, Jill."

She looked at him sternly, then slowly realized he meant it. A softness came over her that made her words feel like whispers on clouds. "It's okay," she said.

"Not just for yesterday," he sighed. "For Gina. For avoiding you all these years. For . . . ," he took in a deep breath and tried to get it all out in one word, "everything."

Her eyes welled with tears, but she stood still in front of him with her hands in her coat pockets. "It's okay. I forgave you a long time ago." She walked toward him and took one of his battered hands in hers, holding it up gingerly so he could see it. "That's something you might want to consider doing, too."

She let go of his hand, but he held it there, looking at the wounds he'd inflicted on himself, and remembering the countless others. It wasn't anything he'd considered before, forgiving himself. He wasn't even sure he knew how to start. The stillness hung there between them until Jill spoke up again.

"I always thought it was funny that I was the one who left, but you were the one who ran away."

"Yeah, well," he said. "Sometimes the easiest way to run away is to stay perfectly still."

She nodded to herself and dragged her foot through the gravel. "So what are you going to do now?" she asked.

"You mean today?" he wondered.

"Open-ended."

"Well, I'm going to go pick up Tess later."

Jill smiled. "You two are quite a team, huh?"

"Classic story," he shrugged. "Boy makes girl. They fall in love. There are some co-dependence issues. I'm a little bossy, she's a little needy. But we're pulling for a 'happily ever after' scenario."

"Here in Pinely?"

"That's where we are."

"Don't you ever think——" she started. "I mean, what if she grows up and realizes. You know, that you gave up your whole life for hers. Isn't that going to be an awfully big burden for her to carry?"

"I hadn't really thought of that," Eric answered, because he honestly hadn't. He pondered on it for a second or two before something resembling an answer came to him. "I guess . . . ," he said, hesitantly, then more sure of himself, "I guess it's better than having loved something else more than I ever loved her."

There was a hint of sadness in her voice the way she said, "Yeah." She looked over Eric's shoulder at nothing in particular then sighed one more time into the wind. "Yeah."

"It's not that bad here," Eric said, surprised that such a thing would ever come from his mouth.

"It just doesn't seem right though."

"What?"

"That you're doing this. Tending bar. Driving a hearse. You're so much smarter than that. You could . . . I don't know. Why don't you open a bookstore or something?"

"Why don't I open a gay dance club while I'm pissing away money?"

She gave him a confused look.

"No one around here reads," he explained. "Ask my mom. Or better yet, get a look at her cross-stitching collection."

"So what are you going to do?"

"I'm going to go pick up Tess."

"Right," she nodded.

The sound of wheels on gravel came grinding toward them and Eric turned to see Beth's car shining in the afternoon sun. Jill waved at her sister, then stuffed her hands back in her pockets. "That's my ride," she said to the ground as much as to Eric.

"Back to school, huh?"

"I guess so." The way she said it made it seem like the most impossible task on earth. "One last push, then I'm out in the real world."

Eric tried to imagine what her real world was going to be like. He couldn't picture anything specific, but he was certain it would be entirely different than his own.

"I'll be back for Christmas," she said, with a little lift in her voice. "It'd be good to see you then."

"Well," Eric smirked, "I imagine I'll be here."

"Yeah. But it'd be good to see you this time."

Eric nodded and tried to think of something reassuring to say, but was cut off by the sudden hug Jill gave him. It was soft but firm, and somehow said more than they'd managed to say to each other all week long. No good words were coming to Eric for a proper good-bye, so he just held her for a second longer and hoped that would do. When it was over, Jill turned toward the house and met up with her sister at the door. Just before she walked through, she turned and smiled at Eric once more. "If you ever need a lawyer . . . ," she said, holding her hand to her head like a telephone.

The way she said it made him hope he would need a lawyer. That he'd need her. But somehow, despite all the evidence to the contrary, he knew he wouldn't.

Driving his mother's car exhausted him more than walking, and now that he wasn't in a hurry anymore, he wished he could just abandon the four-wheeled beast and make do on foot. Unfortunately, that wasn't an option, so he was forced to concentrate on maneuvering the thing through Pinely's Saturday "traffic" in a simple effort to keep it on his side of the road and away from the sides of the parked cars. By the time he saw Tremble's Funeral Home on his horizon, he was happy for the excuse to stop and rest for a while. He'd meant to stop by the home and straighten things up a little bit on Friday, but his lunch with Jill, and its muddling aftereffects, had kept him from seeing to that. Usually, on the evening after a funeral or the next day, he liked to be certain things were in a respectable condition. A room full of mourners could create strange tasks for a guy like him to tend to. Broken things in the bathroom. Abandoned tissues in all sorts of unheard of places. The home had to be presentable at all times, because there was no telling when the next customer might come through the door.

As he walked through the parlor, things seemed to be in fairly decent condition. It was colder than it needed to be since Eric hadn't turned the thermostat back up since the crowds of people warmed the room during the service. He adjusted it to a setting more to Mr. Tremble's liking, then did a walk-through of the parlor, picking up scraps of tissue and flower petals, the shrapnel of the grieving. It was quiet. Standing at the front of the room, looking out on all the empty seats, he was struck by a strange sensation to shatter the silence with a scream, or a song, or some other distraction. Something to lift the heavy blanket of loss that still seemed to hang over the place. Just as he was working up the irreverent nerve, another sound beat him to it. Someone spitting. It wasn't coming from inside the room, but the sound still managed to dart through the parlor and offer some levity. It was subtle, but Eric was glad to be spared the effort of working up a whole production of some kind. He looked at the side door and noticed it was ajar, just enough to let a sliver of light and a spittle of sound leak through.

As he stepped outside, Mr. Tremble lobbed a large, brown mess of spit into the bushes beside him.

"What are you doing?" Eric asked.

"It's warmer out here," Mr. Tremble answered, with a potent mix of honesty and sarcasm.

"Sorry bout that," Eric shrugged. "I just turned the thermostat back up. It should be fine in a little while."

"What are you doing here?"

"Just came by to tidy up a bit," he explained. "It was a good service."

"Yeah," Mr. Tremble nodded, looking over his shoulder to be sure no one else might be coming through the door.

"The song caught me a little off guard," Eric said.

"The youngest girl wanted that."

Eric smiled as he remembered everyone on their feet, swaying and clapping, and the way Jill's voice had carried out above all the others "It's a toe-tapper," he said.

Mr. Tremble shook his head. "We don't get many of those."

They stood there a while in a silence occasionally punctuated by Mr. Tremble's spitting. After about the third spit, Eric spoke up. "You know that stuff's bad for you," he said, pointing to Mr. Tremble's jaw.

Mr. Tremble shot him a look and pulled the pack of tobacco from his back pocket. "That's what I read," he said, holding the pack up so Eric could see his own alteration of the Surgeon General's warning he'd etched on it the day of the funeral.

"Well they don't lie over there at the Surgeon General's office," Eric said with a straight face. "It's probably against the law."

Mr. Tremble didn't say anything. He just stuffed the tobacco back in his pocket and shot another mouthful of spit into the bushes beside him. Eric told him he'd move all the chairs back on Monday, and stepped quietly through the door and into the parlor. His footsteps echoed when he walked. It was a small room, but the sound still found places to travel and bounce around. As he reached the front door, he noticed a few of the cards from the service scattered about on the table top. He scooted them into a short pile and placed them off to one side, then peeled one off the top to give it a look. The front was standard: Mr. Dupree's name, date of birth, date of death, and various titles in life, all embossed in black on the white card-stock. Eric was curious about which Bible verse had been chosen for the back of the card. Mr. Tremble kept a short list in his office from which almost everyone chose, and Eric knew them all. It was a regular Greatest Hits of God. Occasionally someone would surprise him with something a bit more obscure. But he'd never seen what was on the back of Mr. Dupree's card. Where the Bible verse would normally go, was a short saying in simple block type:

> Don't cry because it's over.
> Smile because it happened.

Eric ran his finger over the card and tucked it in his pocket. Then he opened the door, letting the sunlight spill into the room, and walked down the sidewalk to the car.

By the time he reached Gina's house, he was feeling pretty good. Perspective seemed to be showing him the way to a higher purpose, free of dwelling on details and missed opportunities. It was an elation that was welcome, but short-lived. Even for a guy who wasn't dwelling on details, it was obvious Gina wasn't happy to see him. He picked up on it right away.

"Well, if it isn't Don Juan," she said as soon as he stepped through the door.

At first he thought she might be propositioning him. A bold, new tactic, if ever he'd seen one. But the wave of condescension that carried her words quickly knocked any such notion free from his body.

"Did you just get back from another intense make-out session on school property?" she asked.

Eric was truly perplexed by what she was saying. That didn't even sound remotely appealing. Since he couldn't figure out what she was really asking, he opted to answer the question as it was posed.

"No," he said flatly. "I just got back from the funeral home."

"Oh," she said, momentarily set back by the somber image, a tactic Eric swore he'd have to remember for later. "Did someone else—?"

"No," Eric assured her. "I just went by to tidy up a bit."

His reprieve was undone by his own choice of words. "Well I was doing a little tidying up of my own the other night. Explaining to our daughter why a strange woman was sitting on top of her daddy behind the concession stand at the high school."

Somehow Eric had forgotten about that. He wanted to think it had something to do with his new dedication to the future rather than the past, but he had a feeling it had a lot more to do with all the beer he'd drunk the night before. A proper apology was just starting to form in his brain when a sudden curiosity leapt forward instead.

"How did you explain that?" he asked.

She looked pissed, then tired, then confused. "I don't know," she admitted. "Just a lot of mumbling about you guys being friends and stuff like that."

"That's pretty good," Eric nodded. "I would have just shoved her down and run away."

"Well, we have different parenting styles."

Eric briefly found himself thinking about the kid at the Gas N' Sip, wondering if he had any idea just how lucky he'd been.

Sure, he'd had to clean up a bunch of sodas and a busted machine, but that was nothing in comparison to the sort of mess Eric was truly capable of creating.

"Was she . . . traumatized by it or anything?" Eric asked.

"Teflon Tess?" Gina mocked. "You know how she is. She asked a few questions, I skirted around them, she went out to play in the backyard. Hasn't mentioned it since."

"So it wasn't that big of a deal?"

Gina shrugged. "Not really."

"Then why are you pissed at me?"

The look was mostly disappointment, one Eric was used to getting. But there was another element to it. A caught-with-your-hand-in-the-cookie-jar look that Eric was much more accustomed to giving than receiving. "Do you want me to go get her?" Gina asked, her cheeks flushing red as she teetered on her tightrope.

"It's okay," he said, draping a net for her to see. "We can talk, can't we?"

Her forehead wrinkled, and she took an involuntary step backward. "We can?"

"Sure," he said, reassuring himself as much as her.

"About what?"

That stumped him. He didn't remember ever being asked what he was going to talk about. He just talked. If he had to pre-determine his topics of conversation before he spoke, he doubted he'd ever say anything. Who would ever *decide* to talk about the things that came up at the Legion or with Deke or with Tess?

"I don't know," he said. "Don't you have anything you want to talk about?"

She looked at the floor for a second, as though that's where she kept her conversational primer cards. "How's Jill?" she finally asked, flipping her hair out of her face with one hand.

"Gone."

This surprised Eric. That he knew anything about Jill at all was entirely novel, but knowing with such certainty was what caught him off guard. She was gone. And not just from Pinely.

Gina kept her face down, staring at the pattern in the rug like she was trying to solve a puzzle. Eric hardly heard her when she whispered, "Gone," in a slight voice that he just barely recognized as hers. When she looked up at him, he could tell she was trying not to cry. "So, what does that mean for us?"

There was that word, the one she loved to try to squeeze in wherever she could. "Us," he repeated, looking into her on-the-verge eyes. "Me and you?" he asked, as both a clarification and correction.

"Yeah," she sighed, "me and you."

He didn't want to hurt her feelings, despite the fact there were a dozen highly effective options at his disposal for doing just that. He didn't want to. But he also wasn't going to give ground in this battle of hope she constantly insisted on waging. "Well," he started, choosing his words carefully, "I can't really speak for you."

"No," she said, turning to hide her face from him. "I don't suppose you can."

There was no explaining why he did it. It was like instinctively reaching for a falling plate, the way he reached for her. He didn't want to give her hope, but he certainly didn't want to watch her break right in front of him. She curled into his arms like she'd done it a thousand times before, resting her face against his chest where he could feel her breath against him. He'd considered Gina in such harsh terms for so long, he was surprised at how soft she actually was. They stayed that way for a while until he felt her moving her head toward a new position. He looked down to make sure she was alright and discovered her face coming toward his. Her lips were warm and seemed to spark a memory through his mind in a strange succession. It started as the first time they'd kissed, the only time, in the field that summer, but it transformed into the recently refreshed memory of a *Playboy* model, so that by the end he wasn't kissing Gina at all. He was kissing the fantasy of Ginastevens he'd carried with him for so long. The whole illusion was more detailed and nuanced than he'd ever realized. Minus, of course, the pounding footsteps.

The thunder of feet rattled down the hallway, fast and furious, carrying more energy than mass, sounding their arrival well before they broke around the corner. "Mommy, Mommy, I—"

Eric didn't know what she'd seen. She was faster than she needed to be, really, so anything was possible. All he knew for sure was that she was standing in front of them now, and they were standing closer than she'd probably ever seen them before.

"Hi Daddy," she said, somehow staring at both of them at once.

"Hey baby," Eric smiled, trying desperately not to get stared down by a five-year-old.

"What are you guys doing?" she asked.

That question alone made Eric believe she hadn't seen them. Without a doubt. Or maybe she had. Maybe what she really meant was, "What in the hell do you guys think you're doing?" but simply lacked the necessary vocabulary to convey the thought. Or maybe she was just making conversation. Her expression gave no clues, leaving him frustrated that his own daughter had the upper hand on him, something he thought wouldn't happen until puberty at the earliest.

"Nothing," he finally muttered in his most convincing tone. "What are you doing?"

If she wasn't suspicious before, she seemed to be now. It was as though she could smell fear. "I just came to show Mommy something."

"Show Mommy what?" Gina asked, squatting down to Tess's level. Eric was amazed at how perfectly normal her voice sounded. Like it hadn't come from the mouth that had just been attached to his.

Tess swung her arm around from behind her back, holding a stuffed monster above her head like it was a trophy bass. "I found Mr. Things," she said, her voice cracking with joy.

"See," Gina said, "I told you he'd turn up. Where was he?"

"In my closet."

Gina turned to Eric to explain. "He's been missing for about a week now. It was on the verge of becoming a national emergency." Tess was dancing around with Mr. Things, catching up on old times with the urgency of a postwar reunion. "She's always finding lost things in that closet of hers," Gina said. "She hides them too well."

Eric looked at his daughter, spazzing out in a tornado of giggles and flailing monster arms, then looked at Gina, her body curving just so, like the one he'd admired a few hours before. "I do the same thing," he said.

"Hey Tess," Gina said, trying to break through the joyous fit their daughter had become, "why don't you and Mr. Things get ready to go with your dad for the night?"

Tess stopped her bounding and bouncing long enough to look up at Eric. "Mr. Things doesn't have to come," she said.

"He's more than welcome," Eric offered.

"No, I think I'll just leave him here. But I'll put him in a better hiding place this time."

Gina winced at the thought of Mr. Things coming up missing again and excused herself to go watch where Tess hid him this time. Eric knew he would have done the same thing. But he'd have done it so he could move Mr. Things when Tess wasn't looking. Make her believe he was a happenin' guy who was constantly on the go. That, Eric imagined, is why nature insists on two people being involved in the reproduction process. To balance things out.

Gina came back into the living room first, followed by Tess. They both looked equally proud of themselves. Eric was thankful Tess already had her coat on and was ready to go, sparing him any uncomfortable chatter with Gina. Some people would have wanted to try to sort out what had just happened between them. Eric was not one of those people.

"Okay then," Eric said in a singsong voice that surprised even him. All attempts at seeming casual were disintegrating before his very eyes. "Are you ready to go?" he asked Tess.

She was jittering around, filled with the kind of pure energy scientists would do well to learn how to harvest. "Uh-huh," she said.

"She's still a little wound up," Gina said.

"I can see that. Luckily I have my mom's car, so she'll be able to run a few wind sprints in there during the ride."

"We're taking a car?!" Tess said.

The way she said it made it sound like they'd be taking a spaceship, not an Oldsmobile. But they walked just about everywhere together, so he understood her excitement. Somewhat. Tess ran to the door and looked down the hill at the car.

"You think you can fit in there?" Eric asked.

Tess looked over at him, then back at the car. Her breath frosted the window on the storm door, finally obscuring her view enough that she had to look back at Eric. "What do you mean?" she asked.

Sarcasm was either above or below the radar of a five-and-a-half-year-old. Although Eric wasn't sure if it was something you grow into as you gain wisdom, or sink to as you lose hope. Either way, it wasn't a lesson he was interested in taking up at that moment. So he just smiled and said something about going to see for themselves.

When they stepped outside they found the day was becoming increasingly more whiskey and less soda, a wintry blend that bit into you with every breath. But Eric was happy for the cold air. It felt good against his warm cheeks and tasted like it had never been breathed before. If he couldn't have a fresh start, he could at least have fresh air. Tess hopped down the stairs, leaving Gina at the doorway shouting "be carefuls" and "so longs" in a weightless voice whose only ballast was sincerity. Eric walked along behind, not even looking back when he felt Gina's hand trace gently between his shoulders. He was too certain in his intentions now to let uncertainty have this dance.

Tess used the full momentum of her body to swing the car door open, then climbed inside and all but disappeared inside the glass and steel. Eric got in on the other side and turned the engine over, bringing the wheezing giant to life. Back up the hill he could see the frosty silhouette of Gina standing in the doorway. The cold air had colored the glass of the storm door milky white, so he couldn't make out a single feature on her face. She could be any woman in the world. He waved at the shadowy figure, got Tess buckled up, then dropped the car in gear and headed up the road.

The wipers creaked across the windshield, set to work by an errant motion on Eric's part. He didn't know his mother's car very well, but there always seemed to be an assortment of knobs and levers jutting out for him to stumble over. Tess giggled as Eric tried to figure out what he'd hit to make the wipers come on in the first place. She finally reached over and pushed one of the levers up and made it stop.

"How did you know how to do that?" Eric wondered.

"I watched Grandma," she said.

Eric made a mental note to be more surreptitious around her when doing things like starting the lawn mower or building a fire. He was slowly getting better at most of fatherhood. But the way she could not know something one day, then know it the next, still threw him for a loop. Of course, a large part of what she might learn would come from him. And there were opportunities to teach her things every day. Even things she might not be fully ready for. He'd jumbled one of those the other day, but thought it might be worth another attempt now.

"Hey Tess," he said. A straightforward start with little room for error.

"Yeah."

"You remember the funeral the other day?" he asked. A solid way to ensure they were both on the same page in regard to space and time.

"Yeah."

"Well, I wanted to talk to you about . . ." A pause. Fuck! He was already screwing it up. A long pause indicated hesitancy and uncertainty. There was no time to mince words or pussyfoot around. He was losing precious ground too early in the game. ". . . why I was crying."

"I already know," she said.

"You do?" This was unexpected.

"Mommy said he was a friend of yours and that you're going to miss him. That's why you cried."

"That's right," he said. How could Gina have made it so clear and simple when he was about to turn it into one of the great riddles of mankind? "So you understand?" he asked, just for clarification.

"Uh-huh," she said, staring out the window at the passing scenery.

It really didn't have to be so complicated after all, he realized. Just explain what you're feeling. Kids have feelings too. Somehow, even though he had little to do with the whole thing, he was proud of himself at that moment. As he watched Tess sit, contemplative and quiet, he was proud of her too for not clouding such a simple emotion.

She turned her head away from the window and looked at Eric. "Are you going to die?"

It was all he could do to keep the immensity of the car under his control. This was exactly what he'd been afraid of. A million answers rushed through his head before he settled on one that seemed the most fair. "Not for a long time," he assured her.

Her eyes stayed on him for a while, almost looking through him. "I'll prolly cry when you do," she admitted.

"Well," Eric said, "I probably won't be too happy about it either."

Any attempt to negotiate the car into the garage would have been futile, so Eric pulled into his parents' driveway and parked it there. His dad was sitting in the living room, his feet on the coffee table, watching a college football game and drinking a beer. He was completely defenseless against Tess's attack. It was intended as a gesture of love, but Eric could tell his dad's initial reflex was not the most loving one. Still, once he put his beer down, he managed to hug the poor girl rather than strangle her before she ran off toward the kitchen to unleash further strikes of childish love on her grandmother. Eric knew once Tess was gone there was only a brief window before awkwardness settled in. If he was going to say anything, he had to do it soon. So he sat down on the chair across from his dad.

"Thanks for last night," he said. He could tell his dad had been hoping he might not bring it up at all.

"It's okay," he said, trying to sound like it really was. After a player for the team his dad was apparently rooting for dropped a pass in the open field and his dad had properly dressed him down by calling him a "dumb sonofabitch," he turned to Eric and shrugged as though the weight of the world was on his shoulders. Watching football was apparently very painful for his father, which made Eric wonder why he did it in the first place.

"So how did you get me into my room last night?" Eric asked.

"What?"

"My room," Eric repeated. "That's where you took me."

"Like hell," his dad scoffed. "How would I have gotten you into your room?"

Eric couldn't help but feel he was in the middle of an Abbott and Costello routine, but went with it just the same. "I don't know," he said, "but that's where I woke up."

"Really?" he said. "I left you in the car."

"The car?" Eric admonished.

"I could have let you go to jail," his dad said, looking over the top of his glasses the way he did when he knew he had the trump card. "You must have stumbled in to piss, then gone to your old room out of habit," he said. "The way you do."

Tess launched back into the room in such a flash, Eric began to wonder if she was genetically predisposed to sneak attacks. She was carrying a paper bag in her arms, but still attempting to lope along at full speed.

"What do you have there?" Eric asked.

"Veg-e-ta-bles," Tess said, clearly pronouncing more syllables than the word even had. "Grandma told me to give them to you."

"Praise God!" his dad exalted. "Tom Jacobs unloaded half his garden on us when he heard the frost was coming earlier this week. We've been eating vegetable-everything ever since. Apparently your mother's finally sick of it too, so it's your turn."

"Okay," Eric said, looking down at the bounty in the bag. "Do I thank you, or—?"

"Don't thank anyone, just take the fuckin' things."

Tess's eyes grew wide, and she drew in a short breath of astonishment. "Grandpa," she said in a near-whisper.

"Great," Eric said, standing up from the chair. "Why don't I get my daughter out of here before you have her swearing like a sailor." There was something in the phrase that quickly dissipated his anger. Then he remembered the pirate/sailor confusion he'd had with Gina earlier in the week. "What is a sailor, anyway?" he asked his dad.

"You mean like a guy on a boat?" his dad wondered, happy to be off the hook for his verbal slip.

"Is that all it takes? A boat?"

"I guess."

Eric thought it over for a minute, looking to Tess for help she clearly wasn't up for giving. "So if I'm out on the river fishing, I'm a sailor?"

His dad shrugged. "Well, you probably need a sailboat."

"Oh. Yeah," Eric said, concerned that he hadn't thought of that himself, but glad his dad was still around to help. For lack of a better segue, he declared a sudden "Well" before handing over the keys to his mom's car. "Tell her I said thanks," he said. They nodded at each other a few times, just to make it official, then Eric ushered Tess out the door and on their way to his house.

Something was on her mind. The afternoon had gone smoothly enough, but he could tell she had something to ask. Or worse yet, something to say. But there was no way of coaxing it out of her. She was only five and a half, but she was just as set in her ways as any other Mercer who'd roamed this earth. So he let her have her mental plaything for a while, realizing she'd bring it up when she was ready. She sat at the kitchen counter, watching him take the vegetables from the paper bag and store them in various places. It was truly a cornucopia of produce. While he was busy imagining how much of it his folks must have eaten before they finally gave up and surrendered part of it to him, Tess was sitting silently, figuring something in her head. Most of the tomatoes were overly ripe already, so Eric went to put some in the refrigerator.

"You shouldn't refrigerate tomatoes," Tess suddenly offered.

It struck Eric as odd that she knew the word "refrigerate," or rather that she knew how to use it properly. But it wasn't nearly as odd as her bit of unsolicited advice. "Why not?" he asked.

"God doesn't refrigerate them," she said as though she'd just presided over an open-and-shut case.

"Yeah well," Eric said, a bit put off by her smugness, "God doesn't refrigerate milk either, but that doesn't mean I'm gonna keep it out on the counter."

She stared at him for a second, as though it was inconceivable that someone could counter any argument that had God on its side. "Yeah but cows—"

"—get refrigerated too," he interrupted.

Her eyes squinted nearly shut as she tried to figure out a way to win. He smiled to let her know it was all in fun, but she wasn't in the mood to smile back. After a pause that she seemed to feel went on a little too long, she hopped down from her chair and announced she was going to go play outside for a while. It seemed like a strange way to leave things, but Eric had grown accustomed to such behavior from children. And some adults. She scurried out the back door, a choice for which Eric was grateful since it meant a significant reduction in the Buddy Piles factor, and set to tossing leaves above her head so they would fall all around her, as though she were trapped inside the world's most colorful snow globe.

By the time dinner was ready, an unspectacular mixture of chicken nuggets and garden-fresh vegetables, Tess had apparently tired of her leaf-tossing follies. Dusk was casting its pale light on the yard; and Tess was hunkered underneath the maple tree doing something in front of a small pile of leaves. Eric watched her for a while, as always, curious about what she must be thinking, or making. Amazed that he could still know so little about something he'd had such a hand in creating himself. When he finally did call her in, she sprung up like she'd been anticipating it the whole time, hustled in toward the warm light from the kitchen, and laughed as she jumped through the doorway.

"God doesn't refrigerate anything," she said, pointing at her dad for added emphasis.

He could have left it be. But. "Penguins," he said, with a raise of his still-bruised eyebrow.

She breathed out through her nose so hard he half-expected a booger to launch out onto the linoleum. Her arms flailed free from her coat, and she stomped over to the counter to get her plate. She couldn't seem to figure a way to get everything she needed in her hands, so Eric walked over to see what the problem was. In her right hand was a tiny white flower.

"Where'd you get the flower, Tess?" he asked. A legitimate question since the first frost had come a few days earlier, killing every sort of plant that wasn't covered in bark or buried underground.

"I picked it."

He was certain she must be lying, but was still curious. "Where?"

She pointed toward the back door. "It was growing under the tree. In the dead leaves."

When she held it up for him to see, he could make out the tiny roots at the bottom. Somehow it was true. She smiled and told him to smell it, so he did. It was like a tiny piece of spring-time, too pretty to think about too much. He put it behind her ear, causing her to laugh and say something about being an angel. An argument she won without a single rebuttal.

They read together in her bed until he could tell she wasn't following along anymore. Sometimes she would protest when he tried to stop, but not tonight. He closed the book, and she rolled over, pulling the covers up close around her neck. They ran the checklist together, making sure she'd brushed her teeth, washed her face, gone to the bathroom, all while she watched him with a strange detachment. He wondered if she was just sleepy, or if she still had something on her mind. Her face filled the room with a soft glow that warmed him through. She gasped in suddenly, embracing a yawn with no reserve, and smiled through the dampness the yawn brought to her eyes.

"I love you, Daddy."

Sometimes he didn't want to say it back because it seemed too easy. Like a response instead of an emotion. But he could never resist the impulse to let her know.

"I love you too, Tess."

She watched him cross the room and stand in the doorway for a minute.

"Are you going to marry that girl?" she asked in a soft voice that masked any concern she might have.

"Which girl, honey?" he asked, even though he knew.

"The one you were kissing at the school?"

He searched his answer for any loopholes before he gave it, faithfully and without question, to his daughter. "No, I'm not."

She seemed satisfied by his answer and smiled just a little. When he turned off the lights, he could see her face by the glow of the nightlight on the wall. She was still watching him, apparently not through thinking yet.

"Are you going to marry Mommy?" she wondered, her voice betraying a bit more hope this time.

She might have seen the kiss earlier. Or she might carry this idea with her everywhere she went, wondering why her parents were different, waiting for a time to ask. It was a natural thought, and not nearly as caustic as Eric had once considered. Still, he knew his heart was a different place than he'd ever imagined it would be, and there was only one reason for that.

"No, baby," he answered. "You're the only girl for me."

She smiled at such an idea, letting it overwhelm any other expectation she might have had. Her raven hair covered her face when she rolled on her side, and Eric could just make out traces of hair moving with every breath. These were the soft moments he wanted more of. Tomorrow he would welcome them in.